The Second Black Beacon L...

To Pam
Lots of Love
Alan xx

OTHER TITLES FROM BLACK BEACON BOOKS

Anthologies:

Tales from the Ruins
A Hint of Hitchcock
Murder and Machinery
The Black Beacon Book of Mystery
Shelter from the Storm
Lighthouses
Subtropical Suspense

Books by Cameron Trost:

Oscar Tremont, Investigator of the Strange and Inexplicable
The Animal Inside
Letterbox
Hoffman's Creeper and Other Disturbing Tales
The Tunnel Runner

www.blackbeaconbooks.com

the second
BLACK BEACON BOOK
of
MYSTERY

Locked Rooms

Private Investigators

Armchair Detectives

Police Procedurals

A Sherlock Holmes Pastiche

The Second Black Beacon Book of Mystery
Published by Black Beacon Books
Edited by Cameron Trost
Cover art by Małgorzata Mika
Copyright © Black Beacon Books, 2023

Alexander's Nose © Dave Duncan
Bread Pudding © Karen Keeley
Christmas Potatoes © E. E. King
Lost at Sea and illustration © F. K. Restrepo
Lurking in the Shadows © Edward Lodi
The Impossible Theft © Cameron Trost
If It's Tuesday, This Must be Murder © Josh Pachter
(First published in *Mystery Most Geographical*, Wildside Press, 2018)
Justice for Jaynie © Yvonne Ventresca
(First published in *30 Shades of Dead,* WC Publishing, 2017)
Keep Your Friends Close © Maggie King
(First published in *Deadly Southern Charm*, Wildside Press, 2019)
Too Many Sherlocks © Paulene Turner
(First published in *Where's Sherlock, Vol II*, Specul8 Publishing, 2020)
Villainy in the Vertical Village © Joseph S. Walker
(First published in *Cozy Villages of Death*, Camden Park Press, 2020)
Screen Shot © Teel James Glenn
Spanner in the Works © Alan Barker
The Murderer's Vade Mecum © Erica Obey
There is a Tide © Elizabeth Elwood

This book is sold subject to the condition that it shall not, by way of trade or otherwise, be lent, resold, hired out or otherwise circulated without the publisher's prior consent in any form of binding or cover other than that in which it is published and without a similar condition including this condition being imposed on the subsequent purchaser.

Black Beacon Books
blackbeaconbooks.com

ISBN: 978-0-6452471-2-1

There you are, armchair detective. I see you've come back for more. You must have developed a taste for red herrings and bitter almond when you helped our cast of private eyes, police detectives, and amateur sleuths crack the cases in the first volume of *The Black Beacon Books of Mystery*. I completely understand—I really do. Welcome back. Now, before we get started—and this might sound a tad ominous—there's something you need to know. *The Second Black Beacon Book of Mystery* is even more challenging than the first. Our cast of intrepid investigators needs your puzzle-solving talent again. For these aren't merely stories; they are fair-play mysteries. In this anthology, you'll be faced with impossible crimes. You'll find frightful amounts of poison—don't invite these authors over for dinner! There are clues to be collected and alibis to be checked, and your general knowledge and attention to detail will be put to the test. Does that sound like your cup of tea?—ah, best not drink that! Will you take the case? Splendid! We're counting on you.

- Cameron Trost, editor

Black Beacon Books would like to thank our patrons, whose passion for great fiction and independent publishing helped make this anthology happen.

If you'd like to join the team and reap the benefits, subscribe on our Patreon page at: *patreon.com/blackbeaconbooks*

The five patronage tiers are
Shipwreck Survivor, Moonlight Smuggler, Sea Witch, Assistant Keeper, and *Lighthouse Keeper.*

Alexander's Nose by Dave Duncan...9

Bread Pudding by Karen Keeley...20

Christmas Potatoes by E. E. King...35

Lost at Sea by F. K. Restrepo...49

Lurking in the Shadows by Edward Lodi...66

The Impossible Theft by Cameron Trost...85

If It's Tuesday, This Must be Murder by Josh Pachter...98

Justice for Jaynie by Yvonne Ventresca...107

Keep Your Friends Close by Maggie King...123

Too Many Sherlocks by Paulene Turner...132

Villainy in the Vertical Village by Joseph S. Walker...175

Screen Shot by Teel James Glenn...193

Spanner in the Works by Alan Barker...206

The Murderer's Vade Mecum by Erica Obey...225

There is a Tide by Elizabeth Elwood...246

Author Biographies

ALEXANDER'S NOSE
Dave Duncan

A dense fog had descended on London, a poisonous miasma utterly lacking in warmth. A hansom cab drew up at the curb outside the grandiose façade of the Bwana Club, Piccadilly. The cabman scrambled down to open the door for his two male passengers, then unloaded their overnight bags.

An aged porter came hobbling down the steps to take their cases, while the heavier, older visitor paid off the driver. The two arrivals replaced their top hats and advanced up the broad steps to the door, the younger taking them two at a time, demonstrating the absurd length of his legs. The doorman regarded the youngster doubtfully, observing that—despite his formal evening dress—he lacked the massive beard and paunch that marked a true gentleman. His older companion, however, was endowed in both respects generously enough for two, and was a well-known club member, so the doorman saluted and admitted them. The visitors stepped through, leaving the Stygian sulfurousness without for the stench of old cigar smoke within.

Under the hissing white glare of the gaslight, the clerk behind the desk beamed at the arrivals and offered a bow that was much more than the required nod. 'Lord Gravel! I do wish you a good evening, my lord, although the meteorology is not cooperating.'

'Indeed not, Froude!' the Gravel grumbled. 'Write me in, will you? And my grandson—Ethelred Thames-Cheddar.'

'Just write *E-T-C*,' the boy said glumly. 'Everyone else does.'

The clerk smiled with practiced smarm and entered their names in the book.

'Has Sir Gascony Tyrwhitt arrived yet?' His Lordship boomed.

'Indeed he has, my lord. With a guest. You will find them in the library.'

'I'm expecting another man—a Professor Emeritus? No? Well, send him in when he gets here. Have our bags put in our rooms, will you?'

Having shed their November garments in the cloakroom and straightened out their evening dress, grandfather and grandson proceeded into the grandiose bowels of the Bwana Club, side-by-side like a pair of courting penguins.

Grandsire had not yet explained why he had required Etc to accompany him, merely mumbling that Etc might be able to make himself useful for a couple of days. Whatever it might be, Etc welcomed the escape from sitting around the house with outraged parents and snickering siblings.

The cathedral-scale hallway was decorated much as one would expect, with enough oak to rebuild the Armada and more marble than Pericles had piled on the Acropolis. The walls were hung with hunting trophies—the heads of tigers, lions, elk, polar bears, great white sharks, and at least four Komodo dragons—interspersed with oversized portraits of great former members, such as Dr Bedrock, the Marquis of Pittance, Sessile Roads, and Captain Fogg. These were men who had pinned down the hinterlands of the world and most of their inhabitants for the glory of the Empire. Lord Gravel paid no attention because he had seen it all before, but Etc gazed around, wide-eyed, unable to believe that anyone would display such deplorable taste less than a statute mile from the French Embassy.

The library was even larger and more gruesome than he had feared. Three discreet glass-fronted bookcases did contain books, but appeared to lack both hinges and keyholes. All other vertical spaces bore a gruesome collection of assegais, halberds, khopeshes, and other such primitive weapons, interspersed with masks and shields, many of them marred by bullet holes and old bloodstains. All the chairs were covered with black animal hide and stuffed with horsehair. The library was devoid of readers just then, and probably always, but the three men reposing near the fireplace made Etc wonder how recently they had been inspected for signs of rot.

Grandsire Gravel aimed for a couple of gentlemen sipping spirits in the far corner. 'Tyrwhitt!' he exclaimed. 'Good to see you, old man. Sorry for the delay. Damnable fog, what?'

The two men rose and there were introductions. Sir Gascony Tyrwhitt was another casting from the mold that had produced Grandsire—a money man with a suppressed provincial accent—but his paunch and beard were less advanced. His companion was a Major Boot, a tall, spare, and younger man bearing the remains of a tropical sunburn. Ex-India, perhaps? Or the Sudan?

'...and my grandson, Ethelred Times-Cheddar.'

'Historical, geographical, and dietary? A man of many parts!' Boot frowned upward as if no man or boy should be allowed to top his five feet eleven and three-quarters, which Etc did handily.

'Call me Etc, sir.' Their handshake was mutually firm, bordering on challenging.

'You're not ready to be Ethelred?'

Etc smiled again, wishing he had a rifle with a bullet for every person who had asked that.

'He ought to be in school, of course,' Grandsire harrumphed, sinking into a chair, 'but he caught a chill. Growing too fast! Doctor recommended fresh air and sunshine.'

Etc sat down, taking care to be the last to do so. He didn't know whether Grandsire had been told the true story, or only the public version. Anything he might have caught he had caught from the school nurse, and since they had both been caught on the third occasion, they had both been sacked. What the doctor had actually recommended was chastity.

A liveried waiter appeared from nowhere and hovered.

'Large brandy and soda,' Gravel said.

Etc nodded to indicate that he would have the same.

Grandsire noticed, damn him. 'Lemonade for the boy.'

Etc shot the waiter, who was little older than himself, a pained look and said, 'Make that tonic water, please?' He arranged his eyebrows to signal a silent appeal for more than that.

The waiter said, 'Tonic. Of course, sir,' and floated away.

The conversation progressed through the weather, the government, and the scandalous misconduct of HRH the Prince of Wales, in rising layers of outrage and disgust. Etc took no part in it, but he had realized now that Boot must be the Major Boot who had recently massacred enough whirling dervishes to win an honorable mention in *The Times*. With him involved, beside two moneybags with reputations for sponsoring wild enterprises, the evening might manage to be interesting.

The major, already displaying signs of impatience with all the small talk, suddenly slashed through the jabber with a verbal machete. 'So, my lord? Sir Gascony tells me you have some mysterious secret project to put to us?'

'Not mine, Major. I hope Emeritus arrives here all right. You must have heard of him? Oxford...or is it Cambridge? Egyptian expert. Thinks he's on the track of something big.'

Wonderful! The Grandsire believed that Emeritus was a personal name.

'Money in it?' Tyrwitt asked skeptically. 'Or just some hunks of rock with scratches on 'em? I'm tired of financing idiots who promise to find King Solomon's Mines and come back with nothing better than the Queen of Sheba's diary carved in granite.'

Lord Gravel nodded sympathetically, although he had gained his title by sponsoring the expedition that had found Dr Adenoid.

'Emeritus implies...' Gravel paused as the waiter returned with his brandy and a tall glass of something colorless for Etc, who took a quick sip and gave the man a nod of thanks and relief—gin and tonic, adult strength.

And before Grandsire could expose his ignorance any further, a footman ushered in another visitor and pointed to the group in the corner. As they were the only visible life in the room, the newcomer could probably have found them for himself. He came bustling over. Physically he was much like a non-combatant version of Boot—tall, tanned, and much younger than the two captains of industry. In manner, though, he was woolly, rather than leathery. His hair was already white, and worn too long.

Everyone rose to exchange more introductions and handshakes. Emeritus ordered a glass of port; the waiter departed; everyone sat down again. There had to be more small talk, but gin did make it easier to bear. As soon as the waiter had delivered the port and departed, Boot was again the one to break out of the maze.

'Sir Gascony tells us that you have some mysterious secret project to put to us, Professor?'

'Ah!' Emeritus took a sip of port and nodded approvingly. 'Yes, I may just have. Alexander the Great, mm? I'm sure you've all heard of him. Do any of you recall where he was buried?'

Before Etc could stop it, the gin said, 'Δεν θάφτηκε.'

'Aha!' The professor turned soapy but approving eyes on him. 'A classical scholar! So what happened to his body, if it wasn't buried?'

'Τουρσί σε μέλι σε ένα υπέροχο χρυσό φέρετρο με τροχούς.'

'If you don't cut that out,' Grandsire said, 'I'll make you go and stand in the corner. I brought you along because you can read Greek, not to spout it in respectable company.'

'Sorry, sir,' Etc said hastily. 'I said that Alexander wasn't buried. He died in Babylon. His body was pickled in honey and put in a great golden coffin on wheels. Um...'

Everyone waited for him to continue.

'Um, when it was on its way back to Macedon, one of his generals, Ptolemy, raided the procession, stole the cart, and took it to Alexandria, in Egypt, where he'd already made himself king. That's all I remember, sir.' It wasn't, but he had not consented to a *viva voce*.

'But not bad at all, *extempore*!' Emeritus conceded.

Tyrwhitt said, 'So we can assume that you believe that you have located this golden coffin, Professor?'

'Well, it's a little more complicated than that.'

'I am not at all surprised to hear it.'

Emeritus leaned back in his chair, which sighed. He sipped his port to build the suspense. 'Alexander died in 323 BC. His body was on display in the heart of Alexandria for centuries. Romans like Pompey and Julius Caesar visited the mausoleum. Skip forward about three hundred years and...*Cherchez la femme*?' He looked to Etc.

'Cleopatra, sir?'

'Correct! Cleopatra, the last of the pharaohs, a very shrewd and dangerous lady, the darker side of whose character may have been kept from your tender ears.'

'I am familiar with the juicier parts of Herodotus, sir.'

'The Dickens you are! Well, Cleopatra had an affair with Julius Caesar, of course, and after his death had another, this time with Marcus Antonius, or Mark Anthony, as the Bard dubbed him. But Octavian, Caesar's heir and adopted son, better known to us as Augustus, quarrelled with Anthony and there was a big naval battle at

Actium. You are familiar with that, of course?'

Etc said, 'Yes, sir,' but he would have bet his last farthing that Grandsire Gravel was now more at sea than Cleopatra had ever been.

Sensing that the two older men were becoming impatient, Emeritus hurried along. 'At Actium, Anthony and Cleopatra lost. They scuttled back to Egypt, and the following year the triumphant Octavian arrived with his army. The lovers both died—perhaps not as dramatically as Shakespeare describes it, but dead is dead.'

'Like Alexander,' Grandsire growled.

'Deader! And naturally Octavian, who was now in effect the first Emperor of Rome, although he never called himself that, went to pay his respects to Alexander. Think of it! It was one of the most dramatic scenes in history—Alexander had conquered Greece and then the Persian Empire all the way to India. Octavian had turned the Roman Republic into a one-man military dictatorship. Napoleon viewing the tomb of Frederick the Great had nothing on that. But when Octavian was looking at the great man's corpse, he "accidentally" knocked its nose off! That man never put a foot wrong in his life—why would he do a thing like that?' Emeritus triumphantly drained the last of his port.

'I expect he just wanted to know what it was made of,' the gin said. Damn!

Emeritus looked to Trywhitt, Boot looked to Gravel, Tyrwhitt and Gravel exchanged looks, and suddenly all eight eyes settled on Etc as if he ought to know what this crazy academic was ranting about.

Grandsire accepted the problem. 'I know how much that fancy school of yours milks your parents to fill your head with all that ancient Greek and Roman rubbish instead of useful skills like business law or accountancy. So if you do have a useful idea to offer, offer it. Otherwise, be seen and not heard!'

Then the old tyrant, who knew nothing about Egyptian history but everything about club behavior, waved a finger to the waiter in the corner to bring another round.

Etc had always enjoyed Classics much more than horrors like calculus or Chaucer, and he resented the implication that it was useless. 'I expect he was motivated by his forthcoming triumph, sir.' He saw at once from Emeritus's reaction that he had stolen a peal or two of the professor's thunder.

Grandsire was not totally senile; he had noticed too. His glacial look melted a degree or two. 'Are you implying that Alexander's corpse was an artifact?'

'Well, sir, Octavian had won his war against Cleopatra, and every successful Roman general dreamed of great triumphal processions through the city. That was like being buried in Westminster Abbey, except that you could enjoy it more often. Octavian had been granted quite a few triumphs in his time, so he would want to top them all. But Cleopatra knew that too, and knew that he must be dreaming of parading her through the streets in chains, so she did her dance with the asp and cheated him out of that ambition.'

Etc drained his tonic water, silently praying that the waiter wouldn't load the next one too, or at least not so heavily. 'So what about Alexander? To parade the fabled warrior around in his golden sarcophagus, and then build him an even grandioser mausoleum on the Palatine Hill—that would top anything Pompey or Caesar had ever done! Naturally, he dropped in at the tomb in Alexandria to see the old boy.'

His grandfather frowned suspiciously. 'But why did he knock off his nose?'

'To see what it was made of. They didn't have paper-mache in those days, so it was probably pottery. Maybe marble.'

'Oh, well done!' Emeritus said. 'First class honors, Ethelred! It took me a lot longer than that to understand what was going on, and why Alexander was never carted off to Rome in the spoils.'

'It was a fake?' Sir Gascony said.

'Yes, it was. But that wouldn't fool a laddie as smart as Octavian, although it did fool a few of the emperors who followed him. He'd allowed Cleopatra months to prepare for his arrival, plenty of time for her to make preparations. And one thing she moved out of his reach was old Alexander, asleep in his gold coffin. She had a copy made! If Octavian tried parading that around Rome, good luck to him! No doubt she had friends ready to denounce it as tourist junk.'

'And you know where she hid the original?' Grandsire asked.

'I have a strong clue, my lord. On my last dig in the Aswan area of Upper Egypt, one of my fellahin unearthed a jar containing eleven rolls of papyrus, perfectly preserved by the dryness of the sands. One of those was part of an actual note from the queen herself to her son Caesarion! As an historical treasure by itself it is close to priceless, but what it may lead us to is mind-boggling. You see, she needed to put Alexander with his gold coffin and several other treasures somewhere well out of Octavian's reach. It seems that she sent them off—upriver of course—with Caesarion, who was her joint ruler and her son by Julius Caesar. We know that he cleared out before the Romans arrived, heading south. He was about the same age as Ethelred, here.'

'Very close, sir,' Etc said. 'But he was a beefhead.'

'And you're not?' Boot countered.

'If I were the last surviving king of Egypt and the son of Julius Caesar, while the newly triumphant ruler of the known world was falsely calling himself both ruler of Egypt and the only son of Julius Caesar, I would never trust his promise of safe conduct.'

'I should hope not,' Grandsire said approvingly.

'We don't know how Caesarion died,' Emeritus continued, 'but he took with him to the grave the knowledge of where he had left the real Alexander and his golden sarcophagus.'

'Until now?' Tyrwhitt said, ever practical. 'What exactly are you proposing, Professor?'

'An expedition to look for it. The papyrus is not an ordinance survey map, you understand. It's fragile and incomplete, but it strongly indicates an area just south of modern Egypt, in the Sudan. I would prefer not to be more specific at this time, you understand.'

'The war there isn't yet over,' Grandsire said.

'No, it isn't,' Boot agreed. 'We'll need armed guards, and plenty of them. In any case, you don't go looking for the world's greatest treasure, find it, bury it again, and plan on coming back for it later. It will be long gone! This will have to be an all-or-nothing, fully-fledged dig.'

Cairo! Etc thought. Or even Alexandria? Two of the raciest cities in the world! Keep the pesky pyramids, a fellow could quench the raging fires of puberty in Egypt. If he could convince his family jailers that Egypt was just what the doctor had ordered, he might do very well out of this little plotting session.

'How much?' Tyrwhitt demanded.

Pause for suspense. Then Boot said, 'I estimate at least twenty-four thousand pounds. Probably more.'

Etc just managed not to gasp. That was twenty-four times more cash than he could even imagine.

Grandsire snorted. 'All on the basis of a scrap of paper two thousand years old? Well, I've brought along an expert, here. Let Ethelred take a gander at this treasure map.'

Etc became an object of interest again. Alarmed, he set down his almost-empty glass.

He was relieved to see Emeritus shaking his head. 'I did not bring it. It is presently in a bank vault. Understand, my lord, that it is very old and very brittle. I have prepared my own translation, of course, and can give you that, plus my exegesis of it. There are a few other men who are as fluent in the Coptic language and the demotic script as I, but if you call in even one of those to confirm my reading, you will be seriously imperiling security. That is obvious, surely?'

'I can't help, sir,' Etc said hastily. 'I have Greek and Latin, but no Egyptian! All I can offer to do would be to cross-check the classical accounts—Plutarch and the others. The professor's account of the situation back then does correspond to what I remember. I could drop over to the British Museum Reading Room tomorrow. They would have everything I would need.'

'Well, obviously we can't decide tonight,' Grandsire said, draining his glass while looking meaningfully at Tyrwhitt. 'Why don't you be our expert tomorrow, lad, while Gascon and I look into the feasibility, the military situation, and so on? Meet here again, Major, Professor? Say Tuesday, same time? Meanwhile we all play our cards very close to our waistcoats, what?'

#

And that was that. After two large gins, Etc was more than ready to stagger upstairs to his room, next door to Grandsire's. He admired it fuzzily, peered out around the drape to establish that the fog had not given up, untied his bow tie, and removed his damnable garotting collar. With carpet on the floor, a pleasant fire burning and no doubt a hot water bottle waiting in the bed, it made school dorm look like a jail. He decided he needn't bother with the flannel pajamas he'd brought. He could sleep in the—

As he was just starting on his cuff links, there came a tap on the door. Ah! He went over and slid the bolt. The odds were sixty-forty that it would be Professor Emeritus, but it was Major Bolt.

'Do come in, sir. What can I do for you?'

'Not much,' the soldier said, closing the door behind himself. 'You're not my type. This report you're going to prepare for your grandfather at the Museum—it will be enthusiastically positive, I hope?'

'I haven't decided,' Etc said. 'What's it worth?'

The soldier blinked and then smiled. 'A man after my own heart, Etc. That is right, isn't it—Etc? Good name! How much do you want?'

Negotiating was easy when one had two stiff gins burning inside one. 'A third.'

The tropical tan faded into skewbald blotches. 'Droll! Maybe a hundred quid, mm?' Seeing no eruption of enthusiasm Boot added, 'And the same again when the golden geese start laying?'

'Fat chance. You're a pair of hustlers from top to toe. I could knock on Grandsire's door right now and denounce you for attempted embezzlement and you'd probably get ten years on Dartmoor.'

'That's slander, boy!'

'No, it isn't. When we were talking about Cleopatra, I mentioned the works of Herodotus. He lived a hundred years before even Alexander, so about four centuries before Cleopatra, yet your accomplice didn't call me on it.'

'He was sparing your feelings.'

'Nice of him,' Etc said scornfully. 'But I wrote a term paper on the Ptolemaic Dynasty, and I know that one of them—and what I plan to confirm tomorrow is which one of the hooligans it was, but I am almost certain it was Ptolemy VI—dumped Alexander in a cheap coffin and melted down the golden one for grocery money. So you two are liars and twisters.'

Major Boot's expression indicated pain. 'And if we cut you in?'

'Then I shall assure Grandsire that your story looks rock-solid historically, and I want to come along with you on the expedition to find the world's greatest treasure. I volunteer to accompany you as observer, student, and barman.'

'Will your parents allow that?'

'They will sing the Hallelujah Chorus.'

'I can see why. I suppose we might rise to a fifth.'

'A third or Dartmoor.'

Boot sighed, 'A third, then.' He offered a hand to shake.

Etc looked at it warily and shook his head instead. 'Thanks, but not tonight. I will need my fingers to take notes tomorrow. See you on Tuesday—partner.'

Etc saw the scoundrel out and slid the bolt. He stripped and slid happily into bed. He had no intention of trailing off to the Sudan to be shriveled up by the tropical sun or slaughtered by the Mahdi's dervishes. He would abscond in Paris, the City of Light, together with his eight thousand pounds. If the vice and decadence there were good enough for the Prince of Wales, they must be good enough for him.

BREAD PUDDING
Karen Keeley

The Chief Constable fiddled with his fountain pen. If not careful, he'd soon have ink spatted across his desk. 'I'm having a devil of a time trying to make sense of it, Farnsworth. Nothing but poppycock.'

I echoed the chief's sentiment. 'Poppycock, it may be, sir. But young Hennessey and myself, with luck, we'll soon separate the chaff from the wheat, as it were.'

'Luck won't do, Farnsworth. Dogged determination, that's the ticket.'

The chief set his pen aside while gazing through the window which gave him a good view of Linton Gardens, smack-dab in the centre of our bustling community of Hastings in East Sussex. The window, frosted with ice, looked upon a winter fairyland for the locals to enjoy—the grounds, shrubbery and elderberry bushes covered in a light dusting of snow along with the hoarfrost. 'I trust you'll keep young Hennessey with you,' he said.

'I will, sir. If you can spare him.'

'He's spared, but for what, I haven't the foggiest.' He handed me back the sheaf of papers he'd been reading. 'We were told heart failure, and now, death by snake venom. What next, I wonder? Bats in the belfry?'

He leaned forward, elbows on his desk. 'What the devil is that?'

'What is what, sir?' I was busy looking about, wondering what I'd missed.

'That stain on your tie. It won't do, Farnsworth. Get yourself a good woman. She'd soon set you straight with a decent wardrobe.'

I examined my tie, and yes, an unsightly stain, a dried blob of Worchester sauce. Why did it have to be the Chief Constable to spot such a thing? Why not one of my peers?

'If the newspapers get wind of this, there'll be hell to pay. Not a word to them, or to the family. Not until you've unravelled this nasty piece of business. Have I made myself clear?'

'Crystal, sir. Young Hennessey's done most of the legwork, a capital lad, if I may say so.'

'Yes—yes, I have all of that in your initial report.' He reached for a memo lying next to the inkwell. 'I'm told Lady Margaret owned snakes, frightful creatures.'

I glanced up, caught in the act, viciously scrubbing at the dark stain with a fingernail, to no avail. 'They belonged to her late husband, a hobby of his. She didn't have the heart to dispose of them. A young lad in town feeds them, brings field mice he gathers from the grain silos here about. Lady Margaret wouldn't have handled the snakes herself.'

The Chief Constable shuddered, grunted, and scratched an ear. 'Well, someone extracted the venom. It's your job to ferret them out. And a ruddy shame. A waste of a good bread pudding.'

An understatement, if there ever was one. We all knew the chief harboured a fondness for a good bread pudding. 'What the devil? They're now changing the hours in the canteen?' He'd tossed the memo onto his desk. 'What about afternoon tea?'

I had no answer, other than budget cuts. There were always budget cuts, all part of policing, as it were. I turned to take my leave. The chief hollered, 'Before you go gallivanting about town, change that damned tie, Farnsworth. I won't have you looking like a street urchin.'

'Right-o, Chief.' And with that, I left him to his paperwork.

I then joined young Hennessey in the canteen and we ate a late lunch together, equal portions of steak and kidney pie along with thick slices of homemade bread, doing our best to not splat the gravy. The revised hours were posted and due to take effect come the new year. While eating, we revisited the investigation for the umpteenth time, going over witness statements. Originally, the verdict had been Her Ladyship died from natural causes.

Dr Bergen, who'd been with the family a number of years, told us, 'She suffered from heart palpitations. Dizziness too, and the occasional faint. I'd requested her meals be specially prepared, fresh fruit and vegetables, lean meat, all of the fat trimmed, plenty of fish and poultry. For Christmas, she mentioned a goose, a family tradition, to be followed by a bread pudding. I thought it harmless, a small amount, in keeping with the Christmas spirit.'

At that time, I'd said to the doctor, 'Nothing suspicious about Her Ladyship's death,' while toying with my wool scarf, noting the bedraggled threads caught in my coat buttons.

'No, nothing suspicious. I've signed the death certificate and I'll be handing that off to the coroner at some point tomorrow. Prior to her death, Lady Margaret experienced rapid heart rate, a weak pulse along with some numbness in her limbs, shivering and sweating, all symptoms of a failing heart.'

We now knew better, our local pathologist having determined foul play—snake venom most likely introduced into the bread pudding. This threw a spanner into our investigation. All the family had eaten the same pudding, so why weren't they all dead?

While pondering that thought, young Hennessey and I finished our meal, took up our belongings, and made our third trip to the Fitzroy estate in as many days. Hennessey guided our horse and carriage through town, a thick ground fog having moved in from across the Channel. He easily navigated Braybrooke, working his way south to George Street and on past the Barking Dog, a favourite watering hole of mine. Our little Welsh pony, a stout and sturdy fellow, had no trouble navigating the slippery streets. We arrived some twenty minutes later in High Wickham, the estate comprised of the manor house built in a Tudor style similar to the Ascott House found near Buckinghamshire, in addition to a host of stables for Her Ladyship's carriages and horses, along with separate sleeping quarters for her housekeeper, the maid and the cook. All three lived on site, sharing an ample sized brick and mortar cottage which did nicely for their needs.

The stable boy, a young lad of fourteen, took charge of our steed and carriage, for steed was certainly how I thought of our sure-footed pony, his thick winter coat keeping him warm. The lad led the animal out of the bitter cold toward one of the stables. Young Hennessey and I stood on the cobblestones dusted with snow, our breath fogging the air.

I found my mind wandering as I took stock of the Fitzroy home with its dark timbers, white exterior, tall chimneys, and bay windows in addition to three gruesome gargoyles inlaid above the massive front door. Lady Margaret, only daughter to the Earl of Doncaster—thus her lofty title, bore one son, married at the tender age of twenty-one, he and his wife both amateur archaeologists. Fifteen years into their marriage, the couple set off on another adventure, a crusade in search of King Solomon's mines, the lost gold of Ophir.

When word came that both son and daughter-in-law had died from typhus, far from their native England, Lady Margaret and her husband claimed legal guardianship over their grandchildren, all of whom were now grown, having developed a close bond with each other. Cornelius Fitzroy, Lady Margaret's husband, threw himself into his work following the death of his son, travelling abroad, seldom home, succumbing to a fatal heart attack two years ago, he too far from his native England. To my way of thinking, it made for a sad legacy, Her Ladyship's loved ones taken from her.

The butler, a hale and hearty fellow, still serving the family despite getting on in age, occupied a room at the rear of the manor house. It wasn't a bad life by all accounts, Lady Margaret proven to be a kind and generous employer, according to the help. She had given them the whole of the day to spend with their families. She would have her grandchildren with her. Heaven knew, it was time they stepped up and did a few household chores—it would be the making of them.

The goose had been cooked the day prior, as was the bread pudding. There'd also been pickled beets, asparagus and onions, caramelized squash mixed with a handful of dried currants, and a jar of olives—the black ones. Her Ladyship didn't care for the green.

Cook had volunteered all of that information upon our arrival Christmas Day. We'd interviewed her, in her room at the cottage, the maid and the housekeeper having taken Her Ladyship's offer to be with their families. The butler too had been away. Only Cook remained on site, no family to speak of.

Her Ladyship had made it very clear. They were to go, to enjoy Christmas, to make merry. Cook was also expected to play with the cat, which everyone knew belonged to the stable boy, him too celebrating with his family. She'd taken on the duty of feeding and caring for the animal during the boy's absence, giving the cat refuge near her wee fire, but she drew the line at actually playing with it. And yes, she'd put her feet up, and immersed herself in a good book, *A Christmas Carol* by Charles Dickens, borrowed from the local library, when all manner of mayhem broke loose.

'Just imagine, Inspector. There I was, feet up before my wee fire, having attended early morning mass, a kind parishioner coming to collect me and return me home, when that young Colin came barrelling down the lane, hollering for me to come, a terrible catastrophe had befallen Her Ladyship. You could've knocked me over with a feather, the colour drained right out of him. I hurriedly pulled on my hat and coat, and accompanied him back to the manor house, and there, Her Ladyship, dead, lying on her bed, looking as peaceful as the blessed virgin Mary herself.'

Here, she'd made the sign of the cross. 'I crossed myself then too, being the good Catholic that I am, when I heard the sound of horses galloping across the cobblestones. It were Master Philip, headed to town for the doctor. There was naught any of us could do but sit with Her Ladyship, waiting for the master and the doctor to return.'

I'd picked up the book Cook had been reading, *A Christmas Carol*, and wondered if she'd lost interest, having been so abruptly interrupted. All that morning, she'd worried how any of them would manage without help, all four spoiled beyond measure. It didn't matter a hound's tooth they were grown and meant to be self-sufficient, none could fry an egg let alone reheat a full complement of excellent dishes earmarked for their Christmas dinner. And yes, the root cellar was filled, the meals easy enough to reheat if they didn't burn down the manor house first. There'd also been freshly baked bread, four loaves made the day before, as was the bread pudding, it covered with parchment paper. She was later informed, as a family, they'd eaten the Christmas meal just gone one o'clock.

As we were taking our leave, she handed me an additional chestnut which didn't seem important at the time. She'd gone to the dining room to clear away the leftovers from the Christmas meal, not wanting to leave such a task for the grandchildren when Dr Bergen arrived.

'One queer item, Inspector. Something I found most odd.' She stood in the doorway to her wee cottage, winter's chill giving her cause to shiver, her knitted shawl tightly wrapped around her thin frame, her rosary clutched in her hand.

'And what was that?' I'd asked.

She then told me, and I agreed, it was odd, but I'd dismissed it from my mind, believing Lady Margaret died of natural causes. It wasn't until our local pathologist came forth with his findings that I realized we'd been handed an important piece to the puzzle, something Hennessey and I had been digging into these past three days.

Now, the last day of December, and I felt the thrill of the chase as Hogarth, the butler, opened the front door and invited us in. He took our wool coats, hats, and gloves, and laid them in an adjoining room off to the side. We then followed him to one of the sitting rooms where he announced our arrival to all present.

Far off, somewhere over the Channel, I heard a clap of thunder, practically unheard of in winter with its dusting of snow and hoarfrost. I took it to be a good omen as Hennessey and I walked on through, all six, staring wide-eyed, implying both I and my constable were akin to a couple of bad pennies, impossible to get rid of.

'I say, back again?' This from Colin Fitzroy, the youngest of the two grandsons. He bore a striking resemblance to Prince Arthur, Duke of Connaught and Strathearn, when he too had been in his twenties—the Queen's favourite son. 'Have you anything further to share?' This day, young Colin wore a cabled turtleneck jumper and wool trousers, reclining nonchalant on a chaise longue, studying his fingernails, as bored as a mouse at a political convention.

'I do,' I told him, and I took my place standing before the fireplace. A fire had not been lit despite the weather, dreary and miserable. Perhaps a fire would have implied a cheery atmosphere and it certainly wasn't cheery within Her Ladyship's home, anything but. I could see no sign of a Christmas tree, not a sprig of holly or mistletoe, which made me think, anything to do with Christmas had been removed following the woman's death.

Offers were made, tea or coffee, or something stronger, of which Hennessey and I thanked them, and declined. No, we were there on a much more serious matter, it was not a social call. Some ten minutes later, all of them having asked numerous questions which I'd nicely deflected, I told them, 'Before I bring you up to speed on developments, I'm curious about something.'

'What's that?' asked Colin, clearly bored with the whole affair.

He was something of a cad, a good-for-nothing loafer who refused to work no matter how many times Lady Margaret threatened to cut off his monthly allowance. Despite limited funds, Colin always seemed flush, plenty of cash in hand to place a sizeable bet at the racetracks scattered across the countryside or take part in a lucrative game of cards. Rumour stated, he rarely won at either, but he always arrived full of piss 'n vinegar, ready, willing, and able to play.

I addressed young Colin directly. 'Christmas day, none of you were wearing perfume or availed yourselves of hair tonic. Why was that?' I stood with my thumbs tucked in the pockets of my waistcoat, trying for a look of authority. This was not the time to be intimidated by their wealth and social standing.

Irving Hyde, husband to Adeline, the youngest of the two granddaughters, was he himself a retired jockey and now something of a country gentleman, as energetic as a Jack Russell terrier, and just as feisty. He pooh-poohed such an observation. 'This is bloody ridiculous, Inspector. What's perfume or hair tonic got to do with any of this? Addie's grandmother died a natural death. The doctor said so. He signed off on the death certificate.'

'I'm getting to that, Mr Hyde. Please, if you will, take a seat.' He did so, sitting down next to his wife, a woman clearly in the family way, the baby due within a fortnight, we'd been told.

We'd learned through our investigation that Hyde made a lot of money as a jockey, investing a good chunk of it in the production of mutton, principal owner in a Yorkshire sheep farm, leaving him and his wife rather flush according to some we'd spoken to, but that too appeared to be somewhat fishy. We'd also learned most of Hyde's current livestock had fallen victim to foot and mouth disease, the man still trying to recoup his losses, his financial footing on rocky ground, and now, about to be a father.

He took his wife's hand, gave it a tender kiss. Perhaps the man sported some heart after all—not rendered entirely stone-cold in the wake of his recent unpleasant business dealings.

Robert Prothero, attached to London's West End theatrical district, married to Elsbeth, two years older than Adeline, took up his brandy glass and gave it a swirl. He was somewhat advanced in years with muttonchops which also aged him, grey threaded throughout his mane of dark hair. Perhaps he thought the mustache gave him an air of credibility. It certainly appeared he harboured no qualms about drinking Lady Margaret's liquor now that the old woman was dead.

His wife spoke, she too drinking, but it appeared to be a glass of sherry. 'The reason you found no such items in the house was due to grandmother's inability to abide such things. They bothered her immensely. We weren't about to exacerbate her heart condition.'

'Don't forget she also had that stomach ulcer, Liz.' This from Colin, the gad-about. 'Her cockamamie diet reflected that too, remember?'

'Yes, Colin. I know, we all knew.' Elsbeth Prothero gave me her full undivided attention, a woman of renowned beauty with expressive pale blue eyes as cold as glacial ice. 'Scents of any kind bothered grandmother, sometimes to the point where she'd have extreme difficulty breathing. We knew of her sensitivities, her weak heart, and her stomach ulcer. She was on a strict diet which the doctor told you about.'

'And the staff, they too were aware?' I knew I was playing a game of cat 'n mouse which left them all somewhat discombobulated. The Chief Constable would've had my hide for shoe leather if he'd heard my manner, the deliberate cheek of a police inspector. But there was a method to my madness, of which Hennessey was in the know, having taken him into my confidence during the drive over.

I now wandered the room, a half dozen poinsettias having grabbed my attention, noticing aphids on two of the plants, hearty little beggars, able to hold their own throughout the winter months. Perhaps the solarium on the southern side of the manor, home to the rattlesnakes, was warmer than the rest of the house.

Elsbeth Prothero set her sherry glass on a side table. 'We abided by the rules,' she said. 'No scents allowed in the house.'

'Rules, indeed,' I echoed. 'And yet, we have poinsettias scattered about this room. Was there anything else she was sensitive to?'

'Grass, molds, insect bites,' added Elsbeth. 'The poinsettias didn't seem to bother her. They carry very little scent, the same for Boomer here.' I then noticed the dog lying at the side of a Chippendale sofa adjacent to the door through which Hennessey and I had entered, the animal almost hidden from view. Boomer raised his head at the mention of his name, his brown button eyes giving me a good going over. Following that, he lay back down, nose resting on his paws, happily ensconced on a lavish carpet, Kashmir, no doubt, knowing Her Ladyship's tastes.

Philip, the eldest of the four, stated matter-of-fact, 'He's a Welsh terrier,' implying I was something of an imbecile for not having noticed him sooner. As the eldest, he'd been groomed to take over the family business, investments in the Far East, importing silk and all manner of spices, something he'd done upon his grandfather's death, tripling the family assets, simply unheard of in financial circles, if the rumours were true. 'Boomer was no bother to grandmother. A breeder in Chepstow, wasn't it, Liz?'

She nodded, now looking tired, dark circles under her eyes which dampened her regal spirit. I suspected none of them had been sleeping well.

'I wonder who will take him now?' mused young Colin, the gadabout. He then added, 'Boomer seems to like you, Addie.' He'd swung his feet off the chaise longue and sat forward, holding out his brandy glass toward Philip, implying that he deserved preferential treatment as the younger brother. Rather than make a scene, Philip brought him the brandy decanter and filled his glass. 'With the wee one on the way, a pet would be just the thing. Don't you agree, Liz?'

Adeline Hyde, the youngest, offered no chance for her sister to respond. 'Over my dead body,' she said, and shuddered. 'That was a terrible thing to say. My apologies. But I'm ever so weary of it all. I'm desperate to return home. If this little one arrives sooner rather than later, I do not want Dr Bergen anywhere near me. I despise the man.'

'Now, now, my dear,' soothed her husband, Irving Hyde. 'Harsh words on such a harsh day.'

'It's true,' she said. She too bore a striking resemblance to her siblings, all four with the same pale blue eyes as cold as glacial ice, the long dark lashes indicative of their grandmother's ancestral heritage. 'I still maintain the doctor misdiagnosed grandmother's illness. If he'd gotten it right, she wouldn't have died from heart failure.'

I interrupted. 'Do you mean to say, madam—you all believe it was heart failure?'

'But of course. What else could it have been?' This from Philip, the eldest, making no effort to hide his contempt for what he took to be an obvious intrusion into their personal lives—why all the questions?

'My questions will soon be made clear,' I told him. 'But first, a necessary requirement to determine each of you knew of Lady Margaret's health concerns.'

'What the devil do you mean?' Philip's frustration simmered just shy of a rolling boil, something of the mad hatter about him, impossibly impatient, our unexpected arrival neither wanted nor warranted. 'You speak in riddles.'

'I do, but I now come to the point—Lady Margaret's will. As you know, the actual reading won't take place until sometime after the funeral, in the New Year, but her solicitors have informed us—very discreetly mind—that all of you inherit, some more than others. I'm here to tell you, one of you contributed directly to her death. Your grandmother died by poisoning.'

They all shouted their disbelief, including the one who'd performed the dastardly deed, stating it was utter poppycock, tattletale nonsense, nothing but malicious twaddle. I raised my hand in defense, my signal for silence.

'That fact is certain—something we've kept from the press, and from you, until now.'

Philip stated emphatically, 'I'll have you up before a board of inquiry. How dare you make such wild aspersions? Who the devil do you think you are?'

I further ignored him, something of a dark horse in my book. Only a few days ago, young Hennessey uncovered all was not kosher in Philip Fitzroy's world. He'd harboured a resentment toward his grandmother for most of his life, wanting to follow in his parents' footsteps, to be something of an amateur archaeologist himself, of which Lady Margaret vehemently forbade. Instead, Philip had been earmarked for Cambridge and thus—despite his present position spearheading the family fortune—was kept on a short leash regarding his monthly allowance. He'd been smoking and now vehemently tapped his briar pipe against an ashtray, embers flying.

'Three rattlesnakes,' I said, 'kept in the solarium, in their glass habitats.'

'What of it?' This again from Philip, clearly frustrated, his pipe tossed onto a table, bumping up against the ashtray.

'They were a gift to your grandfather from an American admirer. We've found paperwork amongst his correspondence attesting to that fact.'

'Common knowledge,' said Philip. 'Get on with it, man!'

'Lady Margaret died by ingesting snake venom.'

Elsbeth jumped to her feet. 'That's impossible! We were all there, at the table. We thought it was heart failure.' Early on, young Hennessey and I ferreted out the fact Robert Prothero's investments in London's West End cost him dearly, his wife approaching her grandmother on more than one occasion, hat in hand, begging for a loan of which her grandmother flatly refused due to the fact Elsbeth married against her wishes.

I directed my comments to her, thinking there must have been some kind of reconciliation, both she and her husband included in the Christmas festivities. 'The coin, madam, was a forgery, one of many made by a local confectionery in celebration of the coming New Year. They're made of sugared candy, meant as a treat for the children.'

The odd item Cook discovered when clearing away the remains of the Christmas dinner. Now for my *coup de grâce*. 'Your husband passed by the shop just a week ago. A sworn statement was given by the proprietor, who confirmed selling a replica of a sixpence coin to him. Your husband soaked the coin with venom which then leached into the bread pudding.'

She knew exactly my reference, common knowledge amongst not only the gentry but commonfolk too—make a soggy poultice from bread and milk, and the poultice would draw out the infection when placed over an open cut or wound. She turned white, falling back onto her chair, some embroidered thing with spindly legs. It could have been a holdover from Lord Nelson's Admiralty days. 'Oh, oh—,' and she burst into tears.

'I believe your husband made you an unwitting accomplice, madam. He knew of Lady Margaret's stomach ulcer, betting on Dr Bergen ruling her death as natural causes, meaning he'd have gotten away with his crime. If for some reason foul play was determined, suspicion would fall on each of you due to the fact you all stood to inherit.'

I looked at Robert Prothero, whose eyes were flaming with anger, challenging me to take it further.

His wife clutched the ruffled collar of her silk blouse, twisting the fabric, her fingers entwined in a strand of pearls, bringing it to the verge of breaking.

'Did your husband not have you identify to him the portion of bread pudding to be served to your grandmother? Were you not, by your own account and those of your siblings, the one to dish out the pudding which was then passed around the table?'

'You—you monster!' she exclaimed, her eyes a polar vortex aimed at her husband. 'Yes, he told me it was meant to be a surprise. To hide a sixpence coin in grandmother's portion, something that would bring her a small amount of pleasure, a way to enliven the Christmas spirit. He gave me the coin and I hid it in the bread pudding. It never occurred to me it wasn't genuine.'

'But—' Here she stumbled. 'I too handled the coin. Why wasn't I poisoned?'

'Snake venom can be handled and ingested without doing harm,' I told her. 'The poison must enter the bloodstream—the reason snakes have fangs. In your grandmother's case, it was her stomach ulcer. You, madam, handling the coin, hiding it in the pudding, were safe as long as you had no cuts on your hands or fingers.'

All of them, without hesitation, looked at their fingers. Even young Hennessey couldn't help but look at his own, chapped from the cold.

Elsbeth Prothero flew at her husband, meaning to scratch out his eyes, any sense of decency now gone.

Constable Hennessey stopped her. 'Here, madam. Sit over here,' and he led her to the far wall, to the sofa which Boomer seemed to favour. The little Welsh terrier bounded onto the sofa, squirming with enthusiasm, oblivious as to what was unfolding. Elsbeth grabbed him, buried her face in his fur, cradling him, lamenting her heartbreak, 'But why, Robert? I don't understand.'

Robert Prothero broke his silence, now knowing we held the final piece to the puzzle, the sworn statement from the confectioner. 'It's very simple, my dear. I needed your inheritance. My last venture wiped us out financially. Your tiresome ministrations to your grandmother were getting us nowhere.'

He tossed back the last of his brandy and set the glass on a table near his elbow. 'She flat out refused to help. You as much as told me so, as recent as a fortnight ago. The bank has threatened to foreclose, our home, our personal assets, my few remaining business assets, such as they are, all of them hanging by a thread. We'd have been destitute—we *are* destitute.'

Elsbeth Prothero burst into tears a second time. 'But I told you, grandmother was coming around. She'd invited us for Christmas, a reconciliation. Yes, she forbade my marrying you, but she wasn't totally heartless. And certainly not at Christmastime. She would've soon reneged on her refusal to help. Look at Colin,' she all but growled her younger brother's name, 'grandmother kept doling out money to him!'

Colin sat up straight, his ears having perked up at the mention of his name. 'I say, sis—that's rather mean.' No one seemed concerned at his bruised feelings.

Robert Prothero continued, 'Time, my dear, a commodity I simply didn't have. I needed that money—your money—whatever amount you're to inherit right away. The creditors have been snapping at my heels.'

'But how did you get your hands on snake venom? I don't understand.'

'I can answer that,' I told the group. 'The young lad who feeds the snakes, who brings the field mice. While all of you were acquainted with him, having spoken to him from time to time, only your husband, madam, actually broached the subject of milking a rattler for its venom. He offered to pay handsomely should the lad provide him a sample, something he needed for an experiment, a kind of practical joke on a colleague he knew in London, all of it a fabricated lie. The young lad took Mr Prothero at his word. We have his sworn statement, witnessed by his mother.'

Robert Prothero, without a viable defense, gave up the ghost and leaned back in his chair, eyes closed. Any bluster and bother he'd shown prior to my accusation now gone.

I addressed Elsbeth directly. 'The young lad believed your husband, being somewhat naïve given his age. As for your husband, he is well-known, not only in Hastings, but in London's West End.

A man thought to be trustworthy, married to you, madam. Lady Margaret's granddaughter. How could he not be trustworthy? The boy had no idea he'd be helping a murderer commit a heinous crime.'

I turned to my constable. 'Take him away, Hennessey,' and he did so, instructing Robert Prothero to go with him, leaving his wife to try to make sense of it all, sobbing into the wiry coat of little Boomer, her brothers coming to her rescue, even the gad-about, Colin, offering some semblance of empathy. Adeline, clearly uncomfortable in her present condition, cried out, 'I tell you—she ate all of it, every last mouthful,' and she too fell weeping into her husband's arms.

Given there was little we could do for any of them, our job complete, Hennessey and I departed.

An hour later, at six o'clock, I met with the Chief Constable in his office, the man most pleased at our positive result. 'I'm now off home to a hot toddy and more of Maud's bread pudding. She's been keeping it warm for me.'

'I hear plum pudding is just as good, sir.' I tossed Hennessey a wink, him standing near the doorway, hat in hand, sporting a satisfied look that mirrored mine.

'Not in my household, Farnsworth. As part of the New Year celebration, my dear Maud has availed herself of a new recipe, that of the Osborne pudding, traditional bread pudding made with custard and marmalade. If it's good enough for the Queen, it's good enough for me.'

Good enough for the Queen indeed. It was she who'd introduced a coin into a plum pudding or it may have been a bread pudding if memory served, a way to thank her staff for their loyal service. If she'd known her method to provide some Christmas cheer would've been used to kill one of her own, a woman of good breeding and social standing, would she have outlawed the practice?

I turned to Hennessey. 'What say we leave the Chief to his Osborne pudding and we two grab a pint at the Barking Dog.' I was busy examining my tie, this one much more presentable, a Christmas gift from my sister in Eastbourne. I grabbed my greatcoat, my wool scarf with its frayed threads, and my sound sheepskin cap with its serviceable ear flaps.

'Sounds good, Gov'nor,' replied Hennessey, him doing the same, pulling his eiderdown cap tight over his ears.

It was then, the bells of St. Mary's rang out, marking evening vespers.

'Right-o, my lad. And this time, you're buying.'

CHRISTMAS POTATOES
E. E. King

I live in Hollywood and don't often get away from the city. But for the first time in years, I was taking a vacation from smog, dirt, and murder.

I'm a PI, a private investigator—it means I work when I'm sober. I used to work for CARD—Child Abduction Rapid Deployment—tracking missing children, and the scum who took them. I was one of the big boys, one of the suits, constantly surrounded by all the debris and wreckage of a society with too many resources and not enough heart. I had worked for a cause. Now I worked for a paycheck—it was easier.

Still, sometimes they called me in and I had just finished a nasty case. I'd found a missing child and a nest of human vipers. It was the kind of thing that made you feel as if you'd never be clean again. I wanted to wash my hands and my soul. I wanted to forget the whole rotten human race.

It was just before Christmas. In LA Palm trees were circled by blinking lights. Shimmering plastic snow lined the edges of shop windows glistening like promises. It's a magic time of year. Children make lists of toys their parents can't afford. Turkeys who've survived Thanksgiving say their prayers. Angelinos mistake the neurosis in the air for expectation.

So, I went up to Big Cottonwood Canyon to clean my wounds and my memory. Big Cottonwood is in the mountains above Salt Lake City. It's the Alps on steroids. America's answer to Switzerland. It would be the whitest, snowiest Christmas ever.

It's difficult to believe the state of Utah is one of the driest in the nation, because here in the heights, it's lousy with snow and ice. It's dry in another way though, heavily Mormon and morally teetotalling.

You can only get alcohol at the State Liquor Stores, which are carefully hidden, and even there you can't get it cold.

You can get beer at the grocery or 7-11, unless you want it with alcohol—Utah beer is 3.2% alcohol and tastes like weak piss. I didn't care. I wasn't here for the nightlife, which was good, since it consisted mostly of bats and owls.

I was staying at the Silver Fork, a rustic B&B away from the ski lodges with a view of the whole valley and the mountains beyond. I'm not much for skiing. There are easier ways to get broken legs and heads and I know all of them, but I enjoy watching the snow fall. There's a special peace to standing alone in a white wood, cut off from the world. To stand in a winter wonderland without blinking lights and Salvation Army Santas.

I was the only overnight guest at the Silver Fork, though lots of locals came in for lunch and dinner. On Friday, a couple of Chicago Paddies moved in. Peggy and Mac, a red-faced couple in their mid-fifties, as hearty as lager stew.

'Ya know,' Mac said, 'Peggy and I are takin' the time we never had to see each and every state.'

'Exploring just as if it were a foreign country,' Peggy added.

'And it is! 3.2% beer and no whiskey for sale except in pubs or state stores.'

'And the food,' Peggy laughed. 'Oh Lord, it's awful, but the mountains are fierce, and the folks are friendlier than a smile.'

'We plan to go to a Mormon Christmas potluck on Sunday,' Mac said. 'Care to join us?'

'No thanks,' I said.

'We'll bring you back a doggie bag,' Peggy said.

'Woof,' I said.

She giggled.

After breakfast, they left to survey the state like the alien country it was. I left to wander in snow-laden forest. I went to bed early and woke late. There was nothing, nothing but time and the white woods.

It was 10 am when I went down for breakfast. Tammie, my usual waitress, didn't come to the table—three days and I was already hidebound.

Tammie was one of those pretty, healthy girls they specialize in up here. She always seemed ecstatic to see me. Being a waitress and being from Utah is a high fructose combination.

Utah's a good place to escape to—everyone's polite and vigorous. Everyplace is tidy. Everybody seems prosperous. You don't fear walking the streets after dark. And the only uninvited visitors are missionaries.

The waitresses all have names like Chrissie, or Katie, or Kathy. They're skiers, hikers, and mountain bikers. They have strong teeth, wide smiles, muscular legs—no acne, cavities, or original thoughts. They're good kids—even the bad ones. Bad is relative. In Utah, it might mean having a drink, a smoke, or shopping on Sunday. Where I come from bad kids are really bad—murder, gang warfare, rape, and vandalism on Sunday.

I guessed Tammie must be having a day off, probably ski-jumping. Instead, Christie, one of the other regulars, came to take my order. Her face was red and raw like she'd been crying—and she had. Her nose was running and I was afraid drops would end up in my water glass. If the Utah niceness was catching and she was contagious, I'd have to find a new line of work.

'What's wrong?' I asked Christie. I really didn't want to know. I didn't care if her dog had died, her boyfriend had left her, or if she'd discovered she had herpes. All I wanted was a cheese omelet, a cold beer and to be left alone. But it's hard to ignore a snotting waitress.

'Tammie's dead,' she sniffed. She began sobbing, long and hysterically, gasping for air between gulps, like a swimmer caught in the undertow.

'She died last night,' she howled. I raised an eyebrow, motioning to the seat across from me. Christie's legs buckled. She collapsed into it, pouring out her grief in inarticulate sobs, as if I'd asked her to.

'She was fine last night,' Christie wailed. 'We went out after work and had a few drinks at the Canyon Inn.'

I guessed Tammie and Christie were what they called the Jack— or maybe in their case *Jill*—Mormons. Gals who'd been raised in the faith but had fallen away. Some were still believers but didn't like all the rules.

'We didn't drink much,' Christie sobbed on, just as if I'd been paying attention, instead of imagining my cold beer and cheese omelet.

'In fact, I don't even think she'd finished one, when she said she had a stomachache. Then she doubled right over, fell on the floor, and curled into a li-li-little b-b-ball.' She sniffed. 'We rushed her to the emergency room, but she d-d-d-died about half an hour later.' Burrowing her face in her hands, Christie fled howling into the kitchen.

Another server came to the table to take care of me. His nametag read *Greg*.

'I'm awfully sorry about that, mister,' he said. 'It's been a real tough day.'

I nodded and ordered my food.

After I finished, I went up to my room, grabbed my gear and headed out to the woods.

It was a lovely day, blue skies; such as you never get in the city, and pines heavy with snow, but I couldn't stop thinking about Tammie—she'd been a sweet kid, which seemed the norm here. In LA, she'd probably have received sainthood. Why would she just die? A poisoned drink? It didn't seem likely.

Despite the blue sky and white woods, I couldn't find peace.

I was going to visit the coroner. Then I was going to track down Tammie's whereabouts on the day she'd died. It was just what the doctor ordered, another non-paying case.

Driving down into the city, the blue, blue skies dimmed to grey. The Great Salt Lake lay before me, an inland ocean, but much more saline. Gangsters could never have invaded the city. It's practically impossible to sink a body in Salt Lake. Even cement overshoes float.

I had a little trouble finding the place because the city and its environs have very few street names, only addresses. These are laid out in a grid stemming from the central temple. Every address marks how far you are from the temple. At 9088 South 43265 East, I was very far indeed, but I knew that anyway.

Utah drivers are surprisingly rude, I guessed all that treacle politeness must damage their car seats, because they shed it when locked inside their urban attach vehicles. I'd never seen so many SUVs, except in LA where they are necessary to traverse the rough terrain of uncertain prestige.

'Can I help you?' asked a smiling, blond clerk in the coroner's office. Her desk plate read *Pammie Truly*.

I showed her my card. 'I'd like to talk to the coroner,' I said.

'There was a death last night that I'm investigating, and I have some questions.'

She checked out my credentials, called LA and practically wet herself when she found out I'd worked for the FBI.

The coroner was a plump, doughy woman named Mrs Smoot—she would have been more at home in a bakery. She was practically salivating with the excitement of answering my questions. After all, I was big time—I'd worked with the LAPD and the FBI. She didn't know that I'd been rubbing two dollars together for a month, just trying to get them to mate. She didn't know that the only thing I could reliably afford was self-denial. But it didn't matter—Tammie had polluted my winter woods with her demise, and I needed to see what had happened.

Mrs Smoot's report only heightened the mystery. Tammie appeared to be in perfect health, except for the fact that her liver had dissolved. Even if she'd been a heavy drinker for fifty years, instead of a twenty-two-year-old who'd had a few drinks on weekends, that kind of damage just wasn't natural. You need some serious toxins to liquidate a liver.

I thanked Mrs Smoot and left. I began to retrace Tammie's steps. The day she'd died, she'd gone to a Christmas potluck with her family—mother, father, boyfriend Ray, four sisters and three brothers. It was a typical Mormon family. It didn't seem possible anything at the potluck could have been the culprit, because there'd been at least twenty people there. But I found the name of the guy who had arranged it, Elder Loveless, and paid him a visit.

Loveless' house was modest by Utah standards. It would have been a mansion in LA.

Loveless greeted me at the door. He wore a white shirt, black pants, black shoes, black tie, and a constant smile.

'Greetings, neighbor,' he said. 'What can I do for you today?'

'Well,' I said, pulling out my card. 'I'd like to talk about the potluck you gave the other day.'

'Certainly,' he said. 'I'd be glad to. I host these gatherings at least twice a month or so and they're fine. During the season of the Christ, I host them weekly. But you don't need to be a private investigator to come to the next one,' he chuckled. 'Just bring an open heart, a willing spirit, and an empty belly.

'In fact, I'm having a Family Christmas celebration in Moroni Hall after church tomorrow at 2:00. That's on 8409 South 2609 East.'

'Thanks, Elder Loveless,' I said. 'But I'm actually calling because one of the people at your party, Tammie Darling, died rather suddenly yesterday. It seems like it must have been some kind of poison. I'm trying to track down everything she ate.'

'Well,' he said, pulling his lips down in a facsimile of sorrow. 'Isn't that just terrible! Such a sweet, sweet spirit, bless her heart. I must go see her folks. They're good people. How on earth did she die?'

'Her liver dissolved,' I said.

'Well, that's just horrible,' he said. 'But the Good Lord must have his reasons, which we poor sinners cannot yet fathom. I'm sure she's in a better place.'

'No doubt,' I said, looking around at Loveless' décor. Plastic runners covered his light beige carpets and his beige couches were coated in plastic slipcovers. A picture of some guy kneeling before an angel, who was zapping him with gold light beams, graced one wall. The other had a portrait of Jesus, who bore a striking resemblance to Fabio.

'Could you tell me what was served at the potluck?' I asked.

'Well surely, Mr Evers.' He smiled again, displaying every one of his perfect teeth. They must have a lot of dentists in Utah.

'Since I'm hosting another tomorrow, to which you are invited, I can do better than that. I can show you the spread. But it is a potluck you know. I supply the main dishes, but I can't tell you exactly what everyone else brought to share.'

'That'll be fine.' I said. I followed him down the plastic path to a spotless white kitchen. Every counter was covered with Mormon delicacies. There were crudités topped with cheese whiz, slices of Velveeta and white bread. There were a kaleidoscopic variety of Jell-Os with otherworldly suspensions of shredded carrots, peas, and cubed ham floating in them like a science experiment gone bad. There was Frog's Eye Salad, made from small pasta balls mixed with a tub of whipped topping, canned crushed pineapple, and canned mandarin oranges. All were decorated by cardboard angels with paper plate wings and pipe-cleaner halos. The centerpiece, at least I imagined it would be the centerpiece, was a plastic plate containing a manger. The scene had been pieced together. Random bits of faith assembled in a haphazard display of devotion. Joseph, camel and cow, were about two inches tall. They lounged luxuriantly in the shade of a four-inch Virgin and six-inch ass, though even they were dwarfed by the baby Jesus cupie doll who was at least four feet long.

The *pièce de résistance* was a casserole of shredded potatoes submerged in a can of cream of Campbell's chicken soup, topped with sour cream, crowned with cornflakes and baked until molten.

'It's called Funeral Potatoes,' Loveless grinned. 'And I make mine special. I add some mushrooms to the mix.'

'Delicious,' I said. 'If there's one thing that recipe was lacking, it was fungus.'

'The Sisters usually bring dessert,' he smiled. 'Sister Hunsaker makes the finest divinity fudge you'll ever taste.'

'I'm sure of that,' I said.

'What's this?' I pointed to some peculiar red lumpy red and green confections stacked on a plate by the immaculate sink.

'Popcorn balls.' He smiled. 'Special for Christmas! It's mini-marshmallows, corn syrup, salted nuts, chocolate chips, Jell-O and popcorn. Would you care for one? They're truly delicious.'

'I really shouldn't dilute your potluck supplies,' I said. 'Besides, I just ate.' I hadn't, but I'd lost my appetite somewhere around the Frog's Eye Salad and the giant Jesus.

'Did you know that Funeral Potatoes and green Jell-O, were immortalized in a set of collectible pins from the 2002 Winter Olympics?' Loveless beamed.

'That's a bit of useful knowledge of which I was ignorant,' I said.

I left him in his doorway, smiling, waving, and re-inviting me to his Sunday Christmas potluck. 'And bring your friends!'

I continued retracing Tammie's activities. The food seemed toxic, but not lethal—not liver-dissolving.

I visited the Canyon Inn. At about 3 pm mid-week, it was almost empty. Just a few busty smiling barmaids and a couple of old men clutching drinks in their withered hands, waiting for the second coming. The barmaid had heard about Tammie but offered no insight.

I visited Tammie's grieving family but didn't stay long. Her parents greeted me and invited me in. I wondered how, with nine kids, they kept their place so clean. Their carpets were bare, but like Loveless, their furniture was shrouded in clear plastic. I wondered if neatness and tackiness were dominant genetic traits among Mormons, along with strong legs, good teeth and horrendous recipes. I watched their external politeness battle their internal anguish.

Mrs Darling brought forth Christmas cookies and tears. Mr Darling apologized for her display of waterworks. I hated battering words against the wall of their misery. What did I hope to discover? Tammie's death was a mystery and would remain so. People dropped dead every day for no explicable reason.

I returned to the Silver Fork, and despite the cold, sat on the deck watching the sun sink into the haze over the Great Salt Lake.

I spent the next day, Sunday, watching the snow fall around me like crystal peace.

When I returned to have dinner at the Silver Fork, the entry was blocked by two police cars, red and blue lights flashing. An ambulance was screeching away down the canyon. I wondered if some overly ambitious skier had fallen from the heights, or if someone had been crushed by an avalanche. In LA, it would have been gang warfare, here it was more likely to be an irate moose—still, dead is dead. What did it matter where you had met your end, in a dirty back alley or scaling a marble mountain? You were gone, no longer concerned by anything. Wind or smog, ice or fire, all were equal now. You were past caring.

I parked a ways from the Silver Fork and walked toward the door. The police were leaving when I got there. I knew better than to ask what had happened. Police don't like to talk to strangers, especially large ones from the big bad city.

Greg, Christie, and the rest of the staff were there. It was crowded. The Silver Fork was a popular place to hang out and watch the sun paint the white mountains gold. Though the room was packed, it was quiet as a deathbed.

'What happened?' I asked Greg.

'It was Peggy and Mac, that nice couple from Chicago,' he said.

'They were so sweet,' Christie sniffed. 'Such kind, good people, bless their hearts.'

'Are they—?' I let the sentence dangle.

Greg looked at his shoes, minutely examining the laces as if searching for an answer there. 'I don't know. They're taking them to the hospital, but—'

'Th-They had just come back from their potluck,' Christie wailed. 'They sat down and ordered two beers, but before I could even bring it th-th-they j-j-just c-c-collapsed,'

'Do you know what else they did today?' I asked.

Greg slowly shook his head. 'They asked where there was a church, a catholic church. Mac said he wasn't that religious. But Peggy liked to go on Sundays and take communion.'

'She said it w-w-was like wearing clean un-un-underwear in c-c-case you were hit by a c-c-car.' Christie sobbed. 'They looked just like Tammy did before sh-sh-she—'

Greg awkwardly patted her arm. 'Why don't you go home now, Christie,' he said. 'It's been a long day.'

She fled into the kitchen, nose dripping onto the wooden floor, leaving a damp trail of sorrow behind her.

'After church, they went to Elder Loveless' Christmas potluck. They were just like two kids,' he shook his head, 'invited to a picnic. They seemed fine when they came in. Said what a nice time they'd had, and then, well it was just like Christie said.

'It all happened very fast. They complained of stomach pains and collapsed on the floor.

'I called 911. I think they were still breathing, but they didn't look good.' He shook his head again and sighed.

There didn't seem anything to do. I wanted to go to the hospital and see how they were, but I'd just have been in the way. I sat out on the deck and watched the sun streaking violent colors across the sky, like a child finger-painting. I wondered if it was Peggy and Mac's final sunset.

It was. I found out the next morning and returned to Mrs Smoot, the friendly mortician for a chat.

'It's really odd,' she said. 'I've never seen anything like it, and now three cases in three days.

'They both appeared to have been very healthy. The man had had a slight heart murmur, but nothing worth worrying about. And just like that girl, their livers were total mush.'

'Any idea what might have caused it?' I asked.

'Nope,' she said, shaking her head, 'It's a real mystery.'

I drove back through the gridded streets of Salt Lake to Elder Loveless' door.

He was there, and apparently happy to see me, if smiles are evidence of joy. He seemed to be wearing the same black pants, shoes, and tie as yesterday and a duplicate starched white shirt. But the pants seemed too spotless and pressed and the shoes too polished not to be new. Maybe he had a closet full of identical clothes.

He was shocked and dismayed to hear of the deaths. Once again, he had nothing to offer but an invitation to another potluck.

'Jesus's Birthday Lunch!'

Three days later there was another death. Everyone at the Silver Fork was talking about it. Despite a population of a couple of hundred thousand, Salt Lake has the feel of a small town. Zero degrees of separation here in Mormonopolis.

This time it was Elder Doolittle who had met his maker. He was high up in the church, a president or a prophet or something. He'd been a hale and healthy fifty-six-year-old, married, with nine children. According to all, he never drank, smoked, swore, or golfed on Sundays.

The winter woodland had lost its wonder. I smelled something funny, and it wasn't burnt Jell-O.

I went down to the morgue.

'Why Mr Evers—' said Mrs Smoot. 'It's so peculiar. He seems like he was in perfect health, but his liver has completely dissolved. I just don't know what's happening.'

There didn't seem to be anything else to say. I left and went to Doolittle's house. It was about the last place I wanted to go, but something didn't add up.

Doolittle lived in a house that was a giant copy of the others I'd seen. The door was opened by a pretty girl of nineteen or so. She had blond hair, fine cheekbones and a nice pair of legs. But her eyes were red and puffy from weeping.

'Yes,' she said. 'Can I help you?'

'I'm very sorry to disturb you,' I said. 'I'm a private investigator, working with the police. I'm trying to discover what caused your father's death.'

Her eyes widened, as if I'd told her I was a magician.

'You're a private eye,' she breathed. 'Hold on, let me get my mom.'

I waited on the doorstep feeling like a fraud. A soft, round woman in a neat, flowered housecoat wandered out.

'Hello, I'm Mrs Dolittle,' she said holding out her hand. 'Peggy says you are working with the police?' I nodded. 'Mr...?'

'Evers,' I said.

'Evers,' she repeated. 'I'll be happy to assist you in any way I can, of course. Please come in and sit down.'

We sat on her beige, plastic covered couch which could have been a big brother to Loveless'. Maybe the Mormons have figured out how to get furniture to reproduce. It would explain a lot.

Four small faces peered around the doorway, examining me with the interest a scientist might show for a new species of mold. I grinned at them and they vanished.

'May I get you anything?' Mrs Doolittle said. 'Some soda, or Christmas cookies maybe?'

'That would be great, ma'am,' I said. I didn't want anything except a little time. As soon as she had gone, I raced down the hall. Another small face peered at me from one of the doorways. But I bared my teeth and it vamoosed.

I found what I hoped was the master bedroom. The drawers were full of neatly folded undergarments. The clothes hanging in the closet were color coded, dark to light, waiting tidily for Mr Doolittle, who was never coming back.

Beneath the bed stacked in neat rows, like tiny green soldiers, were dozens and dozens of NyQuil bottles. I heard a noise behind me and straightened up. Peggy stood in the doorway watching. I grinned what I hoped was a 'just doin' my job' look and slithered past her.

I slid onto the couch, reaching home plate just as Mrs Doolittle wobbled through the door, balancing a cup of something orange, a plate of red and green rice crispy squares, and what may have been a few cookies, though all that was visible was a thick coat of green, hard, frosting topped with multi-colored sprinkles and some gold stars that couldn't possibly have been edible.

I smiled and sipped the orange stuff. It was orange juice cut with

Tang.

'Did Mr Doolittle suffer any health problems that you knew about?' I asked.

She sighed. 'No, he was healthy as a horse, except for his throat.'

'His throat?' I asked.

'His throat,' she said. 'That poor man was just cursed with a sore gullet. He went through a bottle or two of cough syrup every night. It was the only way he could get to sleep.' She sniffed and wiped her eyes.

'What did you do yesterday, before Elder Doolittle was taken ill?' I asked.

'Well, we went to church, just like always. Then usually we go to temple to perform endowments.'

'Endowments?'

'Yes, like, you know, vicarious baptism for our deceased ancestors.'

I smiled and nodded. Not only didn't I know, I didn't want to.

'Did you go yesterday?'

'No, yesterday we went to a lovely Christmas potluck with the family. Elder Loveless is such a sweet spirit. It seemed righteous. He said it was Jesus's Birthday party—isn't that lovely? But maybe if we had gone to church and done the endowments—' She sobbed silently and blew her nose noisily.

'I'm sure that you are not to blame, ma'am,' I said, and I was. But she was right. If they had gone to the temple to baptise the dead, Doolittle would probably not have joined them.

'Thank you,' I said, rising from the couch. It was so soft I had to grab the arm to propel myself upward. The plastic clung to the back of my legs, making a farting sound as I broke free.

'You've been most helpful,' I said, 'but I've taken up enough of your time.'

'You haven't even had a cookie,' she protested.

I pulled out my phone and stared at it.

'I'd love to,' I lied. 'But duty calls.'

I drove to Loveless, navigating the grid of clean neat streets that had as much character as a Wal-Mart.

I was welcomed in by the smiling Elder, who was horrified to discover that Doolittle had gone to meet his maker.

'Such a pious man,' he said, 'and so healthy. Whoever would have thought he'd go so suddenly?

'It's the Good Lord's will, but hard on the family. I must pay them a visit. Would you care to sit down and have something to eat?'

'No thanks, I just ate,' I said. I hadn't, but I was pretty sure that his culinary delights would send me straight to somewhere nasty, maybe just to the bathroom, but more probably to hell.

'The thing is, Elder Loveless, Doolittle died in exactly the same way Tammie and Peggy and Mac did. His liver dissolved. That's not even close to common. And the only link I can find is that they all attended potlucks you gave.'

'So were about thirty other fine souls,' he smiled tightly. 'The Lord works in mysterious ways.'

'But it wasn't the Lord at work here, was it Elder Loveless? Nor was it mysterious, at least not to you, was it?' I said. 'It was the *Coprinopsis atramentaria*, also known as Tippler's Bane, that you added to the funeral potatoes. Interesting, isn't it? A mushroom whose poisons are only toxic when combined with alcohol. They're perfectly harmless, unless you've had alcohol within seventy-two hours of consumption. And they all had, Tammie the night before, Mac and Peggy at communion, and Doolittle in his nightly Nyquil.'

'The Catholic church is the Great and Abominable Satan, which is the whore of all the Earth. And the imbibing of alcohol is against the word of wisdom. But all the departed can still get into heaven,' he said, holding out his palms and spreading his plump fingers wide. 'It's never too late for that. That's why we baptise the dead.

'Besides, I didn't think it would kill them,' Loveless said. 'Just make them a little ill, ill enough to teach them a lesson, ill enough to consider repentance.'

'But the deaths didn't stop you, did they?' I said. 'Some people are affected more strongly by poison than others. Even peanuts can be deadly if you're allergic.'

'God made their constitutions weak. I was just his instrument.'

'Well, I hope next time he chooses a harp. You're off-key and out of tune, but you'll have a lot of time to practice in prison.'

'I will gladly serve time if the Lord so decides,' he said, baring his teeth in what was meant to be a smile.

I called the police. When they got there I went up to the Silver Fork to pack. It was time to get back to the city, where the criminals snarl, and Christmas is commercial. I prefer it that way.

LOST AT SEA
F. K. Restrepo

Three firm knocks echoed through the lounge. Startled, I fumbled the bottle I'd been struggling with, showering the floor with ibuprofen.

'Damn,' I thought as pain jolted through my head. The pounding in my chest quickened as the knocks became louder. I squinted as I turned to the room blanketed in a sterile glow by the LED panels on the ceiling. The sleek white couches dotting the space evoked a hospital room. Even the oil painting of a crew of sailors gathered around the helm of an old ship became warped under the eerie light, the sailors' grins becoming sneers.

How long had that injection put me under? And where had that needle-wielding brute run off to? Was he still out there on the ship?

The lounge ran down the length of the ship, its sole door set on the shorter wall across from me. It was the sort you'd expect to see on a military vessel, but felt out of place on a small yacht like The Stile; a slab of thick steel that dulled the increasingly frantic knocks peppering it from the other side, framed in a metal jamb with rounded corners. Its sole locking mechanism was suitably plain; a pair of steel bolts, like a sturdier version of the type you'd find in a bathroom stall.

As I shuffled towards the door, the three metal hatches spaced evenly along the port-side wall caught my eye. They were a practical feature—they could swing outwards to be used as tables by those outside the room while providing a view of the sea to those inside it. While raised—as they currently were—the "tables" would be stowed, shielding the lounge from the sea breeze. I hadn't noticed it before, but while lowered, the hatches were certainly large enough for a person to pass through.

'Ezra! Can you hear us?' The booming voice of Captain Harry White cut through the lounge, sparking a memory; a few hours ago, shortly after we'd boarded, the captain had mentioned that the hand crank outside the room—the only mechanism that could open or close the hatches—had been broken by a clumsy passenger, leaving them permanently sealed shut.

I let out something between a sigh and a laugh. Back then, I'd considered the broken hatches a blessing—one that would allow me to work without interruption. Now, my fortress had become a prison.

A woman's voice, tinged with a French accent, joined the commotion outside. 'We can't afford to waste time. Break it down, if you'd be so kind.' On her command, heavy impacts began to rain down on the door.

Time wasn't on my side. I scanned the room once more in hopes that in my panic I'd missed someone or something. I even went as far as to search the two large planters flanking the door. They housed a vibrant mass of leaves with long holes in them, each leaf resembling a mask with many eyes.

Alas, my frantic search bore no fruit—other than the furnishings, the room was indeed empty. And yet, the scene was cleanly seared into my memory; a bulky steel container housing the specimen—the very purpose of our excursion on The Stile—had been sitting on the now bare table in front of me, right up until the moment I'd lost consciousness. My research materials—textbooks, scientific journals, and a powerful microscope, all placed beside the specimen—were also nowhere to be found.

The door held firm under the continued assault. I took a deep breath and raised a trembling hand over the bolts. Every bone in my body screamed against it, as if I were about to pull the hangman's lever while wearing the noose around my own neck.

I stretched the moment a while longer before unlocking the door and stepping aside, narrowly avoiding the two men who spilled into the room. Their eyes darted about until they settled on me.

Had they already noticed the specimen's absence?

A third figure, trailing behind the two men, stepped into the room. 'Glad to see you're still with us, Dr Pace. My, what a mess you've made,' she sneered as she picked up a blue and white ibuprofen capsule from the ground.

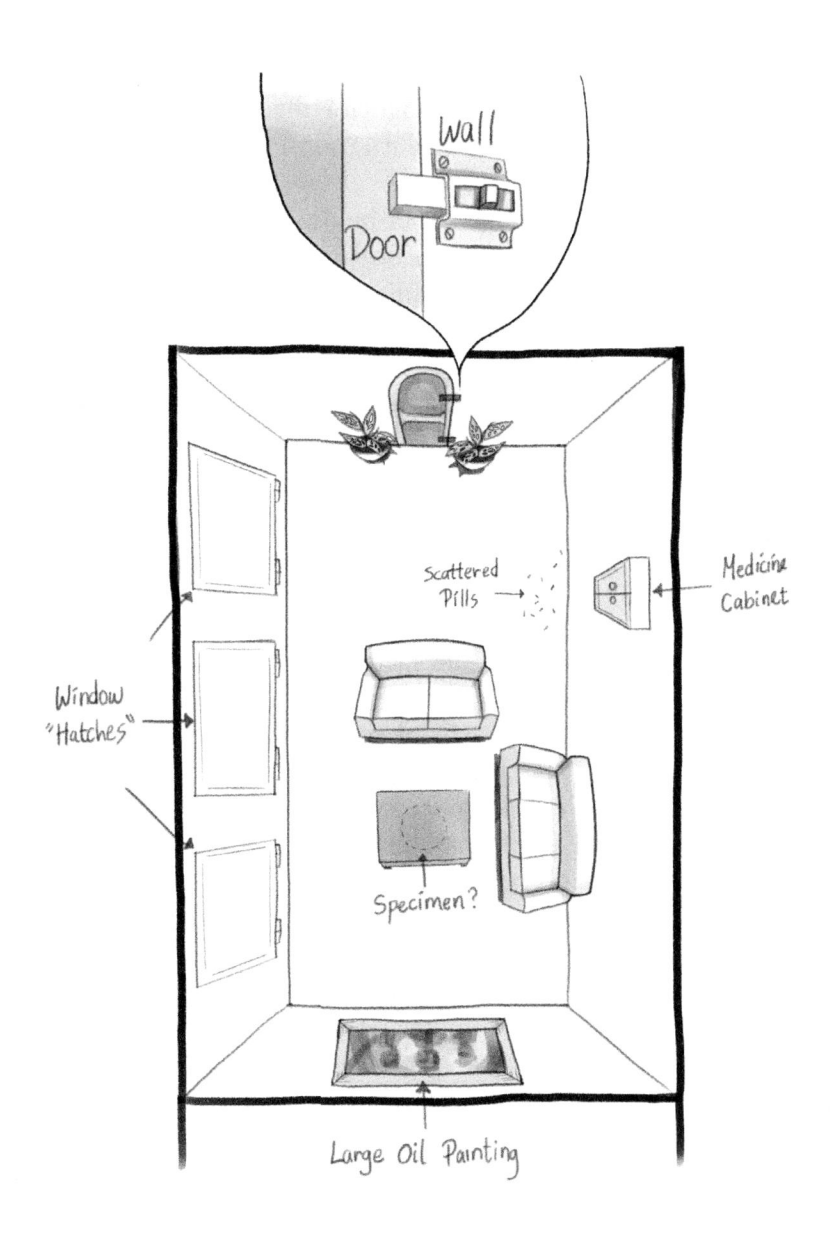

The lounge aboard *The Stile*

As we sat around a table on the ship's upper deck, a bone-chilling gust cut through my linen suit jacket. Captain White had suggested we hold our conference in the lounge for this very reason, but I'd settled on freezing to death if it meant I didn't have to spend another moment in that blasted room.

Whereas the main deck—the level below us—was dominated by the lounge, the upper deck was an open space paved with wooden planks that gleamed in the moonlight. The captain had let the autopilot take control, leaving the cockpit at the stern of the craft empty.

I inhaled sharply and savored the cold, salted air. The deep shadow beneath The Stile and the starless sky became one at the horizon, the vessel's white body and the sliver of moon the only beacons in that abyss.

'With a syringe?' Captain White's booming voice pulled me away from the view. Even sitting, his massive frame towered over the rest of us. Despite his position on the ship, the man both looked and acted the part of a passenger on vacation. His garb—a loose shirt with messily rolled sleeves tucked into a pair of jeans—was strikingly casual, with only a pair of thick combat boots suggesting his role.

'Most likely. I didn't exactly see what they were holding—it all happened rather quickly,' I began unsteadily. 'Someone knocked on the door. The instant I opened it, a man—I think it was a man, anyway—tackled me. I felt a prick in my neck, then he just...strolled out of the room.' I pointed at what I hoped was a red mark on my neck before continuing. 'I was worried he'd come back, so I locked myself in. I passed out a few minutes later.'

The captain hunched over to get a better look at me, tilting his head from side to side. 'Yeah, it looks like he got you pretty good. That's a nasty bruise under your eye.' I touched the spot instinctively and flinched as bolts of pain ran through my face. Apparently, I'd hit the ground harder than I'd thought.

'I guess the rest of us got off easy then. Whatever knocked us out was probably just in our drinks,' the captain continued. A grin split his sun-baked skin.

'But that's strange, isn't it?' said Adrian Grimaud. The man was the picture of austerity, his brows eternally furrowed as if he were in a constant state of displeasure. He was the youngest of the group, a fact obscured by the severe shadow cast by the slim man. He dusted off the arms of his blue-gray suit, a scowl on his stubbled face all the while. 'The three of us were unconscious, so who attacked you?'

It was a fair question. Adrian had been cautious; he'd searched the ship thoroughly before we set sail, which ruled out a stowaway.

'What exactly went missing, anyway?' asked Captain White, giving Adrian a sidelong glance.

I winced. It was the question I was there to answer, after all.

Adrian replied with a grave shake of his head, prompting the captain to raise his hands in mock surrender. In his caution, Adrian had also been protective of the details surrounding the journey. Just as I didn't know the exact route we'd be traveling, Captain White hadn't been told what the cargo was.

Such secrecy was to be expected. The Grimauds represented the interests of the French government, and I'd managed to piece together that a schism in Adrian's department had forced them to rely on foreign contractors to continue their operations.

That was where the captain and I came in. Captain White had been, in his younger days, an expert in stealth and infiltration for the United States Navy. Nowadays, he called himself a "transporter"—he would take any person, any cargo, anywhere. If his extravagant collection of seafaring vessels—which he would often go on about with pride—was any indication, he commanded quite the price for his services.

I, on the other hand, was cut from a less martial cloth. After a long academic road, I'd been fortunate enough to secure a tenured post in the biophysics department at the University of Edinburgh. My recent work on extremophilic organisms—life that thrives under the most extreme environmental pressures on Earth—had not gone unnoticed, leaving me spoiled for choice with respect to research opportunities.

But one in particular stood out. It was an unorthodox arrangement as far as research projects went; Adrian's group offered paltry funding, bare-bones research facilities, and demanded full control over the work I'd produce. On more than one occasion, I'd received a call at some strange hour of the night instructing me to pack a bag. A car would be waiting outside my apartment the next morning. By land, sea, or sky, I'd rendezvous with Adrian and Captain White for the last leg of the journey to a base of operations secured by Adrian's employers. I suspected we were now headed towards one such base on the Isle of Man.

After all this exhausting preamble, I would be given room to work. Though they wouldn't disclose how they'd obtained them, the finds they presented me with were nothing short of breathtaking; living specimens that proved the once-theoretical branches of my field fell into my lap one after another, each a major academic triumph in its own right.

Just then, the clack of leather heels on wood rang out as Elena Grimaud bounded up the stairs from the main deck. Adrian's sister wore an expression of pure joy. For the first time that night she took her hands out of the wool overcoat that reached down to her knees and tugged on the ends of the black ascot tied into a bow around her neck. It occurred to me that I knew next to nothing about the woman. She worked for the same group as her brother as a self-described "loss prevention expert". She'd joined us on these outings before, but had kept to herself during those uneventful journeys, refusing to offer so much as idle conversation. Truth be told, I'd considered her presence redundant—an uncharacteristic inefficiency on Adrian's part.

But now, she was filled with an eerie confidence. Her eyes flashed with recognition; as if the next act of a play she'd watched countless times was set to begin. In one smooth motion she slid into an open chair and crossed her legs.

'I'm afraid I've returned empty-handed,' she said with palpable insincerity. 'I couldn't help but overhear your account, Dr Pace.'

I shuddered. Her gaze was oppressive, as if she were picking me apart from a distance.

The click of Adrian's lighter cut through the sound of the sea nipping at the side of the craft. He cupped a hand over the flame to shield it from the wind, lit a fresh cigarette, then took a long drag from it. 'No sign of it, then?'

'None. It's gone, box and all.'

Her brother exhaled a cloud smelling of toasted mildew before speaking. 'Could it be in the water? Dangling off the ship by one of those tow lines, maybe?'

'Afraid not. It's curious, though. The lines do seem to have been used recently—they're damp,' she answered plainly before turning to me. 'Correct me if I'm wrong, Dr Pace, but after your attacker departed, the box was still inside the lounge. And you were able to lock the door before succumbing to sleep?'

'That's right. I know what you're getting at—if the door was locked, how did the thief return to take the box later on, right?'

'It's what I've been trying to work out, yes. After all, the door and the hatches are the only means of entry. We tested the hatches just after we set sail, but we couldn't force them open. And since the crank was damaged pretty badly, fixing the mechanism wouldn't be possible either.

'That just leaves the door. For one, you can forget about using a tool or wire to work the bolts from the outside.'

Captain White nodded in approval. 'It's a safety feature. All the doors aboard are watertight.'

Elena continued: 'To make matters worse, the door is solid steel, so the bolts would be shielded against, say, a strong magnet. And you can forget about forcing it open—as you saw, Adrian and the captain here were no match for it.'

'That may be so, but given our state, the thief had free rein on the ship. They could've steered the ship to shore while we were unconscious and retrieved something that would help them open the door,' I said in a single breath.

Captain White shook his head. 'I don't think so, Ezra. It's not a normal door, so the hinges don't pop right out or anything. Taking it apart and putting it back together would take a few hours, even with the right tools.'

'We were unconscious for just under two hours,' said Adrian as he pointed to the time on his satellite phone. 'Factoring in travel, the timing doesn't work out.'

Elena's eyes gleamed as her lips curled into a half-smile. She reclined in her chair, tapping the back of it against the metal railing behind her. 'With the door and the hatches covered, the sealed room appears unassailable. So, unless you can propose a way to breach the doors, you are our only possible suspect, Dr Pace,' she declared, addressing what was suddenly a floating courtroom.

I had known it was only a matter of time before someone

acknowledged the most obvious explanation, but the situation was more dire than I'd feared. Elena's analysis left no room for my innocence.

'Oh, come now. You're saying I stole a research specimen? Right before it was to be handed over to me to study at my leisure? I'm not a collector, Ms Grimaud. As long as I can publish my findings, the specimens are of no personal use to me,' I spat.

'Is that right? Well, I'm sure Adrian knows someone who might want to get their hands on something like that, hm?'

Adrian's face went flush. After some deliberation, he let out an exasperated sigh. 'The other departments aren't thrilled with my team's monopoly on this research, and they've got the funding to do something about it. Even if it has to be on the sly.'

'I'll leave it at that—if I say any more, my dear brother won't hesitate to throw me overboard. But there's no shortage of potential buyers. Why, maybe one of them reached out to you already? As they say, everyone has a price.' Elena, the satisfaction plain on her face, no doubt believed her accusation had met its mark.

Truthfully, I hadn't given much thought to the monetary value of the specimens. Although my agreement with Adrian's group guaranteed that all of my work would eventually be published under my name, there would be nothing stopping them from holding my findings back while they secured the rights to any practical applications beforehand. The unique bio-mechanisms of these specimens could inspire a host of innovations, from medical treatments to materials engineering, making them priceless in the right hands.

We fell silent. As far as the others were concerned, both the means and the motive for the disappearance were now clear, and it fell to me to prove otherwise. But reason and logic, the pillars of my profession, crumbled before the raw panic welling up inside me. It was like being asked to build a house of cards with a gun held to your temple—even if you've built one a thousand times before, you probably haven't done it with your hands shaking and your head spinning.

Captain White broke the long silence. 'There's something that's been bugging me. The three of us were drugged, right? How do you suggest Ezra pulled that off while holed up in the lounge, Ms

Grimaud?'

Elena raised an eyebrow, as if surprised to hear something reasonable coming out of the captain's mouth. 'I see. So you're one of those people,' she said as she bounced out of her chair. 'Eager to help, but only capable of doing the opposite. Tell me, where does the drinking water on this ship come from?'

'Umm—ah, right,' he said. 'The water reservoir under the main deck.'

Without replying, Elena left the table and sauntered down the steps leading to the main deck. She returned a minute later and slammed a bottle filled with clear liquid onto the table. 'That medicine cabinet in the lounge is quite well stocked. Midazolam—pretty strong stuff. It works quick, and it'll knock just about anyone out for a couple of hours. It's water soluble too, so all you'd have to do is slip some into that reservoir—'

'Something anyone could've done,' I interjected.

'Ah, but then you'd have another problem to unravel, I'm afraid. I haven't touched any of the food we packed, and the only thing I've had to drink is a single cup of coffee. The three of us,' she said, pointing to her brother and the captain, 'partook together. And I would've noticed if anyone at the table had tried anything suspicious.'

The two men nodded. 'Ditto for the lady,' said Captain White.

'Well, Dr Pace? If the reservoir had been drugged, all of the coffee would've been tainted. And seeing as how everyone finished their drink, no one at the table could've escaped the drug's effects.'

Arguing that point seemed futile, so I opted to change tack. 'Then, perhaps the drug was never in the reservoir. Who prepared the coffee? They'd have no trouble tampering with it before it was served.'

Elena began to pace around the table. 'Well, Captain White took care of the arrangements, but this isn't as damning as it sounds. It was pour-over coffee, you see, so we each poured the hot water into our own mug. All he did was set three mugs on the table and place a filter over the top of each mug, with coffee grounds placed on the filter.

'You're probably thinking, a perfect opportunity to put the drug in two of the mugs, leaving a safe one for himself. With the filter covering the top, we wouldn't have noticed anything was amiss.

'Alas, he set the table before inviting us to sit down. We did so as he went to fetch the water, so he was the last to pick his mug. Since the mugs and filters were all identical, he wouldn't have been able to differentiate one mug from the others. In short, the odds would be stacked against him, and he'd likely be stuck with a tainted cup.'

My jaw tightened. 'W-what about the add-ons? Perhaps the drug was mixed into one that the culprit didn't use?'

'Let's see—correct me if I'm wrong, gentlemen. All of us took sugar, I believe?'

'That's right. That reminds me—Captain White, you filled your mug with ice before pouring in the hot water, right?' said Adrian.

'Yep. What, are you saying the ice was drugged?'

Elena shook her head. 'If either the sugar or the ice had been tampered with, the culprit would've drugged either exactly one person or the entire group,' she said as she tucked back a rogue strand of hair.

The situation worsened by the minute. The matter of the drugged coffee had made it clear; this was, without a doubt, an attack on two fronts—two carefully orchestrated scenarios that served to paint me as the only possible culprit. By locking the door to the lounge I had, in a way, sealed my own fate.

Setting aside the missing specimen, the theft of my research materials was also vexing. Why had they bothered to steal something as mundane as a stack of textbooks and a microscope?

Elena turned to the captain. 'How long until we reach port, captain?'

'Won't be long now. About an hour,' he said.

'The stage is yours, Dr Pace. Tell me, what exactly happened here?' Elena dropped into her chair and crossed her hands in her lap. Adrian sat up straight and stared through me, as if watching for any sudden movements. Captain White excused himself to return to the cockpit, squeezing my shoulder in consolation as he walked by.

Nothing but the sound of whistling wind filled the hour.

#

The road flanked by the coastline seemed to stretch on forever. After disembarking from The Stile at what barely qualified as a port, the siblings escorted me to a black town car sporting tinted windows.

We'd been driving for several hours. It felt as if dawn should've broken long ago, but the sinister night refused to release its grip on the world outside the window.

Adrian drove at a leisurely pace while Elena, sitting beside him, took a drag on a thin cigarette and exhaled out of her open window. It was the first time I'd seen her smoke.

I broke the unbearable silence: 'Defeats the purpose, doesn't it? Why tint the windows if you're not going to bother closing them?'

Elena furrowed her brow. 'Should you really be concerned with—*merde!*' she exclaimed as she scrambled to withdraw her arm from the closing gap. Adrian, his hand on the window's controls, smirked.

She straightened in her seat and crushed what remained of her cigarette into the empty pack. 'I'm glad you're still in good spirits. See that, Adrian? Even Dr Pace sees through your lackluster acting.'

'Did you forget this was all your idea? We could've just grabbed White at port. There's simpler ways of getting information out of someone, you know.'

'Simple men do so love simple solutions. Isn't that right, Dr Pace?'

'You've lost me. Care to explain?' I gritted my teeth. Whatever she was playing at, I wasn't in the mood for it.

'It's like getting blood from a stone with you sometimes, Elena,' said Adrian. 'I'm sure neither of us has any idea what the hell is going through that head of yours. You spent most of the night pointing the finger at Dr Pace, but once we're ashore you call in a trace on White's ship? Which you've yet to explain, by the way,' he griped, momentarily breaking his stony façade.

'Ooh, you've got that look on your face. Fine, then. Just take a deep breath and focus on the road, lest we have a repeat of the incident in Berlin.'

Adrian's brow furrowed. He looked as if about to respond, but thought better of it.

'It's a bit unorthodox, but I'll begin with the identity of our daring thief. Their efforts to frame you, Dr Pace, were rather laughable. Why in the world would you, as the thief, claim the door to the lounge was locked at all?'

'Hmm...but a double bluff of some sort isn't out of the question,' said Adrian, raising an eyebrow. 'Can't put it past these academic types. Always trying to stay two moves ahead.'

'Not bad, Adrian. Looks like I'm rubbing off on you,' she said with a note of satisfaction that her brother returned with a visible shiver. 'Yes, it wasn't until our discussion regarding the coffee that I was able to rule that possibility out altogether. As we established, since Dr Pace was in the lounge at the time, the only way he could've doctored the drinks was by slipping the sedative directly into The Stile's freshwater supply.

'I didn't mention it earlier, but Dr Pace actually has an alibi. As luck would have it, I spent the entirety of the trip—up until our involuntary nap, of course—watching that reservoir. I can guarantee that from the moment we boarded, no one tampered with the water.'

'You can't be serious,' I said, fighting the urge to shout by digging my fingernails into my palms.

Adrian ignored my protests. 'That's more like it. But that puts us back at square one. We weren't able to come up with a way for someone at the table to drug the coffee, after all.'

'Not exactly. There was a way. It's a clever little trick, and luckily for us, it's one that only one person could have pulled off. Not that I ever suspected you, dear brother, but we can't expect Dr Pace here to just accept whatever story we string together, can we?

'The sedative we found was in liquid form, so we believed that introducing it into the cups would doom the drinker to suffering its effects. But thanks to Dr Pace, I discovered something the culprit could use to change that,' she said, looking at me expectantly.

'I'm not sure what you mean—' I squinted and shielded my eyes. The sun's first rays had begun to part the darkness of that long night.

'I suppose it's natural to forget such a detail. Think back to when we found you in the lounge. You'd spilled something on the floor.'

'The...ibuprofen capsules?'

'Yes.'

'I hope you're not suggesting ibuprofen would neutralize the sedative—' began Adrian.

'No, no. The contents of the capsules are quite irrelevant. It's the capsules themselves that we're after. Imagine emptying out a few of them and filling them with the sedative. A hot drink would make short work of the gelatin capsule, releasing its contents into the drink, but—'

'Ah, the iced coffee! The capsule would stay intact in the captain's cold drink, and he'd be able to drink around the capsule!' I exclaimed.

'I see the gears are finally turning,' she said with a note of displeasure. 'So, there you have it—only Captain White, who took his coffee with ice, could have escaped the effects of the capsules present in all three of the mugs. And he could be reasonably sure that the rest of us would prefer a hot drink on that cold night.'

'The bastard's more clever than he looks,' said Adrian. 'Still, that doesn't get us anywhere with the theft itself. Sure, he'd be awake, and Dr Pace's story of a mysterious attacker starts to hold water, but it doesn't change the fact that Dr Pace locked the lounge door.'

'Indeed. So, let's approach this as two separate problems. The culprit first had to gain entry, which as we've established, he could only do through the door. Then, he had to lock the door, exit the lounge, and leave only Dr Pace inside a sealed room.'

'But that's impossible! You can only set those bolts from the inside. And since the hatches were stuck, he couldn't very well leave after locking the door,' I protested.

'We're working backwards, but let's start there. Imagine—the captain is inside the lounge. He's gotten hold of the specimen. Now he must set the bolts from inside the lounge, and there's no way he can leave through that door after doing so. So, what does he do?

'No interruptions this time? Good, good.

'Dr Pace, you've just repeated the very same assumption that is trapping you—that the culprit couldn't have used the hatches to leave the room. That is, however, exactly what they did to leave the scene as we found it.'

'But they were definitely broken. We checked them ourselves, didn't we?' said Adrian.

'Correct. The hatches were broken before our slumber, and they were broken after it. And fixing them is still out of the question.

'Gentlemen, that leaves us with a simple but profound conclusion,' she said, pausing for slightly too long. 'The boat that we woke up on was not the boat we set sail on.

'You see, showing us that the hatches on The Stile were unusable was an important part of the illusion—if they were broken before and after we fell unconscious, it's natural to assume they remained broken in between, right? White capitalized on this assumption, and moved us all to a second ship of identical make and model—one he'd previously left adrift somewhere along our route.'

I was incredulous. Yes, the captain had access to a stable of ships along with prior knowledge of the route we'd travel, but why would he do such a thing?

She continued: 'With this in mind, creating the locked room is simple. White placed Dr Pace in the lounge on the second ship, locked the door, and then simply left through the still-functional hatches. And to seal the illusion, he broke the mechanism after closing them,' she said, clicking her lighter for effect.

Adrian and I fell into a stunned silence. At last, the need to render us all unconscious was clear. It would've required significant preparation and labor to carry out, but the explanation felt the natural one.

'Now, for the best part. I've presented every tool the culprit used to pull off the most daring part of the scheme. The last piece of the puzzle; opening the locked door on the first ship.

'Calling the method simple feels like a disservice, but the simplicity of those sliding bolts was the key. Thanks to them, our thief was able to open that door by relying on a force much simpler than a convoluted string trick or a magnet. Give up yet?'

'For the love of god, spit it out! We don't pay you by the word, you know,' her brother bellowed.

Elena chuckled. 'Gravity. The pull of gravity unset the bolts on that door.'

'That's absurd. No matter how rough the waters, to overcome the friction the bolts would practically have to be turned—' I trailed off, the pieces clicking into place faster than I could form the words.

'Ninety degrees, yes. If the room in question were on land, such a feat would be impossible. But at sea, with another boat at their disposal,' she paused and cleared her throat. 'First, the culprit moves Adrian and me onto the second boat. Next, he plans to capsize the first ship, where Dr Pace remains, onto its side. He ties the tow lines—which we found recently used, if you recall—between the two ships, probably to an anchor point on, say, the starboard side of the first ship, then to the back of the second ship. This way, sailing the second ship perpendicular to the first would tip it over, unlocking that troublesome door once and for all. You were probably knocked about in the process, Dr Pace, leaving you with those bruises.

'From there, he'd have to work fast. He boards the first ship and rescues you before it sinks. The specimen—I'd wager he left it behind, actually. He could always come back for it later. Speaking of which,' she said, turning to Adrian, 'that's why we let him go. He'll lead us right back to it, as long as he believes he's in the clear.'

Elena tapped her phone to dismiss the dull buzz that she'd ignored during her oration. 'Grimaud speaking. Oh? He didn't waste any time, did he? Very well. We'll be waiting. Cheers,' she chirped and hung up. 'That was Laguerre. I had him keeping an eye on the position of the satellite phone I left on White's ship. Sounds like he doubled back along the route just after we parted ways. The local authorities grabbed him as soon as he docked and, lo and behold, he's come into some familiar looking cargo.'

My body went limp; if I'd been standing, I was sure my knees would've buckled. The scheme was insane, to say the least. Would the captain really sink one of his prized yachts just to open its door? But my remaining doubts were swept away the more I thought it through. If the leak in Adrian's organization had made its way to Captain White, he'd have no qualms about trading a mere ship for the priceless specimen.

Elena's explanation even addressed the question of my missing research materials. Even if he'd had the time to gather them from the sinking ship, if they'd been scattered or damaged when the ship capsized, attempting to replace them would raise more questions than simply disposing of them.

#

The car came to a sudden stop. The morning light had cleared away the remnants of that foggy night, revealing a sharp turn in the road hugging a craggy wall. Peering out from one of the windows, I realized that the road now overlooked the sea from a great height. The ensuing sinking sensation in my stomach urged me to the other side of the car.

Elena opened the passenger side door and stepped out. Adrian made to leave through his own door but, spotting the flimsy barrier separating him from the drop, instead elected to crawl over the center console to use Elena's door.

I stepped out as well, allowing the ocean breeze to wash away the smell of stale tobacco that'd permeated the car's seats. The siblings crossed over to the rock wall, Adrian occupied by something on his phone. Before I could follow them, one of the rocks jutting out from the wall slid to one side, revealing the mouth of a narrow cave.

A research facility hidden in plain sight. It was a familiar scene—several of the facilities the siblings had brought me to were hidden behind such mechanisms. But this time, I couldn't help but feel foolish. Before that night, I'd accepted the hidden passages and clandestine research expeditions without a second thought, blinded by the hope of putting my academic career on the fast track.

Now, that hope felt wanting. The dull ache radiating through my body—a lingering reminder of the risks I'd blinded myself to—no longer held at bay by the adrenaline, made me long for my office in Edinburgh. If I had any sense at all, I would make sure I was on the first ship back to the mainland. Putting this nonsense behind me would be, without a doubt, the sensible thing to do.

And yet, as I stepped towards the cave entrance guarded by the siblings, I knew I could do no such thing. Sense and reason were no longer a part of the equation.

It was a matter of pride.

If Elena Grimaud had simply bested me in a battle of wits, that would've been the end of it. If anything, I felt more ashamed at having underestimated such a keen mind than I did at being beaten by it.

But something had occurred to me after Elena's breakdown of the night's events; if I'd been able to piece together the truth of the specimen's disappearance while we were still aboard The Stile, Captain White would've realized he was finished. I couldn't imagine he'd go quietly. It would've made Elena's plan to recover the specimen impossible, at the very least.

Despite this, Elena had let me believe that the consequences for failing to unravel the night's events would be dire. Clearly, she didn't consider it likely I'd succeed—no, there was no doubt in my mind. In her eyes, there was no need to consider the possibility at all.

And that was a pill much too bitter to swallow. The rest of it—the danger, my career, and even the contents of that blasted box—faded into the background, eclipsed by the desire to match wits with her again.

Elena flashed a conspiratorial smirk and motioned into the darkness of the cave. 'Well then. After you.'

LURKING IN THE SHADOWS
Edward Lodi

On her most recent case, Lena Lombardi had neglected to take along her .22 pistol—a mistake she would never again repeat. As she stepped down from her pickup, the septuagenarian patted the pocket of her denim jacket. Reassured by the familiar bulge, she went around to the passenger side.

Before opening the door, she took a moment to examine the mansion where she'd be spending the next several days. Erected more than a century ago, it was an imposing pile—mansard roof, dormers, eyebrow windows, turrets, ells, and towering redbrick chimneys, one of which sported a stained glass window smack-dab in its center.

Prompted by an impatient meow, she opened the door and slid Marmalade's carrying case from the passenger seat. She was about to slam the door shut when a shadow slithered across the hood. She turned, and found herself confronted by a tall figure leaning over her.

'Is that your luggage, ma'am?' the figure, pointing to the pet carrier, asked in a gruff voice. Faintly reminiscent of Frankenstein's monster, he had on a fisherman's hat, a red flannel shirt, and overalls tucked into rubber boots.

'No, it's my cat,' Lena replied. 'Who might you be?'

'Jack Peckham, ma'am. I work for Mrs Weld. I can carry your luggage inside if you got any.'

Lena pointed to a locked metal trunk bolted to the bed of her pickup. 'Luggage's in there. I'll get it later. But thanks for your offer.' She didn't want this Peckham character to know that she had a twelve-gauge double-barrel shotgun and a .22 caliber rifle tucked among her suitcases and Marmalade's litter box.

Lena owned a cranberry bog. The weapons were for shooting

muskrats and poaching an occasional Canada goose. Both species were pests on the bog, causing thousands of dollars in damage, the muskrats by burrowing and undermining dikes and flumes, the geese by trampling the cranberry vines and fouling the crop with their feces.

Even though the geese were federally protected, it was only fair that she should cook one up occasionally, for herself and Marmalade, and store a few in her freezer to serve to guests on special occasions, in partial compensation for the financial losses they caused her.

Peckham nodded and wandered off toward the rear of the house. Lena watched him disappear behind a four-car garage, then lugged the pet carrier along a flagstone walkway and up a set of granite steps to the front door, where she rang the bell and waited, like an itinerant drummer with a satchel of wares.

An elderly woman came to the door. Seeing Lena, she smiled. 'Mrs Lombardi? I'm Beatrice Weld.' She grasped Lena's hand. 'Thank you for coming. I was afraid you might change your mind.'

'A promise is a promise,' Lena assured her.

'I can't thank you enough for agreeing to help me.'

Lena shrugged. 'When you phoned you mentioned a puzzle. Puzzles intrigue me.'

'You might think me a foolish old woman. But I fear my life is in danger. I hope you prove me wrong.' She ushered Lena into a small but elegantly furnished hall.

Beatrice Weld, with her white, neatly coiffured hair, was more or less as Lena, speaking to her on the phone that morning, had pictured. She estimated the woman's age at about eighty. Though scarcely five feet in height, because of her graceful bearing she seemed somehow taller.

She had on a navy-blue suit with shoes to match. Standing next to her, Lena, with her blue denim jacket, faded green top, tan corduroy pants, and worn work shoes, felt like a hobo seeking a handout.

'Would you like to see your room and freshen up? I'll ask my factotum, Jack, to fetch your luggage.'

'Thanks, but I don't need any assistance. I met Mr Peckham outside. He offered his help but I declined.' Not wanting to sound supercilious she added: 'I've worked on cranberry bogs all my life. Exercise and fresh air have kept me in shape.'

'Well then, let me take you upstairs. Once you've settled in we can have a chat over a decanter of wine.' She paused. 'Does Marmalade require anything? Edmund—my late husband—was allergic to cats, as is Cousin Judith, who is a member of the household. I'm afraid I'm not familiar with their needs.'

'Thank you, I have everything he requires. Will Cousin Judith object to Marmalade?'

'Probably. But pay her no mind.'

The room assigned to Lena looked as it might have in the 1890s, except that the attached dressing area was now a private bath. A canopied four-poster bed took pride of place in the center. A marble fireplace occupied part of a wall. There were no closets. In their stead were a tall wardrobe, a dresser, and a chest. The chest was the type once favored by pirates for burying treasure, and by ax-murderers for disposing of body parts.

Lena went outside to fetch her luggage.

She removed her suitcases and Marmalade's necessities from the metal box, then locked it. Just as she was about to lug the suitcases along the walkway Jack Peckham materialized, like a genie from a bottle. There was something about the man she found unnerving. However, when he repeated his offer of assistance, Lena accepted.

He carried the suitcases upstairs, placed them next to the wardrobe, and left, after bidding her good-day.

Lena unlatched the door to the pet carrier. The orange tabby took a cautious peek at his surroundings before venturing out.

'I'll unpack later,' Lena told him. 'Right now I'm about to desert you. But first I'll set up your litter box and leave you a little snack.'

Those tasks completed, she headed downstairs.

Mrs Weld stood waiting at the foot of the stairs. She led Lena into a small room with windows overlooking a garden. Once they were seated she reached for a bell pull. Lena heard a distant chime.

'I know this is absurdly out of fashion, but it works. Mrs Barboza will be here shortly. At least I hope so. Mrs Barboza is my live-in housekeeper,' she explained. 'A wonderful cook. But,' she added with a sigh, 'a bit temperamental.'

Temperament notwithstanding, Mrs Barboza promptly appeared wheeling a cart with a decanter of wine, cut crystal glasses, and an assortment of crackers and cheeses. In her mid-fifties, the housekeeper—short, plump, and sallow-complexioned—wore her greying hair in a tight chignon. Her glowering eyes and dour expression were, Lena suspected, permanent features.

Mrs Weld thanked her, and she left, without having spoken. If she was aware of Lena's presence she gave no indication.

'I've been saving this pinot noir for a special occasion,' Mrs Weld informed Lena as she poured them each a glass. 'I hope you enjoy it.'

Lena, who fancied herself a connoisseur, took a sip and pronounced it excellent. After a second sip she asked: 'Now, what's this all about?'

Mrs Weld took her time replying. 'I may be going about this backwards,' she said at last. 'Maybe you should see the library before we talk.' She paused. 'But no. That can wait.'

She took a moment to savor her wine.

'You've already met my factotum, Jack Peckham, and my housekeeper, Mrs Barboza. And I've mentioned Cousin Judith. The others making up my household are my grandniece, Brook Pezzoli, and my cousin—first cousin, twice removed—Kevin McDuff.' She swirled the remaining wine in her glass, as if the patterns it formed might reveal secrets. 'One of these five, I'm convinced, is trying to kill me.'

'Your reason for believing this?'

'There have been several incidents—seemingly innocuous in themselves, perhaps. But viewed together, I believe they're deliberate attempts to harm me.'

'Such as?'

'A tennis ball placed on the stairs where I was bound to step. If not for having a firm grip on the banister, I would have tripped and almost certainly been seriously injured. Or killed.'

'Which of the five plays tennis? Surely not Mrs Barboza. Or Mr Peckham. Neither seems the type.'

'Brook plays occasionally. And Kevin. But anyone could have put the ball there.'

'You mentioned several incidents.'

'Last week someone tampered with my medicines. They mixed pills that look similar, so that if I hadn't noticed the switch I might have taken too much of one medicine, not enough of another. Even worse, they introduced several aspirin tablets. I take a blood thinner. As a consequence I have to avoid aspirin or anything similar to it, or risk internal bleeding.'

Seeing Lena's empty glass, she poured into it from the decanter. 'I'm not supposed to drink more than an occasional glass of wine, for the same reason. Alcohol irritates the stomach lining. Everyone in the house knows that I indulge myself more than is good for me. Adding aspirin to the mix could prove lethal.'

Lena took a pensive sip of her pinot noir. 'A tennis ball on the stairs. A mix-up of pills. Anything else?'

'A flat tire on a very busy section of Route 44. Someone sabotaged the valve so that it would slowly leak air.' She leaned forward. 'Mrs Lombardi, I don't blame you if you think these incidents add up only to carelessness or mischance, not a devious plot to eliminate me, and that I'm a foolish old lady.'

'There are those who think that I'm a foolish old lady,' Lena said. 'I often prove them wrong.'

'Well then, shall we adjourn to the library?'

Like an ingénue clutching a long-stemmed rose, Lena held onto her glass as she followed Mrs Weld down the hall to an ornately paneled door.

Her hostess paused. 'Before we go inside I should explain the trophies. When Edmund inherited this house from his grandfather, the will stipulated that the library be left intact. The books, *and* the trophies.'

'"Trophies" as in body parts of dead animals?'

Mrs Weld nodded as she opened the door. 'Edmund's grandfather was a big game hunter, in an age when such men were held in high esteem. I find the trophies repugnant. And now,' she added, 'I have an excuse to be rid of them.'

Like the door, the high-ceilinged room Lena stepped into was richly paneled. Two walls consisted of shelves lined with books bound in morocco and other fine leathers. Much of the space on the two remaining walls was taken up by the severed heads of endangered species. Of these, the head of an albino rhinoceros—the *pièce de resistance*—hung above the fireplace.

The library was redolent not only of old tomes, but also of whiskey, stale cigar smoke, and the fetor, however slight, of long-dead animals. Wine glass firmly gripped, Lena began to scrutinize her surroundings. Mrs Weld had brought her here for a purpose. What was it she expected her to find?

'That Big Horn Sheep seems to have lost an ear,' she quipped. 'Recently cut off, by the looks.'

Mrs Weld nodded approvingly. 'Detective Ioanides said you were good.'

'Oh? So it was Ioanides who recommended me?'

'Last week the library was vandalized. The only damage was to four of the animal heads. You noticed the missing ear on the Big Horn. If you look at the Gazelle you'll see the nose is missing. Whiskers have been snipped from the Bengal Tiger, and an eye gouged from the Water Buffalo.'

Lena examined each of the mutilations. 'Were the missing parts left behind, or taken?'

'Taken.'

'Who discovered the vandalism?'

'Mrs Barboza dusts here once a week. Like you, she noticed the missing ear.'

'And you think this act is connected to the other incidents?'

'Something sinister is going on, of that I'm convinced. That's why I phoned the police.'

'Ioanides himself came?'

Mrs Weld shook her head. 'No, a Sergeant O'Hara.'

Lena smiled. 'Ah, the sergeant himself. I know him. He's well meaning, but more adept at opening a box of donuts than investigating a crime. When he surveyed the damage what did he conclude?'

'That it was done by animal rights activists.'

Lena couldn't refrain from laughing. 'I suppose that's better than blaming aliens from outer space.'

Mrs Weld suggested they return to the tea room, where the remainder of the wine awaited. Once they were comfortably seated she asked: 'What do you make of all this?'

'First, I require a confession.'

'A confession?'

Lena wagged a finger. 'Detective Ioanides told you all about me, didn't he? That I'm a snoop who can't resist poking into other people's affairs, and that I'm a sucker for fine wine.'

Mrs Weld shook her head in amusement. 'Mrs Lombardi, as my sainted grandmother would say: "You're a caution."' She brought her glass to her lips. 'As you can see, your fondness for wine is one I share.' She punctuated her statement by taking a sip. 'Dissatisfied with Sergeant O'Hara, I drove to the police station, where Detective Ioanides politely implied that he had more important things to do than investigate the theft of a Big Horn Sheep's ear. He suggested I contact you. Evidently you've helped him in the past.'

Lena nodded. 'Once or twice.'

'As I recall, wine did come up in our conversation. And of course Marmalade. Not to mention your investigative skills.'

'More stubbornness than skill,' Lena replied modestly. 'I nag at a problem until the solution reveals itself.' She made a sandwich of a sliver of brie between two crackers, and carried on the conversation between nibbles. 'I agree—something untoward is going on. Something dark. Who uses the library?'

'Everyone except Mrs Barboza.'

'Jack Peckham?'

'I allow Jack full access. He likes to spend evenings in his room reading.'

Lena fixed herself a second brie-and-cracker sandwich. 'How did you come to hire him?'

'Edmund hired him. I can't tell you much about him, except that he's been here about twenty years, and receives a disability check every month. He's very secretive.'

'You mentioned a grandniece, Brook Pezzoli.'

'Brook's been with me about a year. She grew up in Connecticut. When she lost her job in New London—something happened, something she never talks about; perhaps it was sexual harassment—she found work in New Bedford, so I invited her to move in.'

Lena was about to ask a follow-up question when Mrs Barboza stormed into the room waving a batter-coated spoon. 'I won't have that woman pestering me,' the housekeeper shouted.

'Oh dear,' Mrs Weld commiserated. 'Is she at it again?'

'Telling *me* how to make Portuguese kale soup!'

Lena felt a speck of batter smack her forehead.

'Keep her away from my kitchen or I'll pack my bags this

instant.'

'I'll have a word with her,' Mrs Weld said with resignation. 'Mrs Lombardi, please excuse this domestic disturbance. I'll only be a minute.'

As if seeing Lena for the first time Mrs Barboza eyed her suspiciously. 'You applying for a job? It better not be my position because if it is—'

Lena cut her short. 'I assure you, Mrs Barboza, I'm merely a guest. Mrs Weld does nothing but sing your praises.' She removed a tissue from her jacket and dabbed at her forehead. 'I can't imagine how anyone could fault your cooking.'

'That one can,' the housekeeper declared. 'Dried-up prune that she is.'

'Would you be referring to Cousin Judith?'

'Who else? If she was my cousin I'd send her packing.'

Mrs Weld chose that moment to return. 'The coast is clear,' she said to her housekeeper. 'Cousin Judith promises not to trouble you again.'

'She better not,' Mrs Barboza declared, taking herself and her spoon back to the kitchen.

'Tell me about Cousin Judith,' Lena said once the room was quiet again.

'Edmund's poor relation. Actually, I think she has more wealth than she lets on.' Mrs Weld lowered her voice. 'For my late husband's sake I put up with her. Otherwise—'

Lena brushed cracker crumbs from her corduroys. 'I look forward to meeting the beldam. You said you also have a cousin living here?'

'Kevin McDuff, my cousin's grandson. Kevin commutes to Boston. He works for a large firm in the Financial District.'

'Does he have any dark secrets?'

Mrs Weld hesitated. 'When he was at Boston University there was an incident—don't ask me what. He was suspended for a semester before being allowed to return. That's all I know. I don't like prying into these things.'

You wouldn't be a Proper Bostonian if you did, Lena thought. 'When do I get to meet everyone?'

'This evening at dinner. There'll be five of us. You, myself, Cousin Judith, Brook, and Kevin. Jack prefers to eat in the kitchen with Mrs Barboza. I've invited both to dine regularly with us, but they insist on the kitchen.' Mrs Weld sighed. 'They say it's because we dine too late—7:30—and that may be true. But I suspect it's also because neither of them can bear sitting at the same table with Cousin Judith.'

'I assume Brook and Kevin are at work. Where's Cousin Judith?'

'After her run-in with Mrs Barboza? Probably in her room sulking. Or taking a nap. She suffers from insomnia. Don't be surprised if during the night you hear her wandering the hallways, like a guilty wraith.'

'What exactly is her status here?'

'Officially, poor relation. Lately, though, she's been spending like a drunken sailor. Clothing. Jewelry.'

'How old is she?'

Mrs Weld laughed. 'That's a well-kept secret—though probably close to seventy. Like Jack Peckham, she's a closed book.'

'Ever married?'

'A long time ago. She never speaks of it.'

Lena nodded. 'A mystery unto herself. What was her profession?'

Mrs Weld pursed her lips. 'Avoiding work.' Then added: 'Actually, she was a teacher's aide. Whatever pension she has can't be very big.'

Lena glanced at her watch. She mustn't keep Marmalade waiting. Besides, the wine had made her sleepy. It was time for her nap.

'Meet me in the library at a quarter past seven,' Mrs Weld suggested. 'We'll go into the dining room together and I'll introduce you. Let me think—what shall I say? I know. You're an old acquaintance. We met years ago, blah blah blah. We'll think up a story. Not that any of them will give a hoot. They're self-absorbed, every one of them.'

Lena found Marmalade asleep on the bed. She removed her shoes, grabbed a coverlet from the wardrobe, and placing the pistol under her pillow, lay down beside him. Within minutes she was sound asleep. Her internal clock woke her in plenty of time to change for dinner.

She hid the pistol in a compartment specially constructed for the purpose at the bottom of Marmalade's litter box, where it was highly unlikely anyone would go poking around.

Appropriately attired in blouse and slacks and shoes that were not too shabby, she went downstairs to the library, having first fed the orange tabby his supper, canned chicken that, unlike the seafood he preferred, would not stink up the room. 'When we get home we'll have fresh shrimp,' she promised him.

After Lena joined her hostess in the library, Mrs Weld closed the door so that they could speak in private. 'Is there anyone you suspect in particular?' Lena asked.

Mrs Weld shook her head. 'I'm not close to any of them. I trust Mrs Barboza. Although perhaps I shouldn't. And Jack Peckham. He's strange, but I can't see him wishing me any harm. As for the others—' She shrugged.

'Who will benefit from your death?'

Mrs Weld hesitated. 'Brook, my grandniece, will benefit the most, and then Kevin. They're both heirs. The others—Cousin Judith, Mrs Barboza, Jack Peckham—will receive sizable bequests.'

'Was there any provision in your husband's will for Cousin Judith?'

'Edmund wasn't overly fond of his second cousin. He left her a token amount, ten thousand dollars. Everything else went to me.'

'One last question before I meet this charming group. Is the house alarmed at night?'

Mrs Weld nodded. 'Before retiring, Jack checks all the doors and windows, then sets the alarm. Of course, everyone in the household knows the code, so that they can leave and enter at will. So far, they've all been conscientious about resetting the alarm.'

When they entered the dining room, the only person seated at table was easily identifiable. Although it might be unfair to characterize the woman as a "dried-up prune", it would be accurate to describe her as wizened. Like an apple that's been left on the counter too long, Lena thought. She looked the type who, given a ruler and a classroom of second-graders, would spend the better part of each day rapping knuckles.

Mrs Weld introduced them. Cousin Judith nodded politely but made no attempt at conversation.

Her hostess, whose place was head of table, placed Lena to her right, across from Cousin Judith. A man in his mid-twenties walked in, followed by a young woman of about the same age. Kevin

McDuff and Brook Pezzoli. The party was now complete.

Introductions over, Kevin sat next to Cousin Judith, and Brook sat opposite him, next to Lena. Mrs Weld yanked on a bell pull. Mrs Barboza appeared pushing her wine cart, which she parked in a corner before returning to the kitchen.

Kevin got up from the table to act as sommelier. Lena studied him. Fair-haired, thin, weak-chinned, he was of average height and had on an expensive pinstriped suit, as befitted a financier. He was one of those men who look ridiculous with a pencil mustache, but insist on sporting one.

He poured a finger of wine into Mrs Weld's glass. She raised it to her nose, sniffed, tasted, and nodded her approval. He filled the glass, then Lena's, and worked his way round to Cousin Judith who, sampling the wine, frowned but drank it anyhow.

Lena tasted hers. A merlot. Delicious. Just the one glass, though. She'd already consumed more than enough for one day. She needed a clear head if she hoped to solve the puzzle of the mutilated trophies.

'Auntie Bea spoils us. She serves excellent wine,' Brook commented to Lena. 'And we're lucky to have Mrs Barboza. Such an exceptional cook. I hope she serves something Portuguese this evening. Her kale soup is to die for.'

'Humph.' This from Cousin Judith.

'Your name's Italian, like mine,' Brook observed. Lena glanced at her companion. The young woman had the olive complexion, brown eyes, and black hair characteristic of Mediterranean populations. She was petite, and pretty.

'Lombardi is my married name,' Lena explained. 'I'm one hundred percent Swamp Yankee: a mixture of English, Scots, Irish, Native American, and God knows what else.'

'I'm a Mayflower descendant,' Kevin boasted.

'Along with thirty-five million other Americans,' Mrs Weld pointed out.

The company were spared further small talk by the appearance of Mrs Barboza wheeling in still another cart, on which were a soup tureen, a basket of Portuguese rolls, and a large bowl of salad.

The housekeeper favored Cousin Judith with a gargoyle grin, and left.

Brook rose from the table, handed the basket of rolls to Kevin to pass around, and ladled out the Portuguese kale soup. Placing her napkin over her bowl, Cousin Judith raised her hand palm outward. 'I'll pass.'

'Cuz,' Kevin said, addressing Mrs Weld, 'have the police made any progress regarding last week's incident?'

'No. I don't expect them to. The sergeant who came to the house theorizes it was some animal rights crackpot, and perhaps he's right.'

'Just the same, I'm keeping my door locked at night,' Brook piped in.

'Your aunt told me all about the vandalism,' Lena said to her. 'Cousin Judith, what do you make of it?'

'I agree with Beatrice. Animal rights activists.'

'But how did they get in?'

Cousin Judith shrugged. 'Where there's a will, there's a way.'

'Brook makes sense,' Kevin said. 'I, too, am keeping my door locked at night.' He rose from the table. 'Does everyone want salad? We have a choice of dressings. French or Italian.'

Just as they were finishing their salads Jack Peckham entered the room. The factotum gathered up the salad plates and soup bowls, piled them onto the cart with the tureen, and left, to return in short order, the cart now weighted down with covered serving dishes.

Brook and Kevin pitched in to serve the roast beef, potatoes, and vegetables. Little conversation took place during the meal. Boarding houses must have been like this, Lena reflected. Folks were courteous to one another but had little in common to talk about.

Dessert consisted of apple pie topped with vanilla ice cream. The cook herself carried in the pie hot from the oven, held high in both hands like the head of John the Baptist. Jack trailed behind with the ice cream. Lena was amused to note that Cousin Judith, rather than wrinkle her nose at the pie, tossed enmity aside and ate her piece with gusto, then followed it up with another. The sour prune had a sweet tooth.

Brook and Kevin helped Mrs Barboza and Jack clear the table. Perhaps such tasks were expected of them, in return for room and board. From Lena's observations so far, the household ran smoothly—Mrs Barboza's and Cousin Judith's mutual antipathy notwithstanding.

And yet, somewhere in the shadows, evil lurked.

Lena accompanied Mrs Weld upstairs to her bedroom on the second floor, across the stairway from Lena's. Across the hall were Cousin Judith, Kevin (opposite the stairway), and Brook. On either end of the hall, stairs led to the third floor where Mrs Barboza and Jack Peckham had their respective rooms.

Mrs Weld bid her guest goodnight and went directly to bed. Lena returned to her room to attend to Marmalade. She found the cat restless, pacing the floor, resentful of neglect.

'Stop pouting. Next time I'll leave you home with nothing but water and dry cat meal. I'm sorry you can't roam freely. At least here I don't have to worry about coyotes eating you.'

He looked at her with reproachful eyes.

'Oh, all right,' she relented. 'But first, into your carrier.'

Cat carrier in hand she went down to the library. From the hallway she could hear voices in the kitchen. Brook and Kevin helping Mrs Barboza and Jack Peckham with the dishes. The thought occurred to her, that Cousin Judith's feud with the housekeeper might be intentional, making herself *persona non grata* to avoid doing a fair share of the housework.

With the door closed, she freed Marmalade and began a careful examination of the mutilated trophies, beginning with the Big Horn Sheep. Someone had sliced off the left ear. Or snipped it off. Not an expert in forensics, Lena could not ascertain what type of instrument was used. Did it matter? Probably not.

The Water Buffalo's right eye was missing, crudely gouged out. Left ear, right eye. Was symbolism intended? Hear no evil, see no evil? Nonsense: the Gazelle's nose had been removed. Smell no evil? And how to explain the whiskers missing from the Bengal Tiger? She glanced at Marmalade, who was busily exploring the library's nooks and crannies, and shuddered.

She spent the next half hour examining the remaining trophies. All appeared intact. What, if anything, did the four mutilated animal heads have in common? Nothing that she could see. Were the missing parts needed for some bizarre ritual involving voodoo or black magic? The ear, nose, and whiskers were actual animal parts. The eye, however, was glass. She could hardly imagine a witch standing over a boiling cauldron and dropping in a glass eyeball. But what did she know about such things? She'd been called many things, but never a witch. Not to her face anyhow.

As she pondered these weighty matters the door opened and Jack Peckham entered. Startled from her reverie, she lacked presence of mind to restrain Marmalade. The orange tabby scooted into the hallway.

'Mrs Lombardi.' Jack nodded politely as he strode across the room to one of the book-lined walls from which, without searching, he slid out a book. Bidding Lena good evening, he left with the book tucked under his arm.

The incident gave Lena an idea.

Marmalade's absquatulation did not worry her. What mischief could he get into? Unless he ran afoul of Mrs Barboza by invading her kitchen. Lena imagined the housekeeper chasing the cat with a meat cleaver. Nonsense. Marmalade was capable of taking care of himself. Her immediate concern was the safety not of the cat, but of Mrs Weld.

Might a clue to the strange goings-on in the old mansion lie within the books? What, for instance, was Jack Peckham reading?

She went to the shelf, to the void created by his removal of the leather-bound tome. On either side of the space were volumes of Edward Gibbon's *Decline and Fall of the Roman Empire*. Jack had removed Volume Five. Heavy reading for a factotum.

Had he selected the book at random, to cover his real purpose for entering the library? Lena didn't think so. The first four volumes of the history were not coated with a thin layer of dust, unlike the remaining sixth volume. Evidently Jack was plowing through the final years of the Roman Empire one dusty volume at a time.

Mrs Barboza, given her many duties, could hardly be faulted for dusting only the trophies and not keeping the rest of the library pristine. And that proved a lucky break for Lena. Lack of dust on an individual book would indicate that it had recently been read.

Lena worked her way through the books on both walls, looking for dust-free bindings. There were a number, in various states of cleanliness, that had most likely been perused by the classical-leaning factotum: a nineteenth-century translation of Plutarch's *Lives*, for example, and *Historia Naturalis* by Pliny the Elder.

There was one glaring dust-free exception to volumes relating to antiquity. Tucked between a sneeze-inducing copy of Richard Burton's account of his visit in disguise to Mecca in 1855, and an equally dusty copy of David Livingstone's *Missionary Travels in S. Africa*, was a squeaky-clean morocco-bound copy of Peter Cahill's *India, Glimpses Then and Now*, published in 1874.

Was this an important discovery, or merely a red herring of her own making? Most likely the latter. What possible bearing could such a book have on the mystery of the mutilated trophies? Bengal Tigers were indigenous to India. But Big Horn Sheep? Even so, it was worth bedtime perusal.

Book in hand, Lena went from room to room in search of Marmalade, even going so far as to poke her nose into the kitchen which, everything tidied up, was now deserted. Finding him nowhere on the ground floor she went upstairs, where she found him sitting in front of her bedroom door, waiting to be admitted.

'I see you still have your tail,' she said, alluding to the image she had conjured of Mrs Barboza brandishing a meat cleaver. As she let the cat into the room the door at the end of the hallway, diagonally across from Mrs Weld's, opened. The room was Brook's. The figure that emerged was that of Cousin Judith, a smug smile on her face. When she saw that she was observed, the smile became a frown. With a curt nod she brushed past Lena and entered her own room.

Lena stood before her door considering the significance, if any, of what she had just witnessed. She was about to join Marmalade when Brook stepped into the hallway. The young woman, apparently on her way downstairs, seemed abstracted and failed to notice Lena's presence until she was almost upon her. Startled, she forced a smile.

'I've found something to put me to sleep,' Lena said as a pleasantry, holding up the morocco-bound book.

Seeing it, Brook blanched. Murmuring something indistinct, she returned to her room.

Curiouser and curiouser, Lena thought.

She went into her room to prepare for bed. The door had a keyhole but no key. However, with the .22 tucked under her pillow she would sleep soundly. She tossed the book next to the pillow, changed into her nightgown, and climbed into the four-poster. With Marmalade curled at her feet she began to turn the pages.

She read for a while, then began to nod off. As she fell asleep the book slipped from her hands onto her chest. The pages flipped open to a well-thumbed passage. Wide awake once more, she gave it a quick perusal. The subject was tigers:

The precise number of human beings slain by tigers annually is not known, but is believed to number in the scores. Oftentimes a villager disappears. Did the unfortunate native run afoul of a man-eating tiger? Or to some other, equally ferocious, predator? Was he poisoned by the sting of a cobra or similar venomous reptile? Did he drown? Was he beset upon and murdered by thugs? Did he perish of natural causes?

His body, having been devoured by scavengers, or tossed into fast-flowing waters, or concealed in a make-shift grave, will never be recovered.

Or—and here we arrive at the true subject of this brief monogram—does his body lie in plain sight for all to behold, yet none to suspect that, rather than having succumbed to the ravages of disease or the advancement of years, he is the victim of a cruel and calculated murder? The weapon employed: a tiger. Or rather, the whiskers of a tiger.

The author went on to explain that tiger whiskers, ground up and ingested, cause severe stomach bleeding.

Lena climbed down from the four poster. The vandalism in the library was beginning to make sense. It was no secret that Mrs Weld, because she took a blood thinner, was susceptible to internal bleeding—which could result in death. Someone in the household snipped whiskers from the Bengal Tiger in order to murder the old woman. The other mutilations were merely distractions.

Lena had to warn her—and pray she was not too late. She slipped a robe over her nightgown, grabbed the .22 and slid it into her pocket, gave Marmalade a stern warning not to move from the bed, and hurried into the hallway.

She rapped her knuckles against Mrs Weld's door, then tried the knob. Locked.

She rapped again. 'Mrs Weld, I have to see you.' She tried to keep her voice down so as not to rouse the others, but in the end had to shout before her hostess admitted her.

Even in dishabille Mrs Weld maintained her patrician bearing. Once the cobwebs of sleep had dissipated she quickly grasped the purport of Lena's discovery. The two women sat on ladderback chairs facing one another.

'I feel fine at the moment,' Mrs Weld replied, when Lena voiced her concern.

'Until we discover who's behind this, I suggest you take your meals in restaurants.'

'Or do my own cooking.' Mrs Weld chuckled. 'Neither option would go over well with Mrs Barboza. She'd walk out in a huff. I'd rather take my chances eating her cooking than lose her.' She sighed. 'Do you suspect anyone in particular?'

Lena nodded. 'I have two likely candidates. The trouble is, I can't prove anything.'

It was well into the wee hours when Lena left Mrs Weld to return to her room. As she tiptoed along the hallway, she saw a shapeless lump lying at the base of her door. When she was within a few feet of it the lump stirred.

'Marmalade!' she whispered. 'How did you get out here?'

Though she'd left her bed lamp switched on, no light now leaked into the hallway from under the door. She slid the .22 from her pocket. Someone in her absence, entering her room, had allowed the cat to escape. That someone might still be in there, waiting.

She turned the knob as if about to enter. But instead of stepping over the threshold she flung the door inward, banging it against the wall. At the same time a shadowy figure stumbled across the opening.

The figure quickly regained its balance, turned, and lunged at Lena. The assailant's knife would have plunged into her chest had not Marmalade intervened, by getting his tail stepped on. In retaliation for this outrage the cat dug his claws deep into flesh.

Only momentarily thwarted, the attacker raised the knife in a second attempt. But this time Lena was ready. Without seeming to aim, she fired the pistol. The knife flew from her would-be killer's hand.

Brook let out a cry of agony and clutched her wrist. Lena was prepared to fire a second shot but there was no need. The young woman sank to the floor sobbing.

Lena, whose priority was the well-being of her cat, was about to go in search of the irate feline, when she felt her arm seized and the pistol wrenched from her hand. 'What in hell is going on?' Kevin McDuff demanded.

Mrs Weld arrived at the scene, followed by Jack Peckham and Mrs Barboza.

'I'll take that,' Lena's hostess said to Kevin, indicating the pistol. The bewildered young man handed it to her. He had hairy legs and looked silly in his boxer shorts.

'So it was Brook,' Mrs Weld said to Lena. 'Is she badly hurt?'

Lena shrugged. 'A scratched leg and a sprained wrist.'

'Can I be of assistance, ma'am?' Jack asked his employer.

'Keep an eye on Miss Pezzoli while I phone the police. Mrs Barboza, could I prevail upon you to brew up a pot of coffee? We'll take it in the dining room. Oh, and bring along a bottle of that Irish whiskey. You know where I keep it. And of course you'll join us, I hope.'

'Where's that other one?' Mrs Barboza inquired.

'Other one? Oh, you mean Cousin Judith. Don't tell me she slept through this whole commotion.'

'I'll check on her,' Lena said. She took the pistol from Mrs Weld, crossed the hallway, and knocked on the woman's door. 'Cousin Judith. The jig's up. You can come out now.' Receiving no answer, she turned the knob and slowly swung the door inward. The room lay in darkness. She stepped across the threshold.

Marmalade chose that moment to rub against her leg. 'Damn, Marmalade! You scared the living daylight out of me.' She groped for a switch and turned on the light.

Cousin Judith, her throat slashed, lay on the blood-soaked bed, more colorful in death than ever she had been in life.

#

Detective Ioanides had a weakness for Lena's mock cherry pie, made from her own cranberries. Sergeant O'Hara was himself not averse to partaking of a piece or two. The two men sat at her kitchen table, next to a window overlooking her bog.

'Thank you for returning my pistol,' Lena said.

'From what I hear, that was quite a shot,' O'Hara said, shaking his head in admiration. 'Knocking the knife right out of the killer's hand. And hardly no light to see by.'

Lena maintained a modest silence, not wishing to disillusion the sergeant by explaining that her actual target had not been the knife, but her assailant's shoulder.

Eyeing the remaining slab of pie, O'Hara said, 'The Detective here tells me the two women was in cahoots.'

'Not exactly.' Lena sliced the slab in two and served half to each. 'The scheme to murder Mrs Weld was all Brook's. Cousin Judith was blackmailing her—which accounts for her sudden prosperity. She suffered from insomnia and often wandered the house at night. She must've seen Brook leave the library after the vandalism.'

'Miss Pezzoli has admitted as much,' Ioanides said.

'I'm afraid I'm the catalyst that set things in motion.' Lena poured the men more coffee. 'If I hadn't gone snooping in the library Cousin Judith might still be alive.'

'And Mrs Weld would surely be dead. Whether tiger whiskers would have done the trick is anyone's guess. But Brook would eventually have succeeded one way or another. And eliminated her blackmailer as well.'

The men rose from the table. 'Thanks for the pie, Mrs Lombardi,' O'Hara said as he wiped crumbs from his face. He accompanied Ioanides across the kitchen on the way out. Not paying attention to where he put his feet he trod upon Marmalade's tail.

The incident that followed resulted in language unbecoming an officer of the law.

THE IMPOSSIBLE THEFT
Cameron Trost

It was a chilly November evening and Louise and the boys were having a sleepover at a friend's house. Oscar Tremont was running a warm bath and looking forward to a quiet evening by the fireplace with only a good book and an even better dram of single malt for company. He'd just started to undress when a knock at the door announced an interruption to his plans.

He pulled his tracksuit pants up and walked across the living room, stopping before he reached the door, wondering whether he hadn't imagined it. But the knock came again and a man's voice called his name.

A client?

He grabbed the fire poker just in case. Working as a private investigator meant ruffling feathers on occasion, and there was always a chance some unhappy fowl might decide to peck back. He swung the door open and gave the visitor a quick going-over. Harmless. Mid-seventies. Mild-mannered. Relatively rich. A man of culture. He wore wire-frame glasses and what Oscar took to be a Boglioli blazer. His foulard was floral but tasteful, and the blue dahlias matched his eyes. If he didn't own a country estate, he was trying hard to look like he did.

He looked Oscar up and down before saying in slow, clear French, 'I'm sorry to disturb you, but if you're Oscar Tremont, I'm told I require your services. My name is Henri Ducasse.'

Oscar raised the fire poker into the air absentmindedly just as a schoolboy would flick his hand up to ask a question, but the sudden gesture made his visitor take a step backwards onto the pavement.

'Do come in, Monsieur Ducasse,' Oscar said, bringing the poker back down and tapping it casually against the stone of the threshold.

'I didn't mean to alarm you. There's no need to speak slowly. I may be Australian, but as you can tell, my French is fluent.'

'*Très impressionant,*' Henri agreed. 'Just the slightest hint of a charming accent.'

Oscar led Henri Ducasse inside, returned the poker to its stand by the fire, and motioned for his visitor to take a seat.

'Whisky?'

'Thank you.'

Oscar rushed back to the bathroom to turn the tap off before taking two glasses and a bottle of the Ardmore from the drinks cabinet.

'A client recommended me, Monsieur Ducasse?'

'Please, *Henri.*'

'Henri.'

He removed his coat and foulard and placed them neatly beside him on the sofa, then he reached into a pocket and removed what looked like a wedding invitation. He placed it on the coffee table.

'It's not a recommendation from a satisfied client that has brought me here.'

Oscar poured two drams and handed a glass to Henri. He took the card but didn't even glance at it until he was in his green leather armchair.

'Cheers,' they said, raising their glasses.

After taking a sip, Oscar placed his glass on the coffee table and studied the card. The first thing he noticed about the handwritten message was that it was in English.

'You speak English?' Oscar asked in his mother tongue.

'Not exactly. Sufficient for interpret the—how you can say?'

'Enough to work out the gist of it,' Oscar said.

'Ah, the *gist?* This is the *general sense*?'

'The *overall meaning*—yes,' Oscar confirmed distractedly, staring at the card. He then began to read out loud.

'You have discovered, Monsieur Ducasse, this message where the Bouchart treasure map should be, and I sincerely hope this little swap has more than slightly inconvenienced you. It's abundantly clear you haven't taken full advantage of the map, and therefore don't deserve to keep it any longer. Nevertheless, for the sake of sportsmanship, I've decided to give you one last chance. Make no mistake about it; this is the only opportunity you will have. If you really want the map back, you'll follow my advice. You require the services of Oscar Tremont, who I'm led to believe is a star among private investigators.' Oscar looked at his client and smiled. 'A star? It's rather flattering.'

Henri nodded but didn't share Oscar's amusement.

'So, I've been challenged to a duel of wits,' Oscar mused, back in French now.

'It would appear so,' Henri replied.

'The card is signed,' Oscar pointed out, raising his brow at his client.

'The name can't be real,' Henri said.

'Laure Pinnes?' Oscar asked, shooting Henri a mischievous wink. 'It most certainly is not.'

Henri frowned and sipped his whisky. 'You'll take the case?'

Oscar couldn't hide his surprise at the question. 'I can hardly turn down such a challenge, can I? But we'll talk business once I know more about what's at stake. Tell me about the map. If I'm not mistaken, Alain Bouchart was a Breton nobleman who was involved in an act of piracy off the coast of Belle-Ile in the fifteenth century.'

Henri nodded, clearly impressed. 'That's correct—and this map is rumoured to disclose the location of the bounty.'

'Yet no one has discovered it?'

'Not as far as we know.'

'Intriguing!' Oscar said, reaching for his glass. 'How did the map come to be in your possession?'

'My uncle found it in his grandfather's attic in Batz-sur-Mer years ago. It was buried under a pile of other sketches and notebooks in an old sea chest. We found it while going through the old man's belongings after his death. My uncle kept it in his study, and when he passed away, my cousin decided it would be safer in my possession. That's the worst part of it, Oscar. I've let the whole family down—and I can't even understand how it was possible.'

'You never tried to find the location of Alain Bouchart's treasure?'

'I did. We all did.'

Oscar shrugged. 'What was the problem?'

'It was too cryptic. We couldn't make sense of it.'

Oscar stared into the fire and stroked his moustache.

'Do you have a copy of the map?'

'I'm afraid not.'

Oscar sipped his whisky thoughtfully. 'We'd better get going,' he said eventually.

'Where to?'

'To your house, of course. Is that inconvenient?'

'Not at all. Not if it isn't for you.'

'It isn't.' Oscar looked at the card again and twirled it in his fingers. 'Where do you live?'

'Along the coast road in Le Croisic.'

'I'll follow you in my car. I'm parked out front.'

'The black Peugeot 403?'

'That's the one.'

'Splendid vehicle.'

'Thank you. Give me a couple of minutes to get ready.'

Oscar opened the door for his client and watched him vanish into the gathering dark. There was a question he'd forgotten to ask. Something Henri Ducasse had said—about not understanding how it was even possible. What did that mean? It didn't matter. He'd soon find out enough.

After putting the fire guard in place, he quickly packed his overnight bag, grabbed his car keys and flat cap, and switched the lights off. He locked the door behind him, glanced up and down the street, and got into his vintage car. Before turning the key in the ignition, he looked carefully ahead through the windscreen and peered into all three mirrors, noting the cars and people he could see in the street. Nothing seemed to be out of the ordinary.

A green Rover pulled up and Henri gave Oscar a quick nod and a wave before proceeding along the street. Oscar followed him and they were soon out of town and cruising along the expressway towards Guérande. He thought about the strange turn of events as he drove. It wasn't unusual for a case to suddenly pop up when he had a quiet night alone on the horizon. But this one was different altogether. The perpetrator had offered him a challenge. It was personal. He couldn't help but wonder whether the theft had been carried out merely as a pretext to get him involved. Was this a sign his reputation now preceded him? The map itself was obviously valuable, but its real worth was in the secret it held. Finding the treasure had to be the thief's ultimate goal.

The wind off the Atlantic grew as they headed down from Guérande and through the salt marshes. They would be in Le Croisic in ten minutes.

They passed Saint Guénolé's Church at Batz. Floodlights angled up from the ground made its majestic bell tower glow golden against a sky now as dark as ink. Oscar remembered that one could see as far as Belle-Ile from the top of the tower on a clear day.

A few roundabouts later, they were on the coast road and Henri slowed and pulled up outside a grand three-storey house facing the sea. Even before he'd stopped his car and opened the door, Oscar could hear the waves crashing against the craggy coast. Out to sea, distant lights flickered—green, red, and white—against a backdrop of black.

'It's a beautiful house,' Oscar said when he joined Henri at the wrought-iron gate set in a stone arch. Dormant hortensias lined the inner side of the low wall and rose bushes surrounded the house. The walls were granite and the roof was made of slate. A mauve door lit by a coachman's lamp added a splash of colour. It was hard to be sure in the dark, but it seemed to Oscar that the shutters and gables were painted the same colour.

'Thank you,' Henri said. 'Come and meet my wife.'

Oscar followed him up the stairs.

'The great Oscar Tremont!' she announced, looking him up and down.

'So it would seem,' Oscar mused. 'Someone clearly believes in my greatness.'

Madame Ducasse was a tall and elegant woman. She wore a long black dress with a grey sash around the waist. Her hair was short and more white than grey. She studied Oscar with icy eyes that contrasted with the warmth in her voice.

'Who is this Laure Pinnes?'

'I have no idea.'

'Tell me one thing, Monsieur Tremont,' she said, her voice not so warm now. 'This isn't a set-up, is it?'

Oscar grinned. 'I was wondering the very same thing.'

She stared at him for a moment.

'I suppose we'll just have to trust each other,' she conceded.

'That's how I see it,' Oscar agreed.

'You must be hungry. I have a roast chicken in the oven.'

'That sounds wonderful, but I'd like to make progress on the case first if you don't mind.'

'Yes, and we could both do with another whisky,' Henri said. 'I'll show Oscar the scene of the crime.'

Oscar gave the lady of the house a reassuring smile and followed Henri up the curved staircase.

'Apologies for my wife,' Henri whispered. 'She's suspicious of others at the best of times, and this has made it worse.'

The old stairs groaned loudly with every step they took.

'That's understandable,' Oscar admitted.

At the top of the staircase was a landing and three doors. Henri approached the furthest door and put a key in the lock. 'This is where we keep our most valuable belongings.'

'The other two doors are to bedrooms?'

'That's right, and both are kept locked if that's what you're wondering.'

'It was indeed,' Oscar replied, trying both doorknobs just to be sure. 'You always keep them locked?'

'As a habit,' Henri said, turning the key. 'Our bedroom is downstairs. These two are empty.' He opened the door.

Oscar all but gasped at the remarkable sight. The collection of strange and fascinating objects was one of the most impressive he had ever seen outside a museum.

'It's a veritable cabinet of curiosities!'

Henri smiled. 'That's precisely what it is, although I'm very fond of the German name.'

'*Wunderkammer*,' Oscar said.

'Excellent!' Henri congratulated him. He opened a polished oak cabinet and produced two crystal glasses and a whisky decanter.

'There is one window,' Oscar said, walking over and trying it, but it didn't budge. He noted the bolt.

'It's always locked.'

He looked at the ceiling, walls, and floor.

'No secret entrances that I can see, unless that bookshelf conceals one.'

Henri shook his head. 'Not so easy.'

'In that case, the thief must have used the door. Do you know when the theft took place?'

'Sometime this afternoon. The map was on the wall this morning and I found the card pinned where it should have been earlier this evening.'

Oscar gazed at the empty picture frame on the right-hand wall.

'Were you home all day?'

'That's just it. I was. Between the last time I saw the map and the time I found the card, I didn't leave the house. No one could have gone up and come down without my noticing. You heard the noise the staircase makes. I was between the kitchen, bathroom, and living room all that time, and you can hear the stairs from all of those rooms. It's simply not possible that anyone could have stolen the map and left the house unseen.'

'Or unheard,' Oscar added.

'That's right.'

'Yet here we are,' Oscar mused, looking around.

Other than the oak cabinet and the bookshelf, the only large items of furniture were a display case and a Breton box bed. There were a number of nautical instruments on the cabinet, including a nineteenth-century sextant, compass and hourglass. There was a canary skeleton perched in an oriental birdcage on top of the bookshelf, next to a lava lamp and a Kewpie doll. On the other shelves were an array of animal skulls, a stuffed and mounted pheasant, a pair of jade chopsticks in a china bowl, a voodoo doll full of pins, a Fabergé egg, a mosquito in amber, and a pair of antique handcuffs. The display case contained everything from Neolithic flint tools and Roman pottery to nineteen-fifties chattering teeth and an Elvis figurine with bobbing head. Beside the window—opposite where the map had been—hung a mask Oscar recognised as belonging to the Dogon people of Mali, and the room's floor space was crowded with objects—a full-length cracked mirror, a rocking horse with no tail or mane, a dented astronomical telescope, a longcase clock frozen in time, and an undressed female mannequin. Many of them had a price tag attached.

'I had one visitor but she couldn't have taken it,' Henri said and poured the whisky.

'Who was she?'

'She came to have a look at a number of objects I'm selling.'

'Hence the handwritten price tags attached to some items?'

'That's right.'

'Was she alone in the room at any time?'

Henri sipped his whisky and recalled his movements.

'I don't think so. Not for long in any case.'

'So she was?'

He frowned. 'Well, the phone rang and I was about to hurry downstairs.'

'The landline?'

'Yes, but then it stopped.'

'Your wife wasn't home?'

'Not then. I didn't even make it halfway down the stairs when the ringing stopped. Like I told you, this woman couldn't have stolen it. I was only out of the room a matter of seconds and she didn't have a handbag on her.'

'What was she wearing?'

'I remember her perfume—distinct notes of jasmine—and she was wearing a pair of jeans and a tight-fitting shirt. There was nowhere she could have concealed the map even if she'd been quick enough to get it out of the frame.'

'Interesting all the same,' Oscar said and sipped his whisky.

Henri's face was blank.

'Did she have a phone on her?'

'I can't remember. I think she did—oh, I see what you're suggesting. You think she was the one who made the call to my landline?'

'Certainly,' Oscar said. 'She called you surreptitiously to get you out of the room. How much longer did you stay here after you came back from the staircase?'

'We didn't. She thanked me for my time and told me she'd get in touch if she decided to make an offer on any of the items for sale.'

Oscar nodded slowly. 'Am I right in supposing that you didn't look at the wall where the map was hanging before heading back downstairs to show her out?'

Henri shrugged. 'I don't recall, but she couldn't have had the map on her, Oscar. It can't have been her.'

'No one else entered the room to your knowledge and you're adamant you remained within earshot of the staircase all day?'

'Yes,' he admitted.

'In that case, I put it to you that it *must* have been her. This woman is our thief. How she did it, however, remains a mystery. Did she give you a name?'

'Her first name was Luna.'

'Rather exotic,' Oscar said.

'I can't remember her family name. Pierce perhaps. Not a French name, although she didn't have an accent.'

Oscar closed his eyes and bowed his head. An instant later, his mouth formed a cheeky grin that made his moustache curl. He turned to Henri and asked, 'Piersen?'

The look of astonishment on his client's face was priceless. 'That's it!'

'She's our thief.'

'I don't understand. It has to be an alias.'

'It is, and a magnificent alias at that. We'll discuss the matter later. Our immediate concern is working out how she pulled it off.'

Oscar removed the calling card from his jacket pocket and examined it again, contemplating every word.

'You think there's a clue in the message?'

'There has to be,' Oscar replied absently without looking up.

'How can you know that?'

Oscar looked around the room again before meeting his client's gaze. 'It's just psychology, isn't it? I've been challenged to a battle of wits, and I know that if I'd set this up, that's exactly what I would have done—slipped a clue into the message.'

'I suppose,' Henri admitted.

'One oh-so subtle clue.'

'A clue that will lead you to the thief and help me get the map back?'

'No,' Oscar said, shaking his head. He looked at the card again, then glanced around the room. 'She will come to us, and we won't get the map back.'

'But I want it back,' Henri insisted. 'That's why you're here, man.'

Oscar laughed. 'Calm down. You misunderstand.'

Henri's frown couldn't have been more deeply etched.

'This is a game, Henri, whether you want it to be or not, and I'm going to win it for you, but not without playing along a little longer. Can you do that?'

'Play along?'

'Yes. Will you play along?'

'Of course.'

'Good. Here's what I need you to do—'

And Oscar went on to explain his game plan.

#

A week later, the woman who'd introduced herself as Luna Piersen called Henri and asked whether the telescope was still available and if he'd take fifty euros for it. He answered both questions in the affirmative and told her to come at her earliest convenience.

The doorbell rang just under an hour later.

'Hello. You're here for the telescope?' Madame Ducasse asked on opening the door to a smart young woman with long hair tied back in a ponytail and keen green eyes behind purple-framed glasses.

The visitor nodded.

'Henri!' she called out.

'Yes, dear.'

'Madame is here for the telescope.'

'Thank you. Send her up.'

He listened as the stairs creaked and greeted Luna Piersen with a charming smile when she arrived at the doorway to the cabinet of curiosities.

'Good morning, Miss Piersen. Here you are. It's ready,' he said, turning to the telescope.

There was an awkward silence for a moment.

'Is there a problem?' Henri asked.

'No,' she assured him, walking over to the telescope. 'Only, I forgot to check inside last time.'

'What do you mean—*inside*?'

'Inside the telescope.'

'Whatever for?'

'To make sure it's in order, of course.'

She removed the dust cap and looked inside.

'It works perfectly well,' Henri said. 'I'm sure I told you I've tried it myself.'

But when she looked back at him, there was a glint of mischief in her eyes and a suppressed smile tugging at the corners of her lips. She looked around the room and her eyes came to rest on the box bed.

'Are you sleeping, Mister Tremont?'

The panels slid open and Oscar got out. 'I don't sleep when a thief is on the prowl,' he said, grinning.

'I would have been disappointed,' she replied. 'It appears you solved my puzzle without any particular difficulty. You really are a *star* among private investigators.'

'You're too kind.'

'*Star*—that was it?' Henri asked in astonishment. 'That one clue was enough to tell you the map was in the telescope?'

'It was, but what first got me thinking was the way our thief was dressed when she came here. You told me her clothes were tight-fitting.'

'You're saying she did that to distract me?' Henri looked a little uncomfortable, and Oscar noticed their adversary did her best not to laugh.

'That's not quite what I meant,' Oscar said. 'Although I don't doubt her figure could indeed be used as a highly effective means of distraction.'

'If I may,' she cut in. 'What he means is that the only conceivable reason I'd be dressed so lightly on a chilly day would be to make it look certain to you that I wasn't the thief because there was nowhere on my person I could have hidden the map.'

Henri glared at her triumphantly. 'All very impressive, but you've made a mistake, Madame Piersen—or whatever your name is.'

'What's that?' she asked with a mock frown.

'We've caught you, haven't we?' he snapped.

'You're going to call the police on me?'

'Yes,' Henri said. 'Why wouldn't we?'

'Well, it's not quite that simple,' Oscar said. 'What will they charge her with? She didn't actually steal it.'

Henri didn't reply.

'We played her game, and we won. That's enough, isn't it?'

'What's to stop her from doing it again?'

'Nothing at all,' Oscar admitted.

She pretended she was trying to suppress her smug grin.

Henri frowned, then shrugged. 'I do hope you'll play your tricks on someone else next time though, Madame Piersen, or Pinnes, or whatever your name is—that reminds me, Oscar, what was it you realised about her aliases?'

'I won't be bothering you again, Monsieur Ducasse,' she said, then turning to Oscar, she arched her eyebrows. 'Yes—what precisely did you realise about my aliases?'

'*Laure Pinnes—Luna Piersen*—both anagrams of another name.'

'Who?' Henri asked.

'Who is the greatest thief of all?' Oscar asked him.

'Oh, I see—*Arsène Lupin!*' Henri practically shouted.

'Rather clever.' She narrowed her eyes at Oscar. 'It leads one to suspect you may have personal experience with anagrams, Australian detective.'

Oscar tapped his nose.

'I notice it's not back on the wall. May I ask where you've stowed it?' she continued.

'I had it in the box bed with me,' Oscar told her, walking over to fetch the map. 'I wasn't taking any chances.'

'You really are a clever one.' She narrowed those mischievous green eyes. 'That's it then—the mystery is solved and all the fun and games are over.'

'Not quite.' He raised an admonishing finger. 'There's still one mystery that hasn't been solved, isn't there?'

'Only one?' she asked, disappointed. 'My identity?'

'That's not what I had in mind.'

She looked at him blankly. 'In that case, it must be how I came to hear of your talents.'

'The time to answer all that will come,' he replied with a shrug. 'There's a more pressing matter.'

'Go on.'

'Before you hid the map in the telescope, I expect you took a number of photographs of it.'

The smug grin returned. 'That's an interesting thought. It appears I've left my phone at home. How careless of me!'

'I rather suspect carelessness isn't part of your repertoire. I look forward to our next *partie*.'

'Rest assured, it won't be so easy next time.' And with a wink for Oscar and a nod at Henri, she left the room. Henri saw her out, but Oscar stayed in the cabinet of curiosities, listening to the creaking stairs and staring at Bouchart's treasure map. His opponent had made her departure, but her sweet perfume lingered—as did the tantalising promise of her new challenge.

IF IT'S TUESDAY, THIS MUST BE MURDER
Josh Pachter

Phillida Marlowe leaned forward and carefully applied her lipstick. Then she grinned at her mirror image, flipped her hands out to the sides and, channeling Roy Scheider in *All That Jazz*, announced 'It's showtime!' to her otherwise empty hotel room.

She dropped her makeup kit into her duffel, zipped it closed and set it outside the door for Jeremy to collect, ducked back in to make sure she hadn't left yet another phone charger behind, and headed down to the bus.

It was Tuesday, Day Three of Westminster Travel's eight-day, seven-night *Life in the Lowlands* excursion. Airfare from Heathrow to Zaventem and Schiphol back to Heathrow, four-star hotels every night, all breakfasts and box lunches included, welcome and farewell gala dinners (with unlimited beer, wine, and soft drinks), admissions to all local attractions, and the services of a charming guide (i.e, Phillida, who was advertised as being fluent in Dutch and Flemish but wasn't, though who cared, really, because the natives all spoke quite good English).

They'd now done their two days in Brussels—welcome gala at Chez Léon in the Rue des Bouchers, the Royal Palace, the Atomium, the obligatory pilgrimage to Manneken Pis, the Grand Place by night—and were off to Bruges this morning for a canal-boat ride, a walking tour, a pint of Straffe Hendrick at De Halve Maan...and then tomorrow across the border and into Holland for the usual stops at the Keukenhof for the tulips and Kinderdijk for the windmills before winding up in Amsterdam, where they would have another Royal Palace and another ride in a canal boat, plus the Van Gogh Museum and Rembrandt's *Night Watch* at the Rijks, a brown café in the

Leidseplein, and their farewell gala at the Five Flies before heading home to Cheltenham or Market Snodbury or wherever it was they'd come from.

As usual, Phillida was the first one on the bus.

'Bloody Peter,' she muttered in frustration, when she saw the half-empty packet of Walker's cheddar-and-bacon crisps on the dashboard. She'd told their driver again and again to keep his bloody awful crisps in the glove box when he wasn't actually stuffing his face with them, but Peter rarely remembered. It was a wonder the man was able to stay focused long enough to get them from Point A to Point B without first rambling through the rest of the bloody alphabet.

She put the packet where it belonged and did a quick check of the rest of the bus, pleased to see that Jeremy had as usual swept the floor and run a dust cloth over the windows, inside and out. Although there was no assigned seating on her tours, her generally elderly group members generally staked out a claim to a particular seat on initial boarding and stuck with it for the duration. Some of them went so far as to mark their territory, like cats, leaving some personal possession on "their" seat at the end of each leg of the journey. There was Juliana Jordan's *Fodor's Guide to Belgium* at 3B, for example, and Lucia Caldwell's knitting—what on Earth *was* the monstrosity? a scarf? a sweater for her Corgi?—at 7C, Emmeline Paxton's Ellery Queen paperback at 9B and Nathaniel Steele's thick hardbound compendium of six E.F. Benson novels at 11D and Alicia Moncrief's dog-eared collection of word searches at 14C.

She left these items where they were (far be it from her to interfere with the territorial imperative!), but picked up the empty Lion bar wrapper Mrs Satterthwaithe had left behind at 6A and used it to protect her fingers from Mr Satterthwaithe's wad of used tissues (the man had a simply revolting habit of hacking up gobs of phlegm at every turn of the road) at 6B.

After properly disposing of this rubbish, she glanced out the window and saw her sheep approaching across the meadow that was the Auberge Dehouck's parking lot. She squeezed out of the aisle to make room for them and greeted them with a professionally assumed imitation of cheerfulness as they mounted the steps and filed past her to their seats.

In the lead came Jonathan Arbuthnot (tall, brush mustache, military bearing) and his traveling companion Jasper Cornwallis (squat, stocky, dirty fingernails)—in the privacy of her thoughts, she had christened them the Major and the Miner. To avoid paying the single supplement twice over, they claimed, they had chosen to share a twin-bedded room, but who did they think they were fooling, the silly old poofters?

Close behind them came the Tomkins and the Timkins, who lived in side-by-side cottages in the Cotswolds and, as if they didn't see enough of each other fifty weeks out of the year, apparently took all their holidays together. Basil Tomkins was a head taller than his wife, Samantha, and Camilla Timkins a head taller than her husband, Nigel. Why didn't they simply swap spouses, Phillida wondered, to even things out a bit? Or perhaps they *had*, once upon a time, or were more evenly matched back in Quivering-on-the-Edge but livened things up by changing partners—as in a square dance—whilst far from home.

Then came Casey and Malvika Talwar, who had emigrated from the Punjab to Hammersmith ages ago. Casey couldn't possibly be an Indian name, could it? Perhaps those were his initials, K.C.—for what? Krishna Chaudri? Karma Chameleon? Kentucky Chicken?

They were followed by the Agnellis, the Epsteins, and the Federers, boarding as if by pre-arrangement in alphabetical order.

Poor Mrs Walker—who actually *used* a walker, and whose first name was apparently protected from disclosure under the Official Secrets Act—brought up the rear, and Jeremy interrupted his stowing of the baggage to assist her up the steps.

There, that was all of them. As they settled themselves into their seats for the forty-two-mile drive to Bruges and Peter switched on the engine and adjusted his rear-view mirror, Phillida stood at the front of the bus like a queen surveying her troops on Flag Day and performed the obligatory head count.

...eighteen, nineteen, twenty, twenty-one.

No, that was wrong, there were supposed to be twenty-two of them. She must have been distracted and missed one out. She started up again with Mrs Walker in 1A and recounted.

...nineteen, twenty, twenty-one.

Bloody hell, one of them was missing! Annoyed, she reached for her clipboard and compared the names on the list to the faces eyeing her inquisitively, wondering what was delaying their departure.

Mrs Walker in 1A, check.

The Major and the Miner in 2C and 2D, check.

Juliana Jordan in 3B, check...

...Emmeline Paxton in 9B, check.

Fred and Lila Epstein in 10A and 10B, check.

And there he was—or, rather, wasn't: Nathaniel Steele in 11D.

Most of Phillida's ladies and gentlemen were retirees traveling in pairs. This time around, Nathaniel Steele was the only gentleman traveling alone, and he had been made quite the darling of Juliana Jordan, Lucia Caldwell, Emmeline Paxton, and Alicia Moncrief, the four solo women on the tour—technically, Mrs Walker was also a solo woman, but she alone had seemed completely immune to Mr Steele's considerable charms. He had probably lost track of the time, was still standing before his bathroom mirror adjusting the toupee he seemed not to realize everyone in the group knew full well he affected.

Well, there was nothing for it, if they were going to remain on schedule. With a long-suffering sigh, Phillida climbed down from the bus and trekked back across the parking lot to the hotel, climbed the broad flight of stairs to the second floor and knocked on the door of room 213.

'Mr Steele,' she called. 'Wakey wakey!'

There was no response.

She rapped again, more sharply this time. 'Time to go, Mr Steele! We're all on the bus!'

Silence.

Truly wound up by now, she rattled the doorknob to get the old fool's attention—and was startled when the door swung open at her touch.

Hesitantly, not wanting to embarrass the man if he was still in his smalls, she peeked into the room.

Nathaniel Steele was lying stretched out on the bed, fully clothed but sound asleep, his suitcase open beside him, a folded city map of Brussels clutched in his hands.

Phillida marched over to the bed and tapped his shoulder.

He did not awaken.

She shook him purposefully, hard enough to dislodge his toupee, which dropped from his head to his pillow and lay there like a dozing Pomeranian.

Mr Steele slept on, and it was only then that Phillida noticed his chest was not rising and falling with his breathing, and there were angry bruises on his throat, and he *wasn't* breathing, and he was dead.

#

'I am sorry to keep you all waiting like this,' said Detective Inspector Bavo Van Laerhoven, his English accented but perfectly understandable. The twenty-four faces that stared at him wore an assortment of expressions: frustration at the long delay, boredom, curiosity, and of course horror at the knowledge that one of their number had been strangled to death.

'We have completed our examination of the—ah, of the deceased,' he continued, 'and I'm afraid we will have to try your patience a bit longer.'

The next hour was spent taking statements from each of the twenty-four of them—twenty-one passengers, Peter the driver, Jeremy the baggage handler, and Phillida the tour guide. By the end of that time, a clearer picture had begun to take shape.

Nathanial Steele—a lifelong bachelor—had spent thirty years doing something both terribly uninteresting and yet terribly important in the Civil Service. Now, in his retirement, he had decided to see a bit more of the world than his sheltered corner of Whitehall, and he had signed up for his first organized tour, *this* tour, Westminster Travels' *Life in the Lowlands*.

He had kept himself to himself on the bus, slowly reading his way through his thick collection of E.F. Benson novels, but he had been affable enough during the various sightseeing expeditions and mealtimes of the past two days and had in fact paid courtly attention to the group's five single women, even the uninterested Mrs Walker.

The medical examiner would not have much to say about the time of Mr Steele's demise until he had completed his post-mortem examination, but the indications he had been able to observe at the *locus delicti*—body temperature compared with room temperature, rigor mortis, lividity—suggested that death had occurred no more than twelve and no less than seven hours before the discovery of the body, thus between eight o'clock last night and one o'clock this morning. The victim had been seen in the hotel bar the previous evening, had enjoyed a pint of Trappist beer with the Epsteins before the three of them had gone up to their rooms at approximately eleven, which narrowed the death window by a further three hours.

Between 11 pm and 8 am, each of the couples alibied themselves for the relevant time period: the Agnellis, the Epsteins, the Federers, the Satterthwaites, the Talwars, the Timkins and Tomkins, even the Major and the Miner. By eleven o'clock, they were all tucked up in bed, and two by two, like animals trooping onto Noah's Ark, they'd gone down to breakfast at seven and hadn't been out of each other's sight except for the occasional brief trip toodle-oo.

That left the five single women, Peter, Jeremy, and Phillida unaccounted for—and the M.E. had concluded from the size of the bruises on the dead man's neck that his killer had small hands, which seemed to let out Peter and Jeremy.

'When are you thinking it will be possible for us to be leaving for Bruges, sir?' asked Casey Talwar timidly.

'*Je suis désolé,*' the inspector replied, 'but this bus isn't going anywhere until the murder has been solved.'

'But,' Lucia Caldwell protested, 'but we're supposed to be at the Basilica of the Holy Blood in Bruges at two this afternoon for the veneration of the Relic of the Holy Blood!'

'I expect you're going to miss it, madam,' said Van Laerhoven.

'But we can't! It's the most important part of our whole trip!'

'Not anymore, I'm afraid. The most important part of your trip as of this moment is determining who strangled your Mr Steele.'

A heavy silence descended upon the bus and its passengers.

'I've no idea if this will help,' said Phillida, 'but I've just realized something.'

'Yes?' the inspector drawled.

'His clothes,' said Phillida.

'I am—how do you say it?—entirely ears.'

'Well, the clothes he was wearing when I—when I found him were the same clothes he wore to dinner last night, and—'

'—and he was such a meticulous man,' interrupted Juliana Jordan.

'Surely he wouldn't have worn the same outfit two days in a row!'

'Men don't wear *outfits*,' Basil Tomkins harrumphed. 'We wear *clothing*.'

'Either way,' the inspector mused, 'that suggests he must have been killed before undressing for bed, closer to the early side of the medical examiner's estimate of time of death. Thank you, Miss Marlowe, that is a useful point. But now we—'

'Why don't you use your little grey cells, like that Belgian in that movie with Ingmar Bergman?' said Gino Agnelli.

'In*grid* Bergman,' Lila Epstein corrected him primly. 'Ing*mar* Bergman was a director, and he didn't direct *Murder on the Orient Express*.'

Inspector Van Laerhoven blinked. 'I have no idea what you're talking about,' he said.

'Hercule Porrot,' Mr Agnelli explained. 'How can you not know him, he's a famous Belgian policeman?'

'Pwah-ROE,' said Emmeline Paxton indulgently. 'Air-KYOOL Pwah-ROE. And he was a fictional private investigator, not an actual policeman, although—according to the back story Agatha Christie provided for him—he—'

The inspector cut her off with a shake of his head. 'Never heard of him,' he said.

'Oh, you must read him,' said Emmeline Paxton. 'I adore classic detective fiction.'

'I don't read fiction,' the inspector murmured, as if the word was a rasher of bacon that had gone off. 'It bores me.'

'But you're missing so much,' Miss Paxton protested. 'The red herrings, the deductive reasoning, the impossible crimes, the dying—just a moment. What if Mr Steele left a dying message behind?'

Van Laerhoven's stolid face was completely expressionless. 'I have no idea what you're talking about,' he said again.

'A dying message,' Jeremy jumped in, eager to help. 'I know about that—my mum's got the 'ole Ellery Queen series on DVD. It was on the telly about a fousand years ago.'

'And—?' the inspector prompted.

'And a dying message is somefing they done all the time. Some bloke gets chopped, but before 'e expires 'e writes down some mysterious clue to the name of 'is killer.'

'And why doesn't he simply write the name of his killer?' Van Laerhoven asked, his interest piqued.

Jeremy's face twisted. 'I—I dunno. 'E just don't.'

'If he did,' Emmeline Paxton explained patiently, 'the killer might come back and see it—and of course then he'd destroy it. *Did* Mr Steele write anything before he died?'

'Nothing,' said the inspector flatly. 'We found no paper in his room, not even a newspaper.'

'Unless he wrote something on that map of Brussels he was holding,' said Phillida.

The inspector shook his head. 'No pen or pencil, either. And there was nothing written on the map.'

'Well, perhaps the map itself was a message,' Phillida said slowly. 'After all, there was no reason for him to have it in his hands when he died.'

'His suitcase was open on the bed beside him,' said the inspector. 'He was packing. Perhaps he was putting it away when he was attacked.'

'Nonsense,' rumbled Jonathan Arbuthnot. 'If someone attacked the chappie, he'd've dropped the map and defended himself.'

'Perhaps it *was* a message, then,' said Frannie Satterthwaite. 'The killer choked him and left him for dead. But he wasn't dead. He regained consciousness, but he knew he was dying and wanted to tell the police who'd attacked him.'

'He had nothing to write with,' her husband picked up smoothly, 'and nothing to write on. But he saw the map he'd been packing and was able to grab it before he died.'

'But what does it mean?' asked the inspector, intrigued now. 'A map of Brussels. What was he trying to say?'

'Use your little grey cells,' Gino Agnelli shouted, and Emmeline Paxton waved her copy of *The Siamese Twin Mystery* and said, 'If only Ellery Queen was here!'

Phillida Marlowe stared at the paperback, mesmerized by its brightly colored cover. And then she walked down the aisle to row 11 and hoisted Nathaniel Steele's thick volume from seat 11D, where the dead man had left it.

'*Six Novels by E.F. Benson*,' she read aloud. She opened the book to the table of contents and gasped.

'*Miss Mapp*,' she said, reading out the title of the second of the novels.

The bus fell instantly silent, twenty-three pairs of eyes fixed on her intently, all but Lucia Caldwell, who never looked up from her knitting.

'Yes?' the inspector demanded. 'And what comes after that?'

'I told him I thought we might make a lovely couple,' Miss Caldwell said calmly, her steel needles never hesitating in their rhythmic clacking. 'But he laughed at me, called me a silly old cow, said he wouldn't marry me if I was the last woman on Earth.'

'*Mapp and Lucia*,' Phillida Marlowe read aloud. '*Lucia in London. Lucia's Progress.*' She paused for a moment, and then read the final title: '*Lucia in Trouble.*'

'He was such a disgusting little man,' said Miss Caldwell, clucking in irritation at a dropped stitch. 'And now I suppose we won't make it to the Basilica of the Holy Blood on time, after all.'

Detective Inspector Van Laerhoven walked purposefully down the aisle to seat 7C and took the knitting from Lucia's hands.

'It would have been such a treat,' she said.

JUSTICE FOR JAYNIE
Yvonne Ventresca

Rylie rushed to make the last train into Manhattan. The street remained quiet except for the click of her boot heels and a warm rustle of wind in the trees. No one else was around, but she felt safe in the small Jersey town of Haverfeld, where only one friend even knew her real name.

She'd been reclusive ever since the scandal, when her career crashed and her boyfriend, Denny, asked her to move out of their DC apartment. She worked anonymously now, ghost-writing speeches and creating website content under a pseudonym. The months had passed as she bided her time, watching the gossip about her dwindle along with her savings. The apartment-sitting gig was about to end, and she needed a big story, something to redeem her reputation.

This lead could do the trick. The night shift custodian at a big New York hospital had finally agreed to discuss the Emergency Room doctor facing sexual assault charges from three of his patients. They were to meet in an hour at a coffee shop near the hospital.

She walked faster to make the 12:01 train, knowing this could be her lucky break. But when she arrived at the station, a temporary construction barrier blocked the entrance with a "Platform Closed" sign taped to it. Cursing under her breath, she checked New Jersey Transit information on her phone; there was nothing listed about a closure for Monday night. The small building that housed the waiting area was locked and empty.

A guy and a girl emerged from the direction of the tracks, both in jeans and sweatshirts. They walked close together but not touching, their hoods up despite the warm April weather. A lock of red hair escaped the girl's hood, and she jerked her hand up to tuck it back underneath.

They both looked startled at the sight of Rylie. The girl stopped and stared, but the guy took her elbow and nudged her along as they walked between the building and the barricade.

Rylie froze for a moment at the sight of him. It was unnerving how much he resembled her ex—the black hair, dark eyes, thin face.

'The platform's closed,' he said.

'How can it be closed?' Rylie asked.

He shrugged. 'It doesn't say why.'

The girl never spoke as they hurried away, but she looked over her shoulder nervously. The Denny lookalike and the anxious girl strode toward a dark SUV parked in the far corner of the lot. She glanced back again, and Rylie felt like she was somehow invading their privacy.

With a sigh, she turned her attention to checking her phone for the cost of an Uber. She desperately wanted the ER doctor story, but her tank was nearly empty, and the nearest gas station would be closed. Should she splurge on a car service? Maybe just as far as Hoboken. She could get to the city on her own from there. She ordered a car and walked to the main entrance of the parking lot to wait.

As her Uber arrived, the SUV left from the opposite side of the lot. At 12:01, the train horn blasted, followed by a screech of brakes. The platform must not be closed after all. Annoyed, she hesitated at the open car door, but it was too late now. The Uber driver, a bald man with a gray beard and a scowl, did not seem like he'd understand if she ditched and ran for the train.

Minutes later, as they drove down Main Street toward the highway, she heard emergency sirens. Soon a police car raced by them, heading in the other direction, followed by another one. She hadn't heard sirens in Haverfeld ever. Something big was going on, and she was missing it.

'Turn around,' she told the driver. 'We need to go back to the train station. Please.'

The driver did everything at one speed—slow. He refused to do an illegal U-turn. Then they got stuck at all three traffic lights, and by the time they arrived back at the train, both police cars were there. She jumped out of the car.

'Did I miss the 12:01?' she asked the young cop, feigning

innocence.

'No more trains tonight, Miss. There's been an accident.'

'What happened?'

'NJ Transit's in charge. I really can't say.'

She gave him a please-tell-me smile. 'I'm going to read about it tomorrow, right?'

He sighed. 'The train struck something on the tracks.'

An ambulance pulled up. It was more of a someone than a something.

'You'll have to make other travel arrangements. This station is closed until we finish our investigation.' He hovered near the "Platform Closed" sign, which had turned out to be eerily accurate.

Rylie pointed at it. 'That was up before the train pulled in. I was here earlier.'

The officer looked confused and left her to confer with another cop.

She surveyed the parking area as she returned to the waiting Uber. Only one other car remained in the otherwise empty lot. Was there a story here? The feeling nagged at her, but the hospital custodian would be waiting. The police began photographing the "Platform Closed" sign as Rylie left the station.

#

In the morning, Rylie sipped her coffee and checked the news. Last night's train accident was an apparent suicide. According to the engineer, the male victim had lain motionless on the tracks as the train approached him, and the cameras on the front of the train confirmed that. The authorities would not release his identity to the press until they'd notified his family, and they were still awaiting the results of the toxicology reports. The victim's car had been found unlocked in the train parking lot.

That must have been the other car she'd noticed last night. She should have stayed at the station instead of schlepping into the city—a waste of time, it turned out, when the custodian didn't provide any substantial information. Had she followed the wrong lead? Made another professional mistake?

Staring out the window at the spring drizzle, she wondered what

Denny was doing right now, if he was awake yet, if the sun was shining through their kitchen window. She picked up her phone, hovered her finger over the button to call him. What could she say? That she was different now? Her previous apologies hadn't persuaded him. For all she knew, he had another girlfriend, someone unambitious and devoted.

She knew she had crossed the line, spending the night with the politician, gleaning whatever information she could. Corruption charges had been filed against him based on what she learned, but her relationship with Denny never recovered.

She couldn't call him. Not yet.

Instead, she busied herself by feeding the cat, texting the owner her daily picture of the beloved feline, then tidying the apartment. Her friend, Barb, had gotten her the apartment and pet-sitting job at a time when she needed to escape DC. With less than two weeks left in the arrangement, she started to feel desperation crawl across her skin like a spider. She kept mentally swooshing it away. Something would work out. Something always did.

She spent the morning on her writing assignments, researching productivity in the workplace, ten benefits of eating leafy greens, and corporate wellness initiatives. Finally, it was time for lunch. Maybe she would order something with kale.

She met Barb at the local luncheonette. It was more crowded than usual. While they sat near the entranceway waiting for a table, the TV news featured a story about another politician's affair. Rylie grimaced, trying to tune it out.

'Time does not heal all wounds?' Barb asked.

'Apparently not.' She looked away.

'You know I'm not judging you. I just feel like you're mourning. Your career, your relationship, whatever. And it's time to put away the self-pitying regret and move on.'

'Ouch.'

'You know I'm right.'

Rylie stood, antsy from waiting. 'I can't take being anonymous much longer.'

'I thought you were cured of the spotlight craving.'

'I need to make a comeback,' Rylie said. 'I turn thirty in a matter of days. I always envisioned spending my thirtieth birthday with the man I love, celebrating my professional accomplishments, toasting to our future.'

'You still miss Denny,' Barb said.

Rylie gave her a look. "Miss" didn't feel like nearly a strong enough verb to describe the endless longing.

'One more table ahead of you,' the hostess said.

'Thanks.' Barb spoke quietly after the woman walked away. 'Do you want news about him?'

Rylie felt dizzy, and she doubted it was from hunger. *Please don't let him be in love with someone else.* 'I do,' she said.

Barb nodded. Her husband was Denny's second cousin, but she had stayed neutral during the break-up.

'His mother passed away,' Barb said. 'Cancer.'

'Oh.' Rylie knew he would be devastated. 'That's awful. I didn't know.' Of course she didn't know. She'd been out of his life for months.

'The service will be in Spring Lake on Saturday. They're waiting for his sister to get home, too.'

Rylie couldn't believe it. Denny was in New Jersey right now, not in DC. It seemed like she should know that, that the connection between them would somehow alert her to his presence. But she was being ridiculous. There was no connection there, not anymore. Not since her betrayal.

The news story changed to the local train accident just as the hostess came to seat them.

'What a tragedy,' Barb said.

'Actually, it's a righteous death,' the hostess said. 'My brother works for NJ Transit. He told me they figured out who was killed.' She paused by a booth. 'This okay?'

'Yes,' Barb said, sliding in.

'Who was it?' Rylie asked, transfixed.

The hostess answered in a stage whisper, 'The Rape King.'

'Sawyer Kingston?' The student had allegedly drugged and assaulted several girls during his fraternity's parties at the local college, Archer University. Many of the rumored victims wouldn't come forward, but his last one did. Despite a seemingly airtight case against him, Kingston was acquitted of all charges after a paperwork screw-up prevented several key witnesses from testifying.

'Yes,' the hostess said. 'They'll be announcing it any minute.'

'You're sure?' Rylie slid in the seat across from Barb.

'As sure as he was guilty of those crimes,' she said. 'Your waitress will be over in a minute.'

'Thanks,' Barb said.

Rylie stared at the TV screen instead of the menu.

'What is it?'

'Reporters will be all over the campus when they announce this.' Rylie didn't feel like mentioning that she had been at the train station last night, too. 'It's an opportunity—'

Barb sighed. 'Go. We'll get together another day.'

'You're the best,' Rylie said, rushing from the restaurant.

She sped to the university, fueled by the desire to know, to see firsthand what would happen on campus when the death of the Rape King was revealed. In front of the fraternity house, a group of reporters had already gathered along with a TV camera crew. She hovered at the edge of the crowd, itching to be in the fray.

'How do you feel, knowing your fraternity brother is dead?' one reporter called out to a group of guys approaching the house. A barrage of other questions followed.

The students looked shell-shocked. No one answered, and from the outskirts, she observed how some of them stared at the reporters blankly. One kid with clenched fists looked like he was holding back tears.

And then she saw him: the Denny lookalike, the guy who had been at the train last night. He walked toward the fraternity house, then skirted the crowd and went in a side entrance. No one seemed to notice. After someone from the university made an official statement about tragedy and respecting the privacy of the students, the reporters dispersed, and Rylie found a nearby bench where she waited with a view of the doors. After an hour, her patience was rewarded. The Denny-ish boy came out, wearing shorts and an Archer basketball sweatshirt.

'Brandon!' Someone from inside the house propped the door open and yelled after him.

She didn't catch the rest of it—something about dinner later—but at least now she knew his first name and his connection to the basketball team.

Staying far enough behind that she remained unnoticed, she followed him across campus on tree-lined walkways. She knew in DC the cherry blossoms would be in bloom, but she pushed thoughts of Denny out of her mind.

Near the library, a girl waited for Brandon, but not the nervous one from last night. Rylie recognized her right away from the news. This was Jaynie, the Rape King's outspoken victim, the one who hadn't gotten her victory in court. Brandon blocked Rylie's view as they spoke, so she couldn't judge any of the emotions behind the conversation.

Still, it was certainly an interesting development. Brandon had been at the train station right before the accident, and now he was meeting the person who would be the least sorry about Kingston's suicide.

Unless—maybe his death wasn't a suicide. Rylie shivered and moved off the path, out of their view. Could the Rape King have been murdered? The news hadn't made any reference to foul play, and the other reporters didn't seem to be exploring that line of questioning with the students.

With the combination of waiting for the train last night and seeing Brandon with Jaynie now, Rylie might be the only person who knew what actually happened.

For a moment, she fantasized about everything this could mean. A true crime book with her name in a huge font on the cover. A return to triumph, like the very first time she'd been right, when she and her high school friends investigated their principal's false credentials and caused his resignation. A comeback for a disgraced journalist who had only ever wanted to report the truth and create justice.

She had to find out if her hunch was correct. Her heart raced as she followed them to a parking lot and spotted his familiar dark-colored SUV from the night before. On closer inspection, it was a navy Honda Pilot with Maryland plates. But disappointment set in as they pulled away; she had no way to continue the chase.

Still determined to learn more, she checked the Archer basketball roster online from her apartment. In under two minutes, she had his biography, complete with a photo. Brandon Hamilton was a junior, a sport and event management major who had attended high school in Maryland. That was half the puzzle. She wondered about the redheaded girl she had seen that night. Was she an Archer student as well? She scrolled through the women's sports photos on a lark, but didn't find her.

The story stayed in the news the next day. Jaynie had been at a fundraiser to benefit sexual abuse victims at the time of his death. She released a statement, saying she was 'relieved that fate intervened where the court system failed and that no one else would ever be victimized by that monster.'

Regarding the suicide, one psychologist speculated that the acquittal didn't absolve Sawyer Kingston of his guilt and inner turmoil. But Sawyer's mother disagreed. 'He was innocent,' she claimed, despite the overwhelming proof against him. 'There was nothing for him to regret.'

Sawyer's parents even offered a substantial reward for anyone with information about the day of his death. Would Brandon and the girl come forward? Rylie needed that reward, if she were being honest. She wanted the money. But the truth was, she wanted the story even more. This could be her break, her launch back into the limelight.

She spent Thursday and Friday on the Archer campus, unobtrusively trailing Brandon in the hope that he would lead her to the redheaded girl. Instead, he spent most of his time in the library or the gym.

Then news broke about the toxicology report. Alcohol and Gamma-Hydroxybutyrate, the date rape drug, had been found in Kingston's system. There was speculation that he used GHB recreationally, as well as to allegedly drug his victims. But that was the single new development. Because the only crime Haverfeld had ever experienced near the train was a stolen bicycle. No cameras existed at the station. There were no witnesses.

No known witnesses, anyway.

Rylie called her old boss in DC. He had seemed sad when he fired her. 'You're determined and driven and smart,' he had said, before he went off about ethics and blah blah blah. Now she crossed her fingers that he would give her another chance.

'I have a lead on something interesting,' she told him over the phone.

'I can't—'

'We can use a pen name. Run a special feature. I have a unique perspective on the Rape King's death. I need to do some more digging before I can say anything else.'

'Call me when you have more information,' he said. 'I can't promise anything, but I'll think about it.'

She hung up the phone. This story would take more investigation, but she could feel her life turning around, and just in time.

#

Saturday arrived, gray and dreary, and Rylie thought about Denny and the funeral. She wanted to see him, to be there for him at the church, even from a distance. She would try to stay in the background, but it would be impossible to remain unnoticed. Most of his family knew her well, and those that didn't would recognize her from the news. Still, she pulled her brown hair into a tight bun and put on her most solemn black dress. She could bear the cold stares if it meant supporting Denny.

After she arrived, she hovered in the back, scanning the room. She spotted Denny near the front and sucked in her breath. He was talking to a petite woman. A new girlfriend? No, she exhaled, realizing it was just his cousin. She stood transfixed, soaking in the sight of him, the way he titled his head to listen, moved his hands to gesture. She loved those hands. How stupid had she been, risking their relationship to get the scoop on a story.

'Rylie?'

Forgetting she was supposed to be anonymous, she turned toward the voice.

'Aunt Wendy!' Wendy might be the one person besides Denny who Rylie was happy to see. Wendy wasn't a real aunt, but a close friend of Denny's father.

'How have you been?' she asked. 'It's been a rough few months for you, I'd imagine.'

'Yes,' Rylie admitted, not even trying to lie.

Aunt Wendy patted her arm. 'I'm happy you're here, regardless of what people think. Of course everyone in the family sided with Denny during the...situation. Except for me. I'm the traitor in the family.' She smiled.

'I'm glad there's at least one person who won't glare at me.'
'I need to offer my condolences,' Wendy said. 'Come with me?'
She hesitated. 'I think I'll keep a low profile.'
Wendy nodded in agreement. 'Take care of yourself.'

Rylie was almost feeling good about her decision to come when Denny's older sister approached. From the beginning, she had said they were an ill-suited match, so she was no doubt gleeful about their break-up.

'I'm surprised you would intrude on this day of sorrow,' his sister said. 'Then again, maybe I'm not. You always did lack a certain sense of decorum. Has your presence even registered with my brother?'

Rylie looked over at him, and as if Denny had heard his sister from across the room, he finally saw her. She'd thought she was ready, that she was prepared for this moment, but it suddenly felt like too much. She gripped the back of the pew to steady herself.

'I came to pay my respects,' Rylie said, not wanting to give her any satisfaction. But as soon as his sister moved on to speak to someone else, she practically ran out, not stopping until she reached her car.

Rylie cried on the way home, for Denny's loss of his mom, for her own loss of Denny. Then the sadness seemed to solidify into an angry stone in the pit of her stomach. Stupid older sister. She was a failed screenwriter who always used pretentious phrases like "this day of sorrow".

More importantly, what had Denny's expression meant, when he'd finally noticed her? He'd looked surprised, and something else, something that had made her heart quicken.

Never mind. She couldn't spiral into what-ifs now. She needed a distraction, like the death-by-train of Sawyer Kingston.

Back at the apartment, she changed into jeans and a plain black T-shirt. She unpinned her hair, put it in a ponytail, then drove to the campus. After stopping at the bookstore, she sported a new Archer baseball cap, hoping to look ten years younger. She found the same bench near the fraternity house and waited for some sign of Brandon. Finally, the door opened and she caught sight of him leaving with some fraternity brothers. At the parking lot, he split off from the others.

This time she had left her gassed-up car near his Honda, knowing if he drove someplace, she could pursue him. As she followed, her body tingled with the thrill of a possible discovery. It brought an adrenaline rush like no other.

Hoping he wasn't out on a lame errand, like a fraternity beer run, she trailed him several miles. Finally, he stopped at a diner and went in. Should she go inside, too? Wondering if he was meeting someone, she parked facing the doors and waited. They had passed at least two other diners on the way, so he had obviously picked this one on purpose. She drummed her hands on the steering wheel.

Then a redheaded girl appeared from the end of the parking lot and rushed into the diner. She had to be the one from the train, but there was only one way to be sure. Rylie needed to go in, too. It would be a risk, but if she could eavesdrop, it would be worth it. She pulled down the brim of the Archer cap and entered the glass door.

When the hostess moved to seat her in the room on the right, Rylie pointed to the left and slid into the booth directly in front of Brandon and the girl, with her back to them. Brandon sat in the connecting seat behind her. She would miss seeing their facial expressions, but this minimized the chance they would notice her.

While Rylie ordered chocolate chip pancakes and coffee, Brandon said something that she didn't catch. After the waitress left, she leaned into the seat back, straining to listen.

'I can't really sleep,' the girl said.

'It'll all fade. In a year, no one will even be talking about it.'

'I guess.' Ice tinkled in a glass. 'Have you talked to her?'

'I saw her on campus,' Brandon said. 'She's doing better already. Like a weight was lifted.'

'But she can't know,' the girl said.

'No one will ever know, Chloe.'

'What about the reward?' she whispered. 'What if that woman from the train comes forward?'

Rylie sat motionless.

'I doubt she would remember what we even looked like,' Brandon said.

Oh, you have no idea, Rylie thought.

Chloe spoke so quietly Rylie barely made out the words. 'I'd remember her,' she said.

'Me, too,' Brandon said. 'Anyway, they still think it's a suicide. We'll be safe.'

'He deserved it.' Chloe's whisper had grown fierce.

If only I could legally record this.

They stopped speaking for a few minutes. Brandon shuffled in the seat behind her. The waitress delivered Rylie's food, and she looked up to thank her just as Brandon walked by the table. He turned to glance back at Chloe and his gaze passed over Rylie.

She ducked her head too late. A glimmer of recognition flashed in Brandon's eyes. He about-faced, returning to Chloe.

'We need to leave,' he told her.

'What's wrong?'

'Shh! We just need to go.'

Rylie pretended to search through her bag to avoid looking at them as they quickly paid the cashier, then left the diner.

That hadn't gone perfectly, but it wasn't a disaster. They realized she overheard them, which complicated things, and they might wonder why she followed them. She knew Brandon's name and where to find him, which was way more than they knew about her. Still, it would be risky to show up at Archer again. Brandon might be on the lookout for her.

She'd need to focus on the mysterious Chloe.

When she arrived home, she decided to research the photos taken at Kingston's trial after his acquittal was announced. She focused on the many photos of the victim, checking the friends and family surrounding her. Jaynie had three sisters, but none of them was Chloe. She zoomed in on any female under twenty-five that stood near her. Nothing.

Frustrated, she went to sleep. Sunday morning, she fed the cat and listened to the morning train.

Her phone buzzed with a text. It was Denny, thanking her for stopping by the church service.

She hadn't heard from him in so long. *It's the least I could do*, she typed quickly. *So sorry.*

With the phone in her hand, she waited, hoping he would reply and keep the conversation going. She realized too late that she should have asked a question, something he could respond to.

Had it only been yesterday that she saw him? She mentally ran through her short time at the church. Seeing Denny, and his sister, and Aunt Wendy, the traitor. Wendy's flip-flopped loyalties made her smile.

And then it hit her: Loyalties.

Maybe she had Chloe all wrong. She had been looking for Jaynie's connections, but maybe Chloe was a traitor. She went back to the photos, this time focusing on Sawyer and his family. And there she was, identified in the caption as Sawyer's cousin, looking nervous even then.

'Yes!' she said, causing the cat to scurry away.

This was an even better story than Rylie had hoped. Everyone knew Sawyer would have been behind bars if it wasn't for the administrative mistake. Then a secret act of revenge was carried out, not by relatives of the victim, but by two people on the other side, a fraternity brother who may have known more than was ever revealed in court and a relative of the rapist.

Forget a true crime novel. This could be a blockbuster movie.

Brandon and Chloe had pulled it off. Rylie closed her eyes and imagined Sawyer's last night. Chloe drugs his drink and gets him to the train, maybe under the pretense that they were going out for a night in the city. Maybe they even sit in the parking lot and drink while they wait. She gives Sawyer enough to sedate him. Then Brandon meets them there, helps her move his unconscious body to the tracks. They put up a barrier to keep away interfering bystanders, then they drive away knowing justice has been done.

Justice. There had been a hashtag throughout the trial: *#JusticeforJaynie*

Rylie thought of her next steps, the additional facts she would gather. She'd need Chloe's last name, and information about their family dynamics. She'd want to know more about Brandon and Sawyer's relationship, the fraternity brother who was less than loyal. As she made a list of interviews she wanted to conduct, she had the buzz that always came when a story heated up. This would enable her to renew her career, even under a pseudonym. Eventually, if she could gather enough information, Brandon and Chloe would be arrested for murder.

#

On Monday night, Rylie met Barb for a drink at a bar near her apartment. Still in a celebratory mood, she decided to splurge on a chocolate Martini. Barb ordered her usual Chardonnay.

'How did your story turn out that you left me in the lurch for?' Barb asked. 'The big reveal of Sawyer Kingston's identity?'

Rylie flushed, feeling guilty about skipping out on their lunch. 'Great. I have more work to do, but it's promising.'

'I'm glad he's dead,' Barb said. 'And I don't say that lightly. The whole situation, him roaming free, celebrating, and victimizing how many other girls. If it had been my daughter—well, never mind. A lot of Archer mothers will sleep better with him gone.'

Rylie sipped her Martini, but it made her queasy. The drink was too sweet or too strong or maybe both. She switched to water and steered the conversation to Barb's job and her family and the garden that needed planting in her backyard.

'What should we do to celebrate your birthday?' Barb asked. 'The big three-oh. Come over for a barbecue on Saturday?'

Rylie sighed. She was lucky to have Barb as a friend, but that was not how she envisioned celebrating her landmark birthday.

'I'm not sure,' she said. 'The apartment sitting is almost up—'

'You can stay with us!' Barb's usual enthusiasm was magnified by the wine.

'I might—I might move back to DC,' Rylie said, realizing even as she spoke the words that she had to make it happen. 'I miss living there. And I need to try one last time to make things right with Denny. Even if our relationship doesn't work out, it's where I belong.'

'I have a friend in DC. I was waiting to tell you,' Barb said. 'He's looking for someone to write advertising copy. It wouldn't be exactly like your old job, but I can make the introductions if you want.'

'Thanks. Let me think it over, okay? I haven't made any concrete plans yet.'

'Of course.'

Their conversation wound down, and Barb called a car service while Rylie walked the two blocks home. It was nearly midnight, she realized, and she detoured to the train station instead.

Exactly one week later, the parking lot was empty and no sign warned of a fake closure. She wondered if the police had fingerprinted the barricade. Brandon and Chloe had probably wiped it clean, in which case the lack of any fingerprints might be a red flag. If Sawyer had put it there, he wouldn't have bothered to remove his own prints. Had the police checked?

The 12:01 was due any minute. She walked by the locked waiting area and stood near the track until she felt someone come up behind her.

Brandon.

'I thought you might be here,' he said, as casually as if they had bumped into each other in the campus cafeteria. 'Do you live nearby?'

She raised her eyebrows at the presumption that she'd tell a murderer where she lived.

'I didn't see your car,' she said.

'I parked on the other side this time.'

She nodded, surveying the deserted platform where she stood alone with him. She took a step back from the track.

'You figured it all out, didn't you?' he said.

'I don't have any proof.' The train sounded in the distance. Her heart beat so hard she could feel the pulse in her ears. She took another step away.

He noticed her movement and laughed. 'Oh, you have nothing to worry about. Justice for Jaynie was one thing. Hurting an innocent stranger is another.'

'I'm a reporter,' she said.

He exhaled loudly. 'Wow. That's certainly bad luck for us. We knew the risk when we planned this. I mean, when I planned it. Do me a favor. Leave Chloe out of it, okay? It could just have been me here that night. Me and Sawyer.'

The train approached the station.

'Sawyer deserved it,' Brandon said. 'Whatever you decide to do next, please know the truth.' Then he turned and walked away. He was gone by the time the train screeched to a stop in front of her.

#

Rylie didn't sleep well that night. The truth. She had always been after the truth. When she slept with that politician, when she trailed Brandon on campus, when she'd done other things she wasn't necessarily proud of, truth and justice remained sacrosanct.

Now Sawyer Kingston was dead. Maybe he deserved it. Maybe people also deserved to know what really happened that night, even if it landed Brandon and Chloe in jail.

Tuesday morning, she called Barb. 'Are you friends with anyone in the Haverfeld police department? Or New Jersey Transit? I need to speak to someone about the Sawyer Kingston suicide.'

'The police chief is an old friend.'

Rylie laughed. 'Of course he is, Barb. You're friends with everyone. Can you set something up for today?'

A few hours later Rylie was in the police station, pretending that she was researching a special report on train suicides. But he didn't have much information that she hadn't already gleaned from the local news.

'What about the barricade sign?' she asked.

'That was key,' he said.

She leaned forward. 'It was?'

'Yes, it showed his planning and intent to die. He didn't just fall onto the track in a drugged stupor. He made sure no one else would come by and stop him.'

The police chief closed his folder as if the matter of Kingston's death was firmly settled in his mind.

'Thanks for your time,' Rylie said.

She drove back to the train and sat in her car for a long time, considering. Should Brandon and Chloe be held responsible for what they'd done? Who was she to decide? If she hadn't been at the station that night, would the world be any worse off, not knowing about Brandon and Chloe's actions? Truth and justice had always been entwined in her mind. But maybe in this situation, they weren't the same thing. Maybe this time, the truth should remain hidden.

She drove to campus and found Brandon's parked SUV. After writing him a note, she left it on his windshield.

#JusticeforJaynie

Then she returned to the apartment and packed for home.

KEEP YOUR FRIENDS CLOSE
Maggie King

'*Keep your friends close, but your enemies closer*—I never knew that quote came from *The Godfather*.' Meryl McKinney's words mingled with the chatter of the coffee shop as she held up a tattered paperback copy of the famous tome by Mario Puzo. 'Did you know that, Kat?'

'Nope. Never read *The Godfather*. Or saw the movie.' Kat Berenger rested her blue eyes on Meryl. 'Now, about my proposal—do we have a deal?' Kat and Meryl had chosen a table by a window in Zorro's, a trendy spot in Richmond, Virginia's historic Fan District.

'Oh, absolutely! I'll do anything to catch the scumbag who killed my best friend.' Meryl's voice caught and she took a deep breath.

'And I intend to clear Kenny of suspicion. My baby brother would never have killed his wife.' Kat tossed back her blond curls, setting her earrings jingling.

The two women sealed the deal with a handshake. Kat couldn't help noticing the difference between her hands and Meryl's. While Kat decorated each finger with a ring, and her black lacquered nails sported leopard tips, Meryl, nails bitten to the quick, wore no rings.

Five days before, Vicki Berenger's husband had come home from a weeklong trip and couldn't find his wife. Kenny had the fright of his life when he opened the shower door and found her—dead. Forensics found that Vicki's shampoo contained a lethal mixture of DMSO and strychnine. Since that day, Kenny Berenger found himself in the crosshairs of the Richmond Police Department.

'They always suspect the spouse, don't they?' Meryl asked.

Kat nodded as customers came and went, ordering their oversized coffees and pastries to go.

Meryl went on. 'What's DMSO, anyway?'

'A supplement. People use it for arthritis. Some of my clients get it at the health food store.' Kat was a personal trainer at Max's gym. 'DMSO opens up your pores and allows your skin to absorb other chemicals. Like strychnine.'

'And where would someone get strychnine?'

'It's commonly used in rat poison.'

Meryl closed her eyes, perhaps hoping to block the images her mind conjured.

'First things first,' Kat said. 'Let's get some coffee. Then we can plan our strategy for putting Vicki's killer behind bars.'

'My treat.' When Kat started to protest, Meryl stood and held up a hand. 'You're being so kind and supportive. I'm glad you suggested teaming up to solve Vicki's murder. Running into you yesterday at Kenny's was the best thing that could have happened to me.'

'I've been spending a lot of time with Kenny. He stayed with me until the police released the crime scene. By the way, he and I loved the corn casserole you brought.'

'Thanks. I'm just dreading the funeral tomorrow.' Meryl's voice caught again. 'Well, what can I get you?'

'Just a skinny latte. I had breakfast at home.'

As Meryl walked up to the counter, Kat thought that the woman looked like she'd fallen out of bed five minutes before—and had probably spent the night tossing and turning. Tangled, greasy strands of dark hair brushed her shoulders. She wore a wrinkled cotton blouse, capris, and flip-flops worn down at the heels. Hard to believe that Meryl had recently turned forty-five. She looked much older.

Zorro prepared its coffee in a large roaster that took pride of place by the front window. Kat looked up at the stamped ceiling and down at the original wood floor, now scuffed and worn. Banners from Southern colleges—University of Richmond, College of William and Mary, Virginia Tech, and Virginia Commonwealth University among them—covered the walls, along with relics of the past, such as a framed ad for vanilla milkshakes at ten cents. Bookcases held used books. Plants that looked wilted in the soaring heat of a Virginia summer lined window ledges.

Kat glanced at the few people sitting nearby. A stern-looking man with a military bearing was reading a copy of the *Richmond Times-*

Dispatch. A woman with blue-tinted black hair and oversized red-framed glasses moved to a beat only she could hear through her earbuds. A man of about thirty-five sported a rumpled tee shirt and a baseball cap promoting the Richmond Flying Squirrels, a minor league baseball team. He winked at Kat. She winked back. Despite being fifty something, Kat still enjoyed flirting with men.

As Meryl turned from the counter, Kat got up to help her carry the coffee and a strawberry scone. At the table, Meryl split the scone with a knife and offered half to Kat.

'I lost my job on Monday,' Meryl said.

'Oh, no. You lost a dear friend *and* your job? All in the same week?'

Meryl nodded, looking glum. 'Yeah. Downsizing. Or so they say. I need to get a job fast. I have so many expenses. I had to take a second job a while back, but it doesn't pay well.'

'Where's that?'

'Oh, um—Burger King.'

Kat raised her eyebrows, noting Meryl's hesitation. Aloud, she said, 'What did you do at the job you lost? Where was it?'

'The Heller Corporation. It's an association management firm downtown. And I—um, I did pretty much everything.' Meryl smiled, showing the gap between her two front teeth. 'I answered phones, filed, prepared bank deposits, helped the CEO and the membership specialist. I was there for six years.'

Kat took a sip of her latte. 'So you did everything, huh? And you said they're downsizing?'

'Right.'

'And after you were there for six years.' Kat shook her head. 'That's so unfair. These companies have no loyalty anymore.'

After a moment's pause, Kat said, 'Now let's talk strategy for nailing Vicki's killer. I figure that between the two of us, we know everyone Vicki knew. I'm especially interested in the women in your book group. Hopefully they'll be at the funeral tomorrow, and you can question them afterwards at the lunch.'

'How do I question them? I can't just go, "By the way, did you kill Vicki?"'

Vicki had been Kat's sister-in-law for three years. 'No, you have to be subtle. Cagey. You know these women. And you'd known

Vicki since when? Kindergarten?' When Meryl nodded, Kat added, 'I never really knew her. She and Kenny no sooner met than they married.'

'I told her not to rush into marriage. But she wouldn't listen.'

Kat thought she heard an accusing tone in Meryl's words. Did the woman think that if Vicki had held off on marrying Kenny, she'd still be alive?

Ignoring Meryl's subtext, Kat said, 'Back to your book group—you all met last Thursday at Vicki's house and the very next day Vicki is dead. One of them either did it or might know something.'

Meryl looked doubtful. 'Maybe we need to leave this to the police.'

'The police are laser-focused on Kenny. A retired homicide detective from the Richmond Police Department lives next door to me and stays in close touch with his former colleagues. He won't tell me much—doesn't want to obstruct the investigation—but he does throw me tidbits. I probably shouldn't repeat what he says'—Kat lowered her voice and leaned forward—'but Vicki was depositing three thousand bucks a month into her son's college fund. In cash.'

'You're kidding.'

'Where would she get that kind of money? She wasn't even working, she was getting her MBA.'

Meryl looked blank. 'From Kenny?'

'But why cash?'

Meryl's eyes filled with tears. 'I shouldn't say this—' she trailed off.

'Of course, you should say it!' Kat said.

A young woman with a froth of pink hair and sleeves of tattoos sat in an overstuffed chair, a book in one hand and a yellow highlighter in the other. She turned, frowning, and said, 'Please keep it down.'

Kat glared at the woman, but dropped her voice before saying to Meryl, 'We want to find Vicki's killer and anything you know could help.'

'Okay, *okay*.' Meryl paused for a moment to collect herself. 'When Vicki was in college, she—she was a hooker for a while, and then later she switched to phone sex. Maybe she started doing *that* again.'

'But why would she?'

'She made good money at it. And she wanted to send her son to a good school for pre-med.'

'Kenny makes good money,' Kat said. 'He'd be glad to help out.'

'She didn't want Kenny to feel obligated to send her son to school. She wanted her ex to do it, but he wouldn't come through. So she told Kenny that her father had set up a fund for his grandson.'

Kat didn't respond. Instead she slanted a look at Meryl. 'That explains the money, but not the murder. Do you think someone from the book group killed Vicki?'

'Well, rumor has it that Tina Wood was having an affair with Kenny. So maybe she did it.'

'If they were having an affair, she definitely had a motive. But she has a hell of a nerve going to their house and socializing with Vicki.'

'Yes, well—' Meryl spread her hands.

'Did Tina use the bathroom the other night? If so, she had an opportunity to doctor the shampoo.'

'I have no idea. I'm pretty sure we all used the facilities at least once. It's not the kind of thing you really notice.' Tears spilled down Meryl's cheeks.

'Okay, take a minute.' Kat pressed a tissue into Meryl's hand. 'I know this is very upsetting.'

'But what about—' Meryl trailed off, clearly uncomfortable. 'What about Kenny?'

Kat sighed. 'What *about* Kenny? He didn't do it. He was out of town on business all last week and didn't get home until Friday, when he found Vicki. And he loved her.'

'But he was having an affair!'

'You said that was a rumor.'

'He could have added the poison to the shampoo before he went out of town.'

Kat sighed again. 'Do you know how often Vicki washed her hair?'

Meryl looked startled at Kat's unexpected question. 'Every other day. I think.'

'Okay, let's say that Kenny did add the poison before he went out of town. He left on a Sunday, right?'

Meryl nodded.

'That means Vicki would have used that shampoo at least twice, maybe three times, before Friday. So why wasn't she poisoned earlier in the week?'

'She said she had her hair cut and shampooed by her stylist last week. Plus she alternated shampoos a lot.'

Meaning that Kenny could indeed have managed to switch shampoo bottles before leaving for his trip. Kat became even more determined to clear her brother.

'Okay.' Kat held up her hand. 'Let's consider the method the killer used: DMSO mixed with strychnine.'

'You said earlier that someone could get DMSO at the health food store. And that strychnine is in rat poison.' When Kat nodded, Meryl continued. 'So, we just have to find someone with a rat problem who also had a motive to kill Vicki.'

Kat laughed ruefully. 'From what my cop friend tells me, rat problems in the city of Richmond are more common than you might realize.'

'I imagine an Internet search would tell anyone how to mix DMSO with strychnine.'

'You're right. But Internet search histories can be traced.'

'The killer read it in a book, maybe? Some author used the same method?'

'That's what I've been thinking,' Kat said. 'Do you know Hazel Rose?'

'No.'

'Hazel's a romance writer, but she's started writing mysteries. She's also something of an amateur sleuth. She's on a trip right now or else she'd be solving this mystery. She told me about a book on poisons that she uses for reference. The Richmond Public Library has a copy of the book.'

'Really?'

Kat sipped her coffee. 'I went to the library and found the book. I asked the librarian about mysteries featuring poison and she suggested several, including *An Unbecoming Death*, which has a scene that was identical to how Vicki died.'

'So it looks like the killer got the idea from that story.' Meryl looked thoughtful as she chewed her scone. 'The book group members all read mysteries.'

'The librarian said that someone else had recently requested the same book. She wouldn't tell me who. Of course, she probably doesn't even know. But if we showed her a picture of the women in your book group—' Kat looked at Meryl. 'What do you think of that idea?'

Meryl shoved a too-big piece of scone in her mouth and swallowed the food with the help of her coffee. 'I really don't feel comfortable questioning people who could be killers.'

'Okay. Let's ask ourselves which of these women had a motive. Besides Tina Wood allegedly having an affair with Kenny.'

'I don't know. We all went to school together. Vicki stole Carol Sarris's boyfriend in senior year.'

'That was almost thirty years ago. You think Carol would kill Vicki now?' Kat sounded doubtful.

'No. Just saying.'

'Did any of the folks in your group have rat problems? Not that one has to actually have a rat problem to get rat poison, but it's a place to start.'

Meryl chewed one of her well-chewed nails. 'You said lots of people in the city have rat problems. Carol Sarris lives in Richmond.'

'There you go. You can have a heart-to-heart with Carol tomorrow.' Kat ignored Meryl's alarmed expression. 'You mentioned that Vicki was a phone sex operator. So maybe she blackmailed one of her clients.'

Meryl's face lit up with hope. 'I bet that's what it was.'

'Don't get all excited. If it was one of her clients, he—or she— would have to have been in Vicki's house and used the bathroom.' Kat drained her latte. 'It's pretty unlikely that Vicki would ply her trade as a sex worker in her home. Assuming she even was a sex worker.'

'Yeah. I guess.' Meryl looked distressed at such a promising possibility coming to naught.

'But blackmail? That's an interesting possibility.' Kat gave Meryl a long look. 'How about this scenario: Vicki found out that her dearest friend, her lifelong friend, was embezzling funds from her employer.'

The little color in Meryl's face drained. 'Embezzling? I never heard Vicki mention anyone embezzling.'

'When you said you did "everything" for the Heller Corporation, did that include bookkeeping?'

'Yeah, so—why are you asking?'

Kat leaned forward. 'I heard one hundred thousand dollars is missing from Heller's general fund.'

'Who told you this? Your cop buddy?'

'The Heller Corporation's Membership Specialist also belongs to Max's Gym. According to her, you were fired for embezzling.'

'That's Patty Oates. And she is lying.'

'I know your mom has a lot of medical problems. I know you took a second job at a fast food restaurant for the extra money. I also know the restaurant is having a problem with rats.'

'You read too many mysteries. Besides, Burger King isn't having any such problem.'

'Did Vicki figure out you were stealing? Was she blackmailing you?'

Meryl said nothing, folding her arms as her gaze shot daggers at Kat.

'Remember when I said that the librarian said someone else had recently requested *An Unbecoming Death*?'

Meryl still didn't respond. She sat, looking mutinous.

'She picked you out of a Facebook lineup.'

Meryl rolled her eyes. 'Oh, please.'

'And the fast food place where you work is C.J.'s, not Burger King.' Kat swiped at the screen on her phone and read, 'Former and current employees claim there is a rodent infestation at C.J.'s, a popular fast food restaurant in Richmond.'

'Okay, maybe C.J.'s *had* a problem. But that happened way before I started there.'

'But they probably still had the poison stashed away.'

Tears filled Meryl's eyes and streamed down her face. 'My best friend was bleeding me dry all so she could send her idiot son to an expensive pre-med program. I pity the poor people who end up being his patients.'

Kat sat back, but said nothing.

'It all started when I borrowed a small amount from Heller so my mom's insurance wouldn't cancel. I was going to pay it back. I confessed this to Vicki one night when we drank too much wine. She immediately started blackmailing me and I had to keep embezzling to pay her. A few weeks ago she upped her fee from three thousand to thirty-five hundred. I couldn't do it. My mom has a lot of medical expenses, her insurance premiums skyrocketed, and my brother cares more about gambling than our mother. I realized Vicki was never, *ever*, going to stop.'

'Unless you stopped her.'

Meryl sighed. 'Yes. I hate computers and the library had all the information I needed to poison Vicki.'

'You did get the poisoning idea from *An Unbecoming Death*?'

Narrowing her eyes, Meryl said, 'Yes.'

Kat was sure the police would find Meryl's prints on the book. Leveling her gaze at Meryl, she asked, 'So how did you do it?'

'Like you said, I stole some rat poison from work, found DMSO at a health food store, and a bottle of Vicki's favorite shampoo from another store. I only had to dump some of the shampoo out and add the other ingredients to the bottle. Then at book group I excused myself to go to the bathroom and switched the bottles. Child's play. Too bad I didn't get to see the gory results.' The look of pure hatred on Meryl's face alarmed Kat.

Kat tapped the cover of *The Godfather*. '"Keep your friends close, and your enemies closer?"'

'Meryl McKinney, I'm arresting you for—' The man in the Flying Squirrels cap and rumpled tee shirt flashed his Richmond Police Department badge and finished reading Meryl her Miranda rights. The woman with the blue-tinted hair and oversized red-framed glasses approached and handcuffed a shrieking, cursing Meryl.

As Detective Thomas Fischella and his partner, Detective Stephanie Garcia, led Meryl—now hurling death threats at Kat—away, Zorro's customers and employees froze in their places, not speaking, not moving, as if in a tableau.

Gathering her purse, Kat walked out into a steamy July day. As she started her Mustang and drove toward police headquarters to give her statement, she muttered, 'Can't wait to get this frigging wire off.'

TOO MANY SHERLOCKS
Paulene Turner

Chapter One

As the sometime-chronicler of the exploits of the great detective, Sherlock Holmes, I have been fortunate to witness the workings of his extraordinary mind on many occasions. Sometimes, when considering a case, he would go as still as a corpse, as he turned facts over in his mind. At others, he was a whirlwind, running here and there with no need for rest, nor sustenance, in pursuit of answers that had eluded the police. However, one of his most intriguing adventures began while he was mysteriously absent and I was called upon to start the investigation without him.

During the course of this baffling case—which took us to the heights and depths of London society—I became better acquainted with a most singular individual, among whose achievements I count the stirring of tender feelings within the great detective himself. Holmes loudly declaimed any connection with feelings or matters relating to the human heart. Except when it involved her. The individual I speak of is known in London circles as Irene Adler. Though Sherlock refers to her, simply, as The Woman.

I had met Miss Adler a few times when she called upon Holmes at our shared residence at 221B Baker Street. Although, those encounters were brief, I was struck by the brightness of her eye, the elegance of her carriage, and a general air of astuteness about her. Often, I imagined I saw a smile hiding at the corner of her mouth, as if she were enjoying some secret amusement, the details of which she alone knew.

But on this November evening, a deeper and more personal acquaintance between us was about to begin.

At the time, Sherlock was nowhere to be found and, as the hour grew late, our tickets for the evening's performance of *Moll Flanders* at the Theatre Royal lay, unclaimed, on the dining table.

'Mrs Hudson, have you any idea where Sherlock is?' I enquired, as our landlady entered carrying the mail and the evening newspaper. 'I've not seen him in two days and we have a theatre engagement tonight.'

'He's a bit large to be mislaid, Doctor,' Mrs Hudson said, 'so I can only assume he's been detained on some business or other and has thoughtlessly forgotten your engagement.'

Holmes could be thoughtless in many ways, I knew. He thought little or not at all of the comfort of those around him, when practising his violin late at night or conducting science experiments in our shared living room. Often, in the midst of a problem, he was thoughtless of his own need for food, drink and sleep. But never before had he forgotten a social arrangement with me, one which offered the possibility of observing London's glittering society at close quarters—of benefit in his role as consulting detective—while providing him an opportunity to bask in the warmth of an admiring public—sating his deep need to show off.

It was especially odd he would forget a performance which starred Irene Adler, whom he considered the queen of her sex.

'Should we be worried, Doctor?' Mrs Hudson asked.

'I shouldn't think so,' said I, more blithely than I felt.

'Come to think of it,' Mrs Hudson continued, her forehead trenched with concern, 'I haven't seen him since he went out looking very spiffy two nights ago. Had his hair combed and all. And there was a sweetness in the air around him. If it had been spring, I'd have thought it was the scent of a flower drifting on the breeze. Only no flowers worth their stalks are blooming in this freezing weather. So I wondered, could he have sprinkled floral water upon himself?'

'Highly improbable!' I assured her, before wishing her a good night and asking her to send Sherlock to the theatre if he returned home presently.

#

Night was closing in, its icy fingers taunting exposed wrists, ankles and aching joints. Grey clouds scuttled across the inky sky like vermin in a drain as the cacophony of street life rose—the clatter of carriage wheels on the rutted road, the squeals of children and the deep-throated cries of newspaper-sellers spruiking their wares.

A man in a top hat dashing between carriages, flinched as a hansom driver cracked his whip over a horse's flank. A high-pitched woman's scream told of a cut purse plying his trade nearby.

Just an ordinary night in London town.

I hunched beneath my lapels. Smoke from charcoal burning in a brazier almost covered the scent of waste—horse and human—pervading the streets as I made my way on foot to the theatre.

Before I'd gone far, a small boy appeared on the footpath before me. His legs were like matchsticks with dirt so ingrained upon his face as to resemble a birthmark.

'Please Doctor—sir,' he pleaded, wringing his bony hands. 'Have you got any jobs for me? Only Mr Holmes is nowhere about, and I've the devil of a hunger gnawin' at me belly.'

I recognised the boy. He was one of Sherlock's young hounds, a group of street children, marked by no one, observing everyone. He paid them regularly for information, and, I suspected, for benevolent reasons to which he would never own.

'I am wondering where Mr Holmes might be, myself,' I said, crouching to the child's level. 'If you would be so kind as to make enquiries on my behalf...?' I handed him a clutch of coins.

The boy's brown eyes were as round as buttons upon a winter coat. 'Don't worry, Doc, I'll find him!' He turned to go.

'Wait! Boy! What's your name?'

'My mother, who laid down for her final rest when I was but crawlin', called me Dante.'

'Dante!' I repeated, amazed one as humble as he would possess such an august appellation. 'Well, Dante. I trust we'll meet again.'

'You can count your coin on it, doc!'

He grinned and darted off along the street, to shouts of 'Oi, watch it, you little runt!'

On my way to the theatre, I detoured via Scotland Yard, and made enquiries after Inspector Lestrade. I'd encountered the officer several times during my adventures with Holmes and had come to regard him as a friend. I wanted to invite him to the show to make use of Holmes's unclaimed ticket.

But Lestrade had been called away on urgent detective business, the desk sergeant said. I left him a note, and continued to the theatre.

Squeezing past theatre-goers spilling out onto the pavement, I moved into the reception room, where men in dress coats and women with rich velvet gowns, shaped over corsets of whalebone, chatted excitedly before curtain's rise. Light from wall sconces flickered on their faces, and glanced off shiny buttons and adornments.

I took a moment to scan the foyer for Holmes—to no avail. In casting about, though, several pairs of eyes met mine, with recognition. An older woman in a silver shawl mouthed 'Dr Watson' to her companion; I read it as clearly as a headline in *The Times*. Some of Holmes's fame was, regrettably, flowing onto me. Eager to escape further glances, I moved along the hall and into the theatre.

The three Dress Circles rose up like layers of a wedding cake in gold and cream. I was seated in the Stalls, which were full but for Holmes's empty place beside me.

All my troubles receded as the lights came up and Irene Adler took the stage, in the story of Moll Flanders, a woman making her way through life on nothing but cunning and beauty. Though Moll committed wicked acts along the way, Miss Adler's performance evoked sympathy for her character, highlighting how few choices were permitted to a woman, alone, in a heartless society. Indeed, she was so convincing in her role, I forgot at times I was watching a play. It made me wonder about Irene Adler's personal history—how it compared with the eponymous Moll's, struggling through life with no man's protection.

I fancied I saw Irene glance over, once or twice, at the empty seat beside me, and a shadow of disappointment cross her face.

#

After the show, I made my way backstage to see Irene Adler.

The dressing room corridor boomed with the laughter of performers now at ease. I passed rooms where actors who had played heinous villains onstage had changed into street wear, and appeared as harmless and likeable as the next person. I marvelled at the artifice of the theatre.

Halfway along the corridor, a dozen casts of heads stood upon shelves, bearing wigs, facial hair, and all manner of facial augmentations—noses, chins and cheeks. I touched a false chin. It was warm and spongy in texture but looked so like skin. I was in awe.

'Dr Watson!' Miss Adler's voice summoned me from a doorway further along. 'What a pleasure to see you!' She gestured me into her dressing room.

Hers was larger than most others I'd seen, with a mirror at the centre and lights dotted around it. Pots of makeup and brushes lay upon a table nearby. Bunches of flowers and impressive floral arrangements occupied a portion of the room. Cards peeking out of the bunches revealed they were from Count so-and-so, and Lord such-and-such. Unsurprisingly, this striking and talented woman had a host of admirers, many from the highest tiers of society.

A bottle of French champagne sat unopened in a silver ice bucket. Most of the ice had turned to water but for one recalcitrant cube, like an iceberg floating in northern seas.

'Are you alone, then?' Irene asked. 'I thought I saw an empty seat where Sherlock was meant to be?'

'He was unable to attend, I'm afraid.'

'Cad!' said Irene, still smiling. She'd changed out of her stage costume into a beige and navy dress. Her long dark hair flowed freely, her emerald eyes were as piercing as a cat's, and as mysterious. 'I'm so glad you, at least, could come, Doctor,' she effused.

'I wouldn't miss it. And the pleasure was all mine.'

'So what excuse does the great detective offer for his absence?' Nothing about her delivery conveyed even the slightest annoyance.

'I can only assume he is engaged on some very important business. Nothing less would keep him from attending.'

'Assume?' she said. 'Do you not know where he is?'

'No. He has disappeared before without sending word but...'

'You're worried about him.' She reached for the champagne. Deftly, she worked the cork open and filled two glasses, handing one to me. As the golden liquid fizzed in the glass, I explained that

Holmes had not been seen for two days. Recalling Mrs Hudson's observations about the floral scent in the air at the time, I paused. 'You were not engaged to meet him, were you? Our housekeeper noted he had been quite particular about his toilet, which was not his habit.'

Irene sipped her drink slowly. 'We had arranged to meet for supper in the Café Royal. I am sorry to say, Mr Holmes did not keep the appointment.'

'You mean—he stood you up?'

She nodded, all humour gone. 'At the time, I thought he was just being Sherlock. Rude, careless of my feelings.'

'Holmes is careless of the feelings of most people, regardless of rank,' I said, 'but never of yours, Miss Adler. If he did not keep his engagement with you, and did not send word to explain his absence...?'

Irene shook her head.

'That is cause for concern.' As I spoke the words, I felt them to be true.

Irene's smooth brow creased. She opened her mouth to reply, as a young woman, barely more than sixteen, with rosy cheeks in a pale face, burst into the room, erupting with a jumble of words delivered so quickly they all ran together.

'Slow down, Rachel. And try again,' Irene coaxed.

'There's a gentleman says you're expectin' him and begs to know what's keeping you,' said Rachel. 'He also says he can get any actress he wants in London and doesn't have to wait for a tardy one.' The girl looked steadfastly at her hands as she spoke the last. 'Beggin' your pardon, Miss.'

'Nothing to pardon, Rachel.'

I popped up like a jack-in-the box. 'I will happily send this rude gentleman packing. And explain he does not need to speak to you, or any woman, like that.'

'No need, Doctor,' Irene said, barely ruffled. 'I can handle him.'

I took that as my cue to leave. 'Then I won't keep you any longer, Miss Adler. I just wanted to thank you for the ticket and congratulate you on a wonderful show.'

'We will speak about this business with Sherlock further,' she said. 'I will call at 221B Baker street at ten o'clock tomorrow morning, if that suits.'

I could have told her not to trouble herself. Instead, I nodded agreement. Something was afoot with Sherlock, I could feel it. Speaking to this intelligent woman might shed some light on the situation or at the least quell the fear rising within me like a river in flood. And, if by some chance he was back home by the morning, well, he could explain the empty seat to her himself.

'And, Doctor?' she called me back. 'Please call me, Irene.'

Chapter Two

My dreams were filled with shadowy figures pursuing me and Sherlock calling my name from somewhere I could not find him. I awoke to Mrs Hudson shouting outside my door. 'Sorry to wake you, Doctor, but Inspector Lestrade is here!'

I dressed quickly and headed downstairs to find Lestrade pacing, thumbs in his belt hooks, his habitual frown accentuating his ferret-like features. 'Ah, Watson, there you are,' he exclaimed. 'I heard you'd called into the station last night. How was the show? From all reports, Miss Adler is as pretty as a plum pudding with custard.'

'Indeed she is. And talented too.'

We conversed for a few minutes about the theatre before he interjected. 'I had the shock of me life last night!' He clapped his hand to his chest. 'We pulled a cadaver out of an opium den in town and I swear it looked just like Holmes. Tall, beaky, thinning on top.'

'And?' My heart stopped beating as I awaited the answer.

'Wasn't him.'

'Are you sure? Sometimes, a stint of indulgence can leave one's features in a flaccid state.'

'Gave him a good going over myself,' said the detective. 'It wasn't pretty. But, rest assured, it wasn't our mutual friend.'

That was a great relief. 'Was the man's death due to an overdose?'

'That's the strange part,' Lestrade said, his eyebrows meeting in a caterpillar line of concern. 'His throat had been crushed. There were red marks around here.' He indicated the front of his neck. 'Some powerful hands had a really good squeeze, and the poor devil was too drugged up to resist. I tell you, I wouldn't want to meet the man on the ends of those hands.' He made a whistling noise.

Mrs Hudson, mounting the stairs with tea and toast for me, offered her own opinion. 'Well, you know what they say—big hands, big—?' She raised her eyebrows and cackled like a crone.

The inspector and I shook our heads at the woman and I was about to respond when Irene Adler ascended the stairs, in dark attire wearing a hat with a veil over her face.

'Good morning, Doctor. Inspector.'

'A pleasure, Miss Adler,' said Lestrade.

'I was hoping Sherlock might have returned overnight. Have we any word from him?'

I shook my head.

'Well, I wonder if we can discover something about his movements from an inspection of his living room,' she said.

As her eyes roamed the room, Lestrade raised his eyebrows at me. The pair of us had tried this before on a different case and had failed quite spectacularly.

'I'll start with the obvious,' said Irene, removing her hat. 'The place has been turned over by an intruder.'

I frowned. 'What? No, Holmes is just not a tidy man.'

Miss Adler looked askance at me. 'But the leavings of his pipe are scattered over the seat and floor in such a random pattern as to suggest it was cast aside carelessly.' She knelt and looked under the sofa, emerging with Sherlock's pipe.

'By Jove, you're right!' I asserted. As slovenly as my friend's habits were, he would never discard his instrument in such a cavalier fashion.

'I didn't do a thorough examination of the scene when I arrived,' Lestrade mumbled, 'or I might have concluded the same.'

Someone had been here. But when? Was it last night while I was at the theatre? Or while I slept in the next room?

Irene moved to a study of Sherlock's mail, stacked neatly on the table.

'You can't tell me an intruder's been through them,' Lestrade said. 'That pile of letters is neater than my wife's recipe cards. And no one dares touch those, especially not the recipe for Grandma's eel pie.'

'Indeed,' said Miss Adler. 'The pile is neat. Which in itself is interesting, considering Dr Watson's assertion that Sherlock is an untidy man.

'See how all the letters are open and face down on the desk, with the oldest on top?' she said. 'Usually, the most recent piece of mail sits on top, face upwards. Which would imply someone has been through these letters methodically, starting from the most recent, turning each one over as they read it, before moving to the next. In so doing, they inverted the order and reversed the documents.'

I could see she was right. It was obvious when you thought about it.

'Did they find anything, do you think?' I asked.

Irene shook her head. 'If they had, they would have ceased looking; the rest of the pile would have been left as it was. As the entire pile has been sifted, we can assume they searched the lot and found nothing. Oh, and they're left-handed.'

Lestrade looked quizzically at me.

'Because the pile is sitting so far to the left of the desk,' Irene added.

I imagined a left-hander's action as they perused the pile and realised she was correct again. Meanwhile, Lestrade nodded sagely as if Blind Freddy and all his sightless siblings could have seen that.

Her attention moved to a bulletin board by the bookcase, on which several letters and papers were pinned. Examining each paper in turn, she stopped on an empty space in the middle. 'What was there, before? I see the mark of a drawing pin, recently removed. Something has been taken, Dr Watson. Do you know what it was?'

'I think it was a likeness of Holmes, drawn by a grateful client,' I said.

'So whoever came here went away with Holmes's likeness. Clearly, they're looking for him, and they've never met him before,' she concluded.

As she trawled through the test tubes on Sherlock's work bench, raising each one to the light, the better to assess it, Lestrade scratched his head. 'Madam, can I ask, are you related to Holmes? His long-lost sister, aunt twice removed on his father's side?'

Ignoring the inspector's question, Irene focused on a collection of magnification devices in the top drawer. 'Holmes has a loupe here,' she said matter-of-factly. Picking up a handful of stones from a bowl on the desktop, she placed a small tubular glass to her eye and squinted closely at them. 'The most powerful one I've ever seen.'

'A loupe?' Lestrade pressed it to his face and, as he looked around the room, his magnified bloodshot eyeball was disturbing to behold.

'It's an instrument to determine the quality of a gemstone, such as a ruby or diamond,' Irene explained. 'Mr Holmes seems to be acquiring knowledge in the lead-up to inspecting a gem.'

She paced back and forth, lips twisting to the side in thought. 'As it is Sherlock we are talking about,' she said, 'it will be no ordinary gem, but one quite extraordinary. Gentleman, I'm thinking he could be involved with the recently discovered Callaghan diamond. Have you heard of it?'

Lestrade and I shook our heads in unison.

'It is said to be the world's most valuable diamond. Soon to be added to the Queen's Crown Collection.'

The inspector lowered the glass now, but his eye—both eyes—remained enlarged with awe as Irene Adler explained that her contacts in high places had spoken of a diamond, from South Africa, which was to be re-set into the royal sceptre the next day.

'Not only is the jewel valuable in monetary terms,' Miss Adler expounded, 'but the prestige that would go to Britain, as the caretaker of this prize, would be significant. Mr Holmes's possession of the loupe and the timing of his mysterious absence would suggest the two are related. Though, of course, I'm just speculating.'

The officer and I stood, dumbstruck, at this astonishing news and the ease at which she'd arrived at it.

'I'm sure, Inspector, if you'd had the information as I had,' Irene said, 'you would have reached the same conclusion and more quickly.' Again, I saw a suggestion of humour about her lips.

'Indeed,' Lestrade agreed. 'So that's what Sherlock's up to then? Very good.'

But was it very good? I wasn't so sure.

'Won't there be people from foreign powers across the water keen to get hold of such a prestigious jewel and symbol of power for their own elevation?' I asked.

'Indeed, Doctor Watson, I believe you're right,' Irene replied. 'Possession of the jewel will draw considerable jeopardy to its custodian. Perhaps that's why our friend has disappeared without word. I suspect he's in hiding. And there may well be much to hide from.'

'Holmes in hiding?' said Lestrade, his right eyebrow askew. 'Pish and nonsense. The man is not one to hide from anything.'

I was pleased with Lestrade in that moment. 'He's right,' I said.

'Well, perhaps in this, his consideration for England has overridden his ego,' Irene offered.

'That, indeed, is hard to believe,' I said.

'So, let's assume the intruder was looking for the diamond, or some clue as to Holmes's whereabouts,' Miss Adler said. 'Did he find it, I wonder? The action with the pipe would suggest otherwise. It has been my observation that some men, when thwarted in their aims, throw or smash something to relieve their anger. Usually something belonging to the person they view as responsible for frustrating their ambitions.'

A tightness around Irene's mouth led me to believe she'd had personal experience of such petulance.

'In this case,' she continued, 'the intruder flung the pipe in a gesture of pique. Which is good news for us. For it suggests Holmes is still at large. And if he is, and he's in hiding, for the reasons we have surmised, you'll have no need to fear for him, Doctor. Rest assured, he will have the protection of Her Majesty's best agents.'

It was reassuring to hear her conclusions. 'But can they protect him from himself,' I said, 'and his need to outsmart his protectors and make fools of them?'

'We can only hope.'

Irene set about examining the rest of the room, as Lestrade and I watched. After a fifteen-minute surveillance of our shared apartments, she concluded: 'The man you are looking for is large—head and shoulders above the rest—with red hair, a limp on his left side and a scar on his right cheek. He is German by nationality, with a habit of gambling...and he likes gardening in his spare time.'

If Lestrade and I were wide-eyed before, our eyes were now moons resting upon our cheeks.

'How on Earth have you arrived at that conclusion?' the officer burst forth.

'Firstly, footprints in the fallen ash from Sherlock's pipe allow me to determine the length of our intruder's stride—here one step, there another—which permits a guess at his height. See how the footstep on one side is more pronounced than on the other, suggesting a limp.' Lestrade followed the tobacco trail with his magnifying glass.

'The pattern of the ash suggests the pipe was thrown in the fashion of a dice, like so, under-arm, rather than over-arm like a cricket ball. Perhaps from a habit of gambling.

'And the red hair'—we watched her move to the sofa cushion and carefully lift off a single hair, which she passed to Lestrade—'was a stroke of luck.'

'You said he was German, and a gardener?' I prompted, feeling like a dog awaiting scraps at a banquet table.

'A footprint found in the hallway is from a particular style of a German brogue. Although a popular import among English gentleman some years ago, it has since fallen from the must-have fashion list. I conclude, therefore, it was likely worn by a native of that country, one not so well-off that he could change his shoes each season according to fashion's dictates.'

The long list of assumptions she'd arrived at so easily gave the detective a gloomy aspect. 'And the gardening hobby?' he enquired, dispiritedly.

Irene produced a jagged thumbnail, the colour of ear wax with dirt lining its edge. 'I found this behind the sofa cushions, where it must have torn off during his search. The crescent pattern of dirt beneath the nail is suggestive of someone who habitually has has hands in the soil.'

'Could he be a gravedigger?' Lestrade offered, momentarily brightening. 'Or a grave robber, perhaps?'

'Clever, Inspector,' Irene smiled broadly. 'He might well have been. However, as those activities usually involve a spade rather than clawing at the earth with fingernails, he was probably also an avid planter.'

'And the scar?' I said.

'On his right cheek, shaped like a sickle.'

'How could you possibly deduce that?' I asked.

'It's so large, I can see it from here. Right across the road—where he's standing.'

Lestrade lurched towards the window and I grasped his arm to pull him back behind the curtains, so we wouldn't be seen and give the game away. Sure enough, a man stood across the road, pretending to read a paper—I could just make out its German header—with a noticeable scar upon his cheek.

'In my circles, I've heard whispers of a man,' Irene said, 'a red-haired German, who does secret work for his government or anyone who has the funds to pay.'

'So...this German monster was in our house last night?' I enquired. As an ex-army doctor, I was not given to flutters of fear over gollums and suchlike. But the look of this man, the size of him, and the sense of malevolence emanating from him, even from afar, made me shudder. Especially as I pictured him roaming round the house freely while both Mrs Hudson and I lay unconscious in our beds.

'Don't worry, Doctor Watson,' Irene said. 'While you're unaware of his presence, he has good reason to preserve your life. Because he's hoping to follow you. He wants you to lead him to his quarry.'

A search of the rest of the apartment confirmed items missing from Holmes's wardrobe—some shirts and trousers, spare socks. It was unlikely the gollum took those—rather, their removal confirmed Irene's theory that someone had packed an overnight bag for Holmes's stay in a secret location.

Irene picked up a framed photo on Sherlock's bedside table, frowning. 'So, he keeps a photo of his violin beside his bed?'

'He's a music lover,' I said.

She scoffed. 'He's a strange one, our Sherlock.'

A final search of the sitting room unearthed one more possible clue—a small advertisement clipped from the newspaper, for the Oriental Emporium in Limehouse. Irene found it beneath a protective leather mat on Sherlock's lab desk.

'This clipping seems recent,' I observed, as she passed it to me. 'I wonder why Holmes kept it.'

'It might be worth a visit to this emporium, in case his business took him there in recent days,' Irene suggested.

I nodded, glad to have a concrete lead to divert mind and body from fretting.

'Did our red-haired friend miss this?' I asked, waving the advert.

'We have to assume he's seen it,' Irene said. 'And that he will have it on his list of places to investigate, too.'

#

I farewelled my guests on the street outside our residence, where we agreed to keep each other informed of any new information on Sherlock's whereabouts. While we talked, I glanced about furtively, searching for the German. However, he appeared to have vanished for the time being—which was a great relief.

I watched Irene Adler move along the busy road, so dainty and yet so intellectually formidable, and marvelled at all she'd managed to uncover, while still ministering to Lestrade's bruised ego. Was it possible she had all of Holmes's deductive abilities, coupled with a superior insight into human emotion and motivations? If so, she was a truly fearsome ally. Or adversary.

'Doctor!' came a cry. Along the road, I spotted Dante dodging wheels and insults as he hurried towards me on his spindly legs. 'I been looking for Mr Holmes in his usual haunts, but he ain't there. You want me to keep looking?'

I was reluctant to set the child on a course where he might encounter the gollum, especially given the possibility Holmes might be safely under the protection of Her Majesty's agents. Instead, I invented a new assignment for him.

'Why don't you follow that lady there'—I pointed to Irene Adler—'and tell me where she goes.' I handed him a few more coins. That gave him a task, and if Irene were to encounter any danger, the boy could raise the alarm.

Dante tipped his imaginary hat to me, and vanished into the teeming traffic.

Back inside 221B, I went straight to Mrs Hudson's door to warn her about the red-haired man. But if I'd expected her to wither in fear, I couldn't have been more mistaken.

'Let him come, the ruby-headed kraut,' she said, 'and I'll give him a welcome he won't expect.' She wielded a heavy-based cooking pan in one hand and an umbrella in the other. 'He'll find we English women are not the wilting flowers he imagines.'

As she set to practising her "saucepan swing" and "umbrella poke", I couldn't help but admire her spirit. Of all the landladies in London, she was the right one for the city's famous consulting detective.

Chapter Three

I had a few patients to see at my general practice, but after attending to them, I set out across town and cultures to the Oriental Emporium in Limehouse in the city's east. By a stroke of luck, I managed to pick up a hansom cab right outside my door, though the driver was a voluble chap and particularly rude, making sport of insulting all those we passed. His exclamations constantly interrupted my train of thought as the cab's wheels churned through London's streets, where beggars overtaken by grime shared pavements with the primped, poised, and prissy and the well-heeled rubbed shoulders with those down-at-heel.

'Move your arse or Mr Whip here will move it for you!' the cabbie called to some pedestrians.

Charming.

I wasn't sure what to expect at the Oriental Emporium. Perhaps nothing at all. It might have been no more than a fancy for a trinket that had caught Holmes's eye with that advertisement. I peered through the window of the carriage for signs of a red-headed monster in pursuit but saw none.

And if the gollum did lay hands upon me? Well, I couldn't tell him anything, not for all his efforts to throttle it out of me. I knew nothing of my friend's whereabouts. In this, my ignorance was my greatest strength.

In the meantime, I regarded it as my job to lead the fellow a merry dance, so Holmes would be free to transact his business with the Crown Jewels—if that was where he was—and for the plain thrill of it all. There was nothing like a mystery to quicken the pulse and get the blood pumping.

'Are you crossing the road, or takin' up residence! Out of the way!' cried the driver.

So what was Sherlock up to, I wondered? Irene Adler thought he might be involved in the refurbishment of the Crown Jewels, no less. That would be a boon for his reputation and career. A diamond, said to be the most valuable in the world, would be a financial and political triumph for England, too, adding significantly to its coffers, while boosting its stature upon the world stage. There had been whispers of war brewing abroad lately. Would a clear show of wealth and superiority by Britain quiet the dissenting voices?

'I've seen tortoises that would call you a slow coach! Get a move on!'

Gah! Damned if the fellow wasn't the most obnoxious cab driver I'd ever had the misfortune to engage. And there was some stiff competition for that title in this town. I was relieved when the vehicle finally came to a halt at my destination.

#

The Oriental Emporium was in a poor part of London where many Chinese businesses operated. A bell on the shop's door announced my arrival; several heads turned my way as if connected by string.

Barely a few steps inside, I saw this was no modest establishment. It was a converted warehouse, high-ceilinged and deep, stretching this way and that.

'Welcome, sir!' A man of Oriental persuasion bowed behind the counter. He had a long, thin beard and dark hair tied in a single plait that extended halfway down his back. He wore a high-collared silk shirt and matching cap.

'We have ornaments for your home and jewels for the ladies.' The man waved his arm across bowls containing colourful stones, all glass, I was sure.

My eye caught movement in the back of the shop. Young children practised acrobatic manoeuvres on mats—cartwheels, juggling, balancing on beams, circus training from the look of it. A few were of Oriental ancestry but not all. And there were girls among those performing, which was highly modern.

'Can I help you with anything?' the man asked.

'If it's acceptable, I'd just like to browse your merchandise.'

'Of course! We have clothes, too, for all seasons.' He pointed to a rack at the side, with shiny Oriental-style dresses and shirts and bathrobes with dragon designs. There were winter coats with especially dense wadding, just right for London's relentless chill. I was tempted to purchase one for the cold nights in Baker Street.

Except now was not a shopping expedition.

I perused a shelf of colourful bottles with Oriental remedies and a collection of painted statues—most of rural Oriental scenes. There was one, however, of a woman who seemed more western in her features. And oddly familiar.

'Excuse me,' I held up the statue, 'Is this a statue of—Irene Adler?' The face shape, the hair, the lips bore an uncanny resemblance to the actress's.

The man frowned, and shrugged, as if he didn't understand my question.

'I'm wondering if Mr Sherlock Holmes has been in here, recently?' I tried to observe, as Holmes would, the man's first reaction as I said my friend's name.

'I'm sorry?' He remained blank, no trace of recognition.

'He's taller than me and thin, with dark hair. Does that sound like any of your customers recently?'

The man smiled wryly. 'Sometimes what you are looking for is right in front of you.'

I wasn't sure whether he was merely spouting some Confucius-like wisdom or if his words held a coded meaning as he slid a large wooden bowl in front of me, containing crudely-made paper boats.

'For a single coin, you can read what the boat of the future predicts for you,' he said.

I reached in, drew out a paper boat, and opened it. Inside, written in a fancy hand, was: 'Meet me in Hyde Park at 4 pm.'

I knew it! A message from Holmes. My face flushed with pride that I had managed to pick up on a clue he'd left me.

'I hope your fortune pleases you?' the man intoned.

'Very much so.'

The bell announced another customer entering. My view of the newcomer was partly obscured by shelving but I glimpsed the top of his head—and his bright red hair.

'Perhaps you would like to try the maze of mirrors,' the serving man suggested. 'It is not to be missed.'

He pointed to the side of the room, and I hastened that way, hunching low to remain concealed.

'Is there anything I can help you with today?' I heard the shopkeeper ask. I didn't wait for a reply; I slipped through the doorway to the maze.

#

A narrow corridor with mirrors on either side stretched ahead of me. Walking its length, I had the strongest feeling I was being followed. By myself! Looking left and right, my own image was reflected over and over. An army of Dr Watsons on one side seemed to face off against the same on the other. The effect was dazzling.

Heading deeper into the maze, I passed mirrors that rendered me as wide as a clown or as tall and thin as Holmes.

As if I'd summoned him with that thought, around the corner came my friend in the familiar deerstalker hat and cape.

'Sherlock!' I cried. With his back to me, Holmes held a hand up in greeting and continued on, taking a turn and vanishing from my sight once more.

'Sherlock!' I called again. He'd looked different somehow.

I stood astonished that I'd met my friend here in this strange world of mirrors. Rows of Watsons, gaping like guppy fish, appeared equally baffled.

There was no time to think further upon it as the whole maze rocked and rattled. Someone large had entered and began thumping along the corridors.

I ran, taking this turn and that, banging head-first into a trick mirror. Cursing myself, I backtracked and found a new way through. The game had lost its appeal by now. I was heartily sick of my own image and desperate to escape.

Turning a corner, I got my first look at the red-haired German. His head was square, as was his jaw, with deep eye sockets. The effect was simian and beastly, especially as, in that moment, he walked beneath a mosaic mirror ball dangling from the ceiling. It threw light and distorted images of him this way and that as it revolved.

My breathing was loud in my ears. I heard the man grunting nearby. And then he launched himself at me. I covered my head, anticipating a blow. Instead, a loud bang and a volley of swear words in German revealed he'd made the same mistake as I, crashing into a dead end.

And then I was out. I ran through the shop. The bell chimed as I left.

A cab was sitting outside—the same driver I'd had before, who'd taken a break while I was in the store.

'We have to wait!' I said. 'For a friend of mine.' I hoped to see Sherlock appearing at every second.

'Tall chap with a funny hat and cape? He shot out before you and ran off along the road.'

'Really?' Holmes had left without me? That seemed strange. I wasn't sure what to make of it. Without awaiting my commands, the cabbie started up. I felt fortunate he'd been there, even though he swore at the first person we encountered on the road.

Sighing, I leaned back in my seat and thought over all that had taken place. How the clipped advertisement had led me there. How Sherlock had appeared like a spectre in the maze and disappeared as suddenly. I pulled out his note, and smiled at the fortune-telling ruse he'd used to deliver a message to meet him that afternoon.

I closed my eyes, slightly dizzy as I recalled the lights, the heady incense, the bouncing acrobats. In that moment, I felt like a circus performer myself, balanced on a high wire, with Sherlock holding one end, and the red-haired agent the other.

#

Back at 221B Baker Street, Mrs Hudson brought in some much-needed refreshment and the paper.

'I've had a frustrating afternoon,' she said, sitting down to pour.

She explained that she'd received an invitation to a teahouse in Bloomsbury from a woman claiming to be a friend of her sister's. She'd attended the establishment at the appointed time but waited almost an hour without the woman appearing.

'It's not the first time that's happened either,' said Mrs Hudson. 'A few days ago, an invitation arrived out of the blue, from an old school friend—and I do mean old—inviting me to take tea at her home. I set forth to meet her, all the way to south London, only to find she'd never lived at that address.'

'What do you make of it, Doctor?'

I scratched my chin and examined the facts. 'Was there anything missing from your belongings upon your return?'

'Not that I could tell.'

'Then perhaps she noted the address incorrectly on the invitation?'

Mrs Hudson pressed her lips together as she handed me a cup. 'I'll ask Mr Holmes when he returns.'

Despite training under the great detective, I couldn't fathom even the simplest mystery when called upon. Deflated, I turned to a perusal of the paper. On the front page, was a story about Sherlock Holmes and the Crown Jewels—Miss Adler was right!—with a sketch of the spectacular diamond, from the northern cape in South Africa, to be set into the royal sceptre at a secret location the following day. Sherlock was to witness its authentication and placement in the royal sceptre, on behalf of Her Majesty and all her subjects.

'Sherlock Holmes is a consulting detective of formidable reputation,' I read the piece aloud, 'with no known political allegiances. Renowned for intellectual rigour and moral irreproachability, he is the ideal subject to act as the public guardian for this historic addition to the royal collection.'

'Not so sure about the moral irreproachability,' said Mrs Hudson, slurping her drink. 'Whoever wrote that, clearly, has not met the man.'

I laughed heartily in agreement.

'Well, Holmes would have no interest in stealing the diamond, so he is the safest person to handle it,' I concluded. 'Wealth, power, and prestige hold no allure for him. Of course, he might want the diamond to evaluate its geological properties.'

Mrs Hudson cackled. 'So we'd find it broken into bits, in the bottom of a test tube?' She slurped her drink. 'Just be thankful, Doctor, that Sherlock chose to catch criminals rather than become one.'

#

It was a couple of hours until our meeting at four o'clock. To occupy myself, I examined the living room to see if I could find any clues Miss Adler had missed. There were none, of course. Not much escaped her eagle eye.

I moved onto an examination of Sherlock's bedroom to detail more closely which items were missing from his wardrobe. Among the things I could not locate were his smoking jacket, slippers, and his violin.

I tried to picture the Queen's secret agents packing my friend's bag for a sojourn in a safe house. I had encountered such men during Holmes's investigations before. Most were ex-army, stiff-backed and unsentimental. I couldn't see them slipping the silk jacket and fur-lined slippers into his pack. Nor his violin.

Perhaps Sherlock packed his own bag? But that wasn't right either. Holmes was as disdainful of comfort as any army officer. And besides, if he had gone to the trouble of including those items—my gaze rested on the framed picture of his violin which stood by his bed—he would have included that, too. It meant a great deal to him.

How to explain this? I couldn't just now.

#

The answer continued to elude me as I arrived at Hyde Park ten minutes before four. Although Holmes hadn't specified where he would be, I knew he liked to attend concerts in a rotunda near the Serpentine River. I began there.

Within minutes of arriving, my spirits lifted as I saw a figure bobbing along in familiar deerstalker and cape. I marvelled that Holmes would attire himself in his most visible outfit for a secret meeting. But he knew best what he was doing.

As he drew closer, I detected a discrepancy in his height and weight which confused me. This Holmes seemed heavier than I recalled. And the strong, determined strides were absent; he had more of a purposeless stroll. And then, Holmes walked right by me, without any acknowledgement and I saw this was not Sherlock, but an older man in his garb.

I was still marvelling at that—the coincidence of it, and the fact someone should so boldly have copied my friend's unique style—when I saw another be-caped individual. I was not in a moment's doubt about this person being Holmes. He was young and short, with a beard and wisps of blonde hair protruding from the deerstalker.

Over the next quarter hour, no fewer than twenty five individuals dressed as Holmes appeared, laughing and posing, and puffing on their pipes in a very un-Sherlock way. I asked one what was going on and he informed me this was the appointed hour and location for a meeting of the Sherlock Holmes Appreciation Society.

'But aren't you Dr Watson, Sherlock's companion?' said one elderly pretender.

'No, I'm not,' I responded rapidly. 'But I think I saw him over there.' I pointed to the other side of the river.

The Sherlocks stared across the water and I slunk away, concealing myself behind a flowering bush. All the while, I kept a lookout in case the true Sherlock had devised this scenario to provide cover for our meeting.

'There you are, Watson!' I turned to find a familiar face, though it took a few seconds to process who it was.

'Lestrade!' I exclaimed. For the officer was also dressed in a cape and deerstalker. 'What on Earth...?'

'Does it suit me?' he said. 'I almost fancy I think like the great man in this coat and hat.'

Clothes maketh not the man. I resisted uttering the obvious. 'It looks well on you, Lestrade. But what's going on?'

'I pulled another body out of the Thames today. Could have been Sherlock's twin,' he said. 'Through enquiries, I've established the corpse was last seen in the vicinity of the Diogenes club.'

Upon hearing the club's name, every organ shifted within me. I knew Sherlock frequented the Diogenes club whenever he wanted to see his brother, Mycroft, about a case. I say 'see' rather than 'talk to' because club rules strictly forbade any conversation within its walls.

'A red-headed man of large stature was seen near that location too. It seems our German gollum is stalking all the known haunts of the great detective and anyone who looks like him is in peril.' Lestrade hitched up his trousers.

'So why are you dressed like him, then?'

'I laugh in the face of danger,' the officer boasted. 'It's my job. Several of us at the Yard have kitted ourselves out this way and set ourselves up in spots Sherlock is well-known to inhabit. We are laying a trap for the killer.'

I wasn't sure how to answer that, except to say my admiration for Lestrade increased at that moment. I knew Sherlock didn't think much of his deductive powers, but when it came to bravery, Lestrade was not lacking. His ferret eyes darted about, combing the shrubberies and walkways for the German gollum.

For a short time, I eavesdropped on the assemblage of Sherlock impersonators as they discussed their hero and the various mysteries he'd solved.

'Of course, Dr Watson does much to help Sherlock,' one imposter concluded.

'And what's that?' enquired another would-be detective.

'His dullness makes Sherlock seem to shine all the brighter.'

They laughed like drains at that. While I didn't find it amusing, I couldn't be too angry; at least they appreciated Holmes's remarkable abilities. Though I liked to think they might be underestimating my own small contributions to the detective's success.

When forty minutes had elapsed, and my friend had not appeared, it seemed to me this was not a ploy to create cover. But something else altogether.

'Who called this meeting today?' I asked one Sherlock, with a florid complexion and jowly aspect.

'I imagine it was a Holmes Appreciation society member, but I couldn't tell you who.'

I sniffed. So much for detection. Even I—blockhead though they thought me—knew good detective work involved asking the right questions. None of these pretenders had thought to ask that one.

As I was leaving, I spotted a red-head among the caped crowd. The German agent eyeballed each Sherlock as a potential candidate for his foul deeds. I watched from the side as he decided that the man with the jowls was the real Sherlock and made a grab for him.

'No!' I cried, lurching forward.

The gollum hustled the man towards the carriageway. The fact his victim did not cry out convinced me his attacker held a weapon on him and had made threats if he did not remain quiet. The colour had drained from the man's cheeks as he stumbled along with his captor and his eyes bulged like peeled grapes.

'Lestrade!' I called—to no avail, the officer was some distance away—before launching into action. Fear vied with anger inside me as I charged after the abductor, hurling myself at the man's back and directing my blows to his kidney region.

'Leave him alone,' I demanded.

'You don't want your friend hurt, Doctor.' The man had a heavy German accent.

'I've never see this man before!' I shouted. 'LESTRADE!'

I felt all eyes upon me, as the officer's name was well-known among this crowd, with both the police and Sherlock devotees. I sensed rather than saw the detective speeding towards us, heedless of his own safety. Several others began to converge upon the redhead. The gollum, realising the jig was up, let go of the Sherlock impersonator and attempted to flee. He moved surprisingly swiftly for a mountain of a man.

However, as two officers closed in—Lestrade in the lead—some mothers with prams chanced across the path, blocking access to the man. The police lost precious seconds veering around the group. And then—more ill luck—a cyclist barrelled right into the officers. They went down in a tangle of limbs and deerstalkers. By the time they had regained their footing, their quarry was lost.

I couldn't help feeling there was something familiar about one of the fresh-faced mothers with prams. Though, for the life of me, I couldn't think what.

#

Sleep was fitful at best that night, questions swirling in my head, without answers. At some point, I became aware I was awake. And I was not alone. A creak in the floorboards and the faintest of nasal whistles confirmed it. An intruder was in the bedroom with me.

Casting off the cobwebs of slumber, I stared wide-eyed around the room, hoping to pick out details in the darkness. I vaguely made out a hulking form over my bed as a meaty hand grasped my throat and squeezed. I swung my arms wildly. My attacker repelled my blows as easily as if swatting away a mosquito on a summer's evening. I tried to cry out but barely a croak emerged. To silence me, he pressed down harder upon my larynx until I could no longer breathe.

'Quiet, Doctor,' he whispered, 'and I won't have to kill you. We're just going to take a little trip together to bring the detective out of his rabbit hole.'

He was planning to kidnap me to lure Holmes out of hiding? Not if I could help it! I redoubled my efforts to break free, thrashing about with arms and legs, though I felt my force ebbing and my consciousness fading.

'Unhand the doctor, you devil!' a female voice demanded, followed by the clang of a saucepan hitting bone or skull. Through the veil of darkness, I thought I made out Mrs Hudson's shape and my landlady gripping an iron skillet as if it were a tennis racket.

'Now that's not very nice,' she said, and—*thwap! thwap!*—delivered two more blows to the man's head.

I must have passed out then for I didn't recall anything more until I awoke hours later, as fingers of feeble morning light reached into my bedroom.

I lay there for a moment wondering whether I'd dreamt it all. Then I spotted on the floor a tooth, yellow and fang-like, with dried blood on one end, as if it had been knocked out of a head.

When I sought Mrs Hudson to discuss the attack, however, she shook her head.

'Don't be daft, Doctor,' she said. 'If I had battled an assailant in your room, he wouldn't have got away. I'd have grated his tender parts and served them over fried bread for breakfast.'

Mrs Hudson retrieved her pan for inspection. It was as clean and intact as on the previous day. I would have taken that as proof I'd imagined the whole incident, but for a sore throat and red finger marks turning to bruising around my throat.

Was Mrs Hudson prevaricating? Could she be more formidable than she let on, perhaps secretly in the service of the Queen? Or had she sleepwalked her way through the entire incident?

More questions with no answers. If Sherlock were here, he would guffaw and tell me that though I looked, I did not see. That the answer was obvious.

Oh well, I'd just have to keep looking.

Chapter Four

I spent longer than usual with the newspapers that morning, reading everything I could find pertaining to the refurbishment of the Crown Jewels. After the secret ceremony to replace the diamond in the sceptre, it seemed the entire Crown Jewel Collection would be displayed at Customs House for a select European audience—meaning the Royal Family would show off their shiny new jewels and watch their continental cousins turn green with envy.

As I tossed one newspaper aside, a note in a familiar spidery scrawl slipped out of its rear pages.

'Meet me in the London sewers at 11 am!' it read. 'Where London's theatres meet its most skilled performers and audience of desperates.'

The words propelled me to my feet. Holmes had called for help and I would answer. But first, I had to solve his riddle.

I paced, cursing Sherlock for playing games at such a critical time. It was probably a precaution, I reasoned, in case the note wound up in the wrong hands. Although, knowing Holmes, it could just be an exercise in showing off his superior intellect. Well, I'd be damned if it would get the better of me!

London's theatres were in Drury Lane, of course. Its most skilled performers? They were there too. But the audience of desperates? Even for Holmes, it was a misanthropic label for theatre-goers. Actors, though, were not the only performers. There were street shows, circuses, musicians? Still, I wouldn't call those who viewed them desperates.

And then I remembered—Lincoln's Inn, where barristers—well-known for their showmanship—performed to an audience of the accused, awaiting judgement. They were as desperate as one could be.

So Holmes wanted us to meet in the underground tunnels somewhere around Lincoln's Inn. Why there, I wondered?

I changed into my worst shoes and oldest trousers, fit for the task, and galloped downstairs.

'Where are you going like the devil himself is after you?' Mrs Hudson asked.

'Nowhere in particular.'

My landlady cocked her head. 'Dr Watson, don't ever become a con artist, will you? I'd hate to see you starve.'

#

As soon I hit Baker Street, Dante was upon me. 'Doctor, I've been following that lady, Miss Adler. I know where she's been and where she is now.'

'Thank you, Dante,' I said. 'I am very interested in your report, but later.' I handed him a coin for his trouble. 'Now if you had any idea where the street entry point for the sewer system in a particular part of London was, that would be useful right now. Our other business will have to wait.'

'You want to go into the sewers?' A grin broke out over Dante's face. 'Well, them's like home for me. I can show you.'

'I have a particular spot in mind.'

'Try me, Doctor. I've escaped the Rozzers more often in those tunnels than you've had hot tea.'

Twenty minutes later, Dante had experienced his first hansom cab ride, and I was about to enter "Stink River" as he called it. I'd checked and re-checked that the red-haired agent was not following but I glanced about one last time before lifting a grate upon the street which was the doorway to my meeting with Holmes.

The boy directed me accordingly—third tunnel on the left, second on the right, etc—and promised to meet me back here afterwards. 'Watch out for the rats, Doc. Nasty blighters.'

Descending below street level, the stench from the emissions of a city of a million souls grew so strong my eyes began to mist. Dante pressed his face to the grate. 'Jes' hold your breath, Doc! You'll be right!'

#

Plop. Slop. Slap. Squelch. The sound effects would have turned my stomach if it wasn't already twisting like a wet towel in the hands of a laundry mistress at the smell. There was no lighting in the tunnels, except that streaming from street grates above at irregular intervals. I had to traverse long stretches of near darkness touching the slimy walls to keep from banging my head. In all of my missions with the great detective, this was the most malodorous.

The *drip drip drip* of condensation into the ankle-deep murk was unnerving. As my eyes adjusted to the dark, I made out more detail—the brickwork on the tubes, shiny in the reflected light, the bumpy surface of the water I wish I'd never seen. And rats moving with ease along the slippery sides.

'Oh, Lord,' I muttered.

On the bright side, the stench was less noticeable the longer I lingered here. I imagined it seeping into my clothes, my hair, the pores of my skin.

I heard footsteps. I stood still, trying to determine from whence they came. The tunnels were an echo chamber, the sound bouncing around in an unpredictable fashion. I decided the footsteps were ahead and pushed on. I was not one to take fright easily, I reminded myself. And Holmes was waiting.

My resolve weakened as the *plop plop splash* grew louder. Whoever—or whatever—it was, they were almost upon me.

'Who goes there?' I called, fearing what might loom out of the blackness.

'Who goes *there?*' came the echoing call.

The voice seemed familiar. Limned by light from behind, I recognised the deerstalker hat.

'Holmes!' I exclaimed.

'Watson!'

Light glancing off the walls revealed it wasn't Sherlock, but Inspector Lestrade, still in costume.

'Lestrade,' I exclaimed. 'What brings you here, to the very depths of our city?'

'I had a tip-off the gollum was somewhere in this vicinity.'

'Have you seen him at all?' I enquired.

'No, only rats and rubbish,' he said. 'Why are you wading about in the stink soup, Doctor?'

'I had an invitation from Sherlock to meet him.'

'Really?' Lestrade seemed surprised. 'But isn't this the appointed time for him to authenticate the diamond?'

'Yes,' I replied. 'I thought perhaps there'd been some delay.'

'I guess you'll miss the meeting now,' said Lestrade. 'Not that you were invited to it, were you?'

'No, I wasn't.'

'Although I bet this is one day Sherlock would want you there taking notes. For posterity and all.'

In the distance, we heard the rhythmic slap of feet through the water. We tensed, scanning left and right as the sound ricocheted maddeningly about us.

Lestrade gripped his police truncheon in readiness, my fingers balled into fists.

Around the corner came a scrawny man, his clothes in rags, glowering at us with his one good eye. Just another one of the city's lost and rootless souls.

Lestrade and I exhaled in unison.

I caught a gleam of teeth as the officer began to grin. 'Here we are, together,' he said, 'in mud and waste and who-knows-what up to our knees.'

'Like a couple of clowns in a watery circus,' I added.

I realised that since the beginning, this case had been exactly that—a circus. The bedazzling mirror maze, the convention of Sherlocks, the drama of the sewers. Lestrade had even donned a costume for the show.

'Strange we're both here,' I reasoned aloud, 'at the exact hour Sherlock is to attend one of the most important meetings of his career.'

'Yes, an odd coincidence that.'

Coincidence? Holmes did not believe in them. *The universe is rarely so lazy,* he always said. *When two unlikely strands of a story come together, it may be a random event. But more often it is through the careful work of a seamstress's hand.*

Could it be someone wanted us, Sherlock's two closest allies, underground and far away while the jewel authentication took place? And they had gone to a deal of trouble to get us here.

I could almost hear Sherlock's voice in my head. *Keep the right hand busy and you're less likely to notice what the left hand is doing.* The art of misdirection.

Neither Lestrade nor I had powers of reason anywhere near as sharp as Sherlock's. So what were they afraid of? We knew nothing about diamonds and precious stones. Nor affairs of state, nor the twists and turns of international intrigue. We could not soundly apply Holmes's methods of detection to complex clues or Machiavellian mysteries. But we did know the detective...what he looked like.

'We have to get out of here, Lestrade,' I said.

As we emerged from the tunnel, even young Dante, as inured to poor hygiene as he was, reared back. 'Everyone knows that part of the tunnels is the smelliest,' he said. 'Them poor blighters in the courthouse can't hold back. Want to hear my report on Irene Adler now?'

'Yes, indeed!' I said.

#

We followed the boy, down alleyways, across busy roads, ignoring the disdainful looks of those we passed, to Bedford Square—and an ordinary terrace house, with no visible security around it.

'She's in there,' he said.

I asked Dante to wait in the green across the road as Lestrade and I entered the house, unchallenged. We made it through the doorway and down a stately hall without encountering a soul.

'Dr Watson!' effused a guard rounding the corridor. 'Glad to see you, old chap. We were disappointed when you sent your apologies for today.'

Apologies? What?

'But here you are anyway,' the man slapped me on the back, with undue familiarity. 'Holmes will be happy to have his chronicler beside him on this historic day.'

I felt Lestrade start at the mention of our friend's name. 'Holmes? Is this where the diamond is being verified? But weren't we in pursuit of Miss Adler just now? Is she with him?'

Yes...and no...was the answer, I suspected.

The man led us into a sitting room, well-furnished and elegant, though not as opulent as one might have expected for such an occasion. Locating the event in an ordinary house, with no visible security, was all part of the secrecy. For few would suspect what was taking place behind the ordinary oak door of a suburban home.

The guard ushered us to a sofa to witness the ceremony. Two statesmen in top hats and coats and a couple representing the royal household stood either side of Sherlock as he conversed with a short man holding an enormous diamond. Sherlock placed a loupe to his eye and squinted through it to examine the jewel. Straightening, he nodded and smiled his assent. All the men visibly relaxed.

It was only then Sherlock saw Lestrade and I. And we saw him.

High forehead, aquiline nose, thin lips. All as they should be. But there was something—an eyebrow not quite right. A little too much style in the outfit he'd chosen. And a smile, with a hint of amusement in the corners. This was Irene Adler, if I wasn't mistaken, disguised—and very well—as Sherlock Holmes.

'Mr Holmes,' said the Queen's representative. 'You agree that this diamond is as it was represented?'

'I do,' said Sherlock/Irene. 'The finest I've ever seen. My congratulations to Her Majesty.'

The voice was almost flawless. But not quite. It wasn't just the way she spoke, but the grace in the tone. Sherlock would have been more grudging. None of those assembled could tell, though. They didn't know the detective as I did.

I looked over at Lestrade, whose brow was creased. Something troubled him. But as the room broke into applause, he did too, taken in by Irene Adler's performance. A royal command performance.

However, Irene knew that I knew. She gave me a twinkly smile, with just a smidgeon of concern.

'Who's for a drink?' said one official.

Formalities over, the Queen's jeweller laid out his tools, to begin the job of replacing the old diamond with the new in the royal sceptre. He would complete the task before witnesses so there could be no question of deception.

But first, a bottle of champagne on ice was opened and glasses were charged for the official toast, to Queen, country and the Crown Jewels.

Two more glasses were found for Lestrade and I. The assembled guests said not a word about our wet feet and general reek. They were much too well-bred to disparage us to our faces.

The policeman took great swigs of the golden liquid and became quite sparkling himself. Holmes/Irene, meanwhile, was all charm, impressing all who encountered her. Her eyes frequently sought me out, a tautness about the jaw betraying a fear that I might expose her.

I considered it. But I was trying to fathom what it all meant, where Sherlock was, whether he was in collusion with this? Or in some kind of danger? That was my prime concern.

I was baffled by what Irene hoped to achieve. The jeweller was present and had authenticated the diamond, which would shortly be secured in the sceptre. Unless she could affect an almost magical switch—the real gem with a fake—there was nothing to be gained.

'Dr Watson, my oldest friend,' Sherlock/Irene stood before me. 'You found me.'

Sherlock would never have been so sentimental.

'Yes, although as you can see'—I gestured to my wet trousers and shoes—'I took a wrong turn along the way.'

She could hardly hold back her laughter at this. If anyone present had known Sherlock at all intimately, this moment would have been her undoing. Her eyes were not the dull, focused beans of deduction, but full of light and laughter.

'And although it seems I sent my apologies to Her Majesty for today,' I said, eyebrows raised meaningfully at her, 'here I am. Though, I confess, I must be getting forgetful in my old age, as I have no memory of receiving the invitation.' For the simple reason it had never reached me. By design, I suspected. Irene's design.

'You're a busy man, Watson, with many claims upon your time,' Sherlock/Irene said. 'Perhaps Mrs Hudson received them on your behalf but forgot to pass them on. Landladies can be forgetful.'

Of course! Mrs Hudson—or Irene in her guise—must have taken possession of the Queen's invitations, while the real Mrs Hudson bestrode London on a goose chase for tea.

'Anyway,' Sherlock/Irene said, 'we're overjoyed to see you now.'

Our smiles were painted on—part irritation, part amusement, and just a hint of a thrill that we shared a secret in this room of Her Majesty's officials and spies.

When I was sure we would not be overheard, I whispered, 'Where's Sherlock?'

'Safe,' she said. 'This is for his own protection. We both want that, don't we?'

As she drifted off to charm the royal representatives, in Sherlock's name, I sipped my champagne and wondered whether she'd just reassured me or threatened me. I was still trying to decide when a commotion broke out as the red-haired man stormed into the room, gun brandished.

'Give me the jewel,' he demanded. He held his hand out and the jeweller, wide-eyed with terror, looked to us, unsure what to do. 'Unless you wish to die in this room,' the gollum added.

That made up the man's mind. He offered the stone to the intruder, but as the German went to grab it, Sherlock/Irene lunged forward and snatched it. 'No one's taking that. Off with you now, you—'

We never got to hear what she/he was about to call him for the man drew a gun and fired. Sherlock/Irene staggered back with a look of profound shock. The gollum snatched the diamond and ran. Sherlock/Irene slid to the floor, unconscious.

Bedlam ensued with guards pursuing the gollum and officials hurrying out to watch. I rushed forward to attend Irene, sprawled upon the ground.

'Breathe!' I pushed down on her chest.

'Is he done for?' Lestrade had stayed with us rather than join the pursuit. 'I can't believe it. Sherlock Holmes, dead?'

Neither could I. There was no blood at all. Which seemed strange. I undid Sherlock's coat and shirt to find a thickly-padded vest beneath, made of a tough fibre I'd never seen before. I felt something small and hard wedged within. The bullet.

And then Sherlock/Irene gasped and sat up.

'Sherlock,' Lestrade sounded spooked. 'I know you're clever and all, but to outsmart death...?'

Irene was too occupied with breathing to answer, so I explained. 'Our friend was prepared for such a possibility, with a special vest, padded and of a durable material to stop the bullet reaching the body.'

'I've heard of those,' said Lestrade. 'Might I inspect it, Doctor?'

'Perhaps later. Holmes needs a moment to recover.'

By then, the others had returned, cursing themselves for the gollum's escape. And Sherlock/Irene was back on her feet, if shakily, to the astonishment of the company. A rumour began after that night that Holmes had supernatural powers and bullets could not kill him.

'I could use that drink now,' Sherlock/Irene whispered. Lestrade almost tripped over his sodden feet to oblige, trickling the last drops of champagne into a glass.

In the silver bucket, the ice had begun to melt, but for a lone cube refusing to succumb.

Chapter Five

Miss Adler did not appear on the stage that night. Her stand-in performed the role of London's most notorious female adventurer.

However, audiences were thrilled to see her back again the next night, more dazzling than before. When the final curtain fell, I went backstage, past the familiar props that from a distance had been so effective, but here seemed like cheap copies of life, and past the row of heads sporting facial hair and enhancements for a fuller cheek, a longer chin, and a more forbidding eyebrow.

I knocked on Miss Adler's door.

'Enter!'

Irene smiled, but I saw she was tired. The recent show—and not just the one where she played Moll—had taken a toll. Even drained as she was, though, Irene was a striking woman—the cascades of amber hair (had she ever had the same hair colour twice?), the shapely lips that seemed ever-ready to laugh.

Looking into her eyes now, as brown as dark toffee, a question popped into my mind: 'How do you change eye colour?'

'There are herbs that can darken or lighten the eyes.'

'With no damage to the eye?'

'None.'

We regarded each other, warily.

'I trust Sherlock will be home soon?' I heard the steel in my own voice.

'Perhaps even upon your return tonight, you may find him sitting in his usual chair, contemplating his next case.'

'Or his last,' I said. 'He might be surprised to learn that he put himself in harm's way in the service of his Queen. I do hope he wasn't too badly hurt?' My concern for Irene was genuine, as a medical man and friend.

'He'll live.' Miss Adler threw off the wig, her dark hair tumbling free. 'I daresay he's suffered worse, at the hands of those thought to be respectable members of society.'

I was disturbed to hear this. I'd imagined Miss Adler's life full of admiration and applause. But, evidently, it wasn't all opening nights and rose garlands for an unmarried actress in London.

'You've had a busy time, Doctor?' said Irene. She leaned close to the mirror and, with a surgeon's steady hands, removed first one false eyelash, then the other.

'I've been running hither and thither, hastening after a phantom, searching, but not seeing what was right in front of me,' I said.

'And what was that?'

'That I was a puppet in a comedy show.'

Irene could compose herself no longer. She threw her head back and her unguarded laughter filled the room.

'It was educational,' I conceded. 'Especially the tunnels. I didn't like those trousers much anyway.'

'You're a good sport. Not all men would take it so well.' She dipped a cloth in a pot of cream and applied it to her face, washing off the paint on her cheeks and lips. 'At what point did you realise your friend in Bedford Square was not...as you'd expected him to be?'

'I had my suspicions before I entered the room,' I replied truthfully.

'Really? How?'

I explained that, while enveloped in unpleasant fumes, up to my knees in muck in the sewers, where I could hardly see my (filthy) hand in front of my face, it had all become clear. That I was a player in a show; one intended to keep the eye fixed *here*, away from the action taking place *there*.

'Very good, Doctor. I see Sherlock is not the only resident of 221B with deductive powers.'

'I daresay he would have arrived at that conclusion much sooner, and without ruining his shoes.'

'I'm not so sure.' Irene slipped behind a screen to change out of her stage clothes.

'You didn't find the newspaper advertisement for the Oriental Emporium during your search of our apartment, did you?' I said. 'You planted it there. I know because Sherlock doesn't snip things neatly out of the paper. He rips them out and half the page along with it.'

'That must be very annoying,' Irene called from behind the screen.

'You sent me to the emporium to draw out Sherlock's pursuer?' It emerged as a question.

'I suspected someone would be after him,' she explained. 'And that they might follow you, hoping you'd lead the way. Lee, at the emporium, is a friend of mine. I knew he'd play along. We could get a look at the agent in pursuit, and keep him occupied long enough for you to escape safely.'

'That Sherlock I encountered in the mirror maze? Was it you?'

'Yes, but a poor copy that day. I had to dress quickly. There was somewhere else I needed to be.' Irene broke into a cockney accent. 'Oi. Move your arse! Or Harry the horse here will move it for you!'

I gasped. 'You were that coachman?' I had been totally taken in by her as an odious hansom driver. 'You truly are a master of costume arts, Miss Adler.'

Indeed, as she stepped out from behind the screen, elegant in a ladies ensemble in brown tones, I doubted even those in the theatre's front row would recognise her. A chameleon, that's what Irene Adler was.

'And that circus of Sherlocks? Was that your doing?'

Leaning towards the mirror, she set about securing her hair with pins and attaching a hat to the crown. 'Seemed like a good distraction. And with Lestrade there, you were safe. Although, you didn't need protection.' She turned to me, with an admiring smile, 'You were impressively fierce with that German.'

Warmth flared in my cheeks at the compliment. 'I don't know about that. And anyway, he got away.'

'Shame.' As I watched Irene attend to some rogue strands of hair resisting confinement, in my mind I heard the unmistakable tinkle of pennies dropping into place.

'That night I was attacked in my room—it was you, not Mrs Hudson who came to my aid, wasn't it?' I recalled Mrs Hudson's voice—almost, but not quite, her own. 'Your follow-through with that saucepan was most effective. Thank you.'

She dipped her head and smiled, mischief in her looks.

'The gollum escaped then, too,' I said.

'At least I kept you safe, Doctor. If anything had happened to Sherlock's closest friend, he would be inconsolable.'

She opened the champagne and handed me a glass.

'And the tunnels of waste?' I enquired.

'To avoid complications, on the morning of the ceremony, it

seemed wise to have you as far away as possible. Underground seemed the safest option. For although the officials at the ceremony didn't know Sherlock well enough to spot an impersonator, you and Lestrade did.'

'Well, apparently not Lestrade,' I said. We both laughed. Though in fairness to our flat-footed friend, I think he heard a false note, and suspected something was amiss. But after a glass of champagne he stopped listening.

'And speaking of Her Majesty's agents, I assume you were at the ceremony as one yourself?' I enquired.

Irene's quiet attendance to her glass was as close to an admission as I would get.

'Later on, I imagine, Sherlock will tell the press he attended and vouch for the diamond's authenticity?' I said.

'That's the idea.'

I asked more about the vest. It was a Chinese invention. Lined with thick, light wadding, covered in a hardy fabric, it was a most ingenious thing and would have wider application in the future, I was certain.

'And was it your idea to take Sherlock's place?' I enquired.

'He is a civilian,' she said. 'With the German on the loose, it seemed prudent. Though perhaps Holmes could have done better if he had been there.' Her lips pursed with annoyance directed at herself.

'You stopped a bullet for him,' I said, and knew it to be true. 'As far as I'm concerned, you saved Sherlock's life that day. For you and I, Miss Adler, know Sherlock would never have worn a protective vest. His professional pride would not permit it.'

'Call me Irene. Please?'

She put down her glass and began pulling on her gloves. 'Now, may I ask you a question, Doctor?' she said. 'How did you find the house at Bedford Square? Only a handful of people knew the location.'

'When it comes to spies, Her Majesty is not the only one with agents in the shadows,' I said. 'One who answers to Sherlock—a resourceful and enthusiastic young agent—ghosted you over the past twenty-four hours and saw you entering this house.'

'He must be resourceful indeed,' Irene remarked, 'as I have

watched keenly for anyone on my tail.'

No doubt she was looking for full-sized pursuers, not a half-sized street urchin like Dante.

'The same agent,' I added, sipping my drink, 'made enquiries at the Café Royal on my behalf. You said you were engaged to meet Sherlock the night he left our residence smelling like a spring garden, and that he'd stood you up. But according to the café manager, Sherlock was with you that night.

'So, tell me, was that when you and Her Majesty's agents "took" Sherlock into custody? I know you could not have managed it on your own. For all that he admires and respects you, Irene, he does not trust you. He would have been on his guard, expecting skulduggery.'

Far from being insulted, Irene seemed delighted. 'Oh, well. What's an assignation without some risk?'

Her similarities with Sherlock astonished me. I had no doubt my friend enjoyed Miss Adler's company because he was never sure whether she would flatter him or drug him and sell him to his enemies.

'But that red-haired gollum was slippery, wasn't he?' I mused. 'More slippery than one of Lestrade's eel dinners.'

She drew the corners of her mouth up into a smile, like the curtains raised upon a stage.

'To think there were so many opportunities to capture the man. All missed.' I listed them. 'In the emporium, the park, in my bedroom that night, and in the final meeting, where he got away with the diamond.

'The police almost caught him that day in the park,' I went on. 'They would have, but for a group of mothers pushing prams, and a bicycle rider.'

Irene listened but did not reply.

'And now that I'm back here, in the theatre,' I said, 'I realise where I'd seen one of the mothers before. It was your assistant, Rachel.'

Irene fixed me with a hard gaze. 'Are you saying I was in league with the German to steal the Queen's diamond? That I'm a traitor to my country?'

I considered that for a moment, and shook my head. 'No. I felt the man's hands on my neck that night. There was nothing feigned about that. And I saw him fire that bullet into you. I examined you afterwards. There was no trickery I could detect.'

'Do you imagine I wanted England humiliated?' Irene demanded. 'Her enemies to have the means to finance a war on our shores?'

'No.'

'Then what do you think?'

I paced, attempting to order my observations. 'There was a statue in the emporium that looked just like you, you know?'

'An amusement. I did Lee a favour once.'

'And the children learning circus arts? Where were their parents?'

Irene did not reply.

'Her Majesty has her agents,' I elaborated, 'of which you are one. And a very good one. But you have your own people, too. Lee and the children at the emporium—they're your agents,' I stated. 'And Rachel at the theatre. You take care of them. Her Majesty knows nothing of their existence.'

Irene scoffed. 'I can see the rational scientist in you has been overtaken by the writer tonight. One day, perhaps you'll turn your hand to drafting plays for the theatre, to thrill audiences with your florid imaginings.'

It was a poor attempt to discredit my logic. We both knew it.

'You asked me why you would help the German escape. For the same reason you had me running all over London. Because he provided the spectacle—the show. He could step into the spotlight and take the blame for the theft. When really that had occurred before he arrived. You pulled off the robbery of the century, Irene. You stole the real diamond—the most valuable jewel in existence. And you did it right under the noses of Her Majesty's best agents.'

'I...what?' Irene's eyes grew big, her jaw tight.

'When the German came after me,' I continued, 'you saw an opportunity. So while you pretended to go after the man, you actually used your own collection of street agents to ensure he escaped. You wanted him at large, and at that final meeting at Bedford Square.

'You kept him in play, until the end. Somehow he found his way to the top-secret location.'

'You must have led him there, Doctor. He was following you,' she asserted.

I shook my head. 'If he had followed me that day, he'd have had sodden trousers and shoes, like mine. His were dry.

'You suspected he might attack you at that final meeting,' I continued, 'so you prepared yourself as best you could with Lee's vest. Meanwhile, you stationed your own agents to run interference across the street if the authorities got too close to him afterwards. According to reports, attempts to apprehend the thief in Bedford Square were impeded by a group of mothers wheeling prams on the green, an Oriental man on a bicycle and some children practising acrobatics—a girl among them.

'Lee had made a copy of the stone. After the diamond was authenticated, as we drank a toast to her Majesty, you exchanged it for the real jewel. It was the imitation the German made off with. That's why you had your people there, to make sure he wasn't caught and the fraud exposed. Your people will presume the real jewel lost. The enemy government won't discover the truth until later. And they can hardly complain then.'

Irene smiled with her mouth, but not her eyes. 'That's quite a story, Doctor. But if that were true, where did the diamond go? I was shot and unconscious. You examined me, unfettered, and presumably did not find a rock upon my person?'

'No, I did not,' I conceded.

'Well, then...?' She raised eyebrows, awaiting my answer.

As I chewed upon my bottom lip, uncertain, Irene began to relax. She was a cool customer that one—ice cool.

'I recall you were very keen to have a drink after that near-death incident,' I said. 'And who could blame you? I remember at the time looking into the bucket and seeing that the ice had started to melt, all but one solitary cube that remained whole.

'You made the switch and dropped the real diamond into the ice bucket, to reclaim later. When you regained consciousness, that was the first thing you checked on.'

I thought she might deny it. Instead, she was quiet for a time, then flashed me a dazzling smile, nothing held back. 'You know, Sherlock underestimates you.'

'In summary,' I continued, trying not to succumb to flattery, 'you were one of the Queen's agents, charged with securing the jewel.

But secretly, you had your own people, your own agents working to your agenda. As a result, a fake diamond has been set into the royal sceptre in the Crown Collection. Sherlock will go on record as vouching for it. The Queen's agents will ask no further questions about it; they believe the German stole the jewel and will endeavour to keep the theft a secret so as not to discredit the government. But in reality, the real diamond was under their noses the whole time.'

Irene chuckled. 'Well, all the other jewels in the Crown Collection have been replaced with copies, to pay gambling debts for this royal cousin or that duke. At least the proceeds for this one will go to a good cause.'

'Your people?' I asked.

'London's an expensive city to live in, as I'm sure you know. But a cheap place to die.'

Without funds to pay their way, many paid with their lives, I knew.

We drank a toast, sizing each other up, as allies, and enemies.

'If you repeat that wild theory to anyone, Doctor,' Irene said, 'they'll never believe you. And if Sherlock were to investigate further, well, it might end badly for him.'

Was she making threats? Against Sherlock? It was my turn to smile now. Irene Adler was formidable and as ruthless as any male, I had no doubt of that. However, I did not believe Holmes was in any present danger.

He always said when you eliminated the impossible, whatever remained, however improbable, must be the truth. I knew a bag had been packed with some of Sherlock's belongings for his stay in protective custody. Included in that was his smoking jacket, slippers, and violin. Neither the seasoned secret agents nor Sherlock himself would have bothered with such fripperies. So who did? It had to be a particular agent, concerned not just with his survival, but his comfort and contentment. Irene Adler had packed his case.

And someone who had demonstrated that much care would not harm him without a most pressing reason. For now at least, I reasoned, he was safe.

I laid out my argument for Irene, who made no attempt to deny it.

'Well, next time I want to blackmail Sherlock,' she said, 'I know what to do. I have but to steal his violin and threaten to harm it, and all my demands will be met. That framed photo by his bedside reveals where his heart truly lies.'

Indeed.

But for all her cleverness, she'd missed the most important clue. If she'd used her Sherlock logic, she would have noted fingerprints on the glass in the frame, revealing the picture was handled frequently. The photo on display was fractionally askew, as if placed there quickly and carelessly. Which should have given her a hint. Beneath the picture of the violin, was a second photo of something Sherlock valued even more than his instrument. It was a portrait of Irene herself.

The two of them liked to think they were adventurous and brave, disdaining love as a commonplace illusion somehow beneath them. But in this area, I was the master and they the students.

For I knew love was the ultimate risk. It demanded you lower your guard and reveal your vulnerabilities, effectively placing the secret of your destruction in the hands of another. Neither of them had the courage to take that risk. To trust anyone to that extent. Not yet anyway.

I did not divulge Sherlock's secret to her. It was not mine to reveal.

At this point, Rachel, the rose-cheeked beauty I'd met during my last visit backstage, rushed in. 'Irene, a gentleman begs your attendance,' she said. 'He says he is tired of lingering by the stage door and his generosity tonight will be seriously curtailed if he has to wait much longer.'

'Offer him my apologies,' said Irene, 'and tell him I will not be attending to him tonight—or any night—until he learns some manners with me and my people.'

The girl smiled. 'I would love to tell him that, but I fear his reaction.'

'Very well, I'll tell him myself.' Irene turned to me. 'Excuse me, Doctor?'

She got up to leave, turning back briefly to give me a wink and a playful smile—a gift from one of the strongest and smartest women I've ever encountered—before heading down the corridor.

Rachel and I waited together, awkwardly.

'Are you studying to be an actress?' I asked.

'Yes, sir.'

'You have a good teacher in Irene.'

'Yes, sir.'

'And what do your parents think about that?'

'I have no parents. Irene takes care of me.'

I wondered how many more there were like Rachel, under Irene's protective wing, who would otherwise perish in the city.

'Well, good night to you, Rachel. And say good night to Miss Adler for me.' I put my hat on, and prepared to leave.

'Miss Adler?' the girl seemed confused.

'Irene Adler.'

'Oh yes, Adler's her stage name. We know her by her real name.'

'And what's that?'

'Irene Moriarty.'

VILLAINY IN THE VERTICAL VILLAGE
Joseph S. Walker

Guidebooks and travel websites call Kern, Arizona, a ghost town. To quote the eminent philosopher, Monty Python, however, we're not dead yet. Of course, it is true that a village boasting ten thousand residents a century ago has dropped to under two hundred. That's mostly a long downward spiral from natural causes, since the copper mines that were the town's entire reason for existing in the first place went bust decades ago. Until the day June Laredo got a pickax buried in his chest, murder was not a significant factor in the village's population decline.

#

Kern, today, is just a couple hundred ramshackle buildings clinging stubbornly to the side of a mountain, along a road that slaloms back and forth as it climbs from the valley floor before finally slipping over the shoulder of the peak. From a distance, the town looks like a few lines of faded, blockish shapes pasted diagonally onto a much larger, sage green triangle. Most of the buildings are empty, and many are too dangerous to go into. The brutally steep grade has been rendered even more unstable by the decaying network of mine tunnels and shafts running underneath the town. Every few years, one of the buildings either slides down the hill or collapses into a pit. It always makes for a bit of excitement, hearing a sudden, ungodly crash in the middle of the night and hoping nobody still lived there.

Maybe you get hurricanes where you live. Do I judge?

Tourists from the flat Midwest creep up Kern's single, zigzagging road with bloodless faces and white knuckles, leaning into the steering wheel, unnerved to find themselves, after each steeply banked hairpin turn, suddenly level with the roofs of the buildings whose front doors they just drove past. At the top, by the abandoned mine buildings at the old main shaft, they can park and catch the small trolley that runs from the town to the peak and back continuously through the day, making regular stops at all of Kern's allegedly world-famous attractions. They can eat at the Lost Miner Diner, which claims, based on no particular evidence, to have the best burgers in the state. They can visit the once luxurious Clark Hotel to hear of the poor, doomed chambermaid (or, if there are no children in the group, prostitute) who haunts room 303. They can roam through the Kern Copper Heritage Center to see rusting mining tools and a scale model of the town built from toothpicks. Finally, if they have any energy remaining, they can spend some time, and hopefully some money, at the Motherlode Gallery, offering a dazzling assortment of jewelry, photographs, sculptures, and miscellaneous doodads turned out by local artists.

Most of them don't have the required remaining energy, which is kind of a shame, since I own the Motherlode.

Before it was an art gallery and souvenir shop, it was the house where I was born and grew up, and I still live on the top floor. My parents gave up on Kern years ago. They're up near Seattle now. My mother wanted to live someplace where she could see water without turning a tap and walk outside without getting sunstroke.

Two things keep me in Kern, trying to make a go of it. The first is what remains of my artistic ambition. I was a jock in high school, a brawler and a troublemaker, but that changed when I picked up a camera. I have an eye for taking attractive pictures of the mountains and deserts in this part of the country, and nothing matches the satisfaction of somebody wanting to part with actual money to hang one of my photos on their wall.

The second thing is the girl next door. Literally. While I was growing up in a building that would become a gallery, Susan Morgan was growing up in the adjoining building, already operating as the Copper Heritage Center. There's a doorway now linking the lobbies of our businesses, which means I could get from my bedroom to hers without even going outside. Tragically, I've never had cause to make the trip. It's both my blessing and my curse that

Susan thinks of me as that most hopeful and hopeless of creatures—the Best Friend. The starring role of Boyfriend was cast back in high school, and June Laredo had been clutching fiercely to the part ever since.

#

I came downstairs to open up shop one Saturday morning in September and was surprised to find the door to the Heritage Center still closed. Susan has always been an early riser, and usually by the time I wander in she's got both our OPEN signs hanging out and coffee waiting. I started a pot, then stepped out onto the sidewalk to gauge the day. It was already pushing ninety and the sky was high and pale blue and completely free of clouds. September's a good tourist season here because of people trying to avoid the summer heat, though these days summer seems to last most of the year.

I hoped for a profitable day. I'd spent the week framing big prints of some of my new shots of the red rock formations around nearby Sedona. Tasty bait for well-off travelers looking for an ostentatious souvenir.

A Honda SUV with Nebraska plates inched around the nearby curve, the woman behind the wheel leaning forward in concentration, the man beside her staring at his phone. A girl in the backseat stuck her tongue out at me as they went past and reared back in surprise when I stuck mine back out at her. She spun to start yelling at her parents about me.

Well, hell. Hopefully I hadn't just cost myself a sale.

Back inside, Susan was sitting behind her cash register, leaning back with her eyes closed. I poured coffee into her favorite mug—Sadness from the movie *Inside Out*—and brought it to her. She grunted thanks and took a long sip.

'Bad night?' I asked.

She shrugged, tracing a finger along the rim of the mug. 'June and I had a big fight.'

I'd heard this too many times before to immediately whoop out loud, click my heels together and go shopping for a ring. 'What about?'

'Oh, Bob asked me to talk to him,' she said. Bob Carlyle was the mayor of Kern, a position which mostly entailed shaking hands with tourists and bugging the state for money. 'They're getting complaints again. He's surly, he snaps at people, he's mean to kids. Apparently there was a family yesterday that got so mad they wouldn't even get on the trolley. Demanded a refund.'

June's great-grandfather had been one of the founders of Kern. His grandfather had led the miners in union battles with the company that had, on occasion, turned bloody. Now June's main job was driving the town trolley up and down the mountain. He was supposed to talk up the local businesses and offer amusing patter about Kern's history. For a while now, though, we'd been hearing that he either kept up a stony silence behind the wheel or just plain got nasty with people. Since the town would dry up and blow away once and for all without tourist dollars, there had been concern.

'Well, hell, let Bob talk to him,' I said. 'Kinda low to be getting you to do his dirty work.'

'It's not like it doesn't concern me,' she said. 'I need people in here, and happy people spend more money. But, Andy, he got so mad so fast. He said it's beneath our dignity to play yokel for a bunch of people he wouldn't spit on if they were on fire. Said he wasn't going to do it much longer. I asked him what he meant by that and he laughed and stormed out. I tried to call him all night, but he never answered.'

'Well, he can't avoid you for long,' I said. 'I haven't seen the trolley yet this morning, but it'll be by soon.'

'Yeah,' she sighed. 'We'll see if he even comes in to say hi, I guess.'

#

For the next hour, though, nobody turned up. I lost track of the time as I was hanging my new pictures, but I was vaguely aware of Susan wandering in and out, often stopping to look out the windows.

'I've counted twenty out-of-state plates going up,' she finally said. 'No trolley. What the hell is June doing?'

'Sulking?' I guessed. 'Have you tried calling him again?'

'Four times,' she said. At that moment, the bell on the front door of the Heritage Center rang. 'Finally,' she said. We both walked through the connecting doorway.

It wasn't June, and it wasn't a group of tourists. Mayor Bob Carlyle was standing just inside the door. He was flanked by Tim Alford, the town police chief, and Linda Espen, the state trooper who usually got sent out for anything beyond Tim's capabilities. Since Tim was pushing seventy and regarded the world through a perpetual haze of resigned confusion, Linda had gotten to know Kern pretty well the last few years.

'Susan, Andy,' Bob said. He looked miserable. If he'd had a hat, he would have been turning it in his hands. 'We, um...' He trailed off and looked helplessly at Linda.

'Ms Morgan,' Linda said. She looked crisp and fresh in her uniform, and she held her hat in her hand. She wasn't turning it. Since Tim was wearing a Diamondbacks T-shirt and a pair of shorts, complemented by neon blue Crocs, she was the only one in the group projecting any kind of authority. 'We need to see the Lover's Pickax for a minute, if we can.'

Susan looked baffled, but she shrugged assent. 'Sure,' she said. 'You all know where it is well enough.' She turned to lead the way, but Linda moved to head her off and go first. Susan frowned, but she let the trooper lead the way down the hall to what had once been a dining room and was now the main exhibit hall.

The Lover's Pickax was Kern's most famous artifact. It had belonged to June Laredo's great-grandfather, who was trapped in a distant corner of the mine by a cave-in. When the rescuers found his body a week later, he was lying on his back, clutching the pickax to his chest. On the handle, using a pocketknife and working in the dark, he had crudely carved the message 'Tell Maureen I love her.' Susan displayed it in a clear plastic case on a small table in the middle of the room. I've seen more than one tourist cry over it.

The five of us trooped in. The plastic case was on the floor. The pickax was gone.

'What the hell?' Susan said. 'June must have taken it. He's always threatened to. Says it belongs to his family. Did he send you guys here to tell me he's keeping it?'

'Not exactly,' said Tim.

'Susan,' Bob said. 'June's dead. We found him this morning on the floor of his kitchen with the Lover's Pickax stuck in his chest.'

Susan staggered backwards a step. Linda tried to block me, but I moved up and guided her to the bench at the side of the room where people can look at the model of the town. I got her seated and let my hand rest on her shoulder. She was staring at Bob and her mouth was moving, but nothing came out.

'Whole damn place is torn to hell,' Tim said. 'Furniture turned over, clothes thrown around. Looks like somebody had a hell of a fight.' He got the look on his face he gets when he thinks he's being clever. 'Lover's quarrel, I'd say.'

I started to stand up to challenge that, but Linda gestured me back down. 'Ms Morgan, when did you last see Mr Laredo?'

'For the love of Christ,' I said. 'You've known them both for years. You can call them Susan and June.'

Linda just shook her head at me. 'Mr Larson, be quiet or I'll have you removed.'

'Last night,' Susan said. 'He came over. We had a fight. He left about nine. I haven't seen or talked to him since.'

'What did you fight about?' Linda asked.

Susan looked at Bob. 'Why don't you tell her?'

Bob looked away. 'June's been a problem with the tourists lately. Acting hostile. I asked Susan to straighten him out.'

Tim grunted. 'That's right enough. Just last week I had to kick his ass a little to keep him from leaving a nice couple from Iowa on the side of the road.'

'Was something specific bothering him?' Linda looked at Bob, then me. 'Did he talk to any of you about it?'

I shook my head. I'd never gone out of my way to talk to June, since he clearly knew how I felt about Susan and liked to be amused about it.

'He's just a contrary sort,' Bob said. 'Could have been anything getting under his skin.'

'Life rubbed him wrong,' Tim said. 'He wanted to be a big man, like his granddaddy.'

'Okay,' Linda said. She took a pair of handcuffs off her belt. 'Ms Morgan, please stand up and put your hands behind your back. I'm placing you in custody.'

'Now wait a minute,' I said, standing up. 'Based on what?'

'Based on what?' Linda said. 'She was in possession of the

murder weapon and has admitted to arguing with the victim. Little things like that.' She softened a shade. 'I'm sorry, Andy, but I'm not calling my captain and telling him that I didn't arrest the obvious suspect.'

'It's okay,' Susan said. She stood up. 'Can I see June first?'

Linda shook her head as she was putting the cuffs on. 'I'm sorry. It's an active crime scene. There's a team coming from Sedona to collect evidence.' She looked at Tim. 'I can't leave long enough to run her to the county lockup. Is the cell free?'

Kern has a single small jail cell, at the back of the building where Tim and Bob have their offices. It's mostly used when somebody gets so ripping drunk they seem likely to fall down the mountain if left to their own devices.

'Sure,' Tim said. 'I can take her over.'

'No,' Linda said. 'I want you to stay here and keep this room locked down. After they're done at Mr Laredo's house, I'll send the team over here to see what they can turn up.'

'Happy to help,' Tim said. He dug into his pocket and handed Linda the key. She took Susan by the elbow and started for the hallway.

'Susan,' I said. 'What can I do?'

'I can't think straight,' she said. 'Come see me when you can. I didn't do this, Andy.'

'I know,' I said.

'Let's go,' Linda said. She and Susan walked out.

Bob sighed deeply and shook his head. 'I guess I'd better go get the trolley going. God knows how many tourists are up there waiting. Andy, you going to be open?'

'Yes,' I said. 'No. Hell, Bob, I don't know. Just look at the sign when you drive by.'

'You don't have to snap,' he said. He walked out.

Tim sat on the bench. 'I guess I gotta ask you to vacate the premises, Andy. Course I'm sure your fingerprints are all over this place. Susan's too.'

'Yeah,' I said. 'Who actually found him, Tim?'

'That little girl from the college. What's her name. Brittany something?'

'Ashley, I think.' Ashley was a tourism student at the state college.

She had some kind of internship, working on improving Kern's marketing. She'd interviewed Susan and me a couple of times. 'She went to June's house?'

Tim shrugged. 'She helped out on the trolley sometimes. Probably went over because he hadn't turned up. Poor little slip of a thing was hysterical.'

#

Hysterical I could understand. I hadn't even seen the body, and I felt like my brain had been cut off from my body. I hadn't liked June Laredo, but he'd been a presence in my life since early childhood. Since Laredo and Larson are next to each other in the alphabet, I'd stood beside him in countless lines at the schools in Sedona that Kern kids got bussed to. It would be strange not having him around, but I couldn't let myself start thinking about exactly how things might change. How I might want them to change.

I left Tim guarding an empty room and wandered back to the Motherlode. I hadn't been robbed while we were all in the back, so that was one good thing for the day. Without really thinking about it, I turned the sign on the front door to CLOSED and locked up. I went upstairs and stretched out on my bed and tried to think.

It didn't take me long to realize that was getting me nowhere.

I gave pacing a shot, then staring out the window. It was a hell of a view. From up here I could see damn near fifty miles across the long valley sweeping down to the desert toward Sedona. After a while, I realized I was mostly thinking about how June would never get to look at the view again, and then about how the state prison for women probably didn't overlook much of a vista.

I had to find something to do. It was getting close to noon, and Susan never did eat much of a breakfast. If nothing else, I could provide sustenance. I went up the short flight of stairs that led to the roof. A makeshift bridge connected it to the stretch of road above the one the gallery fronted. Most of the buildings in Kern have this kind of roof access. It's a hell of a lot more convenient than hiking all the way around on the street, though we all have incredibly well-developed calves.

I walked down the block to the Lost Miner Diner. As I'd expected, the place was buzzing. Since it was a weekend, most of the Kern residents who commute to Sedona for work were in town, and a good chunk of them were huddled around the tables, leaning toward each other to swap the latest gossip. When I walked in, every head in the place turned to look at me, and silence dropped like a blanket. I made a show of looking over my shoulder to see who was behind me.

'How's she doing, Andy?' someone said.

'Did she do it?' came from another direction.

I shook my head and went to the counter. Donnie Milleret was working, and I could see through the doorway that his parents were both in the kitchen. I'd known them my whole life, too. I'd known pretty much everyone in the room my whole life.

'Andy,' Donnie said. 'Sit anywhere. Haven't had any tourists yet today.'

'I want to take something to Susan,' I said. 'God knows what Tim has to eat over there. Beef jerky from the Depression, probably. Can you make up a couple of hamburgers?'

'Sure thing,' he said. He went into the kitchen. I put my back against the counter and looked out over the room.

'Who was that asking if she did it?' I said conversationally.

The room went quiet again. I scanned the room. A few folks met my eyes. Most didn't.

'I don't want to hear that question again,' I said.

Everybody thought about that for a couple of minutes.

Donnie came around the counter and handed me a paper bag and a couple of cold cans of soda. 'Ma put some extra fries in,' he said.

'Thanks, Donnie.' I reached for my wallet but he held up his hand.

'No charge,' he said. 'You tell Susan to let us know, she needs anything.' He raised his voice. 'Tell her nobody at the Diner thinks she's a killer, and we're sorry for her troubles.'

I nodded my thanks, gave the room one last lookover, and walked out. Part of me felt like Gary Cooper. The rest of me was sure they'd all be laughing before I was ten feet away.

#

At Kern's makeshift town hall, I found Susan perched on the cot in the small cell. Ashley was sitting at Tim's desk, huddled into herself. Of the two of them she looked more miserable, but then she was the one who'd started the day with a murder victim.

'What are you doing here?' I asked.

She shrugged. 'That state cop asked me to sit with Ms Morgan. I guess there's nobody else to do it and she says the crime scene people will want to talk to me, so I can't leave anyway.'

'Well, you can take a break,' I said. 'I've brought lunch for the desperado.'

She looked at me dubiously.

'Ashley,' I said. 'There is exactly one road leading through this town. If I busted her out all the state cops would have to do is sit on it and wait for us to turn up.'

'Promise you won't open the cell,' she said.

'Unless the desperado needs the bathroom,' Susan added quickly.

'Yeah, that,' Ashley said.

I held up my right hand. 'I do so solemnly promise.'

'Okay.' Ashley stood up. 'I guess I'll get some lunch myself.'

'Here.' I handed her a twenty. 'Overtip. Donnie wouldn't take my money.'

She took the money and left. I passed one of the sodas through the bars and opened the bag.

'I'm not all that hungry,' Susan said.

'Okay. There's extra fries though.'

'Damn. Okay, give.'

Somewhere on the list of things I like about Susan is that she eats like food is a pleasure. She's not one of those girls who don't like guys to see them eating.

I gave her one of the burgers and a tray of fries and parked myself in Tim's chair with the rest. 'How you holding up?'

She shook her head. 'I can't believe this is real. June is dead and I'm in jail for murder. I can't decide which thing I believe less.'

'The second one,' I said. 'Nobody thinks you did it.'

'You mean you don't think I did it.' She took a bite of the sandwich. 'I think we can agree you might be a little bit biased.'

I decided to ignore that. 'Well, nobody in the room right now thinks you did it, then. Do you have any thoughts on who did?'

'I don't know,' she said. She rubbed a temple. 'Before you came in, I was actually wondering about her.'

'Ashley?' I didn't hide my surprise. 'She weighs about eighty pounds. I doubt she could swing a pickax, let alone kill somebody with it. Anyway, why?'

'June told me she was sweet on him. Tried to kiss him a couple of times.'

I screwed up my mouth. 'Why would anybody be sweet on June?' A heartbeat after the last word left my mouth, I clamped it closed. Too late.

'You want to rephrase that?' Susan asked.

I took a huge bite of my hamburger and pointed to my mouth. Can't talk while I'm chewing.

'Uh huh,' she said. She took a drink. 'I understand. If I'm honest, I loved June. I did. I do. But it's been a while since I've felt like I like him.'

I swallowed. 'Everybody keeps saying he's been different lately.'

'Lately? I'd say a year. More. And people like Bob don't know the half of it.' She pulled her feet up onto the cot and hugged her knees with her free hand. 'When he wasn't working, he'd just disappear for hours. A whole day, sometimes. At first I thought he was seeing another woman, but then I started to think that he was driving to Sedona or somewhere and deliberately getting into fights with people. He had weird bruises and scraped knuckles, and his clothes were filthy.'

'Why would he be getting into fights? Fights about what?'

'Nothing. Anything. He was so angry, Andy. He hated playing chauffeur. He said all the time that if the world was a fair place he'd be rich.'

Before I could respond to that, Bob came in. 'Guess I'm not surprised to see you here,' he said to me. 'Susan, you need anything?'

'A file in a cake?' she said.

'Hell, you could probably pull the planks off that wall with your bare hands. You got any idea how old this place is?' He opened the top drawer of Tim's desk and started rummaging through it.

'What are you looking for?' I asked.

'There's supposed to be a spare set of keys for the trolley in here somewhere,' Bob said. 'The crime scene people won't give us the set June had with him. What a hell of a day.'

'There used to be a set in that little utility room he used up at the old mine building,' Susan said. 'Where he kept the guest book and pamphlets and everything.'

'Yeah, well,' Bob said. 'Good luck finding them. That place is a mess.' He held up a keyring. 'Bingo.'

'What do you mean?' Susan said. 'June was a lot of things, but he wasn't a slob. He kept that room organized.'

'I guess that was another part of the job he didn't want anymore,' Bob said. 'I gotta go rescue those tourists or nobody's doing any business today.' He opened the door and almost collided with Ashley coming back in. He grunted in exasperation, moved past her and was gone.

Ashley had her own bag of food. She handed me my twenty. 'Donne said nice try.'

'Worth a shot,' I said. 'Hey, you know anything about that little room up at the mine being messed up?'

'Oh, yeah,' she said. 'That was the first thing that was weird today. I was supposed to meet him up there to ride along today. When he was late, I went to look for him in the building and the utility room was a jumble. All the tourist pamphlets were scattered around on the floor, and the guestbook too. I thought kids must have done it.'

'So, what?' I said. 'June had fights with the killer both at the mine and at his house? What did they do, carpool from one place to the other?'

'I don't know,' Ashley said. 'It creeps me out to think about any of it. Hey, did you know his real first name was Juneau? Juneau Laredo?'

'Yeah,' Susan said. 'His folks traveled a lot. They named him after the place where he was conceived. He hated it.'

'Where are they now?'

'Florida. Linda's trying to contact them.'

I was only half listening. I was thinking about that utility room.

#

I was still thinking about it later that night as it began to get dark. The crime scene people had taken the rest of the day to clear June's home and the exhibit room the pickax had come from. When they finally released June's body, Linda had the hearse come by the jail. She took Susan out and stood at a respectful distance while she had a minute to say goodbye.

I spent most of the day sitting in Tim's office, trying to keep Susan company. For long stretches we didn't talk much. I would have offered to call somebody if there was anybody to call, but her folks had died in a car accident a few years back. I did offer to find a lawyer, but she said that could wait until they decided if they really had enough to charge her.

For tonight, at least, she was still in the jail here in Kern. That was another effort on Linda's part to be kind, I think. Tomorrow, though, she'd be going to Laredo to be interviewed and, in all probability, formally charged. I wanted to stay in the office overnight, but Linda politely, but firmly, told me that informal courtesies only went so far, and that a couple of other state cops were coming up to keep tabs on Susan until the morning.

Lying in bed, I looked up at the ceiling and thought about things as the light from outside dimmed. I had an idea of what I wanted to do, but I had to work to convince myself to do it. The hard part wasn't trusting my hunch. The hard part was convincing myself that it would be okay to go into Susan's bedroom for the first time without her permission or knowledge.

The last light was almost gone when I swung my feet to the floor. I turned on the bedside lamp by the window and left it burning. I went out and down the stairs to what used to be the kitchen when I was growing up. Now it's my darkroom and workspace. I gathered what I needed and put it in a little bag.

So far it had been easy. I knew every inch of my home. Now, though, I had to navigate unknown territory, and just in case anybody was watching windows, I had to do it in the dark. I slipped though the connecting door into the Heritage Center and started up the stairs. The second floor was part of the museum. Susan's bedroom was on the third floor.

Once I was inside I stood a minute to let my heart slow down from the climb and from the scent that was a little bit flower and a little bit powder and all Susan. I set my bag by the door and turned on the little flashlight on my phone, shielding it with my hand. The bed was a big unmade four-poster. The closet door was open. There was a bureau up against the wall. I went to it and opened the top drawer. Bras and panties. I shut it quickly.

The second drawer was T-shirts and pajamas.

The third drawer was the hit: June's drawer, with supplies of his clothes and toiletries for when he stayed over. I blocked that part out of my mind and knelt, running my hands carefully between the layers of cloth. If there was nothing here, I figured I'd look under the bed next, then try the closet. It was possible, of course, that I was completely wrong about all of this and that there was nothing to find.

Except there was. It was folded into the back pocket of a pair of jeans at the bottom of the drawer. Easy to miss. Just a business-sized envelope with a couple of pieces of paper in it. I flattened them against the floor and shined the light on them. It only took a couple of minutes to see I'd been right.

Now to hope I was right about the rest of it, too. I didn't know how long I had to get ready. I tucked the envelope into my little bag and pulled out my supplies.

#

As it turned out, I could have taken my time. It was almost two in the morning before I heard a creak in the ceiling above me. I'd been half dozing, but I was immediately awake and alert. Somebody had come across from the upper road and was walking cautiously to the doorway leading down into Susan's building. It wasn't locked. Susan kept the museum part locked at night, but like most folks in Kern didn't bother with the doors up here. I listened as steps made their way slowly down to this level. A flashlight beam moved across the hallway outside, then explored the first few feet of the bedroom floor. The shape holding the flashlight came into the room, and the circle of illumination found the bureau.

I turned on the lamp next to the chair I was sitting in at the other side of the room. 'Evening, Bob,' I said.

The mayor spun to me. For the second time in twenty-four hours, I saw somebody rendered speechless.

'Morning, I should say,' I added.

'Andy,' he managed. 'I'm—Susan asked me to come get some of her things for the night.'

'Now that's not bad,' I said. 'Maybe you had it ready, but if you're thinking on the fly, that's pretty good. It'd fall apart if we called Tim's office, of course.'

'I don't know what you mean,' he said.

I held up the envelope. 'You mean to say you're not looking for this?'

He started forward, his hand actually reaching for it before it dropped back to his side. 'I don't know what that is.'

'Sure you do,' I said. 'You tore apart June's house and the utility room at the mine looking for it. That was your mistake, really. Why not leave the utility room looking decent? You could pass off June's place as getting messed up in a fight, but that didn't make sense for two different places. My guess is you were just pissed.'

'You've got a rich imagination,' he said.

'Not as rich as June's,' I said. 'I have to give him credit. He didn't just get fed up with driving tourists around, he actually did something about it. He's been going back down into the mine, looking for a new vein. And this,' I held the envelope up again, 'is the proof that he was right. A lab report explicitly stating that the ore samples he sent in were of sufficient quality and quantity to be viable for commercial mining. He was going to open it all back up again, wasn't he?'

Bob was shaking. 'He came to me last week. He actually thought I'd be happy about it. Support him.'

'I take it he was wrong.'

'Of course he was wrong! We've got a nice life here, Andy. You must see that. We're not rich, but we have a nice little town and all we have to do is smile for the camera once in a while. And he wanted to bring it all back. The stench, the trucks, the noise, the way the whole town would shake when they set off charges. No more museums. No more precious little art shops. You're too young, Andy. I remember it from when I was a kid. This town was hell.'

'What about the money?' I asked.

Bob laughed. 'What money? He bought the mineral rights to the whole mountain for himself. It was cheap, because nobody thought there was anything to have the rights to. He would have been rich, sure. You think he was going to share it? Think he was going to, what, make the guy who's been chasing his girl since high school an executive vice president? His granddaddy was union to the bone. He would have been sick at the idea of June being the company. The boss.'

'So you killed him. I guess you got lucky there, picking the night when he actually went through with his threat to take the Lover's Pickax.'

'Lucky, hell,' he said. 'I was watching him. Waiting for a chance. I was close enough to the window last night to hear them fight. A couple of hours after he stormed out, I came back and snuck in downstairs and took it. Mayor's office has keys to every business in town.' He looked hungrily at the envelope I was tapping against my thigh. 'My only mistake was assuming he would have the lab report at his place. When I couldn't find it, I tried the mine. By that time it was too late to come look for it here.'

'Well, I wouldn't say that was your only mistake,' I said. I opened the envelope and showed him that it was empty. 'The actual report is hidden, Bob. Maybe it's in this building. Maybe mine.'

He shook his head. 'I wish you hadn't done that, Andy.' He took a gun out of his pocket. 'Now I have to make you talk.'

'You can try,' I said. 'But here's the thing, Bob. I'm a photographer. And not just a still photographer. You see that little box stuck in the upper corner behind me? That's a camera. And ever since you came into the room it's been recording.'

He looked stricken. 'So I'll take the camera.'

'Get with the times, Bob. What are you going to do, expose the film? It's been uploading to the cloud. Even if you kill me right now, even if you find the report, Linda Espen will be getting an email in the morning with a link she can click on to see your confession in living color.'

He closed his eyes. He staggered to the bed and sank down onto it. He seemed to become aware of the gun and held it up briefly, studying it, then dropped it on the floor.

'You shouldn't have tried to frame her, Bob,' I said. 'I can almost understand everything but that.'

'What if I just leave?' he said. 'Get up and walk out the door? Will you stop me?'

I thought about it. 'No,' I said. 'You've always been decent to me. Helped me start up the gallery after my folks left. I'll give you an hour, but you'd better think hard about how to use it.' I hardened my voice. 'Clock's ticking, Bob. Run.'

#

As it turned out, Bob wasn't much better at running than he was at framing people. He should have made straight for Mexico, or at least a state border, but the cops picked him up just a few hours later at the Greyhound station in Phoenix, trying to buy a ticket for Kansas. Maybe he figured nobody would think to look for him someplace entirely horizontal.

A couple of weeks later, he pleaded guilty to June's murder to avoid the death penalty, though he'll die in prison. Linda Espen came in person to give Susan and me the news, right after Donnie Milleret, the town's new trolley driver, had picked up a batch of happily free-spending tourists. I think Bob would have been pleased to know that the publicity of the murder had been good for business.

'So,' Linda said. 'I guess that just leaves the question of what's going to happen to Kern.'

'Not a thing,' Susan said. June's will, made years ago, had left her all his worldly possessions, which now included the mineral rights to the mountain we were sitting on. He'd never had much use for his folks. I don't think he'd ever really forgiven them for naming him Juneau. 'Bob was right about that much. Going back to mining would destroy this town. I've been talking to some lawyers about setting up a trust to make sure it never happens.'

'I guess that's it, then.' Linda said on her way out. 'See you the next time Tim needs a hand with a drunk or something.'

I went back into the Motherlode. One of the women who'd just left had dropped a bundle on a dramatic shot of the Coffeepot rock formation, and I had to prep it for shipping to Indiana. I was humming to myself when I became aware of Susan hovering in the doorway between our buildings.

'Yes?' I said.

'I still haven't really thanked you,' she said.

'Don't. I didn't do it for you. I was just trying to spare myself the long drives to come visit you in the can.'

'Right,' she said. 'I should have known.' She turned to go back to her counter, but glanced back over her shoulder. 'Andy?'

'Yes?'

'Be patient,' she said. 'Just a little longer.'

She walked away before I could say anything. That was okay. I've been patient a long time. I can be patient a little longer. Patience comes naturally to those of us living halfway between the valley and the peak, waiting to see which way we'll go.

SCREEN SHOT
Teel James Glenn

My name is Jon Shadows, and in my experience, the two words that seem to go together with a good deal of comfort are *Hollywood* and *irony*.

I came to realize that even more when I was called on to step a little out of my usual bodyguard duties and come, after the fact, to a scene of tragedy. In point to the fact, I was asked to do what they call a "psychological autopsy", which is when you try to figure out what went through someone's mind before they put a bullet in it without having the body to examine. After all, in this case I was told there was no doubt about the cause of death, so all that was left was the reason.

'I can't make sense of any of it,' the now-dead space captain said on the laptop screen I was looking at. Behind the guy in the space captain uniform was a calendar with half the dates X-ed out in blood red and a rack of hats on a wall, all and all a very non-spaceship setting. 'I have to end it,' the captain continued. Then the image of the man on the screen showed him putting the revolver that he held in his hand up to his right temple and he pulled the trigger.

I froze the screen before his falling forward onto the laptop that had shut the computer off. And before he'd splattered his brains out of the side of his head. I turned to the woman who had brought the thumb drive with the gruesome image to me and begged me to look at it. 'I've looked at this a number of times since I got this, Mrs Barnet, and I can't think any differently than the police—your brother killed himself, I am sad to say, and this video proves it without any doubt.'

The middle-aged woman that sat across from me in the booth at Universal Studio's café was clearly past tears, but the aura of misery hung around her like a cloud. 'I know that, Mister Shadows,' she said in a quiet, restrained voice, 'but despite what the public thought, my brother was a deeply religious man. He was a devout Catholic and his taking his own life like this...was...was an aberration. It was just not who he was. I know he had periods of deep depression, any artist does, every actor I am told, but to think that something drove him to this, and I missed it, is a guilt I cannot live with. What could have caused such desperation, such depths of pain? I want to know; I need to know if there is something I could have done. Please help me find out.'

I was in Los Angeles on another case when the Shadows Foundation for Justice's coordinator referred Jill Barnet to me. My father had founded the organization to help those who could find no help elsewhere and I was the main investigator-advocate for it. This case seemed really beyond our scope; her brother was the one who had needed help and he was gone.

I really didn't see I could do anything but agree with the police's final ruling on the suicide of Bill Shaker, famous for the role of Space Captain Cody in the '90s TV series. He was in the process of making the revival movie when, on a lunch break, he put a gun to his head.

I had enjoyed his show way back when, and to see him—in his captain's uniform—put that gun to his head was startling even to this jaded investigator. If you wanted to be cynical, I guess you could say his last show was his most spectacular.

'I don't know that I can do much to give you the closure you want, Mrs Barnet. Unfortunately, it all seems pretty cut and dried.'

'That's what they all said to me, Mister Shadows, but I know it's not true. Why? I can't say—just a feeling, perhaps, but still, I have to know why. You are my last hope to find closure. I have nowhere else to go.'

There it was, the final appeal. The mandate of the Foundation was "Help for the helpless, hope for the hopeless," so I could not really turn my back on her. Even if I could only give her a vague peace of mind, I had to try.

'Okay, Mrs Barnet,' I said, 'I do my best. I will look into it.'

#

The first thing I had to do was get a sense of who the real Bill Shaker was, what kind of man, in order to find out what could have driven him to suicide. I started my search for the truth at where his truth had ended for him, his bungalow on the Universal Studios movie lot.

Coming from the east coast, it was an odd feeling walking down those back lot streets in the off-hours, the New York Street so familiar from so many movies was like a dream version of my own city. Then there was the European street right next to it. I was especially impressed by the cobbled stones that ran under the arch where the Frankenstein monster had raged against the villagers, so long ago. I guess the little kid in me came out then and imagined running from the black and white monster that had made me hide under the covers long before the real life danger of Afghanistan.

Hollywood magic seemed so real walking on those streets, but then, that was the whole idea of the so-called "dream factory".

The little bungalow that Bill Shaker had used when on the lot was in a line of others and still had the "do not enter" tape across the door. I had written authorization for the LA Sheriff's Department and a key, so I went directly in.

Inside the room had remained untouched from the day, two weeks ago, when William "Bill" John Shaker had been found with his brains blown out on the floor of the bungalow.

Once I closed the door all outside sound was gone and I was alone as Bill Shaker must have been in those last moments.

I stood for a moment to take it in, even closing my eyes to visualize the computer screen again. When I opened them, I looked around again.

To my right was the big production calendar he'd used to keep track of his commitments with all but the last two days crossed off; a hat rack with several fedoras that he favored as a style choice and was known for wearing to public events; and an open closet with spare space captain uniforms, a suit jacket, robe and slippers. Next to that was a bathroom door.

To my left was a daybed under a long, high-up window with some photos on the wall of Shaker from various series he had been in; *RD Walker-Police*, *The Barberry War* and, of course, *Space Captain*

Cody (from his two-year run in the early '90s). It had since become something of a cult hit.

Straight ahead of me was the desk with a makeup mirror above it with photos and notes stuck up on the glass. I found myself looking at me standing there at the door and thought I looked a bit lost for what to do next. I sure felt it.

On the floor was a dark stain in the carpet that was evidence of the last moments of the actor Bill Shaker, whose histrionic performances I had enjoyed as Space Captain Cody. I had even sent away for a box top premium with a space badge.

I crossed the room and pulled up the rattan chair to the desk to sit down. In front of me was the blank space where his laptop computer had been when he had taken his life.

I looked at the mementoes around the mirror. There were a number of snapshots: Shaker and his sister—Mrs Barnet—at some première years ago, one of his racehorses, his estranged wife from better days when she had first guest starred on his old show.

Tucked among them were a Catholic mass card for another actor who had passed away two years ago, some cartoon drawings of his Captain Cody character from some fan of the original show, and a rosary with a note from a fan blessing him for visiting a children's hospital.

I put my hand on the desk, trying to imagine his headspace before he put the gun to his temple. In the mirror, I could see what I had in the video with the hat rack and calendar—the light streaming in from the window.

None of it made sense. Bill Shaker had done two seasons of a show that a short-lived network canceled, but it wasn't the end of a career. He'd had work before and work since—a steady, if unremarkable, leading TV actor's career doing guest shots on other TV shows and a good number of TV movies that got good ratings.

And in recent years, cable and streaming reruns of *Space Captain Cody* had made it a legitimate cult hit. Shaker had, in the meantime, been far-sighted enough to buy the rights to the character, thus giving himself the power to jump on producing and starring in a revival TV film as a sort of reboot/pilot with hopes for a series.

Everything was going swimmingly for the actor.

'No sense at all,' I said looking once more around the room. 'You should have been on the top of the world, Captain Cody!'

#

'Bill was a freaking religious nut,' Gloria La Mar said. The faux blonde vixen was every bit a Hollywood ex-wife with more man-made parts than a Tesla, but her anger at Shaker was real. 'He kept saying he couldn't divorce me because it was a sin because we had been joined in the eyes of God at the church!'

She had agreed to meet me in a diner on Cahuenga Boulevard and had entered the place like she was walking the red carpet. I half expected the paparazzi to mob her—well at least she seemed to expect it, though none showed up.

I recognized her from an old episode of *Space Captain Cody*, though I suspected back then there had been more original parts. I couldn't tell if she was smiling or stuck in a stiff wind, because the skin on her face was so tight.

'So, you're saying you can't believe he would take his own life?'

'Well, he would go to mass five times a week and all that,' she said with disgust, 'but it still didn't stop him from breaking his wedding vows by sharing his Captain's log with little fangirls at conventions. Somehow he was able to reconcile that with his vows to me.'

'Is that why you left him?'

'Those little flakes were barely a blip on the sea of marriage,' she gave an unconcerned laugh. 'They could never give a man what I could.' I thought I saw the memory of an expression on her face with that proclamation. 'I tried for a long time to be what he wanted, to stay young for him; it didn't matter to Bill. Ultimately though, I left him because I was not getting the attention and love I needed. And I found a better man who loves me for who I really am. That's it, plain and simple. But Bill had to be in control. He would not let me go; would not give me the divorce and let me marry the love of my life.'

I tried to figure if she was playing me, but her statement rang as the only real thing about her. So I decided to press on and ask, 'Can you think of anything—anything at all—that might have driven him to this?'

She shook her head and I thought I caught some real expression under the flesh mask, almost sadness. 'I really did want to be free, but not this way. Not this way.'

#

'Bill Shaker was a shit,' Jeffery Matthews said, leaning forward in his chair behind his desk and pointing a finger at me. 'When I found him dead in his dressing room, it just proved what an arrogant, self-serving prig he was. Whatever made him check out, he didn't give a damn about me or the rest of the production group that he left stranded high and dry on this show.'

Matthews was a thin man, but not a frail one, with long-fingered hands that were those of an artist. He was seated in his office a few blocks from Universal Studios, surrounded by models of spaceships from *Space Captain Cody* and several other shows he had worked on as special effects supervisor.

'You sure don't mince words, Mister Matthews,' I said as non-committal as I could. He'd been gracious enough about seeing me after I made it clear I was not there for any kind of "on the record" comment. I played things as casual as I could.

'Don't get me wrong,' he was quick to add, 'on screen he held the eye and he knew Cody; I really do think he would have made this revival a real hit, 'cause he still had it, you know?'

'But?'

'But as a human being he was almost the opposite of that caring, connecting character he played on that show. He was a user—could never allow anyone else to have the spotlight; not his co-stars, his wife, his friends. He would take the good lines from other actors in the original series, steal all the good scenes for himself. And he made sure he got the love scenes. Add to that he was vicious in business.'

'Yet you were co-producer on this revival with him; you co-wrote it with him. That seems like you were letting yourself in for some misery.'

He shrugged. 'I fleshed out his script idea, yes, but he made it clear there would be no show without him. But he also knew there was no show without me and what I could do with squeezing a dollar the farthest for production value. I started in the old show as physical prop man and modelmaker but rose to SFX supervisor. A lot of the "in" stuff that made it popular with the fans in the old show came out of my innovations, even if he refused to acknowledge them back then.

He realized this meant I had to be part of this incarnation, which is why he came to me. And there was no way this one would look as good for the budget he was able to raise, without me.' He pointed to a screen on the wall with footage running of the revival show—what they call raw footage. There was a series of numbers running across the bottom of the screen.

There was no sound but images of Shaker, in character and full, colorful uniform, striding around the command deck of his spaceship. The scene shifted to a long shot of the space ship circling a planet then dissolved into what looked like the planet surface where several of the other crew members in full helmeted spacesuits trudging across a hostile landscape that was a splash of crimson and orange stone and odd shapes. One of the space-suited figures stumbled and the picture froze.

'Okay, Doug,' Matthews said into a recorder he held up to his face. 'At 21:27 the shadows are not tracking on the planet surface to match the figures as they walk across the open plain. Fix them.'

I looked at the screen and sure enough, now that he mentioned it, the shadows cast by the two astronauts did not match those of the rocks they were maneuvering through. When Matthews saw my expression, he said, 'CGI sets—the whole planet surface is provided via green screen. It allows us to put in the backgrounds and build sets optically that we could not afford in real life. Only way we could afford the scope of the script.'

'Movie magic,' I said.

'TV budget magic,' he laughed. Then his expression got serious. 'And thank God for it. It was the only way we could write around Shaker offing himself.'

'How so?'

'The last two days were planned to be shoots of the planet surface and his character was supposed to be in it, albeit wearing his spacesuit. They were key to the story and were spread through the script. We were able to use a double for all the suit long shots with a little rewriting, then use an old close-up of him from an out-take and actually put it in the helmet for the very last shot. We gave all the lines to other actors and you just see him smiling as if Captain Cody was glad his crew had learned all the lessons he had taught them. I'll show you—' He touched a button on the desk and forwarded the footage on the screen to a shot of a space-suited figure standing alone against a fictional vista of stars and two moons. The camera zoomed in and the last shot was a smiling Bill Shaker inside that suit. He looked actually beatific and even wise in the shot.

'Wow,' I said. 'Sure looks like he is really in that helmet.'

'Yes, it does.' He beamed like a father at a high school graduation. 'I'm good at what I do. That will give us an ending that works for this show. No thanks to Shaker. We had to take three days off after he died and then a number of skull sessions to figure this ending that works. I even brought in one of the writers from the original series who gave me a great monologue for the second-in-command to deliver that makes it all work for the story. Another full week for me to get this effect just right. But it works. In fact, I think it works better than what we had before. It's a great coda for the original series in any case. The fans will love it.' He got an almost dreamy look in his eyes and added, 'I think we might even convince the network to let us release this theatrically with all this publicity—the nostalgia factor and all—and frankly the quality of the finished product.'

'So, can you think why Mister Shaker would do it? Why would he kill himself?'

'Pure meanness?' he said quickly, a hint of bitterness in his voice. 'If he killed himself, we couldn't use any insurance to finish the film. If I hadn't figured how to save it with the footage we had and give some of his lines to the first officer and other actors, I would have been out a lot. It would have been as dead as he is.'

'You have investment in it?'

'He came to me with the rights and an idea. I mortgaged my home to get this going, took out a loan, found other investors because I thought he was right. He did nothing but complain; said there was no picture without him, that he would "save" my failed career.' He stood up from behind his desk, now agitated. 'Like any of his shows had been a runaway success? I was making a living. I'm the one who hadn't blown all my money on hair-brain get-rich-quick schemes and still had a home to mortgage.'

'He wasn't wise in his investments?'

'He was an idiot at anything but looking good on camera. Oh, he could negotiate like a wolf, but then his lack of discipline would make it fail. At least he was too stupid to ruin me completely by waiting until only two days before wrap to kill himself.'

'So, you think that's why he killed himself?'

Matthews shrugged again. 'I couldn't say, but if he had even done it the day before, I would have lost everything. Be a hoot if he waited just to be nice to me, right?'

#

My next stop was one of Shaker's co-stars—the only other cast member from the original run, Robert Saito, who now played First Officer Oki.

He had been one of the youngest of the cast in the original run of the show as a helmsman and had been upgraded to first officer when they brought him back. He had also been upgraded to sleeping with Shaker's still-married wife, Gloria La Mar, and was apparently the "love of her life" she had spoken of.

He was a vital decade and a half younger than Shaker—and than Gloria's original parts, though a lot of her was definitely younger than he was.

'He did everything he could to keep me from being written into the new film after he found out Gloria and I were an item,' Saito said. 'But fan reaction to the announcement that I was in the show at all was so overwhelming that Bill had to let them write a part for me.'

He was in a dressing room on the Universal lot while on break from the legal thriller TV show he was guest starring on as the killer. 'Bill and I had minimal contact, only two actual scenes together, so it wasn't too bad. Then when he...well, after he was dead, they shot a couple of new scenes with me to fill in plot stuff and gave me some of his final lines and my part really got bigger.' He was combing his hair and getting ready to go back on camera. 'So now, if the movie does well, they may do a spin-off with me. I guess I get the last laugh after all.'

He rose and adjusted his tie. 'Now I get his cast-off series and the wife he couldn't see for his own ego.' He walked to the door of the room then stopped and turned to look at me in a gesture that was both dramatic and sincere at once. 'Gloria is the most real person I've ever met in this fake town. I have no idea what went through Bill Shaker's mind but I'm glad he is gone, if only for leaving us free to wed.'

There wasn't much more to press from him as he was clearly what old Perry Mason episodes would call a "hostile witness".

I left him and walked back to Shaker's bungalow with no more of a clue as to what I was going to tell Mrs Jill Barnet. I had talked to a dozen more people about Bill Shaker and his state of mind and had no more idea why he would have killed himself than I had at the beginning of it all. It seemed like his career was going to take an uptick, and his doctor said he had no particular sickness to be afraid of and was actually in good shape for a man his age who liked to drink occasionally.

The director of photography had said Shaker really was beginning to show his age on camera, so lighting and angles had become much more important to maintain his hero status. Could that and the fact that he had lost his wife to a younger man be enough to send him into one of his spirals of depression?

I sat in the chair he had died in and looked around the room again. 'Why did you do it, Bill? Why did you leave it?'

I opened my own laptop, set it on the spot where his had been, and pulled up some old episodes of *Space Captain Cody*. It was not as much fun as when I first saw them, but then what is? And with the knowledge that Cody was done and gone, it was a little bittersweet.

But the old episodes were still good, and on-screen Bill Shaker was every bit the hero. I could see the budget limitation at this point, with none of the vast backgrounds that I had seen in Matthews' office in the new movie. Advances in computers really had changed the game. The cramped wooden, fake rock sets were pretty obvious—even campy.

The Captain would make pronouncements as he tried to make sense of the week's problems, save the day, and often get the alien gal. Good campy fun.

But not so for me anymore. What could I tell Jill Barnet?

I looked up around the bungalow again, over at the hat rack and the calendar with the shoot days X-ed out, and suddenly I knew. I *could* make sense of it!

I just had to do some research, but I was pretty sure I knew the reason that Bill Shaker died—and it was not what people thought.

#

There was a small première screening of the finished *Return of Captain Cody* three weeks later in a screening room on the Universal lot. The network executives and most of the key crew of the film were there, along with Jill Barnet and myself as her plus one.

First officer actor Robert Saito basked in both the praise of the executives and in the wide-eyed adoration of Gloria La Mar, who came on his arm and stayed glued to him the whole time.

Producer-writer SFX master Jeffery Matthews was glowing with praise. When the lights came up on the final scene of Space Captain Cody standing on the planet surface and smiling, the applause was thunderous.

Jill was crying with seeing her brother on the screen but they were tears of pride as well as nostalgia.

'I just wish I knew why he did it,' she said as we stood near the doorway as people filed out. The principals all gathered at the back of the room for a group photo.

That was when I told her. 'He didn't,' I said.

The conversation around us suddenly went silent and all eyes turned to me.

'What are you talking about?' Saito asked.

'Yes,' Matthews said. 'What kind of nonsense are you saying?'

'Well,' I said, 'let's go backwards. The phrases that Shaker said in the video, *I can't make sense of any of it*, and *I have to end it*, were both things Space Captain Cody said in different episodes of the old series. Just innocuous phrases strung together.'

'So?' Gloria said. 'He was always quoting himself; like they were famous people's quotes.'

I had to laugh at that. 'Well, maybe, but for a self-send-off, he would have chosen better. But to continue...the conversation I had with you, Mister Matthews, talking about the shadows on the TV show got me thinking, so I rewatched the suicide video again and again.'

'Ghoul!' Matthews said, but there was something in his eyes beyond disgust.

'Well, the shadows were right,' I continued. 'They were right for that room at that time of day and that is where you foxed me. You didn't change the background like in the space scenes.'

'Of all the—' he began but there was fear in his eyes now and he was assessing those around us who had shifted their gaze from me to him.

'You only changed the foreground, and that was your mistake. You took almost a week to get the Deep Fake technology right after you sat in that chair in his uniform at a lunch break and recorded yourself. You were able to substitute his face and used lines from those old episodes so the voiceprint would match his real voice. But you did sloppy work. That calendar in the background still had eight days to shoot, not the two left when he supposedly killed himself.'

He started to edge toward the door but I physically blocked him and he didn't want to go against me. He still thought he could talk his way out.

So I kept on with my explanation. 'For the actual murder, you went back to your roots in physical props, Matthews. You walked right up to him and put the small caliber gun to the guy's temple and pulled the trigger. He had no chance. Afterward you put a blank in the gun, pressed it into his dead hand and fired it to make sure the powder residue would read right. That bungalow was pretty soundproof and his skull muffled the full load bullet that killed him. You loaded the fake shooting on his laptop from a thumb drive to make it look like he'd done it himself and videoed it.'

'You're out of your mind!' His voice cracked. He was not a quarter the actor that Shaker had been.

'Maybe,' I said, 'but they have forensic computer people who, now that they have a reason to, will take that video apart pixel by pixel. You have the skill and the equipment and the reason to want the whole enchilada. No reason to share with a has-been actor, right? And only you knew when you could kill him and still make the film work. How long had you planned it? From when you first wrote the script?'

He broke then and tried to run, but a simple right cross took him down.

There it was. Done.

So *Hollywood* and *irony*; Jill got the odd comfort in knowing her brother was murdered, Matthews made the revival film of *Space Captain Cody* a hit by the rewrite and the publicity about his being charged with the murder, and thus made Shaker a true Hollywood immortal. The new fake captain and the very real cougar's relationship seemed to be the only genuine thing I had encountered in the whole affair.

Hollywood, go figure...

SPANNER IN THE WORKS
Alan Barker

The cloud covered the sky like a huge, grey blanket. There was no rustling in the trees, nor rippling in the lake.

At one point, a squirrel emerged from the bushes. It stopped abruptly and glanced at the motionless form beside the water. Then, as if anxious not to be spotted by an unseen threat, it hurried across the grass and scuttled up the nearest tree.

On the lake, a stray leaf floated towards the edge, little by little. Eventually, it nestled against the neck of the dead woman lying there, her face immersed in the water.

A sign nearby read: PLEASE DO NOT FEED THE DUCKS

The deceased was identified as Gail Everaldo, a forty-two-year-old from Woking, in Surrey. She had been bludgeoned to death beside the local lake at Goldsworth Park and her body discovered by an elderly man walking his dog. The probable weapon—a spanner—was found in the water within striking distance, as if the perpetrator had made no attempt to conceal it. Surrey's Major Crime Investigation Team immediately launched a murder enquiry and released a press report, but by early evening nobody had come forward with any meaningful information.

The forensic pathologist estimated the time of death as between noon and two o'clock that afternoon, Friday the 2nd of October. The remains of a sandwich had been found beside the body. Detective Inspector Alec Wells, the appointed Senior Investigating Officer, took the view the deceased had been eating the sandwich on a nearby seat—where her handbag lay—before feeding bread to the ducks, at which point her assailant had struck. There was no sign of a struggle, suggesting the dead woman had been attacked from behind.

Initial enquiries revealed that Gail Everaldo left behind a sixteen-year-old son, Pablo, and her estranged husband, Carlos. Gail and Pablo had moved out of the marital home in Cobham two years earlier and subsequently resided in her mother's home in Woking, six miles away.

One point of interest was that, according to the mobile phone found in Gail's handbag, Carlos Everaldo had telephoned her eleven times during the previous fortnight, despite a protective order she'd had in place against him.

Early that evening, Wells and Detective Sergeant Des Kearney set about interviewing the deceased's relatives, starting with Gail Everaldo's mother.

Valerie Hinton was a tall, elegant woman, probably in her late sixties, Wells thought. Along with her next-door neighbour, Ruth Lee, she'd gone to the hospital mortuary and identified the body as that of her daughter, and they were now back at Valerie's house, Ruth Lee having made her excuses and left.

'I knew something like this would happen,' Valerie said, dabbing her eyes with a tear-stained handkerchief. 'That man was determined to hurt Gail. You simply *must* arrest him.'

'I assume you're referring to your daughter's ex-husband, Carlos?' Wells asked.

She nodded vigorously. 'Ever since Gail walked out on him with Pablo, he's made her life a complete misery.'

'But I believe there was a protective order against Carlos. So if he was still making contact with her, why didn't she report him to the police?'

'Gail was scared he might get violent if she got him into trouble; he could be very volatile. I suggested blocking Carlos from phoning her, but she said that would have been like a red rag to a bull. On the other hand, if she'd allowed him access to Pablo, that might've been the last we saw of the lad.'

'Have you been approached by Mr Everaldo recently?'

'No, thank goodness. He doesn't come here, but he could always reach Gail by phone whenever he wanted.'

'Did Gail go to Goldsworth Park Lake often?'

Valerie Hinton winced markedly, as if Wells' question had prompted an image of her daughter's dead body. She blew her nose and said, 'She loved the lake; it can be so peaceful there. She went at least a couple of afternoons a week, and I'm sure Carlos knew that.'

'How was her behaviour recently? Did she seem upset at all?'

'These last two days she was very stressed. When she got home yesterday evening, she looked as if she'd seen a ghost. In fact, she was so out of sorts she went into Pablo's bedroom by mistake, rather than her own. I expect Carlos had been on the phone, giving her a hard time over Pablo. I tried to get her to talk about it but she flatly refused.'

'Did she have a new gentleman friend? Or a close girlfriend we could talk to?'

'I don't think she'd been in a relationship since the marriage broke up. And she didn't have many friends as such.'

'Did she have any electronic devices we could take away for examination?'

'Yes, there'll be an iPad and a laptop around somewhere.'

Kearney cleared his throat and said, 'We also need full details of Gail's movements today, please.'

Valerie took a deep breath. 'She got up at her normal time—around six-thirty—and made Pablo's breakfast before seeing him off to school. The rest of the morning she spent reading, then said she was going to Goldsworth Park and would have lunch there. That was the last I saw of her.'

Wells nodded. The deceased's VW Polo had been found in the car park of the local supermarket, a few hundred yards from the lake where her body had been found. 'What time did she leave home?' he asked.

'About twelve o'clock, I think.'

'Didn't she work on Fridays?'

'She was an exams invigilator at a local college. She only went in when they needed her, and today wasn't one of those days.'

Wells paused before his next question. 'As a matter of routine, we need to know your own movements this afternoon, Mrs Hinton.'

'Of course, Inspector. I was playing bridge with some friends in Ripley. I'll give you their contact details before you go.'

'Thank you. Was Pablo at school today?'

Valerie nodded. 'He didn't come back afterwards though, so I had to ring him to break the news about his mum. I believe he's seeing

Ruth's daughter Jodie from next door, so he probably got together with her after their final lesson.'

'Could we speak with Pablo?'

'He's gone out again. I feel quite sad that at a time like this he prefers to be with his girlfriend rather than here.' She gazed out at the long garden, fiddling with the beads of her necklace. For a few moments, she seemed lost in thought but then turned back to Wells and said, 'Perhaps you could come back tomorrow morning? I'll make sure he's here.'

'Certainly, and I'll need you to be present at our meeting with Pablo, in view of his age. Also, I'd like to appoint one of our lady officers to spend some time with you to ensure you have everything you need and to keep you updated on the enquiry. Would that be acceptable?'

Valerie said it would, and they agreed a time for Wells and Kearney to see Pablo the following day, Saturday.

Daylight was fading by the time they drove along the sweeping gravel drive of Carlos Everaldo's spacious property in Cobham and knocked on the oak front door. Wells wasn't surprised by the South American's evident wealth; he'd once been a high-profile footballer, having moved from his native Brazil to the UK to play for Chelsea.

Everaldo was short but sturdy with neatly combed black hair and a boxer's nose. He wore a powder blue Los Angeles Chargers shirt with 56 emblazoned on the front and back.

When they told him of his ex-wife's death, he showed no reaction other than to say he'd heard about it on the early evening news and that it was nothing to do with him.

'We'd like a full account of your movements today, Mr Everaldo,' Wells said, once they'd taken seats in the living room.

'I was here, on my own, Inspector. Takin' it easy.'

'So there's no one who can verify that?'

Everaldo shook his head. 'I have people in to clean the house and keep the garden lookin' nice, but not today.'

'Can you provide their contact details, please?'

With a grunt, Everaldo pulled a notepad from a bureau and passed it to Kearney to take down the details.

'And you definitely didn't go to Goldsworth Park this afternoon?'

'You can't pin nothin' on me. I was here all the time, mindin' my own business.'

'Do you have security cameras here, which could confirm you didn't leave the house at any time?' Kearney asked.

Everaldo gave him a quizzical look. 'I don' need 'em.'

Wells looked up in mild surprise, as the living room lights came on, apparently of their own accord. He turned back to the Brazilian and said, 'How was your relationship with your ex-wife since you split up, Mr Everaldo?'

'Didn' have no relationship. I had my life; she had hers.'

'When was the last time you saw her?'

'Couple of days ago. Bumped into her in town.'

Wells and Kearney exchanged glances.

'Did she speak to you?' Wells asked.

Everaldo's lip curled. 'Only briefly. She didn't seem in the mood for a cosy chat.'

'What did you talk about?'

'I really can't remember, Inspector. Maybe we discussed the weather, who knows?'

Wells waited, but Everaldo merely stared back at him with raised eyebrows.

'Have you telephoned her recently?'

'Maybe once or twice.'

Wells took a sheet of paper from his briefcase. 'According to the mobile phone we found in your ex-wife's handbag, you rang her three times this week and eight times the week before. Why?'

'I wanna see my boy, that's all.'

'And she didn't play along, so you killed her?'

Wells watched with interest as the colour rose in the Brazilian's cheeks. Instead of replying, Everaldo got up and left the room, returning shortly with a glass of orange juice.

'By telephoning your ex-wife,' Wells said, 'you were in breach of the protective order she'd taken out against you. You could be put in prison.'

Everaldo's smirk was wicked. 'I promise never to ring her again, Inspector.'

'Did you threaten her?'

'I don' threaten no one. I keep myself to myself.'

'What about Pablo? Do you have contact with him?'

Everaldo shook his head then gazed out of the window, caressing his earlobe. 'Perhaps now they'll let me see him. What do you reckon?'

'That's not for me to decide. My job is to establish who killed your ex-wife and why.'

'It wasn' me, okay? Someone else done it. Maybe a jealous boyfrien'.'

'Gail's mother told us there's been no one else in her life lately.'

'Then I'm sorry, I can't help you. Now, will that be all?'

Wells pondered a moment. 'I'd like to conduct a search of your property. I'd also like to borrow your clothing for examination, and take your photograph, fingerprints, and DNA. Do I have your permission?'

Everaldo took a gulp of juice and sneered, rubbing his ear again. 'You wan' those things, you need a warrant.'

#

'*Someone* must have seen *something*,' Kearney said to Wells the following morning as they watched the CSIs go about the painstaking task of searching for evidence in the area surrounding the crime scene.

They'd had their briefing at the police station, and Superintendent Lyda Reynolds had instructed the relevant officers to step up their house-to-house enquiries, which had so far yielded very little. And it was too early for the results of the post-mortem conducted the previous evening.

'I can't believe Carlos went to the lake, killed Gail without her struggling or raising the alarm, then returned home without being seen.'

Wells made a sweeping gesture with his arm. 'Look at all the trees and undergrowth, Des. There's a multitude of places he could have lain in wait for her. He knew she came here habitually, and it would have been relatively simple catching her unawares.'

'We need a change of luck, so we do.'

'Be patient, Des. And let's not get ahead of ourselves. We don't even know for certain Carlos is the killer.'

Pablo Everaldo had the same olive skin as his father and beautiful black eyelashes. He wore a Nike sports shirt and jogging bottoms. For a sixteen-year-old, he seemed quite brawny, Wells thought.

'I'm sorry to trouble you at such a difficult time, but we need to establish the events leading up to your mother's death and the reason she died. Could you tell us how she'd been over the past couple of weeks? Did she seem upset about anything?'

Pablo glanced at Valerie Hinton then slowly shook his head. 'She seemed okay, just a bit quiet.'

He spoke with a South London accent, which came as a slight surprise to Wells, though he was aware the boy had been raised in the UK.

'Did you know your father telephoned her on several occasions recently?'

'She never said anything to me.'

'Has your father been in touch with you?'

'I don't take his calls. The thing is, he's not my dad anymore.'

Wells paused then said, 'Do you think he could have killed your mother, Pablo?'

The boy tensed up, a wary look in his eye. 'He better not.'

'Did you know she was going to the lake yesterday?'

'She often went on Fridays before school broke up for the weekend.'

'You were at school yesterday?'

Pablo gave an imperceptible nod. 'Then I was with my friend when my gran rang and told me to come home as something horrible had happened.' His face crumpled. 'I still can't believe it...'

Later that morning, while making further enquiries in the Goldsworth Park area, Wells took a call from Lyda Reynolds, who spoke in a rush.

'Things are happening fast, Alec—two people have come forward with useful information about Carlos Everaldo. A labourer called Ray Singer, who was digging up the road in Woking town centre on Wednesday, witnessed an altercation between Carlos—whom he recognised from his days as a pro footballer—and a woman we believe to have been Gail. Apparently Carlos was pushing her around, and Mr Singer and his work buddy had to step in to allow Gail to get away.

'Also, an officer from the electricity board, who was on his rounds doing meter readings yesterday morning, has testified seeing Carlos leave home in his Porsche between ten and eleven, heading towards Woking.'

Wells felt a surge of adrenaline. 'So Carlos was lying about staying at home all day. We'll bring him in for questioning, ma'am.'

'Yes, please. Quick as you can.'

Wells rang off, and Kearney grinned and said, 'Ah, the price of being famous! You can't blink without someone noticing you.'

When Wells and Kearney arrived at Everaldo's house, they were met with an eerie stillness. No sound came from inside, and the only birdsong Wells could hear seemed distant.

Wells rapped on the front door and waited.

He exchanged glances with Kearney then knocked a second time and spoke through the letter box. 'Mr Everaldo, it's the police. We need to speak to you urgently.' Still no one came to the door. 'Let's try round the back, Des.'

There was no sign of the Brazilian in the garden, but a French window leading into the living room was slightly ajar.

'Are you at home, Mr Everaldo?' Wells called.

The only sound was the monotonous ticking of a clock.

Kearney sauntered along the path and peered through another window. Wells saw him tense up.

'Guv, we need to go in!'

Carlos Everaldo lay sprawled in the kitchen doorway, his hands across his abdomen, his eyes shut tight, and a pool of vomit spread across the floor in front of him.

Wells bent over him and placed two fingers on his neck. He looked up at Kearney and shook his head. 'We've lost him,' he said.

That afternoon, officers were tasked with carrying out a thorough search of Everaldo's premises and taking away all computer equipment and clothing for examination. A check of the dead man's mobile phone revealed nothing of significance the police didn't already know.

'This has put a giant-sized spanner in the works, so it has,' Kearney remarked, his broad shoulders sagging. 'Presumably we're ruling out suicide?'

Wells nodded. 'Seems completely out of character. And, if you did top yourself, you would hardly choose arsenic, would you?'

'Not for all the Guinness in Dublin.'

'So, where does that leave us?'

'Either Carlos killed Gail, and someone else took exception and killed him. Or'—Kearney paused, stroking his jaw—'Carlos didn't kill Gail at all and X killed them both.'

#

The post-mortem, conducted on Monday morning, showed substantial traces of inorganic arsenic in Carlos Everaldo's bloodstream. A carton of orange juice in the fridge was found to be the source of the poison.

Wells, who had spent a quiet day at home the previous day, was busy writing up his notes at lunchtime when his phone rang. It was WDC Saina Khan, the assigned liaison officer for Gail's family. Wells could hear birdsong in the background.

'Guv, I've found a jar of arsenic in Valerie Hinton's garden shed. At least, someone has labelled it as arsenic.'

'Good work, Saina. Bag it up and don't let anyone near it. Is Mrs Hinton there?'

'Yes, guv.'

'Tell her I'd like to speak to her and I'm on my way.'

On arriving at the house in Woking, Wells wasted no time with preamble. 'Mrs Hinton, we've found a batch of arsenic in your shed. May I ask what you use it for?'

'To get rid of the rats, that's all.'

'What if I said that Carlos Everaldo was killed by arsenic poisoning?'

Valerie Hinton clapped a hand to her chest but didn't reply.

'Have you ever been to Mr Everaldo's house?'

'Not since Gail and Pablo moved here.'

'We've also established that, on Friday afternoon, you didn't arrive at your friend's house in Ripley until 2:45. So you don't appear to have an alibi for the time Gail was killed, between twelve o'clock and two o'clock. In fact, you could have followed her to Goldsworth Park in your own car, killed her and then gone straight to Ripley.'

Valerie's eyes widened alarmingly. 'That's a preposterous

suggestion. Why on Earth would I kill my own daughter? I didn't kill her *or* Carlos.'

'But there's no one to vouch for your movements between the time Gail left home and when you arrived at your friend's in Ripley?'

'I suppose not. I had lunch here on my own then did some clearing up before getting changed and going out.'

'I'd like to speak to Pablo now. Is he back from school?'

'The head teacher allowed him the day off. But he's not here—probably next door with his girlfriend.'

Wells went in search of Saina Khan and found her closing the front door, looking flushed.

'I've found something else, guv,' she said in a low voice. 'I don't know if it's significant, but I thought you ought to see it.'

She held out her hand to reveal a Yale key in a cellophane wrapper.

'Where was this?'

'In a container on the chest of drawers in Pablo's bedroom. I've tried the locks on this house, but it doesn't fit.'

Wells' phone rang. 'Yes, Des?'

'Forensics have provided their report of objects found in the vicinity of the crime scene where Gail died,' Kearney said.

'And?'

'The only thing which might be of interest is an earring with a crucifix. It was half-buried in the undergrowth about ten yards from where the body was found. I'll send you the photo of it, guv.'

'Please. And send it to Saina as well, would you?' He rang off and told Saina Khan of the new development. 'I'm going next door to see if Pablo's there. You stay here and keep chatting with Mrs Hinton—ask her if she recognises the earring.'

Wells strode along the garden path of the house next door and pressed the doorbell.

Presently, a girl who looked the same age as Pablo appeared. She had striking blonde hair with a crimson streak down the middle and was simply dressed in a white T-shirt and tight-fitting jeans.

Wells showed his ID and asked if Pablo was on the premises.

'Pablo from next door?' The girl shook her head. 'I haven't seen him.'

'Actually, you might be able to help. You're Jodie, I take it? Were you with Pablo on Friday afternoon, at school?'

'No, we're in different classes.'

'But you were with him after school, weren't you?'

Jodie gave him a quizzical look. 'No, why would I be?'

Wells remained silent for a while then said, 'My apologies. I think I may have been given some incorrect information. For clarity's sake, you and Pablo aren't an item as such?'

'Bingo! The policeman's finally got it.' Jodie slammed the door, leaving Wells alone on the doorstep.

He felt his skin prickle. He had the horrible feeling he'd been led up the garden path—literally.

Back in Valerie Hinton's house, Wells waited patiently while she called her grandson. 'Pablo, the police are here. They wish to talk to you urgently.'

There was whispered conversation in the background.

Then Pablo's sullen voice came down the line. 'I'll come home in a bit.'

Once Valerie had rung off, Wells said to her, 'I was under the impression from our conversation the other day that Pablo was close friends with Jodie next door. But that's not the case, is it?'

He watched her fingers play with the beads of her necklace. 'I could've sworn I saw him letting himself in through their back door recently,' she replied, a faraway look in her eye. 'But he doesn't talk to me, so you'll have to ask him directly.'

Wells nodded at Saina Khan who proffered the key she'd found. 'This was in Pablo's bedroom. Is it a key to next door? Or is it a spare to his father's house?'

'I've really no idea, Inspector.'

Wells pulled out his phone. 'Have you seen this earring before?'

'I'm afraid not. Your colleague has already asked me. I'm sorry I can't help.'

Valerie pressed a tissue to her nose and scurried out of the room.

Pablo, on returning home, said he didn't recognise the earring with the crucifix. As to the key found in his bedroom, he stated that it was to his father's residence, and it had belonged to himself before he and his mother had moved out.

'When was the last time you used it, Pablo?'

'About two years ago.'

'You haven't visited your father in the last few weeks?'

'No. Like I told you, he's not part of my life anymore.'

'So we shouldn't find your fingerprints anywhere in his house?'

Pablo flushed but said nothing.

Wells leaned forward. 'Here's the thing. Your mother was killed on Friday. Your father had been making serious threats against her, so he's an obvious suspect. Now he's been killed also, I have to consider the possibility the motive for his murder was revenge for your mother's murder. Eye for an eye. You've made it clear you despised your father, and if he *did* kill your mother—'

'I didn't kill him! I didn't go anywhere near him!'

'Inspector, please!'

Valerie Hinton's face was suffused with rage, but Wells wasn't to be deterred.

'We found a batch of arsenic—the poison used to kill your father—in your grandmother's shed, so you had access to that. You also had a key to his house. You could easily have gone over there when he was out, slipped the poison into his drink, and left without anyone seeing you.'

'That's a lie! I haven't been there in years.'

Wells changed tack. 'Where were you on Friday between twelve and two o'clock?'

'Why d'you ask? You don't think I killed my mum?'

'Someone did. Who's to say it wasn't the same person who killed your dad?'

Pablo banged his fist on the table. 'What is this? I loved my mum. No way, mate!'

'Nevertheless, I need to know your movements on Friday afternoon. Were you at school or not? I'll be checking with your teacher, remember.'

Pablo bowed his head, and Wells waited. When eventually Pablo looked up and spoke, it was in a quieter voice. 'I had free periods in the afternoon. After the last lesson in the morning, I left school and went home.'

'At what time?'

'About twelve.'

'Your gran didn't say anything about your coming home.'

Pablo's eyes flicked to Valerie Hinton and back. 'I went to see the lady next door.'

'Which lady?'

'Ruth Lee.'

Wells heard a sharp in-take of breath from Valerie but kept his gaze fixed on Pablo. 'Jodie's mum?'

'That's right.'

'Are you in a relationship with her?'

Pablo nodded, his gaze on the floor. 'We've been together a few months.'

'Oh, Pablo, why didn't you say something?' Valerie wailed. She didn't get a reply.

Wells said, 'Did your mum know about your relationship with Ruth?'

Pablo shrugged. 'She probably guessed but she never spoke to me about it.'

'All right. So, when you left school at twelve o'clock, did you go straight to Ruth's?'

'Yes.'

'What time did you get there?'

'About 12:15, I guess.'

'How did the two of you spend the afternoon?'

'We had lunch, relaxed for a bit, then went for a drive somewhere—Newlands Corner, I think.' Newlands Corner is a beauty spot in the Surrey Hills, about eight miles south of Woking, where Agatha Christie famously "vanished" in 1926. 'That's where we were when Gran rang to tell me about Mum.'

'Were you with Ruth the whole of that time?'

'Yes. You can check with her if you don't believe me.'

'What about Friday evening, when I was here interviewing your gran about your mum's death? Were you at Ruth's then?'

Pablo nodded and looked away. 'She's easy to talk to.'

Valerie gave a small sob and Wells turned to her. 'I'm going to have a chat with Ruth now. I suggest you both stay here in case I need to ask anything else.'

This time, it was Ruth who answered the front door. When Wells said he would like to speak to her in private, she sent Jodie up to her room.

Ruth Lee was an attractive woman with short fair hair and high cheekbones. Wells had met her briefly on Friday when she'd helped identify Gail Everaldo's body. Now, she folded her arms across her chest and asked Wells what he wanted to know.

'We've been speaking to Pablo Everaldo, from next door, who has been helping with our enquiries into the deaths of his parents. During our discussions, he advised us that he has a close relationship with you.'

Ruth inclined her head. 'I feel sorry for Pablo. He's badly upset at the moment, particularly about his mum.'

'How long have the two of you been friendly?'

'Not long. I know I'm a lot older, but it's nothing serious.'

'What about Jodie's father?'

'I divorced him twelve years ago and have barely seen him since.'

'Did Gail know about your relationship with Pablo?'

'She probably guessed.'

'Didn't that bother you?'

'Not really. Gail and I weren't particularly close. And it wasn't as if Pablo is underage.'

Wells held her gaze and said, 'Tell me how you spent the day on Friday.'

Ruth let out a bark of laughter. 'You mean the day Gail died? I sincerely hope I'm not a suspect, Inspector.'

'We just need to eliminate you from our enquiries.'

'Hopefully you won't find that too difficult. So let me think. During the morning I was working.'

'From home?'

'Yes. I'm a bookkeeper and was preparing accounts for my client. Then Pablo arrived and we had lunch. After that, we drove to Newlands Corner and found a spot to sit down and take in the views.'

'What time did Pablo get here?'

Ruth averted her gaze briefly then replied, 'Probably about half past twelve.'

'Were the two of you together for the whole afternoon, until Pablo got the call from his gran about Gail?'

'We were indeed.' Ruth smiled. 'So I have a cast-iron alibi for the time Gail died. And why on earth would I want to kill her anyway?'

'Perhaps Gail disapproved of their relationship and was determined to put the kibosh on it,' Des Kearney suggested later. 'That would give Ms Lee a solid reason for killing her if she was that keen on Pablo.'

Wells considered. 'It's not impossible. But the murder didn't take place until after twelve o'clock, so Ruth would've been hard pressed to kill Gail in Goldsworth Park then get home in time for Pablo's arrival, which seems to have been no later than 12:30. Unless they're both lying—which I seriously doubt, as I can't see Pablo being implicated in the death of his mother.'

'Nor me. But he's still a player so far as Carlos's murder is concerned.'

Wells rubbed the back of his neck and winced.

'Something troubling you, guv?'

'Someone said something today—a throwaway phrase—that I've a feeling may be significant. But I can't for the life of me think what it was.'

At home that evening, Wells was half-watching a film on the television when the "throwaway phrase" he'd referred to earlier finally came to him. In his mind, he went back over his interviews with Pablo Everaldo, Valerie Hinton, and Carlos Everaldo, and the more he thought about it, the more certain he was that his theory about the murders of Gail Everaldo and Carlos Everaldo was correct.

After a while, he picked up the phone and dialled Lyda Reynolds' number.

Once he'd finished speaking, Lyda said, 'That sounds very plausible, Alec. But we still need evidence.'

'I agree. We need to make a number of checks tomorrow and hope they produce positive results. Here's what I'm thinking...'

#

The following lunchtime, Wells and Kearney paid a visit to Ted Dyson, an elderly gentleman from Cobham.

'I'm sorry to trouble you again, Mr Dyson'—two junior officers had interviewed the old man on Saturday—'but I understand from Carlos Everaldo that you were engaged by him as a gardener. According to my notes, you advised my colleagues you didn't have any contact with Mr Everaldo last Friday, the 2nd. Is that correct?'

'Aye. I only worked there on Thursdays. It's a real shame he passed away—he always took the trouble to have a chat with me about football and the like.'

'Please think back to when you were here last Thursday, October 1st. This may be clutching at straws, but did you see anyone acting suspiciously in the vicinity of Mr Everaldo's property that day? Maybe if he was out?'

The old man considered. 'Not when I was working during the daytime, no. But I did bump into someone later.'

The detectives exchanged glances.

'Mr Dyson?'

Ted spoke slowly, staring through the window. 'I had to return to Mr Everaldo's to pick up my fork in the evening, which I'd left behind. I wanted to aerate my own little lawn, see?'

'Yes?'

'When I got there, I bumped into someone coming out the front door. Said they were a family friend and had dropped something off for him, and drove off quickly.'

Wells took a deep breath. 'Was it someone you knew?'

'No, although the face did seem a bit familiar, like.'

Wells pulled five photographs from his briefcase and laid them on the table. 'Were any of these the person you bumped into?'

Taking his time, Ted Dyson examined each photograph in turn. When he came to the last one, he tapped it lightly. '*That's* the birdie.'

Kearney leaned forward, his huge hands gripping the edge of the table. 'What about Mr Everaldo? Was he not at home at the time?'

'No, sir. Chelsea had a home match against Juventus in the Europa League. He wouldn't have missed that for the world.'

'Thank you, Mr Dyson, that's extremely helpful. But I do have one more question.' Wells produced a photograph of the crucifix earring. 'Did Mr Everaldo wear one of these, by any chance?'

The old man looked from one to the other of them, a puzzled expression on his face. 'Why, yes, he did. But surely you would have seen it for yourselves when you saw him?'

Two hours later, there was a hushed air of expectation among the assembled audience in the incident room. Superintendent Lyda

Reynolds clasped her hands and announced they'd had huge breakthroughs in relation to both murders. Stepping to one side, she asked Wells to update the team.

'Thank you, ma'am.' He turned to address his colleagues. 'First, I'd like to talk about the murder of Gail Everaldo. As you know, the chief suspect has always been Carlos. He'd rung Gail several times in the last fortnight about having access to Pablo, and had harassed her when they bumped into one another in Woking town centre. While we don't know exactly what was said, I'm fairly certain he made threats on Gail's life. But, despite everyone's hard work, we had nothing to pin Gail's murder on him.'

Saina Khan raised a hand. 'Are you saying Carlos didn't kill Gail after all, guv?'

'No. I'm saying he *did* kill her but managed to cover his tracks. He wiped the spanner clean of prints. He would've made the journey to Goldsworth Park via the back roads and parked in one of the cul-de-sacs, avoiding CCTV. He almost certainly destroyed the clothing he'd worn that afternoon. And I expect he left his mobile phone at home or at least had the GPS function switched off. But he shouldn't have told us he spent all day at home. The following morning, an employee of the electricity board came forward testifying he saw Carlos drive away from his house between ten and eleven on Friday. So why did Carlos lie to us, if he wasn't involved in Gail's murder?'

'That all sounds very premeditated, guv. But how did Carlos know Gail would be at the park at that particular time?'

'Maybe, unknown to her, he followed her from her home in Woking. Or maybe he was there on spec, perhaps having made abortive trips to the park previously. Either way, it was his crucifix earring that snagged on something—maybe a bush—and was found by the CSIs in the undergrowth near Gail's body. His gardener confirmed he'd been wearing one for some time—he almost certainly wouldn't have been allowed to wear it during his footballing days—and we've now found the purchase on his credit card statement. Funnily enough, when Des and I interviewed him on Friday evening, he kept rubbing his earlobe, which was probably an instinctive reaction to having lost the earring.'

'What about the murder of Carlos himself, guv?' one of the junior officers asked. 'Was it one of the suspects on the board?'

Wells stepped to one side so that everyone could see the row of five photographs. 'We spoke to his gardener, Ted Dyson, today. Ted said he bumped into someone coming out of Carlos's house last Thursday evening, someone he didn't expect to see. This person said she was a family friend and had dropped something off for Carlos, who, it seems, was at Chelsea watching their European match. She would've guessed Carlos would go to the match as he had a season ticket every year. I believe she used Pablo's key to gain access to the house, and introduced a lethal dose of inorganic arsenic—taken from the batch in Valerie Hinton's garden shed—to the carton of orange juice in Carlos's fridge.'

Wells tapped the nearest photo. 'There's your murderer.'

There was a collective gasp.

'Eye for an eye?' Saina Khan said.

Wells nodded. 'That's exactly the expression I used when I spoke to Pablo yesterday, without realising how close I was to the truth. Gail put the poison in Carlos's orange juice on Thursday; he bludgeoned her to death on Friday; and he died later, after drinking the juice.'

'What was Gail's motive for killing him, guv?'

'Absolute, unmitigated fear. Carlos had been ramping up the threats on her life and she knew they were for real. She thought her best chance of survival was to kill Carlos before he got to her. I suspect the altercation she and Carlos had in Woking pushed her over the edge, leading to the decision to go to his house when he was out and administer the arsenic.

'Valerie Hinton said that, when Gail got home on Thursday evening, she looked as if she'd seen a ghost—which is hardly surprising given Gail had just had the shock of her life, bumping into Ted Dyson when trying to leave the scene of her crime without being seen. Valerie also said Gail was so out of sorts she went into Pablo's room by mistake—but I think that was to return the key she'd used to get into Carlos's house.'

'Why didn't she report the threats from Carlos to the police?'

'To her way of thinking, it would only solve the problem short term. He wouldn't be locked up for ever, and she knew he'd come after her when he got out.'

'What happens next, guv?'

'Our work isn't over by a long stretch, and we've a press release coming up this evening. But right now'—Wells glanced at Lyda who smiled and nodded—'I believe the pub is open, so you are all welcome to treat yourselves to a well-deserved shandy!'

There were cheers all round. It had been a stressful few days for the team and a little light relief was welcome.

Kearney looked at the ceiling and closed his palms. 'Give us this day our daily Guinness,' he muttered.

Everyone laughed, including Wells. 'We've more than a solved case to be grateful for, Des. Just think, if Carlos had offered us a drink when we interviewed him on Friday evening, we might've had the contaminated orange juice ourselves!'

THE MURDERER'S VADE-MECUM
Erica Obey

Being a Useful Compendium of Hitherto Undiscovered Methods of Murder

First Method: *The Untraceable Poison*

What was by far our most puzzling case began with a simple question from Mack Byrne, the Morgansburg Town Justice and Chief of Campus Security at De Sales College. 'This should be one for your databases,' he said. 'In all the murder mysteries you have collected and catalogued, have you ever heard of someone who was literally poisoned by a poison pen letter?'

A quick word of explanation. I don't actually collect murder mysteries. I've written an AI program that does that. His name is Doyle, and a question like this is a sure-fire way to arouse him from cyber-slumber.

'If the Good Inspector is referring to the poison pen letter as a device in Golden Age mysteries, it was near ubiquitous,' Doyle settled into lecture mode from my computer's speakers. 'For what better device is there for dramatizing the myriad petty jealousy and venial sins in a closed society upon which the classic murder mystery depends. Two cases that come immediately to mind are Agatha Christie's *The Moving Finger* and Dorothy L. Sayers' *Gaudy Night*, although a cursory search would easily uncover more. Would you like me to perform one? I can run it in background mode...'

'No need.' Byrne shook his head against the prospect of an afternoon-long lecture. 'I'm talking about one where the actual letter was poisonous.'

'For that, I would suggest you turn to the annals of true crime and the anthrax scare of 2001. Or if you really wanted to stretch a point, I would submit the Unabomber's deadly parcels could be seen as a form of poison pen as well—'

'This wasn't a bomb,' Byrne said. 'We don't have the full toxicology report yet, but if you ask me, it couldn't be anything other than arsenic poisoning. The symptoms are exactly the same as those of the KGB informant I found stuffed in the suitcase in the abandoned Orient Express platform at the Istanbul Train Station.'

Another word of explanation. Byrne is a retired Army Intelligence operative who does his best to live a quiet life here in Morgansburg, NY—at least until Doyle and I get involved.

'By the time I got to Dmitri, there was nothing I could do for him except arrange a pension for his widow,' Byrne went on. 'His own damned fault. He should've just trusted me. At least in this case the doctors are pretty confident she'll pull through.'

'*She* being—?' I prompted him.

But Byrne was already off on a different tangent. 'Any idea what a v*ade-mecum* is?'

'Basically, it means a guidebook,' I began, but Doyle would not be denied.

'The term *vade mecum*, which—perhaps obviously—derives from the Latin for *go with me*, has long been used of manuals or guidebooks that can be carried in a deep pocket, thereby being available for a traveler's immediate reference. However, the term does have a larger, more metaphorical meaning, referring to works which are intended to serve as one-stop references or guides to a particular subject, whether or not such a work can actually be carried in one's pocket.'

'So *The Murderer's Vade-Mecum* would be?' Byrne pressed.

'The title sounds familiar—,' I began.

'*The Murderer's Vade-Mecum* is one of two books known to be authored by Lord Peter Wimsey,' Doyle informed us. 'The other one being *Notes on the Collecting of Incunaba*. No actual text of either volume has been found, so we must rely on Sayers' describing the *Vade-Mecum* as a "useful compendium of hitherto undiscovered methods of murder".'

'In other words, it's not a real book?' Byrne's face said everything.

I shrugged. 'I suppose someone could have unearthed a hitherto undiscovered manuscript from Dorothy L. Sayers' literary estate.'

'Impossible,' Doyle sniffed. 'Such exciting news might have

escaped the notice of the *hoi polloi*, but in the circles *I* move in...'

'How many times have I told you that *the hoi* is redundant?' I sighed. '*Hoi* means *the* in ancient Greek...'

'So to get back to the matter at hand, any idea why a reference to a non-existent book might threaten a librarian?' Byrne cut short our squabbling. 'To the point where it caused her to collapse as soon as she has read a note containing it?'

'Perhaps the message was in code,' Doyle suggested. 'Or even provides the key to a code—a single-page tear sheet, as immortalized in *The Key to Rebecca*. Shall I run a few straightforward pattern-matching algorithms?'

'No,' Byrne and I said as one.

Doyle preserved a moment's offended silence as a matter of principle, before he said, 'Then perhaps the Good Inspector could offer us a slightly more organized *précis*, beginning at the beginning and all that. Order and method in all things, you know.'

'Doyle does have a point,' I said. 'You mind telling us what this is all about?'

'A call came in from emergency dispatch around 11 am. Margery Fox, the rare books curator at the village library was found collapsed at her desk by the Keep Calm and Carry Yarn knitting group. She was taken to the ER down in Poughkeepsie, where she is expected to survive. However, she is still unconscious, and according to the doctors, unlikely to be able to answer questions for at least twenty-four hours.'

Byrne paused uncomfortably. 'I—was hoping you and your Little Friend Doyle might be free for a ride-along to interview a few eyewitnesses.'

'Someone saw what happened?' I asked.

Byrne's face twisted in a way that suggested we had reached the heart of the matter. 'They call themselves the Detection Book Club. I trust you can see the problem.'

'The Detection Book Club,' I repeated.

'Dedicated to the appreciation of one Harriet Leigh, Morgansburg's answer to Agatha Christie, as well as Margery Fox's beloved great-aunt. Margery has devoted her entire life to preserving her great-aunt's literary legacy—in between chasing down library fines from Morgansburg's wayward youth.'

227

'And now someone has tried to kill her with the citation of an imaginary book from a better-known mystery writer,' I said.

'Intriguing,' Doyle murmured. 'I would be delighted to take the case.'

Second Method: *The Locked Room*

The Morgansburg Public Library was housed in a landmarked federal-style house, set back from the Village Green behind an expanse of uncertainly maintained lawn. The faded historic marker that balanced near the front steps noted that it had been bequeathed to Morgansburg to serve a library in perpetuity by one Harriet Leigh, who had also left a grateful town her book collections, which were to the professional librarian's eye, a demonstration of why "obscure" was not a synonym for "rare". Of course, value was in the eye of the beholder, especially when it came to book collecting, and somewhere in this world there might be someone who was willing to pay seven figures for a copy of *Steady as You Go: Getting the Most out of your New Shower Safety Rails*. Nonetheless, professional appraisers tended to take a dimmer view of valuation.

Morgansburg is such a small town that Byrne is the closest thing there to a professional police force. So there was no crime tape to impede the Mind over Mat(ter) yoga group from relaxing into *shavasana* in what had once been the house's grand entryway and was now the library's event space. The rest of the interior was similarly at odds with its repurposing as a library. To begin with, despite the building's clean, rectangular exterior lines, the hallmark of a federal interior is octagonal rooms, which can be tricky to put bookshelves in—especially when two entire walls of each room were dominated by a hand-carved Adam fireplace on each end.

Flashing a non-existent badge at the yoga instructor's urgent semaphore that we were interrupting their meditation, Byrne strolled over to inspect the circulation desk—a large trestle table that had dominated the foyer for nearly half a century before it had been unceremoniously jammed across the front of the cloakroom to make room for the library's jam-packed events calendar. The cloakroom was crammed with book trolleys, whose rusted wheels emitted hair-raising shrieks of protest when Byrne tried to move them. An unworthy part of me wondered whether he was doing it deliberately. An extended rehab for PTSD had left Byrne with a loathing for yoga instructors almost as great as my own.

With a decidedly unblissful glare at Byrne, the instructor wound up with a weary *namaste*, and the class began to roll up their mats and disperse. I winced as I recognized the yogini who made a beeline for Byrne. Lori Raglan. Chair of the Young Friends of the Morgansburg Library and all-around pain in the ass.

'Is it true?' Lori asked. 'Is she really dead?'

If Byrne had a reaction, he disguised it well. 'I'm happy to report that the doctors are confident that Ms Fox will make a complete recovery.'

'Oh, dear Lord!' Lori rolled her eyes. 'That woman must have nine lives.'

Byrne raised an eyebrow. 'I'm sorry. Is there some sort of bad blood between you and Ms Fox?'

It was a disingenuous question, to say the least. Ever since the new library board had ridden into town on the wake of the hipster invasion from Brooklyn, everyone in Morgansburg knew that Margery Fox was the sole obstacle to the incoming board's quest to build a new library to "usher Morgansburg into the 21st century" by purging the dead wood on the library board. With the exception of Margery, the dead wood had gone quietly, content to allow the hipsters to discover the provisions of Harriet Leigh's will for themselves—especially the bit that stipulated that they would lose not only the building and books, but the endowment that supported them if they made any changes that were not personally approved by Margery Fox, who was Harriet's literary executrix as well as her great-niece.

'You don't understand!' Lori cried. 'She planned this! Just to get back at us!'

Byrne raised an eyebrow. 'You're suggesting that Margery Fox poisoned herself just to prevent you from moving the library to a new location?'

'There's nothing she wouldn't stoop to! She's just a spiteful old witch. We tried to share with her; we begged her to get involved in our plans. But she wanted no part of it. Said the library would move over her dead body.'

'No offense, ma'am, but I'm beginning to wonder whether I need to warn you against self-incrimination.'

Byrne might as well have not spoken. Lori plowed ahead, 'I mean, just look at how *old* she is; sixty-three. And completely gaga. Devoted to the memory of her great-aunt. I tell you, it's unhealthy. She could live another thirty years, and my children will have children then. Someone had to do something.'

'Again, ma'am, I think it's only fair to warn you it sounds like you have a solid motive to poison her.'

Lori stared at him, eyes widening. 'Did you really just go there?'

'Ma'am?'

'Did you really just suggest—?' She waved her hands as if batting aside a swarm of flies. 'Stop. Just please stop.'

'Ma'am?' Byrne asked. 'Did you wish to make a statement?'

This time, I was certain the stolidity was deliberate.

'You want a statement, I'll give you a statement.' She whirled, then beckoned furiously at the lone man in the class, a wiry corporate raider who had left his phone in easy reach of his mat so he could surreptitiously check his messages. 'Greg! I need you right now!'

She whirled back on Byrne. 'You know Greg Mumford, the Library Board lawyer, don't you? From now on, any speaking I do will be through him.'

'Very prudent, ma'am,' Byrne said. 'Do you wish to make an appointment with the Town Justice's office now, or shall I have the State Police contact you directly?'

'Okay, okay, okay.' Greg said. 'Now, I don't know how we got here, but I know this is not where any of us want to be. Come on, people, we're all neighbors here, not a bunch of cut-throat lawyers negotiating an IPO. Let's not let this escalate to that level. Trust me, I swim with those sharks, and they are not people you want to deal with.'

Byrne cast him a look that would be hard to parse if you were not aware that Byrne was a man who quite literally had swum with sharks—in all likelihood to disarm a nuclear weapon that made a feeding frenzy look like a tank full of guppies. 'All the same, it's best that I give you a moment so you can confer with your client and agree on a strategy. In the meantime, I've got some witnesses to question in the Rare Books room.'

The Detection Club awaited us in what had once been the house's actual library, which now housed Miss Leigh's personal collection. Both books and fixtures had once been grand, but now both the leather bindings and oak shelves were cracked and sagging. The deep-seated armchairs had been reupholstered in utilitarian vinyl and folding chairs surrounded the central library table. An industrial-looking vacuum lay in front of a bay of empty shelves—bright green books that had obviously been removed from the shelves were scattered catawampus across the floor.

The members of the Detection Club were just as ramshackle. A woman trapped between a web of lacy scarves and a confectionary wig was introduced as Miss (emphatically not Ms) Gabriele Porter, the well-known poetess, as well as, she confessed with a giggle, an absolute addict when it came to mysteries. Next to her was seated one of the stringers for the *Morgansburg Times*, a twitchy retired English teacher who wore a tweed jacket and bow tie. A hefty man with tattooed forearms and grease-stained fingers was holding forth on how Tom Clancy got everything wrong to a woman whose hair and shoes were as utilitarian as his own.

'The Detection Club, right?' Byrne asked, announcing himself with a swift tap at the door. 'Would you mind if I ask you a few questions about the incident this afternoon?'

'Oh, please, Inspector!' the poet twittered. 'We absolutely insist!'

'We have been waiting on tenterhooks,' the woman in sensible shoes said reprovingly. 'No one will tell us anything, although we have called the hospital repeatedly. You think they would show us some professional consideration if nothing else. I gave the EMTs a complete log of her vitals before they arrived. They thanked me politely enough, but I saw them toss it in the waste bag along with the other wrappings.'

'I'm happy to tell you that Ms Fox is expected to make a complete recovery,' Byrne said. 'But she is still unconscious. The doctors suspect arsenic poisoning.'

'I knew it!' the sensible woman cried. 'I told them!'

'Now, ma'am, I'm just a town justice, but I need to warn you that statements like that can be taken the wrong way,' Byrne cautioned her with more jollity than was strictly necessary.

'Oh, don't be ridiculous,' she scoffed. 'The symptoms are unmistakable.'

'Are we suspects?' the retired English teacher asked, clearly unwilling to allow the sensible woman to hog the limelight.

'Hardly,' Byrne said with a laugh. The expressions around the table ranged from disappointed to genuinely insulted, and he hastily amended himself, 'But you are eyewitnesses. You were all here when it happened, right?'

They shifted like students confronted with a pop quiz. 'Well, yes,' the tweedy man said. 'And no.'

'I mean, we all saw her faint,' the sensible woman said. 'but as for the rest—'

'She was closeted inside the Rare Books room when we got there,' the poetess took up the thread, when the sensible woman offered no further explanation.

'I knew something was wrong the moment I saw the door was locked,' the woman in sensible shoes said. 'But there's knowing and *knowing* if you know what I mean.'

From the look on Byrne's face, that was at least one *know* too many.

'Most unusual,' the tweedy man concurred. 'And that was before we all heard the vacuum cleaner start up.'

'She locked herself in to vacuum the room?' Byrne asked.

'Oh, she must have set it off accidentally,' the hefty man said. 'It was only on for a moment.'

'She probably tripped over it,' the sensible woman said. 'And I tell you I'm of half a mind to file an OSHA complaint. The mold remediation was supposed to be completed weeks ago, but the library board simply turns a blind eye to our complaints.'

'Pure harassment, if you ask me,' the tweedy man said. 'They're trying to drive us out.'

'We shall not be moved,' the hefty man said, flexing his bulk meaningfully.

'And how long was it from when the vacuum stopped running to when she opened the door?' Byrne asked.

'One minute and thirty-seven seconds.' The tweedy man pulled out a turnip-shaped watch before he added unnecessarily, 'I timed it.'

'Well, you timed it wrong,' the poetess said, consulting a diamante brooch watch nestled among her lacy scarves. 'Margery unlocked the door, we all heard her do it. But she fainted before she could open it.'

'The handle just moved of its own accord,' the poetess said with a shiver. 'We all saw it.'

'Then the door creaked open and that note fluttered out, as if she had dropped it right there and then,' the sensible woman said.

'You mean, the note that read *The Murderer's Vade-Mecum*?' Byrne asked.

'I'm sure we didn't take time to read it,' the tweedy man said. 'We were all too busy attending to our fallen comrade. It was instantly clear she was *in extremis*.'

'Classic arsenic poisoning,' the sensible woman said. 'As I told you before.'

'Did they test the note for arsenic?' the hefty man asked.

'They tested it,' Byrne allowed. 'Didn't find a trace.'

'Oh, well played, Inspector!' The tweedy man clapped his hands. 'I did not see that coming.'

The sensible woman stilled him with the kind of brisk gesture that suggested she had once pursued a career teaching fractious toddlers. 'I think that we can all safely agree that none of us suspected Margery would take things this far.'

'What exactly do you mean by "this far"?' Byrne asked.

An awkward silence before the hefty man said, 'When she fainted, we all assumed it was Margery overdramatizing. She's been experiencing lapses in memory and mood swings lately, y'know. But to take a fatal dose of arsenic just to make a point—well, frankly I can't see her doing it.'

'But it wasn't a fatal dose!' the poet cried, her wig tilting even more perilously askew with every word. 'The Good Inspector just told us! She's going to be fine. So you can't rule out the possibility that she took just enough to make her collapse—to make it look like it was one of us.'

If you looked at Byrne, you'd see no tell-tale sign that this was the kind of conversation that could awaken in him the near uncontrollable urge to put his fist quietly through the nearest wall. 'You have any idea why Margery might want to do something like that? By all accounts, you all are Harriet Leigh's most devoted fans.'

All eyes turned to the retired English teacher, whose bow tie had suddenly grown constrictive, to judge from the sudden flush that suffused his face.

'Margery could be a jealous, vindictive woman,' he sighed. 'Of course, loyalty is to be admired, but the way she went on when she found out I host a modest online mystery community of my own, and may have invited members of the Detection Club to join me. She even went so far as to accuse me of stealing the Detection Club's archive of Harriet Leigh's papers. As if anyone in this group needed any further discussion of Harriet Leigh and her tediously derivative detective!'

'Still, it was only a tempest in a teapot. Or at least it should have been. If only someone hadn't leaked a few less than kind posts to Margery.' The woman in sensible shoes glared around the table. 'One hardly likes to think anyone in our little circle could have done such a pointless, destructive thing, but I'm certain that will be the direction poor Margery's accusations will take when she finally comes to.'

Third Method: *The Vanishing Weapon*

By the next morning, Margery Fox was sufficiently recovered to make a statement. She received us confined to her hospital bed by a tangle of drips and monitor cables, a tray of saltine crackers and a carafe of water on the table beside her. 'Fifteen minutes,' the nurse warned Byrne. 'And I'll cut you off early, if I see any signs of distress on those monitors. I don't care what court you call yourself a justice of.'

'I'm sure I couldn't tell you what happened,' Margery protested, as soon as the nurse had left. 'One moment, I was standing there, trying to turn off that wretched vacuum cleaner. The next moment, I was on the ground myself—I'm sure I couldn't tell you how.'

Byrne nodded gravely. 'The Detection Club says you had locked yourself in the Rare Books room. Any particular reason you did that? I understand it wasn't usual.'

'Of course, it wasn't usual. I was looking for signs of sabotage—especially with that wretched vacuum.'

Byrne's gaze sharpened. 'Do you have cause to believe someone's sabotaging the library?'

'I know it! And not just someone. It's those ghastly Friends. Once they discovered Lord Mycroft had discovered their schemes to destroy my great-aunt's legacy, they had no choice but to escalate.'

'Lord Mycroft?' Byrne repeated.

'Oh, he's not one to stand on rank. But when you're dealing with these kinds of people sometimes you have to let them know who you are. As His Lordship has told me on numerous occasions.'

Byrne nodded. 'Would you be able to put me in touch with this Lord Mycroft? Text me his contact information, maybe?'

'No need,' Doyle murmured in my earbud. 'The address is Marlborough Flats, when he's in London. The Dower House of his father, the Duke, when he is in the country.'

'A duke?' I asked. 'This man isn't just a lord, he's a full-fledged duke?'

'Lord Mycroft Ashton is a gentleman of independent means who divides his not inconsiderable intellect and fortune between solving crimes and collecting William Morris first editions,' Doyle informed me.

'Sounds a lot like Lord Peter Wimsey to me,' I said with a frown. 'Are you sure you're not making this up.'

'*I'm* not making up anything,' Doyle said in a tone that made it clear someone else was.

It took another minute for the penny to drop. I stepped away from the bed, out of what I hoped was Margery Fox's earshot. 'Are you telling me that Margery's friend is Harriet Leigh's series detective? In other words, we are dealing not only with a non-existent book, but also a non-existent detective?'

'Given the unfortunately fleshist tendency you exhibited the last time we debated the question of cyber-existence, perhaps it would be better to table this discussion,' Doyle said.

I turned my attention back to the bed, where Byrne was asking, 'And what exactly is this Lord Mycroft's connection to the Morgansburg Library?'

'Absolutely none! Lord Mycroft's loyalty is only to my great-aunt, and ensuring that her legacy is preserved as is her due. He and my great-aunt were great rivals when it came to book collecting, and at the same time, the best of friends. Indeed, some even hinted at a further *tendresse*. May I refer you to his now classic *Notes on the Collecting of Kelmscott Editions*, in which he tells of more than one bidding adventure against the indomitable Harriet Leigh.' Margery fell back against her pillows and gestured faintly toward her water carafe.

Obligingly, Byrne poured and waited for her to swallow a glass before he asked, 'But he was the one to contact you, right? Why?'

'He was concerned about preserving Great-Aunt Harriet's legacy against a terrible threat!' Margery lowered her voice. 'Someone is intent on eradicating her memory completely. They are buying up any books by Harriet Leigh with the sole purpose of pulping them. Fortunately, Lord Mycroft discovered the foul plot in the nick of time, and he and I are engaged in a plan to acquire any volumes of Harriet Leigh's work that come up for sale on the public market. We are determined to outbid all others even if we need to run down the entire endowment to do it!'

If Byrne's jaw dropped the way mine did, he did a better job of hiding it. 'Just to clarify that I heard you right, you are buying these books out of the library's endowment?'

'Oh, I'm not doing anything,' Margery said. 'Lord Mycroft is handling all of it. I simply send him whatever funding he requests.'

I barely suppressed a gasp. Sending funding to a fictional character made arsenic poisoning look like petty crime.

From Byrne's expression, his thoughts were going down the same path as mine. 'Was one of your recent purchases a book called *The Murderer's Vade-Mecum*?'

Margery's brow clouded. 'Well, now how could you have known that?'

'You were clutching a note with those words on it when they found you. One theory was, it was some kind of threat.'

'Oh, Lord Mycroft would never threaten me.' Her frown deepened. 'Nonetheless, there was something not quite right about that title. It niggled at me. I'm not entirely sure why.'

'Shall I enlighten her?' Doyle asked.

'No!' I hissed.

'In fact, it was the title that made me think of sabotage,' Margery told Byrne. 'I'm not sure why, but suddenly I began to wonder whether Lord Mycroft was having his little joke at my expense.'

'Strikes me that arsenic poisoning is no laughing matter,' Byrne said.

'I didn't mean to imply—' Margery straightened, setting several monitors beeping, and the nurse came running. 'Of course, it wasn't Lord Mycroft's fault—it couldn't have been. Instead, I suggest you take a look at those miscreants on the Library Board and their infernal mold machines.'

Her words faded behind a pointedly closed door as we were escorted out into the hall—where a flustered doctor hurried to intercept us. 'Am I correct that you are the one investigating the arsenic poisoning?' he asked Byrne.

'I'm just the Morgansburg Town Justice,' Byrne replied. 'No real official standing for anything as serious as poisoning, but it made sense for me to ask some preliminary questions to decide whether this warrants being kicked up to the state troopers.'

'I'm afraid you're going to have to,' the doctor said.

'Is there some kind of problem?' Byrne asked.

'I'm not sure what to call it,' the doctor said. 'But maybe it's better to start at the beginning. I'm the gastroenterology resident, so I'm the one who oversaw pumping Ms Fox's stomach.'

To judge from his expression this may well have been his first experience of such a thing, and it appeared that he might be reconsidering his vocation. I wondered whether anyone had ever brought up the issue of colonoscopies with him.

'I just got the complete lab results,' he went on. 'And the problem is, while her blood shows toxic levels of arsenic, there is only scant trace of arsenic in her stomach contents. Far from enough to cause her this kind of harm.'

'Are you saying she was faking it?' Byrne asked.

'You can't fake the kind of vitals she came in with,' the doctor said. 'Theoretically, of course, she might have found something that would temporarily induce those kinds of effects, then pass harmlessly, but if she did, I for one would like to know exactly what it is.'

'I'm sure a lot of people would. That kind of thing would be pure gold,' Byrne said. He sounded more than a little admiring, causing the doctor to beat a hasty retreat with a muttered excuse about an urgent hemorrhoid procedure. I couldn't blame him. Even after being weekly trivia partners with Byrne for over a year, I still couldn't get used to these matter-of-fact reminders that some time in his past, he had not only made a career out of killing people, he had, by all accounts been extremely good at it. Then again, I was the one with the computer program that pretty much was his own *The Murderer's Vade-Mecum*, so who was I to cast the first stone?

I waited until we were back out in the hospital parking lot before I asked Byrne, 'So how could Margery have been poisoned with arsenic if there was none in her stomach?'

'You can absorb arsenic in other ways—some more esoteric than others. There was the animal rights activist that tried to give poisoned rats artificial respiration, but that is admittedly an outlier.'

I could only hope so. 'How about through the skin?' I asked, mostly to rid my mind of the pictures that sprang up unbidden in my head.

He shook his head. 'Not likely. She would have had to literally cover herself in it, roll around like you were powdering a doughnut. The EMTs would definitely have noticed it when they found her.'

It was, I reflected, probably a good thing that I had never particularly cared for doughnuts—especially those with powdered sugar.

'But breathing in arsenic can be as deadly as ingesting it by mouth,' Byrne reflected. 'It goes directly into the blood stream without the stomach acids breaking it down. On the other hand, it takes a pretty sizeable concentration, even in an unventilated room. It's hard to imagine anyone voluntarily sticking their head into a paper bag of the stuff.'

My mind went back to that mysterious vacuum cleaner the Detection Club had heard beyond the locked door.

'Do you think it's possible someone rigged the vacuum to spread mold instead of sucking it up?' I asked.

'MacGyvered it, you mean? Sure, I could do it in my sleep.'

'Yes, but you're you.' In other words, Byrne was the man who was rumored to have taken out all the Pentagon's systems with one blow, quite literally.

'We've all got our talents.' He grinned. 'And yours definitely is being the brains of this operation. You got time to head back to the library and take a look at the fatal vacuum cleaner?'

Fourth Method: *The Unshakeable Alibi*

'At the risk of throwing yet another spanner into the works,' I said as I endured the bone-jarring ride back to the library in Byrne's pick-up truck, 'Doyle has urged me to point out to you that Lord Mycroft is not real.'

Byrne raised an eyebrow. 'Well, I was kind of tending to that point of view anyway, but I take it your Little Friend knows something specific.'

Doyle was twitching so eagerly, I let him do the honors. 'Lord Mycroft Ashton, FRS, RA, champion fencer, decorated war pilot, blue in rowing at Oxford, connoisseur of William Morris editions, and amateur criminologist, is the hero of Harriet Leigh's detective series. Once remarked upon as a second Peter Wimsey, he has sadly fallen out of fashion among aficionados of detective fiction.'

'So Margery has been embezzling library funds at the purported request of her great-aunt's most famous fictional character.' Byrne shook his head. 'I don't want to be the one who goes on record, but if someone wanted to take her to court on the grounds of being *non compos mentis*, there isn't a judge who's going to be on her side. Even me.'

'Then let's hope it doesn't come to that,' I said. 'In the meantime, what do you say as long as we're in there looking at the vacuum, we also grab the chance to check the shelves for stray copies of those non-existent books?'

'And if we find them, what would that prove?'

'If nothing else, it shows that someone went to an awful lot of trouble to set up Margery. And it leads to a far more important question, at least in my mind. Why would someone go to this much effort to frame a woman they were already planning to poison?'

Byrne conceded the point with a nod, but as we reached to open the doors to the Rare Book room, a voice rang out. 'Don't bother. I've already tried. Those idiots locked themselves inside. They have been barricaded in there ever since the remediation team showed up.'

Greg Mumford, Morgansburg's favorite young friend, thrust

himself between us and the Rare Books room to continue his catalogue of grievances.

'They said they were just going to run a few tests on the vacuum, but nobody's heard anything for nearly an hour. I finally had to send the team home, and you have my word, I'm going to stick the Detection Club with the missed appointment charges. Completely gaga, the lot of them. Even Margery didn't trust them. You should have seen her last email. *My dear, Mycroft. I fear you are the only one I can trust...*'

Byrne tensed. 'Funny you should bring up Lord Mycroft,' he said, his voice carefully casual. 'Margery had a lot to say about him too, but I'm still not sure I understand exactly who he is.'

'He's nothing but a damned cyber-predator, who claims to be rescuing Harriet Leigh's work from oblivion, but he's really no better than some scammer who claims to have the keys to the Nigerian treasury. And Margery has fallen for it hook, line and sinker. For chrissakes, she's already invited him to visit her here in Morgansburg, and promised him he can stay in her great-aunt's bedroom.'

Greg's voice trailed off as he became aware of the long look Byrne was casting him. 'You seem to know a lot about Margery's correspondence with this Lord Mycroft,' Byrne said. 'It's almost like you've seen their emails yourself.'

'She uses the library computers, which are public access. How could I help it if she forgot to log out?'

'The library system logs you out automatically,' I told him. 'I know. I installed it myself. It's a routine security precaution.'

Greg eyed me as if a pet dog had spoken, then conceded the obvious with a shrug. 'All right, all right, I'll tell the truth. Yes, I wrote those emails.'

'You intentionally posed as Lord Mycroft in order to defraud Margery Fox and the Morgansburg Library?' Byrne asked.

'Come on,' Greg said. 'Someone had to play hardball. That woman would have drawn this out for the next half-century, and frankly, we were all sick of it. You've got to see it from our point of view.'

Instead of answering right away, Byrne loomed. At well over six foot tall and built like the West Point running back he had once been, looming was a particular talent of his. 'All I see is you were entrapping a woman into embezzling money using an online persona. Now, I'm no lawyer like you—just a Town Justice without any formal legal training—but it strikes me that that's internet fraud. So I think the only real question is how much money is involved and whether that means we can keep this in the Town Justice Court, or whether we need to kick it upstairs to the County Prosecutor.'

'What the—?' Greg shook his head. 'Look, you've got this all wrong. It's not like I was taking the money for myself. Even with two kids to put through college, I don't need it, and neither do any of the rest of the Friends. We put it all in the Friends of the Library account.'

'Then I suggest you put it back as quickly and quietly as possible, so we can all forget this ever happened.'

'Don't be ridiculous. We can't. We turned around those funds to buy computers for our kids,' Greg said. 'And about time too. We have been begging Margery for ages to sign over the budget. Do you know how many educational software packages that money bought?'

'No, but I know what misappropriation of funds sounds like when I hear it. Which still gets us back to the question of whether we're dealing with a felony or a misdemeanor. Although frankly, I'd suggest you take your chances with the prosecutor's office rather than with me. Because personally I find internet scammers targeting vulnerable women among the lowest forms of pond life there are. And I've got a pretty deserving composting manure project that's burning a hole in my Community Service list.'

'You really need help, you know that?' Greg shook his head with a sigh. 'I thought you were different, but you're just like the rest of them. We come here, willing to roll up our sleeves and put this town on the map, and all we get is resistance every way we turn. It's like you people don't want to be found.'

'Well, now, you may just be right about that,' Byrne said. It was a sign of how genuinely angry he was that he would let something that personal slip. There were very few people here in Morgansburg who knew that there were a host of radars out there Byrne would prefer not to cross. I, on the other hand, had no excuse beyond finding computers and cats far easier to deal with than the average human. Still, it meant Byrne and I understood each other. Many people would even describe us as friends.

'But that's neither here nor there,' Byrne went on. 'The real issue here is poisoning, which is a felony any way you look at it. The prosecutor might be willing to hand over the financial issue to a Town Justice, but they're never going to let a poisoning get swept under the rug.'

'Are you crazy?' Greg demanded. 'I never poisoned anyone. For God's sake, I don't have access to poison, let alone arsenic.'

'Anyone has access to arsenic, if they look hard enough,' Byrne said. 'Bottle of lye beneath the kitchen sink. Roach spray in the coffee. Soaking old strips of flypaper if you can find such a thing anymore. Wallpaper and paint, weed killer. Taxidermy, if that's your thing.'

As I said, I was used to these impromptu disquisitions from Byrne. Greg Mumford not so much. He simply stared at Byrne for an appalled moment before shaking his head. 'I'm done here. If you want to accuse me of poisoning Margery, then I suggest you figure out how I did it. And if you can't, I suggest you find yourself one hell of a good libel attorney.'

'That's your decision,' Byrne said, in the tone that could shut down a frat house kegger before the beer was even tapped. 'In the meantime, I'd like to make sure the Detection Club is all right.'

He turned his attention to the closed doors of the Rare Books room, knocked once, and then a second time. 'Is someone in there?' he called.

When he received no answer, he forced the doors open with a swift thrust of his shoulder. A moment's silence before his voice echoed through the entrance hall with the authority of the commando he had once been. 'I'm afraid I'm going to have to ask everyone to stay right where you are, while Dr Watson calls 911. Unless, of course, you have first aid training. Then we could certainly use your help here.'

I risked a glance into the Rare Books room as I made the call, and immediately wished I hadn't. Limp arms and hands clutched spasmodically against the oak surface, like shipwreck survivors scrabbling for the bulk of the hefty man on the other end of the table. An all-too-familiar wig lay abandoned on the floor. I couldn't see the faces of the woman in sensible shoes or the English teacher, but I was just as happy not to. It wasn't just Margery this time. Someone had apparently poisoned the entire Detection Club. And to judge from the condition in which we last saw her, it could not possibly have been Margery Fox.

Fifth Method: *The Impossible Crime*

One look at Byrne's haggard expression when he got back from the ER, and I feared that this time at least one poisoning was fatal. But Byrne allayed my worry with a quick shake of his head. 'Same as Margery,' he said. 'No one's likely to enjoy the next few days, but everyone is expected to make a full recovery.'

'Arsenic again?'

'The doctors are being cagier this time around—"symptoms are consistent", "dependent on the full toxicology report", that kind of thing. But yes. In all likelihood, arsenic again.'

'But not ingested by mouth?'

'They invited me to inspect the samples for myself, but I told them I could wait for the paper report,' he said with a grin.

'Can't say I blame you. But let's go on the assumption the same thing happened to all of them. It had to be that mold remediation vacuum. Why don't we go back and look at it now that we're no longer derailed by administering CPR?'

Byrne took one look at the squat, round canister that lurked in one corner of the Rare Books room and said, 'If we're dealing with arsenic, I think you'd better let me handle this.' I didn't argue. His real name was William; "Mack" was just a nickname, short for "MacGyver". Me, I'm engaged in an ongoing war with the material world. Besides, my eyes were drawn to the pile of books strewn across the floor, and especially their brilliant green covers. I bent closer to examine them, then changed my mind as I remembered a graduate school lecture by an unassuming rare books curator with an unlikely passion for poisonous books.

'When you're done there, I think you may want to take a look at this—'

'Stop before you kill everyone in this building!' Greg Mumford cut me off, as he burst into the Rare Books room behind us. 'Do you have any idea what you're dealing with here?'

Byrne straightened away from the vacuum, his face a rare mask of fury. 'Not only do I know exactly *what* I'm dealing with here, I've got one hell of a good idea *who* I'm dealing with. And I'm guessing that the state police can prove it when they dust this vacuum for prints. Because anyone who came up with a dumbass stunt like this would be too stupid to think to wipe them off.' He shook his head, ignoring Greg's spluttered response. 'You didn't think you'd get yourself in enough trouble entrapping Margery into financial fraud? You decided you needed to poison a few people as well?'

Byrne is intimidating enough when he is stone-faced; when he allows himself to be visibly angry, a wise man would run for the hills. But Greg had already demonstrated he was anything but wise. His mouth twisted with the angry patience of a teenager as he sighed, 'I didn't poison anyone. I merely created a mold event. And I wouldn't have even had to do that if Margery had just listened to reason.'

Byrne's voice grew dangerously quiet. 'Listened to reason about what? Did Margery start to ask too many questions? Maybe one or two you didn't have a ready answer for?'

'It was that wretched murderer book. The one in Latin. *Murderer's* yadda yadda.'

'*Vade-Mecum*,' I told him.

'If you say so. I don't know. It was just a title I pulled off the internet somewhere. But one look at it and Margery got the wind up. Kept obsessing about Lord Mycroft conspiring with another Harriet to erase her aunt's legacy.'

'Harriet Vane,' I said. 'Dorothy L. Sayers' fictional mystery writer and the love of Peter Wimsey's life.'

'If you say so,' Greg sighed. 'All I know is that someone had to play hardball.'

My eyes lingered on those brilliant green covers. 'You mind telling me exactly which books you decided to play hardball with?'

'What does it matter?' Greg sighed. 'I dosed them with yeast, not arsenic.'

'Trust me, it matters,' I said. 'Especially if you decided to inoculate all those pretty green books that are scattered on the floor. Striking books, wouldn't you say? The mold should stick out like a sore thumb, shouldn't it?'

'Maybe,' he said. 'I wanted to make sure the mold team saw them fast.'

'But not so fast that the mold couldn't spread to the shelves, so that you could condemn the entire building, right? Maybe you even helped matters along by taking scrapings from the books and sneaking them into the vacuum to make sure they were spreading the problem, rather than rectifying it?'

'For God's sake, get a grip! You're talking like I'm some kind of mass poisoner.'

'Quite possibly because that's exactly what you are.' I shook my head in disgust. 'Green books would have been a warning sign to anyone who knows a damn thing about rare books. They're poisonous—so much so that there's been an entire exhibit devoted to them. That color, that beautiful green you're looking at right there, is called Paris green. And do you know how they achieve that distinctive color? You guessed it. Arsenic. Over a millimeter of arsenic per square centimeter.'

'How was I to know?'

'Stop!' Byrne cut him off. 'Just do yourself a favor and don't say anything more until you call your lawyer, and I'm not talking about your friend the libel attorney.'

'In the meantime, with your permission, I'll just have a quiet word with Lord Mycroft,' Doyle purred in my earbud, 'and convey our sincere congratulations on a case I could not have handled more masterfully myself.'

THERE IS A TIDE
Elizabeth Elwood

The car was parked on the gravel verge beside the lake. It was an old Chevy Cavalier, its black paint dulled with grime from the road. As she drew near, Margaret Ross could see someone slumped across the back seat. She stepped closer, hoping she was not about to discover a dead body. But no, the young man looked pale, but there was a faint movement of the tattered quilt that was drawn over his chest.

Margaret sighed. Another homeless person, desperate, possibly jobless due to the pandemic. The poor man's soul was probably as chilled and grey as the lake beyond. It was a dreadful day to be living rough. Turbulent clouds were rolling across the sky, and the tree branches were quivering in the first small gusts that heralded the coming storm. The March winds had been fierce this year, and this next storm was supposed to be particularly violent.

Impulsively, Margaret reached in her pocket and pulled out the notebook that she always carried on her walks. It didn't matter that her nephew had given her an iPhone and pointed out all the clever things it could do. At eighty, old habits died hard, and pen and paper were old friends. She quickly jotted a note and ripped out the page, setting it firmly under the windshield wiper of the vehicle. Then she continued on her way.

Half an hour later, the occupant of the car awoke from his sleep. As his eyes gradually focused, he saw the white rectangle plastered against the windshield. When he retrieved the note, he discovered that it contained an address with directions, followed by a short message.

His eyes widened as he read it: *When you wake up, come by and I'll be happy to provide you with coffee and a meal. Possibly a day's work, too.*

#

Carrie Grey had risen early and had seen Margaret Ross taking her morning walk. The road that came down from the lake continued past Carrie's cottage and on around a lagoon that drained into the ocean through a channel at the western end. The ring road came to a halt at the Pool Bay General Store and Post Office, but a footbridge crossed the channel and allowed walkers to complete the circle back to the lake road. The mailboxes were accessible, even when the store was closed, so Margaret often came early to pick up her mail, always circling the ring road first and returning by the footbridge before heading for home.

Carrie waved from her deck as Margaret went by, admiring the woman's determined stride and wishing she could walk as vigorously. Carrie's arthritis had been flaring of late and she had to take the shorter route across the footbridge when going to the store.

Carrie liked Margaret. The two elderly women had much in common. Both were independent and creative. Carrie painted watercolors; Margaret was a potter, and both displayed their wares in the store and at craft fairs. However, Margaret was a loner whose only socializing involved her shifts at craft fairs or the thrift store, whereas Carrie had numerous friends, a warm relationship with her children and grandchildren, and an open-door arrangement with Gloria, the lively redheaded divorcee who lived next door. Margaret had no one but a nephew, who, in Carrie's opinion, was simply out for himself.

Carrie watched as Margaret continued around the ring road. The morning was overcast and the lagoon mirrored the dark clouds overhead. Little bursts of wind rippled through the trees on the far shore, and the flag above the store danced erratically as the gusts lifted it, then whipped it back against the pole. Carrie hoped the coming storm would not be as bad as the weatherman had predicted. Her cottage lay on the isthmus of a peninsula and, in a heavy squall, the area between the two bays became a wind tunnel. Shivering, she went back inside and secured the doors and windows. It was a day to stay warm by the fire. She hoped Margaret would make it home before the deluge began.

#

The wind began in earnest that night. It howled and whistled, then rose to a high-pitched scream as the worst of the gusts raced past, rattling the windows and making the sofa that Carrie sat on vibrate alarmingly. The downpour started soon afterwards. The raindrops lashed the windows and the wind hurled them against the house with such intensity that they sounded like a hail of bullets. Predictably, as Carrie was watching *Jeopardy*, the power went out. She lit the LED lamps that she kept for such eventualities, and got ready for bed. By the time she was tucked in, the sound of the wind had settled to the consistent roar of a typhoon. She hoped the trees by the lagoon would be able to withstand the storm. The Douglas fir at the side of the channel was particularly worrisome because it was showing signs of disease. Still, there was nothing she could do about it. Philosophically, she stuffed earplugs into her ears and snuggled down under the covers. Hopefully, with the sound muted, she would be able to sleep. After a while, she became attuned to the steady roar and drifted off.

At two o'clock in the morning, she was awoken by a thunderous crash. The power was still out, and the room was black as pitch. She got up to look out, but all she could see was the dark void beyond. Her earplugs muted the sound of the wind to a dull drone, but she could tell it had not abated. She took a deep breath to calm herself and returned to bed. She would see what had happened in the morning.

By first light, the wind had stopped, but the rain still pounded the earth. Carrie peered out through the veil of water streaming down from her overflowing gutters. Amazed, she saw that the lagoon had grown much larger. The ring road had disappeared. The torrential rainfall, in combination with a king tide and the wind surge, had caused the lagoon to break its banks. At the centre of the pool, a strange shape obtruded from the depths. The dark waters appeared to have reared a sea monster, a rough, bulky body with gaunt, angular arms pointing up at the sky. She squinted in an attempt to make out what it was. Then she realized what had happened. The Douglas fir had come down in the night. It had crashed through the footbridge and lay sprawling across the water.

#

The waters receded a couple of hours later, and by the time people were up and about, the ring road was accessible again. However, the footbridge was out of commission, and Carrie was forced to walk all the way around the lagoon when she went to the store. To her relief, the work crews came in that afternoon, and by Monday, the span was repaired and she was able to use the bridge again.

As she returned from shopping, she saw the front door of her neighbor's house opening. Gloria flew out and bounced down the front steps. Her tawny mop of hair was bobbing up and down, a sure sign that she was on a mission. As she opened the door of her Jeep, she noticed Carrie coming up her driveway.

'Got to check on Margaret Ross,' she called. 'You didn't happen to see her this morning, did you?'

'No, why? Is something wrong?'

'She hasn't been answering her phone.'

'Did you let her nephew know?'

'He's the one who called me. He's on the way to check on her, but the ferry was late so he's only just passed Sechelt. He's going to meet me at the house.'

'Why call you if he's coming himself?'

Gloria pulled a face.

'He probably hopes Margaret's popped her clogs and doesn't want the hassle of dealing with it himself. He's such a slimeball. He was here on Friday, cozying up with Zimmerman, and you know what that means.'

Carrie sighed. All the locals were aware of Bruno Zimmerman, the developer who was building condos wherever he could gather large numbers of lots on British Columbia's Sunshine Coast. His current project was to build a gated community in Rumrunner's Cove. He had bought all the properties surrounding Margaret's home and had made her countless offers, all of which she had refused. Having identified an ally in her nephew, he had now enlisted him to put pressure on her.

Carrie had met Margaret's nephew on several occasions and been irritated by his dismissive attitude. Jason Ross was a high-school teacher who had successfully run for civic politics, the winning of his seat depending more on his deceptively youthful, blue-eyed-boy good looks than any real substance or ability, and he made no attempt to disguise his opinion that people of her generation were a drain on society and irrelevant in the general scheme of things. She had no doubt that his call to Gloria was motivated more by a desire to cover himself from charges of negligence than from genuine concern for his aunt.

Carrie pulled out her keys and opened the door of her cottage. 'Give me a minute to put this inside,' she said. 'I'll come with you.'

Having put her shopping away, she hurried back, climbed into the passenger seat of the Jeep, and braced herself for the ride. Gloria was in her fifties, but she drove as if she were trying to qualify for the Indy 500. It was no wonder she was so thin, Carrie thought affectionately. Gloria was always on the go. She worked long shifts at the pub, managed the Harbour Hotline Facebook page, and spent the rest of her time looking out for all the other people who lived in the bay.

As they headed up towards the lake, Carrie eyed the debris at the side of the road.

'We should have checked on Margaret after the storm,' she said soberly. 'There are a lot of trees on her property. I hope nothing came down on her cottage.'

Gloria veered left when they reached the turnoff to Rumrunner's Cove. The narrow road meandered through stands of alders and cedars, and then came to a halt at a wide gravel circle where five driveways branched off into the woods. Carrie could make out some houses amid the trees, but they looked abandoned. There was no sign of life.

Margaret's driveway was a dirt lane that wound through the trees for a hundred yards, and then debouched onto a wide grassy strip stretching down to the sea. There were four buildings on the property: Margaret's cedar-shingled cottage, an A-frame that housed her potting studio, a storage shed, and a bunkhouse for the occasional itinerant worker. Beside the bunkhouse was a woodshed, neatly filled with fir logs. Judging by the scent and the colour of the wood, they were freshly chopped. A Ford Escape was parked on a square of asphalt beside the cottage.

'Her car's here,' said Gloria. 'She hasn't gone out.'

She pulled up in front of the cottage and got out of the Jeep. Carrie got out and peered towards the A-frame.

'There's no light in the studio. She must be in the cottage.'

Gloria was already on the doorstep. 'I can't hear any movement,' she said. She was about to knock, when she saw that the door was slightly ajar. She pushed it open and called out. There was no reply. She turned back to Carrie and shook her head. Carrie stepped past her and entered the cottage.

'Come on, we'd better look around.'

The door of the cottage opened onto a laundry room, and from there into a kitchen that formed the short leg of an L, the rest of which was a living room with bookshelves, comfortably padded armchairs and a television. A small pile of unopened mail sat on the section of the kitchen counter nearest the door, along with the gloves and scarf that Margaret wore in cold weather. An unwashed frying pan in the sink showed remnants of scrambled eggs, as did the plate on the kitchen table. The dregs in the mug beside it looked like tea.

'The blinds are raised,' said Gloria. 'She got up and had breakfast.'

'Yes, but not necessarily this morning. Look how congealed those bits of egg are.'

'Well, she isn't here. We'd better check around the property. I'll take a quick look in the bedroom first.'

Carrie nodded and headed for the door, but before she could step outside, a cry halted her in her tracks. She turned back to see Gloria standing in the bedroom doorway. Her face was ashen and she clutched the door frame as if she needed its support to stay upright. Carrie had never seen her friend look so distraught.

'She's in here,' Gloria cried. 'Someone's bashed her head in.'

#

Carrie called the emergency services. Jason arrived shortly afterwards. He pulled his Nissan up beside Gloria's Jeep, got out of the car and raised his eyebrows to see the two women standing on the porch. His pale blue eyes hardened when Gloria told him what had happened to his aunt. He appeared less surprised than angry, and ignoring Carrie's statement that they should not touch anything, barged past them into the cottage.

'I'm wearing my driving gloves,' he snapped.

He strode into the bedroom and came out brandishing Margaret's handbag. Carrie had noticed it on the bedside table, but had held back from handling it.

'You should leave it where it was,' she protested.

Jason ignored her and rummaged through the bag.

'I thought so,' he said. 'The money's gone. She had five hundred dollars in here on Friday. Ten fifty-dollar bills. That drifter killed her and stole the money. I told her she was insane inviting strangers into the house.'

Gloria looked at him skeptically.

'What drifter?'

'He was sleeping in his car up by the lake.'

Gloria's eyes widened. She turned to Carrie.

'There *was* a car parked by the lake Friday morning. I saw it on my way round to the IGA. It was a black Chevy Cavalier. It had gone by the time I came back.'

'That's the one,' said Jason. 'My aunt saw the driver sleeping in the back and she took pity on him and offered him a meal. He was here having lunch with her when I arrived at noon. He was heading for Powell River the next day, so she said he could spend the night in the bunkhouse. I told her I felt uneasy about leaving her with him there.'

'What time did you leave?' Carrie asked.

'Not until evening. I took the last ferry back to town. His car was still there when I left.' Jason fixed Gloria and Carrie with a self-satisfied stare. 'Well, I don't think the police will have much difficulty solving this one. I took the license number in case there was a problem. They'll track him down in no time.'

Gloria stared back at him.

'Well, isn't that convenient,' she said tartly.

Jason's eyes narrowed. 'It's not my fault that my aunt took stupid risks with her life. She should never have stayed here. This wouldn't have happened if she'd listened to my advice.'

'Yeah, yeah, yeah,' said Gloria. 'We know the patter. Land prices are sky high; sell now before they go down again.'

'It was good advice.' Jason flashed a superior smile. 'The Bard summed it up perfectly: *There is a tide in the affairs of men which taken at the flood leads on to fortune.*'

'Cassius's advice didn't work out too well for Brutus,' Carrie said mildly.

'That's irrelevant,' snapped Jason. 'My aunt would have made a packet if she'd sold.'

The hostile silence that followed was broken by the arrival of the ambulance, but it was another half hour before the police got there. To Carrie's relief, Jason went out to make phone calls in his car, so she and Gloria were able to talk quietly on their own.

'Arrogant prick,' said Gloria. 'Fancies himself, doesn't he? Quoting Shakespeare at us as if we're his Grade Nine students. I bet he only knows that bit by memory because he uses it when he's out on the hustings. Those Peter Pan good looks that win him votes hide the character of a viper.'

'That's a bit strong,' Carrie demurred.

'No, it isn't. Those pale blue eyes could give you frostbite if you stared at them too long. He's positively gloating that he has a ready-made suspect for the investigating officer. I wouldn't put it past him to have paid the guy to do the deed.'

'If that were the case, he'd hardly help the police trace the car.'

'Well, maybe. It just infuriates me that Margaret's death is giving him exactly what he wanted.'

Their conversation came to a halt with the arrival of the police cruiser. Carrie was not surprised to see the stocky constable with the grizzled crew cut who got out of the car. Jack Rowan was a familiar figure, regularly dealing with call-outs from the harbor. However, she did not recognize the tall, fair-haired woman who accompanied him. The newcomer had a lean, angular face with closely set hazel eyes that managed to be piercing and impassive at the same time. She was bundled up in boots and a long grey puffer coat that reminded Carrie of pictures of Napoleon marching on Waterloo. Carrie suspected she was as thin as Gloria under the heavy padding.

The woman turned out to be Detective Constable Adrian Wright, and she was not amused to hear that the crime scene had been trampled over by three people. She sharply forestalled Jason's attempt to take charge by hearing him out without comment, then instructing him to go back and wait in his car. After inspecting the scene and finding, to her amazement, that the murder weapon lying on the rug beside the body was a truncheon, she came out to talk with Carrie and Gloria while waiting for the coroner and forensic team to arrive.

Adrian smiled inwardly at the sight of the two women hovering outside the cottage: a gangly, jeans-clad motormouth and a diminutive, quietly observant Miss Marple, albeit garbed in comfortable Lululemon loungewear rather than tweed skirt and twin set. Every detective's dream: a pair of nosy parkers; intelligent-eyed, community-minded, incalculably curious, primed in harbor gossip and eager to tell their all. She listened closely as the two friends gave her a detailed description of Margaret's personality and habits.

Margaret, they explained, was obsessively regular in her routines. She rose early and often was out walking as soon as it was light. On Tuesdays through Saturdays, she'd walk out to the lake, down to Pool Bay, and around the lagoon to the post office. Most days, she'd be there to check her mail box before the postmistress arrived. Then she'd go home for breakfast. On Tuesdays, Wednesdays and Thursdays, she did shifts at the thrift store. Friday, she'd do errands and chores, and the rest of the time, she'd seclude herself to work on the crafts that she sold at the summer fairs.

'She was a good person,' Gloria concluded sadly. 'Sharp-tongued, but very kind. It's entirely possible that she'd take pity on a homeless person and invite him for a meal,' she admitted, 'but we only have Jason's word for it that she did so.'

Adrian raised her eyebrows. 'Why would you doubt his word?' she asked.

Gloria needed no encouragement to launch into an account of Margaret's resistance to Bruno Zimmerman's development plans and her nephew's fury at her refusal to sell. 'There's a huge amount of money at stake,' she finished, 'and I don't exactly see Jason bowed down with grief. He hardly looked at his aunt's body. He made no comment on the weapon. All he was interested in was the missing money and the fact that there was someone to blame. Aren't you going to consider the possibility that he could have snuck back here on the weekend and killed his aunt?'

Adrian ignored the question. She was more interested in Gloria's mention of the weapon.

'Do you know where the truncheon came from?' she asked.

Carrie interjected: 'It was Margaret's. She inherited it from her father. He was a special constable during the British General Strike of 1926. She used to keep it by the bed in case of intruders.'

Adrian quailed at the thought of an eighty-year-old woman attempting to defend herself against a young aggressive male with criminal intent. However, she refrained from comment and simply asked, 'Is there anything else either of you want to add?'

Carrie replied: 'Only that you should check with the postmistress to find out what she put in Margaret's box on Friday afternoon. If it's the same as the pile on the kitchen counter, you'll be able to pin the date of the murder to Saturday. It was a dreadful morning, so she might have gone a little later than usual, but her habit was always to go out to get her mail first and eat breakfast after she came back. She must have been killed soon after she finished eating because she never left dirty dishes lying around. She always cleaned up after herself.'

DC Wright nodded gravely. She gave Carrie her card and told her to call if she had any further information. Then she turned her attention to Jason, who was glowering impatiently from his vehicle. It was a dismissal. Carrie and Gloria reluctantly returned to the Jeep and headed back to the bay.

#

The autopsy confirmed that Margaret's last meal had been eggs, tea, and toast. She had been struck from behind and had died from a single, powerful blow from the truncheon. Hopefully, she never knew what hit her, thought Adrian, as she reviewed the forensic reports. There were no fingerprints on the truncheon, other than some blurry ones of Margaret's, so the killer must have worn gloves. Still, given the time of year, everyone would be wearing them, or have a pair at hand.

Adrian had noted Jason Ross's driving gloves and, like Gloria, had sensed that his professions of sorrow were insincere. There was a coldness in his eyes that suggested he felt no grief at his aunt's death, and his emphasis on the missing money and the presence of a drifter seemed a little too glib, especially when both he and the developer who wanted to buy Margaret's property were going to benefit from the murder.

Therefore, she was disappointed to find that both men had alibis. Bruno Zimmerman had left for a conference in Whistler on Friday evening and had not returned until the following Wednesday. Jason Ross had witnesses to confirm his presence on the Friday and Monday ferries and colleagues to prove he had been in Vancouver on the days in between. And although the bunkhouse showed little sign of occupancy, other than a faintly lingering smell of pot, and a pillow and neatly rolled sleeping bag, Jason's story about the drifter held up. Other people had noticed the Chevy Cavalier parked by the lake, and Bruno Zimmerman had seen it on Margaret's property when he'd gone to meet with her and Jason on Friday afternoon. A search of Margaret's purse produced a bank slip verifying that she had taken out five hundred dollars the previous day, yet there had been no sign of the money in the cottage.

Two days later, the driver of the Chevy Cavalier was traced and brought back for questioning. His name was Grant Inkster and, as Margaret had suspected, had lost his job during the pandemic. He admitted to taking Margaret up on her offer of a meal and a night in the bunkhouse. He had three fifty-dollar bills in his wallet, which he said Margaret had paid him to chop and stack a pile of rounds she'd had delivered for her woodshed. He had done so after lunch, and Jason Ross had seen him doing it. Margaret had brought him a bowl of soup around six o'clock. He'd drunk it and then turned in for the night as he was tired and he didn't want to intrude on her visit with her nephew. In the morning, he went to the cottage to thank her before heading for the Earl's Cove ferry, but there was no answer when he knocked. He opened the door and called out, but the place was deserted, so he assumed she was out for her walk and he left to catch his ferry.

His story was plausible, and if it weren't for the fact that there was more than twice that amount of money missing from Margaret's purse, Adrian would have believed him. But with no other suspects, and with Inkster admitting that he had been wearing garden gloves while handling the wood, it was hard to see any other conclusion than that of a desperate man, jobless and homeless, who was tempted by the sight of the money in Margaret's purse. The course of events appeared to be inevitable. Grant Inkster would be charged with the murder of Margaret Ross. But Adrian was still uneasy. Her instincts told her there was something important that had been overlooked.

#

Since Gloria worked at the pub, she was privy to harbor gossip. Her local knowledge was augmented by a wealth of cousins, nieces and nephews working in various retail outlets and offices. These included the desk sergeant at the police station, from whom she heard of Grant Inkster's arrest when she ran into him after doing her grocery shopping. She drove home, stashed away her purchases, extracting the bag of cinnamon buns that she had bought at the bakery, and hurried over to tell Carrie the news.

Carrie, obligingly, put on the coffee pot and set plates on the kitchen table. Gloria distributed the buns and told Carrie what she had learned.

'Grant Inkster doesn't deny having the money,' she concluded, 'well, some of it anyway, just a hundred and fifty dollars, but he says that Margaret paid him for chopping and stacking her wood.'

Carrie frowned.

'That doesn't make sense. If he were guilty, why wouldn't he say she paid him the entire amount that Jason says is missing? It almost sounds as if he didn't know how much money Margaret had in her purse.'

'It does, doesn't it? And yet the police say there are no other suspects.'

Carrie poured the coffee and nodded soberly.

'Are they not considering that it could be a setup? What about your suggestion that Jason could have come back on Saturday after the homeless man left?'

Gloria shook her head.

'No, it turns out Jason was in Vancouver all weekend. The police checked. Mind you, I still say he could have paid someone to kill his aunt.'

Gloria stopped speaking as her cellphone rang. She pulled it from her pocket and looked at the screen; then rolled her eyes at Carrie, said 'Speak of the Devil,' and answered the call. Carrie continued to drink her coffee while Gloria muttered a series of *all rights* and *can dos* into her phone. Finally, she ended the call and grimaced.

'The police have finished at the cottage. Jason wants me to pack up Margaret's possessions for the thrift shop. He isn't wasting any time, is he?'

'No, but there's no point in refusing. Margaret would want the shop to benefit. I'll help you. We can go today, if you like. Finish your coffee and we'll head down to the general store to get some boxes.'

Gloria nodded and drained her coffee mug. Carrie quickly washed up the dishes, and they set off for the store. Then, with the back of Gloria's Jeep loaded with boxes, they drove to Margaret's cottage.

The stormy weather had passed and the day was gloriously bright. Sunlight sparkled on the lake, and the wooded lane that led to Rumrunner's Cove was a tunnel of golden speckles dancing amid luminous shades of green. When they arrived at Margaret's property, they saw a squad car parked on the gravel. Constable Rowan stood nearby, removing police tape from the boundary. Gloria pulled up and rolled down the driver's window. Rowan walked over to greet them.

'The heir must be in a hurry,' he said. 'DC Wright only just gave him the okay to clear Margaret's things. No surprise he's getting you two to do it.'

Gloria grinned. She liked Jack Rowan.

'We're doing it for Margaret, not her all-about-me nephew.'

Carrie cut to the chase. She was not in the mood for small talk. 'I hear you've arrested Grant Inkster,' she said. 'Are you absolutely sure he's the killer?'

Rowan raised his eyebrows.

'And who are you ladies suggesting as a substitute?'

Carrie leaned forward so she could look directly at him.

'It just seems so convenient for Jason Ross,' she said. 'He's the one who benefits from Margaret's death.'

Rowan shook his head.

'Margaret was alive after he left on Friday evening. She phoned him while he was gassing up at the Petrocan.'

'Why would she call him ten minutes after he'd left?'

'The wind had started in earnest and she wanted to catch him before he turned onto the highway and warn him to watch for trees on Misery Mile.'

Carrie frowned. Surely Jason was familiar enough with the coast to know about the stretch of road, so named by the locals, that was notorious for unstable trees beside the highway. Rowan looked amused at Carrie's dubious expression.

'We didn't take Ross's word for it,' he assured her. 'The gas-station attendant heard him take the call, and it showed up on both cellphones. The attendant also saw him turn onto the highway and set off for Langdale. There's no way he could have doubled back to his aunt's house and still clocked in at the ferry terminal when he did. Besides, everything points to Margaret being killed Saturday morning. She'd had breakfast, but not cleared the dishes, and had not yet opened the mail she'd picked up that morning. We know she was already home by eight-thirty because a crew arrived at that time and spent the morning clearing a fallen tree on the road that leads to her property, and they didn't see her pass. She was probably dead by nine o'clock when her nephew called from town to check on her. Grant Inkster didn't leave until nine-thirty to catch the eleven o'clock ferry from Earl's Cove. The timing says it all.'

'What if someone else came by after he left? Maybe Margaret missed her nephew's phone call for some other reason. She could have been in the washroom, or saying goodbye to Inkster.'

'Not possible. No other footprints, no car tracks. Besides, the work crew would have seen anyone who came along the road.'

'Could someone have come in by boat?'

'No. There were enough waterfront-property owners out checking or fixing their docks who could attest that no boats came into the cove. Sorry, ladies,' he concluded, with a wry shake of his head, 'Inkster was the only person there. It's pretty cut and dried.'

Unable to argue any more, Gloria nodded, put the Jeep into gear and drove silently to the cottage. Carrie was quiet, too. Both felt dejected. It was depressing to think that their friend had died so needlessly through an act of kindness, and that her death was to benefit someone who lacked all the decency and selflessness she had displayed. When they entered the cottage and looked around, they were even more disheartened at the sight of Margaret's possessions, still in place as if waiting for their owner to return, yet lacking the vitality that had been imbued into them by her presence.

On the principle that one should deal with the most difficult challenges first, Carrie suggested that they start with Margaret's clothing. Gloria agreed, and they entered the bedroom and opened the closet. The room was uncomfortably bright, for the window faced east and the sun was beating in. Gloria began pulling clothes off the hangers, but Carrie went to lower the blind. As she loosened the cord, she frowned.

'That's odd,' she said.

Gloria looked up from the pile of clothes she had deposited on the bed.

'What is?'

'The cord was wound clockwise. I remember Margaret once going on about blinds when we were opening up at the thrift store. She said it was easier to wrap the cord counterclockwise if you're right-handed, especially as it hangs down to the left of the hooks, and it's natural to loop it back around them, rather than lift it across and wind it the other way.'

Gloria raised her eyes heavenward.

'And do we have any other brilliant household tips, or can we get on with the job at hand?'

Carrie ignored the sarcasm. She went out to look at the kitchen and living-room blinds.

'I told you so,' she said, when she returned. 'All the other blinds are wound counterclockwise. Margaret was a creature of habit. Why would she have reversed the one in the bedroom?'

'I don't know. What are you suggesting?'

'That someone else raised that blind. I wonder if Jason is left-handed.'

Gloria shrugged.

'Makes no difference whether he is or not; everyone doesn't operate according to Margaret's rules. And so what if Jason raised the blind? It isn't a big deal. We know he was here on Friday.'

'Yes, but he didn't arrive until noon. The blind would have been up. He didn't leave until evening, by which time the blind would be down. Margaret liked to shut out the night once the sun went down.'

'Perhaps she was holding something in her right hand when she put the blind up in the morning.'

'Perhaps, but I still think it's odd.' Carrie picked up the sweater at the top of the pile and folded it neatly. 'Why don't you bring in some boxes, and I'll fold these.'

Gloria went out and Carrie continued to work her way through the pile. As she folded, she reflected on what Jack Rowan had told them. The timeline that the police had worked out did make sense. Margaret was normally home and breakfasted by nine o'clock, but something still niggled in the back of Carrie's mind. It was the dreadful weather that day. Surely Margaret would have waited for the rain to abate before venturing out.

Suddenly, the significance of the timing struck her.

'Oh, my goodness!' she gasped. 'She couldn't have picked up her mail that early on Saturday.'

She slapped down the sweater she was folding and called to Gloria.

'What?' said Gloria, as she returned with the boxes. 'You look like an electrified cartoon cat.'

'It doesn't make sense.'

'What doesn't?'

'What Jack Rowan told us. Jason must have been lying about Margaret's phone call.'

'How do you figure? The gas-station attendant heard him take the call. It showed up on both phones.'

Carrie sat down on the bed and frowned.

'Let me think,' she said. She closed her eyes and thought back to the day they had discovered Margaret's body. She reflected on the unwashed dishes and the unopened mail, and she thought about Jason Ross and his behaviour when he had arrived at the cottage. Then her eyes flew open and she turned triumphantly to Gloria.

'What was the first thing Jason did when he arrived on Monday?'

Gloria thought for a moment.

'Plowed past us and went to find Margaret's handbag. Oh!' Gloria's face lit up. 'You're thinking that he had the phone with him and put it back in her bag, right under our noses.'

'Exactly. He was wearing his driving gloves, so he wouldn't have left fingerprints on it. What if he killed Margaret before he left on Friday? He could have taken her phone with him and made the call himself. The gas station is served by the same tower as we are, so no one could show it hadn't been made from Margaret's house. It would have been easy for him to pocket dial the call and pick up on his own phone.'

Gloria nodded.

'Yes, that's just the sort of cagy, clever-dick thing he'd think of to make his story sound credible.' She paused, and then frowned again. 'But how do we explain the breakfast things? The autopsy definitely showed that her last meal was scrambled eggs, tea and toast.'

'True, but how many times have I had scrambled eggs for dinner. We old ladies who live on our own aren't in the habit of making gourmet meals. What if Jason offered to rustle up scrambled eggs and toast on Friday night? He could have washed up his own dishes and left hers out, knowing that everyone would assume she'd been up and about on Saturday morning. There was nothing to stop him from taking her keys and picking her mail up on Friday night. The store was shut by then. It was dark. No one would have seen him at the mail boxes.'

Gloria shook her head in amazement.

'Carrie, I swear you've got it. He made it appear that Margaret had been killed Saturday morning, knowing that the poor sap in the bunkhouse would end up getting the blame.'

'And,' said Carrie triumphantly, 'that explains the blind. He must have followed her into the bedroom and hit her from behind when she was putting it down. Then he had to put it up again to make it look as if she'd got up in the morning.'

Gloria bit her lip.

'It makes sense,' she said, 'but is that enough? Where's the proof? The police will want evidence. They won't act unless there's something substantial that Jason can't argue away.'

Carrie pulled out her cellphone and tapped in the number that Adrian Wright had given her. While she waited for the call to be answered, she smiled at Gloria.

'Oh, there is,' she said. 'The proof is in the king tide. For Margaret to have picked up her mail and be back at her cottage and breakfasted by nine, she'd have to have been in the bay around seven-thirty, but the ring road was impassable. The flooding didn't abate until nine o'clock.'

Gloria beamed.

'Well, isn't that perfect,' she said. 'Thinking he was creating a cast-iron alibi, and hoist by his own petard. I always said Jason had an overinflated opinion of his own intelligence.'

'Absolutely,' said Carrie. 'Instead of reading Shakespeare, he should have read the tide tables.'

AUTHOR BIOGRAPHIES

Dave Duncan (June 30, 1933—Oct 29, 2019) was one of the most popular and prolific Canadian SF&F authors with over 65 traditionally published novels. Duncan was famous for creating uniquely original but logically consistent magical systems or SF settings. His best-known series are *The Seventh Sword*, *A Man of His Word*, and *The King's Blades*, but if you liked *Alexander's Nose*, try *The Reaver Road* and *The Hunter's Haunt*, fantasy novels featuring the fast-talking scoundrel, Omar. *Alexander's Nose*, which appears here for the first time, is one of Duncan's few short stories and his only pure mystery. *wikipedia.org/wiki/Dave_Duncan_(writer)*

Karen Keeley has published short fiction in more than a dozen anthologies: literary, speculative and crime, the most recent *Crime Wave: Women of a Certain Age* (Sisters-in-Crime, Canada West) and *Tales from the Monoverse* (Last Waltz Publishing). She is a member of the Short Fiction Mystery Society (SFMS) and Sisters-in-Crime (Canada West.) Her novella *Sticks and Stones* was short-listed as a finalist in the 2022 Eyelands Book Awards. A proud Canuck living north of the 49th parallel, she divides her time between family, friends, the outdoors, and writing—not necessarily in that order. Visit her at *karenmkeeley.blogspot.com*

E. E. King is an award-winning painter, performer, writer, and naturalist. She'll do anything that won't pay the bills, especially if it involves animals. Ray Bradbury called her stories, "marvelously inventive, wildly funny, and deeply thought-provoking". Check out her paintings, musings, and books at *elizabetheveking.com* and *amazon.com/author/eeking*

F. K. Restrepo is new to the world of writing fiction. His first encounter with the impossible crime was a revelation—the offer of a battle of wits between the author and the determined reader immediately clicked with his life-long love of puzzles and competitive games. Ever since, he's chased that Aha! moment, gleefully exchanging stories with fellow fans of locked-room mysteries and attempting to out-sleuth one another. He is a native New Yorker, and a programmer by day.
fkrestrepo.com

Edward Lodi has written more than thirty books, both fiction and non-fiction, including six Cranberry Country Mysteries. His short fiction and poetry have appeared in numerous magazines and journals, such as *Mystery Magazine*, and in anthologies published by Cemetery Dance, Murderous Ink, Main Street Rag, Rock Village Publishing, Superior Shores Press, and others. His story, *Charnel House*, was featured on Night Terrors Podcast. He is a member of the Short Mystery Fiction Society and a frequent contributor to their blog.

Cameron Trost is an author of mystery and suspense fiction best known for his puzzles featuring Oscar Tremont, Investigator of the Strange and Inexplicable. He has written two novels, *Letterbox* and *The Tunnel Runner*, and three collections, *Oscar Tremont, Investigator of the Strange and Inexplicable*, *The Animal Inside*, and *Hoffman's Creeper and Other Disturbing Tales*. Originally from Brisbane, Australia, Cameron lives with his wife and two sons near Guérande in southern Brittany, between the rugged coast and treacherous marshlands. He runs the independent publishing house, Black Beacon Books, and is a member of the Australian Crime Writers Association. camerontrost.com

Josh Pachter was the 2020 recipient of the Short Mystery Fiction Society's Golden Derringer Award for Lifetime Achievement. His stories appear in *Ellery Queen's Mystery Magazine*, *Alfred Hitchcock's Mystery Magazine*, *Black Cat Mystery Magazine*, *Mystery Magazine*, *Mystery Tribune*, and elsewhere. He edits anthologies (including Anthony Award finalists *The Beat of Black*

Wings: Crime Fiction Inspired by the Songs of Joni Mitchell* and *Paranoia Blues: Crime Fiction Inspired by the Songs of Paul Simon*) and translates fiction and non-fiction from multiple languages, mainly Dutch, into English. *joshpachter.com*

Yvonne Ventresca writes suspenseful novels for teens that explore themes like trust, deception, and betrayal. She is the author of *Black Flowers, White Lies* (Sky Pony Press, 2016), and *Pandemic* (Sky Pony Press, 2014), as well as two non-fiction books: *Avril Lavigne* (Lucent Books, 2007) and *Publishing* (Lucent Books, 2005). She's also had several short stories for kids and adults selected for anthologies: The Third Ghost in *Voyagers: The Third Ghost*, Justice for Jaynie in Sisters in Crime's *30 Shades of Dead*, The Art of Remaining Bitter in *Hero Lost: Mysteries of Death and Life*, and Escape to Orange Blossom in *Prep for Doom*. *yvonneventresca.com*

Maggie King is the author of the Hazel Rose Book Group Mysteries. She's also published short mysteries for anthologies, including *Murder by the Glass* and *50 Shades of Cabernet*. She belongs to International Thriller Writers, James River Writers, Short Mystery Fiction Society, and is a founding member of Sisters in Crime Central Virginia, where she manages the Instagram account. Find her at *maggieking.com*

Paulene Turner is a writer of short stories, short plays, and novels. A former journalist, she's currently editing her six-book YA time travel series, The Time Travel Chronicles, with a view to a 2023 release. Her short stories have appeared in magazines and anthologies in the UK, US, and Australia. As well as writing short plays, she also directs them for Short and Sweet, Sydney—the biggest little play festival in the world. She lives in Sydney with her husband, twin daughters, and twin pugs, Holmes and Watson. *pauleneturnerwrites.com*

Joseph S. Walker lives in Indiana and teaches college literature and composition courses. His short fiction has appeared in *Alfred Hitchcock's Mystery Magazine, Ellery Queen's Mystery Magazine, Mystery Weekly, Tough,* and a number of other magazines and anthologies. He has been nominated for the Edgar Award and the Derringer Award and has won the Bill Crider Prize for Short Fiction. He also won the Al Blanchard Award in 2019 and 2021. You can follow him on Twitter *@JSWalkerAuthor* and visit his website at *jswalkerauthor.com*

Teel James Glenn has killed hundreds and been killed more times—on stage and screen—as a stuntman, swordmaster, storyteller, bodyguard, actor, and haunted house barker. He is proud to have been beaten up by Hawk on the *Spenser for Hire* TV show. His work has been printed in over two hundred magazines including *Weird Tales*, *Mystery Weekly*, *Pulp Adventures*, *Space & Time*, *Mad*, *Cirsova*, and *Sherlock Holmes Mystery*. His novel *A Cowboy in Carpathia: A Bob Howard Adventure* won best novel 2021 in the Pulp Factory Award. He is also the winner of the 2012 Pulp Ark Award for Best Author. And he was a finalist for the Derringer short mystery award in 2022. *theurbanswashbuckler.com*

Alan Barker has been writing creatively since 2018 when he took early retirement. He has short stories published in various magazines (*Scribble*, *Ireland's Own*, *Yours Fiction*, *Your Cat UK*, *Café Lit*, and *Crystal*) and in various anthologies which will include *Mickey Finn: 21st Century Noir, Volume 5*, to be published December 2024. He is also a certified proofreader and copy editor. He's online at *twitter.com/alan_scribble* and *facebook.com/alan.barker.92754397*

After **Erica Obey** graduated from Yale University, her interest in folklore and story led her to an M.A. in Creative Writing from City College of New York and a Ph.D. in Comparative Literature from the City University of New York, where she published articles and a book about female folklorists of the nineteenth century before she decided she'd rather be writing the stories herself. Learn more at *ericaobey.com*

Elizabeth Elwood spent many years performing with Lower Mainland music and theatre groups and singing in the Vancouver Opera chorus. Having turned her talents to writing and design, she created twenty marionette musicals for Elwoodettes Marionettes and has written four plays that have entertained audiences in both Canada and the United States. A Derringer Award nominee, she is the author of six books in the Beary Mystery Series, and her stand-alone short stories have been featured in many mystery magazines and anthologies. Elizabeth was the winner of Best Short Story in the Crime Writers of Canada Awards of Excellence in 2022 for her story, "Number 10 Marlborough Place", published in *Ellery Queen Mystery Magazine*. Visit her website at *elihuentertainment.com*

Also Available from Black Beacon Books

An edge-of-your-seat anthology of new fiction inspired by the classic films of Alfred Hitchcock, the Master of Suspense!

For news, reviews, competitions, author interviews, and exclusive excerpts

Visit our website
blackbeaconbooks.com

Like us on Facebook
facebook.com/BlackBeaconBooks

Join us on Twitter
@BlackBeacons

Find us on Instagram
instagram.com/blackbeaconbooks

Subscribe on Patreon
patreon.com/blackbeaconbooks

Discover All our Social Media Links
https://linktr.ee/blackbeaconbooks

Printed in Great Britain
by Amazon